D0481467

BREATHING BOOKS

Cornelia Funke

RECKLESS

The Golden Yarn

A MirrorWorld Novel

With Illustrations by the Author

Translated by Oliver Latsch

Breathing Books · Los Angeles

MIRRORWORLD was originally inspired by a collaboration between Cornelia Funke and Lionel Wigram.

First Edition: November 2015

10 9 8 7 6 5 4 3 2 1

Book design by Mirada
Printed in Canada

33614056497042

For
The Phoenix – Mathew Cullen
and his wizards in alphabetical order:

The magical bookmaker – Mark Brinn
Wizard Eyes – Andy Cochrane
The Canadian – David Fowler
The Fairy of the Marina – Andrin Mele-Shadwick
The Tamer of Magical Beasts – Andy Merkin

and for
Thomas W. Gaehtgens
Isotta Poggi
and last, thanks to the alphabet only,
Frances Terpak,
who opened the Treasure Chambers of the Getty Research
Institute
for me and Jacob

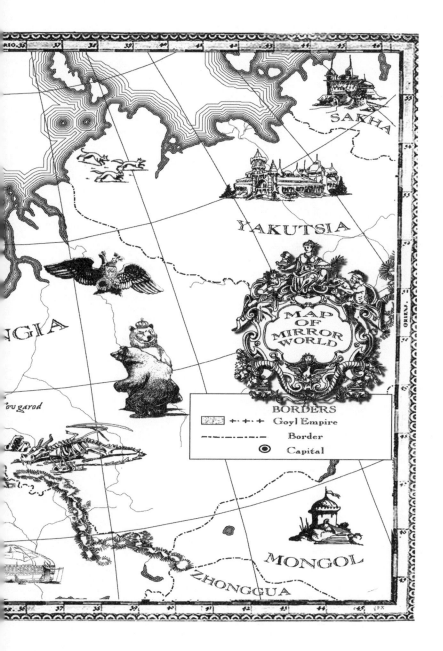

RIO 36   37   38   39   90   91   92   93   94   95   96

SAKHA

YAKUTSIA

NGIA

'ov garod

MAP
OF
MIRROR
WORLD

BORDERS

+ · + · +   Goyl Empire

— · — · —   Border

◉   Capital

MONGOL

ZHONGGUA

ss. 56   37   38   39   90   91   92   93   95   PX

1

THE MOONSTONE PRINCE

The doll-princess was not having an easy labor. Not even the palace garden offered a refuge from her screams, and the Dark Fairy listened, and she hated how those groans and whimpers made her feel. She hoped Amalie would die. Of course. She'd been hoping ever since Kami'en had said yes to the other one in her bloody wedding gown. Yet there was more: an unreasonable longing for the infant who was pushing those screams from Amalie's vapid, pretty mouth.

Through all these months, only her magic had kept the unborn child alive. The child that could not be. "You will save it. Promise me!" The same whispered plea, every time after he'd made love to her. Only that had made Kami'en return to her bed at night. The desire to meld his flesh with human flesh—it made him so helpless.

Oh, how the Doll screamed. As though the infant were being

carved with a knife from her body, the body that only a Fairy lily could make desirable.

Kill her already, Skinless Prince. What gives her the right to call herself your mother?

He would have rotted inside her, like a forbidden fruit, if it hadn't been for the magic the Dark One had spun around Amalie. Yes, the infant was a boy. A son. The Dark Fairy had seen him in her dreams.

Kami'en did not come for her help himself. Not this night. He sent his bloodhound to find her instead. His milky-eyed jasper shadow. Hentzau stopped in front of her, and as usual he avoided looking in her eyes.

"The midwife says she's losing the child."

Why did she go with him?

For the child.

It filled the Fairy with quiet satisfaction that Kami'en's son chose the night to come into the world. Amalie feared the darkness so much, she always kept a dozen gaslights burning in her bedchamber, even though their pale light hurt her husband's eyes.

Kami'en was standing next to Amalie's bed. He turned as the servants opened the door for his mistress. For an instant, the Fairy thought she could see in his eyes a shadow of the love she used to find there. Love. Hope. Fear. Dangerous emotions for a King, though Kami'en's stone skin helped him hide them. More and more, he was starting to resemble one of the statues his human enemies erected for their Kings.

The startled midwife toppled a basin with bloody water as the Fairy approached Amalie's bed. Even the doctors backed away from her. Goyl doctors, human doctors, Dwarf doctors. Their black frocks made them look like a murder of crows drawn in by the scent of death rather than anticipation of a new life.

Amalie's doll face was swollen with fear and pain. The lashes around her violet-blue eyes were congealed with tears. Fairy-lily eyes...The Dark Fairy thought she could see in those eyes the water of the lake that had once delivered her.

"Go away!" Amalie's voice was hoarse from screaming. "What do you want? Who called you?"

The Dark One pictured those violet eyes being snuffed out and that soft skin Kami'en so loved to touch turning cold and flaccid. The temptation to make her dead was so sweet. Too bad the Fairy couldn't indulge it, for a dead Doll would take Kami'en's son with her.

"I know why you're not letting the child out!" the Dark One whispered in Amalie's ear. "You're afraid to look at him. But I won't allow you to kill him with your dying flesh. Deliver him, or I will have him cut out of you."

How the Doll stared at her. The Fairy wasn't sure whether the hatred in Amalie's eyes revealed more fear or jealousy. Maybe love bore fruit even more poisonous than fear.

Amalie squeezed the infant out. The midwife's face turned into a contorted mask of horror and disgust. On the streets, they already called him the Skinless Prince. But he did have a skin. The Fairy's magic had given him one, as hard and as smooth as moonstone, and just as transparent. His skin revealed everything it covered: every sinew, every vein, the small skull, the eyeballs. Kami'en's son looked like Death—or at least like his youngest spawn.

Amalie groaned and pressed her hands over her eyes. Kami'en was the only one who looked at the baby without dread. The Dark Fairy took the slithery body and stroked the transparent skin

11

with her six-fingered hand until it turned as red as his father's, giving such beauty to the small face that now all the averted eyes turned back in enchantment to admire the newborn prince. Amalie reached out for her son, but the Fairy placed the baby in Kami'en's arms. She did so without looking at the King, and when she stepped out into the dark hallway, he didn't stop her.

The Dark Fairy had to pause halfway and struggle for breath on a balcony. Her hands trembled as she wiped her fingers on her dress, again and again, until she could no longer feel the warm body they'd touched.

There was no word for child in her language. There hadn't been in a long time.

2
AN ALLIANCE OF OLD FOES

John Reckless had stood in Charles de Lotharaine's audience
chamber before, once, with a different face and a different name.
Was that five years ago? He found it hard to believe it hadn't been
longer, but those past years had taught him much about time,
about yearlong days and years that passed as quickly as a day.

"These will be better?"

Charles, the Crookback, frowned as his son tried to hide another
yawn behind his hand. It was an open secret that the crown prince
Louis was suffering from the Snow-White Syndrome. The palace
kept silent about where and how the prince had contracted that
malady (as was, in these days of progress, the preferred term
for the effects of black magic). Yet the parliament of Albion had
already seen debates on the dangers (and opportunities) of a
King on the throne in Lutis who could at any moment fall into
a sleep lasting days at a time. The Albian secret service claimed

that Crookback had even gone so far as to secure the services of a child-eater to heal the crown prince. Judging by the yawns Louis tried to hide behind his dark red sleeves, she'd not been very successful.

"You have my word, and that of Wilfred of Albion, Your Majesty. The machines I will build for you will not only fly higher and faster than the airplanes of the Goyl but will also be much better armed."

What John did not mention was that he could only be so confident because those Goyl airplanes had been designed by him as well. Not even Wilfred of Albion knew of his famous engineer's past. His stolen name and new face had shielded John from such exposure, just as they protected him from the Goyl, who were supposedly still looking for him. A different nose and a different chin were a small price to pay for days spent free of fear. His nights were still shattered by dreams that were the legacy of years spent in Goyl prisons. But he'd learned to make do with little sleep. Yes, the past five years had indeed taught him a lot. Not that they had made him a better person—he was still a self-serving coward, relentlessly driven by ambition (some truths were best faced straight on). His imprisonment had taught him that, but also a lot about this world and its inhabitants.

"Should your generals be concerned that airplanes may not be the answer to the military superiority of the Goyl, then I can assure you that the parliament of Albion shares these concerns and has authorized me to address them by presenting two of my most recent inventions."

The authorization had, in fact, been issued by King Wilfred himself, but it seemed best to maintain appearances. Albion was proud of its democratic traditions, though the true power still rested with the King and the nobility. It was no different in Lotharaine, though here the people had a less romantic view of noble and crowned heads — one of the reasons for the armed riots that were currently plaguing the capital.

Louis yawned again. The crown prince had a reputation for being as stupid as he looked. Stupid, moody, and with cruel tendencies that worried even his father. And Charles of Lotharaine was getting old, though he dyed his hair black and was still a handsome man.

John motioned one of the guards who had accompanied him from Albion to come closer. The Walrus (this moniker for Wilfred the First was so fitting, John was perpetually worried he might one day actually use it to address his royal employer) had him well guarded. Albion's King had insisted, over John's well-known dislike for ships, that his best engineer go in person to sell Crookback on the idea of an alliance. The construction plans, which the guard now handed to the King's adjutant, had been drawn by John especially for this audience, leaving out a few vital details he would supply after the alliance was completed. Crookback's engineers wouldn't notice. After all, John was confronting them with the technology of another world.

"I call these 'tanks.'" John had to suppress a smile as his Lotharainian competition leaned over the drawings with an obvious mix of envy and incredulous awe. "Not even the Goyl cavalry can withstand these machines."

The second drawing showed rockets with explosive warheads. There were indeed moments when John's conscience tried to put him on trial. He could have brought inventions into this world that would have made it healthier and more just for its people. He usually soothed his conscience with a generous donation to an orphanage, or to Albion's suffragettes, though that of course brought up memories of his wife, Rosamund, and of Jacob and Will.

"Who is going to manufacture these valves?" an engineer asked doubtfully.

John returned to the present, where he was a man without sons and where the woman in his life was the daughter of a Leonese diplomat and fifteen years his junior.

"If they can make those valves in Albion," Crookback barked at the engineer, "then we can damn well do it here. Or will I have to recruit my engineers from the universities of Pendragon and Londra?"

The engineer's face lost all color, and the King's advisors regarded John with cold eyes. Everyone in the hall knew what the King's answer meant. The decision was made: Albion and Lotharaine would form an alliance against the Goyl. A historic decision for this world. Two nations that for centuries had used any excuse to declare war on one another, now turned into allies by a common foe. The old and eternal game.

John decided to go to the palace gardens to write a missive informing the Walrus and the parliament of Albion of his diplomatic success, even though it turned out to be near impossible to find a bench without a statue towering over it. His phobia against stone statuary was just one of the irritating consequences of his imprisonment by the Goyl.

He finally found a bench under a tree. As he wrote the message that would shake the balance of power in this world, his uniformed guardians used the time to stare after the ladies of the court as they ambled between the pristine hedges. They certainly seemed to confirm the rumor that it was Crookback's ambition to have

16

all the most beautiful women of Lotharaine gathered at his court. John found a little comfort in the fact that Crookback was an even worse husband than he. After all, John had never been unfaithful to Rosamund until he discovered the mirror. And as far as his affairs in Schwanstein, Vena, and Blenheim were concerned, one could certainly wonder whether having such dalliances in a different world actually counted as adultery. *Oh yes, they do, John.*

As he put his signature under the dispatch (with a fountain pen he'd discreetly modernized, after having grown tired of ink-stained fingers), he saw a man rushing toward him across the white gravel paths. He'd noticed the man before, standing in the audience chamber by the crown prince's side. The unexpected visitor wore an old-fashioned-looking frock coat, and he was barely taller than a large Dwarf. The spectacles he nervously adjusted as he stopped in front of John had such thick lenses they made the eyes behind them look as large as an insect's. Fittingly, his pupils were just as black and shiny as insect eyes.

"Monsieur Brunel?" A curtsy, a servile smile. "With your permission: Arsene Lelou, tutor to His Highness the crown prince Louis. Could I, possibly, eh"—he cleared his throat as though his assignment were stuck there like a splinter—"bother you with a request?"

"Certainly. What is it?"

Maybe Monsieur Lelou needed help in explaining some technical innovation. It couldn't be easy to be the teacher of a future King in such a rapidly advancing world. Yet Arsene Lelou's request had nothing to do with the New Magic, as science and technology were referred to behind the mirror.

"My, eh, royal pupil," he lisped, "has for these past months been fielding inquiries regarding the whereabouts of a man who has also worked for the Albian royal court. And since you are a member of that court, I wanted to take this opportunity to ask you in His Highness's name for your aid in our search for this person."

John had heard nasty stories about how Louis of Lotharaine dealt with his enemies, so the man Arsene was asking him about already had his deepest sympathy.

"Certainly. May I ask whom you are inquiring about?" Always best to feign helpfulness.

"His name is Reckless. Jacob Reckless. He is a famous, if not infamous, treasure hunter who has worked in the service of, among others, the deposed Empress of Austry."

John noted with irritation his hand trembling as he handed his signed dispatch to one of his guards. How easily one's own body could turn traitor.

Arsene Lelou noticed the trembling hand.

"A bite from a will-o'-the-wisp," John explained. "Years ago, but I still have that tremor in my hands." He'd never been more grateful for his new face, for he had once looked very much like his elder son. "You may relay to the crown prince that he can cease his inquiries. To my knowledge, Jacob Reckless died when the Goyl sank the Albian fleet."

He was proud of the calmness of his voice. Arsene Lelou would not know that the news John had just related had rendered him unable to work for days. His own reaction to the news of Jacob's death had startled John so much that at first he'd been utterly convinced the tears dripping on his newspaper had to be someone else's.

His elder son....John had, of course, known for years that Jacob had followed him through the mirror. All the newspapers

18

had reported on his treasure-hunting feats. Still, the unexpected encounter in Goldsmouth had been a shock, but his new face had worked even then. It had hidden everything he'd felt at that moment of meeting, the shock and the love, as well as the surprise that he still felt so much love.

That Jacob had followed him had not surprised John. It had been no real accident he'd left the words to guide his son through the mirror in one of his books. (John himself had found the words in a tome on chemistry left behind by one of Rosamund's illustrious ancestors.) John had been fascinated that his elder son had made it his mission to seek this world's lost past while his father was bringing it into the future. In that way, Jacob took more after his mother. Rosamund had also always tried to preserve rather than to change. Could a father be proud of a son he'd abandoned? Yes. John had collected every article about Jacob's achievements, every picture that showed his face or illustrated his deeds. Of course, nobody, including his own mistress, ever knew this. And of course, he'd also hidden from her the tears he'd shed for his son.

"The sinking of the fleet? Oh yes. Impressive." Arsene Lelou swiped a fly from his large, pale forehead. "The airplanes have indeed given the Goyl too many victories. I shall await with burning impatience the day your machines defend our sacred lands. Thanks to your genius, Lotharaine will finally have an appropriate answer against the Stone King."

The toadying smile Lelou gave him reminded John of the icing the child-eaters put on their gingerbread. Arsene Lelou was a dangerous man.

"However, if I may be so bold as to correct you..." Lelou continued with obvious glee. "The Albian secret service may

19

not be as omniscient as its reputation suggests. Jacob Reckless *survived* the sinking of the fleet. I myself had the dubious pleasure of meeting him a few weeks after. Reckless calls Albion his home. And through my inquiries, I've learned that for many of his treasure hunts he relies on the expertise of Robert Dunbar, professor of history at the University of Pendragon. All that makes it more than likely he will, sooner or later, turn up at the Albian court. He does need royal sponsors. Believe me, Monsieur Brunel, I wouldn't have bothered you if I wasn't convinced you could be of great service to the crown prince in this matter."

John would not have been able to name his emotions. They were, again, surprisingly strong. Lelou *had* to be wrong! There had been barely any survivors, and he'd pored over the lists dozens of times. And? What difference did it make whether his son was alive or dead? To give up the only one he'd ever loved unselfishly was the price John had paid for his new life. Yet those years in the dark dungeons of the Goyl had made the wish to be forgiven by his elder son grow like one of the colorless plants the Goyl grew in their caves... And with it had come the hope that the love he'd discarded so carelessly might not be lost for good. He had to admit he'd always been forgiven most readily. His mother, his wife, his mistresses... Yet a son was probably not as eager to absolve a father, especially not a son as proud as Jacob.

Oh yes, John remembered Jacob's pride. And his fearlessness. Jacob had been too young to recognize his father for the coward he was. Fear had dominated all of John's life. Fear of the opinions of others. Fear of failure and poverty. Fear of his own weakness, his own vanity. His incarceration by the Goyl had been a relief at first—finally a *real* reason to be afraid. Cowardice was more ridiculous when one lived where the greatest physical threat came from the traffic on the streets.

"Monsieur Brunel?"

Arsene Lelou was still there.

John forced a smile. "You have my word, Monsieur Lelou. I will make inquiries. And should I hear news of Jacob Reckless, you will be the first to know."

The bug eyes glistened with curiosity. Arsene Lelou had not bought John's story of the will-o'-the-wisp. Isambard Brunel had a secret. John had a strong feeling that Monsieur Lelou was an avid collector of such secrets and that he was also a master at turning them into gold and influence. But John had some experience in keeping secrets, too.

John rose from his bench. Probably not a bad idea to remind the little bug that he was the taller man. "Is your royal pupil interested in the teachings of the New Magic, Monsieur Lelou?"

As a little boy, Jacob had listened for hours while his father explained the function of an electric switch or the secrets of a battery. The same son who years later dedicated his life to the rediscovery of the Old Magic. A subconscious statement against his father? After all, John had never made a secret of the fact that the only miracles he was interested in were the man-made ones.

"Oh, certainly! The crown prince is a great advocate of progress." Arsene Lelou tried hard to sound convincing, yet his slightly awkward look confirmed what was said about Louis at the Albian court: Nothing could hold the attention of Lotharaine's future King for more than a few minutes except dice and girls of any provenance. Recently, though, if the Albian spies were to be believed, Louis seemed to have also developed a passion for weapons of any kind. Not a very good hobby for someone as cruel

21

as Louis, yet possibly an asset for Albion's attempts to modernize both countries' armies.

And you, John, will show them how to build tanks and rockets. No, it wasn't quite true that John had no conscience at all. Everyone had one. But there were many voices in his head that had an easier time reaching him: his ambition, his desire for fame and success—and for revenge. For four stolen years. Admittedly, the Goyl didn't treat their prisoners as badly as the Walrus or Crookback did. Still, he wanted revenge.

3

HIS HOME

The building in which Jacob had grown up rose into the sky higher than any of the castle towers that had intimidated Fox as a child. He looked different in this world. Fox had no words to describe the difference, but she felt it as clearly as she felt the difference between skin and fur. These past weeks had helped explain much of what she'd never understood.

Above her, the stone faces stared from the walls like fossils from a Goyl city, but among all this piled-up steel, the walls of glass, the haze of exhaust fumes, and the ceaseless noise, Fox felt the other world like a piece of clothing she and Jacob wore hidden from sight. People, houses, streets—there was too much of everything in this world. And too little forest that could have offered shelter from it all. It hadn't been easy to reach the city where Jacob had grown up. The borders in his world were more tightly guarded than the island of the Fairies. Forged papers, with her photographed face showing all the lostness she couldn't hide. Train stations, airports, so many new words. Fox had seen clouds from above and nighttime streets that looked like fiery snakes. She would never forget any of it, but she was glad the mirror that had brought her here was not the only one and that she'd soon be going home.

That's what they'd come here for, to go back, and to see Will and Clara, of course. Jacob had talked by phone with Will a few times since they'd come to his world. He'd driven the jade from his brother's skin, but Jacob was aware he could never undo all the things Will had lived through behind the mirror. How much had it changed his brother? Jacob never asked this aloud, but Fox knew the question preoccupied him.

For now, though, she was wondering how Jacob must feel seeing Clara again, even though the past months had made them feel so close it seemed almost immaterial if he kissed others. Almost.

Jacob held open a heavy door that must have been impossible for him to open as a child. Fox squeezed past him, feeling his warmth like a home. A home even in this world. She could tell that Jacob was glad she was here. His two lives brought together. For years he'd asked her to come with him. Now she felt sorry she'd always said no.

Fox looked around while Jacob exchanged polite words with the wheezing doorman. Compared to the shabby house she'd spent her childhood in, Jacob had grown up in a palace. The grilled door of the elevator he now waved her toward reminded her a little too much of a cage, but Fox did her best not to let Jacob see her uneasiness, just as she'd done in the airplane that had brought them here. Only the sight of the clouds had made up for the metal confinement.

"Just one more night." Even in this world Jacob read her thoughts. "We're going back as soon as I've gotten rid of this thing."

Jacob carried the swindlesack that concealed the crossbow under his shirt. The sack's magic still worked. Jacob couldn't explain why. So far, all objects he'd brought through the mirror had lost their magical powers. He claimed it was because of the crossbow, but her fur dress also still worked. Fox had been very relieved. Being able to shift into the vixen's body had helped her not to become completely lost in this strange world, though it hadn't been easy to find places where she could shift unobserved. The dizziness she felt as she stepped out of the elevator reminded her of her childhood, of climbing trees that were always a bit too tall. A window framed Jacob's city: trees of glass, chimney reeds, rusty water-tank flowers.

Fox hadn't seen Will in almost a year. In her memory, he still had a skin of stone, but the joy on his face as he opened the door made those memories disappear like bad dreams. She did think Will looked tired. The mirror had given the brothers very different gifts, and wasn't that just the way magic objects worked? One sister's gold was the other one's pitch.

Will barely seemed to notice how much Fox had changed. Clara, on the other hand, looked at her as though she couldn't believe this was the same girl she'd known in another world. Fox wanted to tell her, *I've always been older than you; that's how the fur works*. The vixen was always young and old at the same time. Fox remembered the closeness she'd shared with Clara—and the feeling of betrayal when she'd caught her kissing Jacob. And Clara remembered, too. Fox could see it in her eyes.

Jacob had made Fox promise not to tell Clara or his brother

25

how he'd nearly paid with his life for getting Will his human skin back. And so Fox had kept quiet about their race against death and instead answered their questions about how she liked this world. Oh, the things we never talk about...

At some point, she asked Clara to point her in the direction of the bathroom. On her way back, she stepped into what she immediately recognized from Jacob's stories as his room. A shelf with tattered books, photographs of Will and their mother on a desk into which he'd carved his initials. He'd carved something else into the wood: the profile of a fox. Fox ran her fingers over the carving, which was stained with red ink.

"Everything all right?" Jacob was standing in the doorway.

Once more Fox noticed how different he looked in the clothes of this world. There was no point in trying to pretend she felt all right. Jacob had told her how on his first trips through the mirror Alma had to feed him medicines for days. But in this world there was no Witch who could help the body adjust to the strangeness.

"Why don't you go back now? I'll join you tomorrow evening."

There were photographs above his bed—not the sepia pictures of Fox's world but fully colored images of faces that meant nothing to her. She'd been so certain she knew every crevice of his heart, but Jacob was like a country she'd only traveled through halfway. She wanted to visit the places he loved in this world, where he came from... But for now this was probably enough. Her body yearned for her world, as if she'd been breathing the wrong air for too long.

"Yes," she said. "Maybe you're right. Will and Clara will understand, won't they?"

"Absolutely." He stroked her forehead, which ached. The noises of this world had settled behind it like a swarm of wasps.

26

Fox had imagined the room with the mirror almost exactly: Jacob's father's dusty desk, and above it the models that looked so like the plane they'd used to escape from the Goyl fortress. The pistols that looked like they came from her world...and maybe they did.

"You're not leaving because of her, are you?" Jacob tried to sound casual, but Fox could hear that the question had been on his mind for hours.

"Her?" They both knew who he meant, but Fox couldn't resist. "The girl in the chocolate shop? Or the girl who sold you the flowers for Clara?"

Jacob smiled, relieved to hear the sarcasm in her voice.

"When you get to Schwanstein, send a telegram to Robert Dunbar." His glance toward the mirror told Fox how much he wanted to come with her. "Ask him what he knows about Alderelves. I want to know how many there were, and how you'd recognize one. Also their enemies, allies, weaknesses... Anything he can find."

Robert Dunbar was one of Albion's most renowned historians. His knowledge had helped Jacob on many of his treasure hunts. He was also half Fir Darrig, hiding his rat tail under his coats, and he owed Jacob his life.

"Alderelves? Have you smelled blood? Are you going to look for more of their magic weapons?"

"No, I think one is enough." Jacob's voice sounded serious. Fox knew he had something on his mind that he didn't yet want to talk about.

"Some things are best never found, Jacob." Fox wasn't exactly sure what made her repeat Dunbar's warning about the crossbow.

"Don't worry." Jacob handed her the clothes she would need in

27

the other world. "I don't have any wish to find the lost Elves. I just want to make sure we haven't already found them."

She should stay, but she had no idea which world he was talking about. She believed him safe in his.

Jacob leaned against his father's desk as Fox stepped toward the mirror. She touched the glass. She already missed him.

4

A Safe Haven

The Metropolitan Museum of Art stood above the constant flow of traffic like a temple, though Jacob couldn't say what gods were worshipped here: the arts, the past, or the human urge to create useless things and then dress up useful things in beauty. The wide steps were teeming with schoolchildren. When Jacob didn't join any of the admission lines, a grouchy guard asked him where he thought he was going, but the guard immediately became chatty when Jacob mentioned Fran's name. She was probably the only curator who brought home-baked bread (after a French recipe from the Middle Ages) or Russian walnut cake for the museum employees. Frances Tyrpak would have fit in perfectly behind the mirror, and not only that but her knowledge of antique weaponry would have served her very well there.

Jacob had borrowed Will's backpack to transport the crossbow. His own bag was so tattered that it was much more fitting for a

29

treasure hunt than for visiting a museum, and even Fran would've found it hard to accept seeing him pull a weapon of that size from a barely palm-sized pouch.

Swords, sabers, spears, maces... One could have outfitted an entire medieval army with the items on display in the Met's Arms and Armor collection, and the halls Jacob walked through showcased only a fraction of that collection. Every modern museum of this world had treasure vaults that often filled entire floors of their buildings. They were, of course, much less romantic than the vaults behind the mirror, but they did preserve their treasures much more effectively: climate-controlled, windowless rooms, precious items hidden in white drawers, in boxes, and behind metal doors. The perfect hiding place for a weapon that should never see the light of day again.

Fran was supervising two men who were dressing the figure of a horseman in a rich armor bristling with gold and silver. Not an easy task, and the stiff mannequin sitting on an equally stiff horse made it even harder for the two, who didn't seem to be adept at their task. Fran had deep furrows in her brow.

"A suit of presentation armor from 1737 Florence." She greeted Jacob with a deadpan voice, as though she saw him in her exhibition rooms every day. "The only time this was worn was for a royal wedding. Quite ridiculous and almost sensationally tasteless, but it's quite a sight, isn't it? I read it was too big for its owner, so he had stuffing added to it and then nearly died of heatstroke." Fran pointed to one of the glass-fronted cabinets along the wall. "That spear you sold me is quite the attraction. But I still don't believe it's from Libya. I will find the truth one day. But it's a gem."

Jacob had to smile. It really was a pity he couldn't take Fran Tyrpak on a trip behind the mirror.

"I admit the spear has its secrets," he said, putting the backpack on one of the padded benches where people could sit and marvel at the artistry of objects whose sole purpose was to kill. "But I promise you, I never lied about where it's from."

Behind the mirror, they called it Lubim, but its borders were almost identical to those of what Fran knew as Libya. The equivalent country behind the mirror was ruled by a deranged emir who drowned his enemies in vats of rose water. The spear brought forth armies of golden scorpions wherever it struck the ground. Jacob had, of course, always assumed it would lose that power on this side, but since the swindlesack and Fox's fur dress had kept their magic, he couldn't be so sure anymore. The spear's thick glass home gave him some consolation. Just two nights earlier, he'd spent hours making a mental list of all the things he'd brought into this world.

Fran's eyes widened behind her tortoiseshell glasses as Jacob pulled the crossbow from the backpack.

"Twelfth century?"

"Sounds about right," Jacob answered as he handed her the weapon, though he didn't have the faintest idea when or where the Alderelves had created it. Should Fran ever have its wood examined, she'd certainly get some very mysterious results.

One of the men dressing the knight lost his footing on the ladder, and a jewel-encrusted arm-guard barely missed Fran's head before it clanged on the floor by her feet. She shot a barbed glance at the man, but her real concern was neither for her head nor for the precious arm-guard, but for the crossbow, which she had pressed to her chest.

Jacob picked up the piece of armor and examined the jewels set into the metal. "Glass."

"Sure. The descendants sold off the original jewels. Quite normal. The Italian nobility was perpetually bankrupt."

Fran pointed at the silver covering the crossbow's handle. "These embellishments look like nothing I've seen before."

"You should avoid touching those for too long."

Fran raised a quizzical eyebrow. "Why?"

"There are...stories about the crossbow. The silver may have been laced with some poison. And there's supposedly a curse on it, one that works even in our godless times. Whatever it is, the last owner of this crossbow succumbed to a fatal madness." *And I met his living corpse.* He could hardly tell Fran that most magical weapons were known to be devious and evil, and more than eager to do their work.

"Who'd believe it—Jacob Reckless is superstitious?" Fran's smile was so incredulous Jacob felt quite flattered. She put the crossbow on the display case next to them. "You acquired this legally, did you?"

"Fran Tyrpak!" Jacob managed to sound truly offended. "Hasn't my paperwork always been beyond reproach?" He'd learned to forge documents and seals from one of the most talented forgers behind the mirror. An indispensable skill when one dealt in goods from another world.

"Yes." Fran eyed the crossbow with obvious desire. "Your papers are always flawless. Maybe a little *too* flawless."

A dangerous subject.

Jacob handed the arm-guard up to the workers.

Fran was not paying attention to anything but the crossbow. "I've never seen such a bowstring," she mumbled. "If I didn't know better, I'd swear it was made of glass."

Her eyes pleaded, *Come on, tell me the truth! What kind of a*

32

weapon is this? Her gaze looked so wise that for a moment Jacob felt uncertain whether he'd come to the right place. Maybe he'd already pushed his luck too far with the spear.

"The string is indeed made of glass," he said. "A very rare technique."

"So rare that I've never heard about it?" Fran adjusted her glasses as she scrutinized the silver. "Very unusual. I think I may have seen a similar pattern some years ago on a dagger. But that came from England."

Another Elven weapon in this world? What could that mean? Nothing good. Jacob felt a sense of danger he'd so far known only in the other world. "Is that dagger in your collection?"

"No. As far as I remember, it belongs to a private collector. I can find out for you. How much for the crossbow?"

"I'm not sure I actually want to sell it yet. Would you mind storing it for me for a while? The dealer I got it from treats his merchandise so badly it would've been better off buried in a bog."

Fran's eyes darkened as if Jacob had told her the dealer was a cannibal, though in her eyes even that probably would've been a minor offense in comparison to ill-treating such a beautifully crafted piece of weaponry.

"Admit it—you got this from one of those crooks who cause more damage to our cultural heritage than all the world's exhaust fumes combined. Which one? Thistleman? Dechoubrant? If it were up to me. I'd have them all executed—by firing squad. But why don't you want to sell this crossbow? You're not sentimental. How is it special?"

Oh, she would have loved the story. The palace of a dead king, the Waterman, the Witch's clock, the marksmanship of a Goyl...

Jacob zipped the empty backpack. "Let's just say I'm in its

debt."

Fran's eyes pierced him as though trying to skewer the truth out of his head, but her fingers were already closing around the crossbow's handle. Like him, she was a treasure hunter, guardian of a lost past that had left only its traces in gold and silver. Too bad he couldn't tell her about the bolt that had pierced his chest and saved his life. Or about the two armies destroyed by this one crossbow. Fran would've appreciated these stories.

"Fine," she said. "I'll have it archived — *if* you'll permit me to let our conservators take a closer look."

"Absolutely. I'd love to know more about its history myself." And about the smith who could make bowstrings out of glass. But there was probably not much to be learned about the Alderelves in this world, even if one's laboratory was as good as the Met's.

"How long shall I keep it for you?"

"One year?"

By then, hopefully, he would have learned how the crossbow could be destroyed. Of course, he didn't tell Fran about this. He'd already tried fire, explosives, and a saw, but these hadn't even left a scratch. Only the fire had made the wood a little darker.

✵ ✵ ✵

A museum made it easy to forget which world you were in. But back outside, at the top of the steps, the noise of the Fifth Avenue traffic gave Jacob such an abrupt reminder where he was he found it hard to handle the wave of homesickness washing over him. Not that the streets of Vena or Lutis were any less noisy. It was surprising how much noise horse-drawn carriages and coaches could make. Below him people were crowding the wide sidewalks on their way to bus stops and coffee carts, but in his mind's eye he saw the castle ruin with the roofs of Schwanstein in the distance. When he spotted Clara at the bottom of the steps, he nearly stumbled into a tourist who was coming up.

Will? Jacob's heartbeat was set racing by all the worries he'd tried to keep at bay ever since he sent his brother back through the mirror. It was ridiculous how any unusual gesture or expression he'd not seen on his brother's face before immediately took him back to those moments in the palace in Vena where Will had nearly killed him. But Clara smiled at him reassuringly, and Jacob slowed so that he wouldn't stumble over his own feet. If this wasn't about Will, then what was she doing here?

Yes, what, Jacob? Oh, he could be such a fool. Naive like a puppy, he stumbled straight into the trap. But the face at the bottom of the steps was so familiar. It still reminded him of all they'd been through together. His memory's soft focus had turned even the Larks' Water into a pleasant anecdote. He noticed she was wearing leather gloves despite the warmth of this summer morning, but he didn't think too much of it.

"What are you doing in a museum so early in the morning?"

Even the question didn't raise Jacob's suspicion. But then she kissed him on the lips.

"Just think of the unicorns," she whispered to him.

And she pushed him into the oncoming traffic.

Screeching brakes. Horns. Screams. Maybe even his own.

He closed his eyes too late.

Felt a bumper break his arm.

Metal and glass.

5

THE PRICE

It was so quiet Jacob assumed he was dead. But then he felt his body. The pain in his arm.

He opened his eyes.

He wasn't kneeling on pavement, as he would've expected, nor lying in his own blood, but on ultramarine-blue wool embellished with silver and woven into such soft thickness as found only in the most precious carpets.

"I apologize for the crude joke. Your brother's bride as a lure — it was simply irresistible. She has the same grace your mother had, though she does lack a bit of the mystery, doesn't she? It's probably what your brother likes about her. He already has too much mystery himself."

Jacob looked up to find the face for the voice. His neck ached as though someone had tried to break it. A man was sitting in a black leather chair a few feet away. The same chair stood in the museum. The museum in front of which Clara had pushed him into the moving traffic. Department for Modern and Contemporary Art. *Get up, Jacob!* He couldn't tell what was making him more nauseous — the collision with the car, or Clara's blank face as she'd pushed him into the street.

The man was maybe in his late thirties, and he possessed a beauty that seemed strangely old-fashioned. His face would have fit well in a painting by Holbein or Dürer. His suit, however, had been crafted by a modern tailor, as had his shirt. He gave an amused smile as Jacob's eyes fixed on the tiny ruby in his earlobe.

"Ah, you *do* remember."

The voice had been different when they last met in Chicago. Norebo Johann Earlking.

"Rubies." He touched his ear. "I've always had a weakness for them."

Jacob managed to sit up, though he had to grab a table for balance.

"Is this your real face?"

"Real? A big word. Let's say it's closer to my own than the one I showed you in Chicago. The Fairies like to make a secret of their names, and we Alderelves like to hide our true guises."

"So the name is real?"

"Does it sound real? No. You can call me Spieler..."

He followed Jacob's glance out the window.

"Fantastic view, isn't it? We're barely a stone's throw from Manhattan. Amazing how easy it is to hide under the mantle of apparent disuse."

The derelict landscape outside the window stood in stark contrast to the precious furniture. Crumbling buildings drowning in ivy, and the unrestrained growth of a forest battling human construction.

"You mortals place such a touching importance on appearances."

37

Spieler got up and went to the window. "Animals aren't fooled as easily. A few decades ago, your lot were almost onto us because some rare heron didn't want to share this island with us." He drew on a cigarette he balanced between his slender fingers. Six fingers on each hand, as on all immortals. Spieler blew the smoke toward Jacob, and the narrow room suddenly became as wide as a palace hall, with walls clad in silver and chandeliers made of elven glass. The only object that didn't change was a marble sculpture of startling beauty. This eliminated Jacob's final doubt about who he was dealing with. The sculpture was of a tree, and captured in its bark was a face frozen in mid-scream.

"*Exile*. At first you try to make it bearable by imitating the familiar." Spieler took another drag from his cigarette. "Yet that gets very monotonous very quickly, and it reminds you too much of all you've lost."

The view from the window disappeared into smoke. The trees vanished, and the water of a river reflected the skyline of a city that seemed strange and still familiar. New York maybe a hundred years ago? No Empire State Building.

"Time. Another thing your kind takes too seriously." Spieler crushed the cigarette into a silver ashtray, and the hall shrank back into the room where Jacob had awoken, with the same desolate view through the window. "Not foolish, trying to disappear the crossbow into the archives of the museum. After all, how could you have known that Frances Tyrpak is a good friend of mine? Of course, she knows me with a different face. A lot of the Met exhibits were donated by us. But I assume you realize you're not here because of the crossbow. Or have you forgotten your debt to me?"

Debt...

Jacob thought he could smell forgetyourself, the mythical flower of the Bluebeards. Yes, his worry over the crossbow had made it easy to forget his debt. Together with the desperation that had made him careless enough to engage in such a magical trade. Careless? There wasn't much choice when you were caught in a Bluebeard's labyrinth.

"There's a charming tale from our world about a Stilt who teaches some useless peasant girl how to spin straw into gold," Spieler continued. "She, of course, tricks him. Even though all he'd asked for was rightfully his."

Today I bake,
tomorrow brew,
the next I'll have
the young Queen's firstborn child.

Jacob had never been too impressed by the Rumpelstiltskin's threat—his mother had to explain to him what a firstborn was. And even now, he doubted he'd ever have children anyway.

Spieler saw the relief on Jacob's face and smiled.

"You don't seem to mind my price. So let me be quite clear: As soon as the vixen puts her first child into your arms, that child is mine. You can take your time with your payment, but pay you will."

No.

No what, Jacob?

"Why should her first child be mine? We are friends, nothing more."

Spieler now looked bemused, as though Jacob had tried to tell him the world was a flat disc. "Oh, please! You're talking to an

39

Elf. I know your most intimate wishes. It's my business to fulfill them."

"Name another price. Any other." Jacob hardly recognized his own voice.

"Why should I? This is my price, and you will pay it. Your vixen will make beautiful children. I hope you don't take too long."

How love suddenly tasted of guilt, all wishes of treason. How clear one's own desires become once they are made impossible. All the nonsense he'd convinced himself of—that he didn't love her in that way, that his yearning didn't really mean anything... Lies. He wanted her forever by his side; he wanted to be the only one in her life, the only one who mattered, the only one who'd give her children, the only one who'd see her grow old.

Never, Jacob. Forbidden. He'd sold his future. That he'd sold it to save her life was little consolation.

"Payment is due only in the world where the deal was struck." It was a pathetic attempt.

"Into which I shall never return lest I want to be turned into a tree? Ah, yes. I'd forgotten about that small detail. But I have to disappoint you again. We shall return. Soon. Some of us, at least."

The Elf stood by the window.

Get out of here, Jacob.

There were two doors. And then what? If the Elf was to be believed, they were on an island. There were a few islands in the East River, and swimming through those dangerous waters was not a very enticing prospect, especially with a broken arm.

Spieler had his back to Jacob. He was talking about the Fairies, about their vengefulness, about human ingratitude. He seemed to like the sound of his own voice. Who else would listen to him?

40

He'd mentioned others. How many had escaped? Jacob's eyes were drawn to a mirror leaning against the wall near the sculpture of the Elf frozen into the tree. The mirror was even larger than the one in his father's study. The frame sprouted the same silver roses, though this one had magpies sitting among the thorny vines.

Spieler was still looking out the window, and the mirror was just a few steps away. Jacob reached it before the Elf could turn. The glass was as warm as an animal, but no matter how hard he pressed his hand over the reflection of his face, the mirror still showed the same room.

Spieler turned around.

"Even your kind can make a sheer endless number of all sorts of mirrors. Do you really believe we are any less inventive?" He went to the desk under the window and leafed through some papers. "Fairy and Alderelf. They once belonged together, like day and night. Did you know that? Our children were mortal, but always exceptional. They would be crowned, declared geniuses, revered as gods. In this world, we can have children with mortal women, but those are often shockingly mediocre."

Jacob stayed standing in front of the mirror. No matter how hard he tried, he couldn't turn away from it. It was as though the glass were peeling layers off his soul.

"It's stealing your face," he heard Spieler say. "Ironically, it was a mortal who came up with the idea to use our mirrors to create more reliable helpers than your kind seemed able to provide. Show yourself."

The air in the room grew warmer, and the sunlight coming through the window broke around two figures of mirrored glass. The whole room was reflected in these figures—the white wall, the desk, the chair, the frame of the window. Their bodies became clearer as the faces took on the color of human skin and the reflections turned into clothes. The illusion was perfect, except for the hands. This time the girl wasn't even wearing gloves: Glassy fingers with silver fingernails rose to touch Clara's face. The boy by her side looked younger than Will, but who could tell how old they were?

"Just a few weeks old," Spieler said.

Could the Alderelf read all his thoughts?

"You've met Sixteen. Seventeen has even more faces than she does, but I thought it might be useful to give him yours as well."

Jacob pushed the girl away as she reached out to him. Her brother, if he could be called that, didn't like it, but Spieler shot him a warning glance, and Seventeen's body turned reflective again until it was as invisible as polished glass. Sixteen did the same, but only after giving Jacob a parting smile from Clara's lips.

"It's an interesting place, that hospital where I stole your brother's bride's face. A good place to watch Death at work. Mortality is such a mystery." Spieler pulled a medallion from his pocket. It contained two mirrors, each the size of a clock face. One was clear, the other much darker. "All I had to do was put the medallion on the table in the nurses' station. You humans love mirrors. You have to constantly make sure you still have the same face. Nothing scares you more than if someone changes it."

Spieler changed into the man whom Jacob had met in Chicago. Norebo Johann Earlking. "The stunted growth, the green eyes... Oberon, the Elf whose Dwarf-sized body was the result of a Fairy curse. I admit I had expected you to catch that allusion. The name was so obvious. I stole the face from an actor who played Oberon on stage. I've always found it entertaining to play with the images

42

your kind has created of us, and of yourselves."

The Alderelf's faces came and went. Some were familiar to Jacob; some weren't. Until he was suddenly looking at a face that for a long time he'd known only from photographs.

Spieler brushed John Reckless's graying hair from his forehead. "Your mother never noticed the difference. I was very fond of her. Too much, I have to admit. But I fear that I, like your father, failed to make her happy."

6

A Visitor for Clara

Clara first noticed the girl as she was talking to one of the doctors about a child with an inflamed appendix. The face seemed familiar, but she had too much on her mind to pay close attention to the stranger.

Will had not slept again, and he still didn't want to talk about what was really keeping him awake. He found excuses, for her and for himself. The moon. Something he ate. A book he'd wanted to finish. He tended to hide worries, wishes, or feelings he was ashamed of from himself and others. It had taken Clara a long time to see that. Her invisible Will. So hard to pin down. Sometimes she imagined a locked room deep in his heart, which even he never entered. Except in his sleep.

But it wasn't just Will. These past weeks she'd felt quite strange herself. As though someone had been inside her head and had taken something away. The feeling was particularly strong when

44

she looked in the mirror in the morning. Sometimes her own face seemed alien to her, or she felt as though her childhood face, or that of her mother, was looking back at her from the misted glass. She'd started to remember things she hadn't thought about in years. Her entire past life seemed to be coming back to her, as though someone had stirred up the tea leaves of her memories. She had not told Will, of course, or anyone. What could she say? *Someone was inside my head and stole something* — a ridiculous diagnosis for a would-be doctor.

Still, she'd been tempted to talk to Jacob about it. It was silly how much she looked forward to seeing him. She tried to tell herself it wasn't Jacob she missed, but the life he lived and the world he lived in, but it was no good. It pained her that she couldn't hear enough of the stories Jacob and Fox told her and Will. Didn't she do everything to avoid reminding Will of the other world? Hadn't she wished the mirror to hell a thousand times over? And yet far too often she caught herself sneaking into that dusty room when Will was out, staring into the glass as though it could show her the world waiting on the other side like a forbidden fruit. Did Will feel the same? If he did, he didn't show it.

Clara was sitting at the nurses' station, finishing some charts the doctors would need the next morning, when the girl she'd noticed before was suddenly standing right in front of her. Clara hadn't even heard her approach.

"Clara Ferber?" The girl smiled. Clara noticed she was wearing gloves, even though it was a hot day. They were made of pale yellow leather. "I'm to give this to you. From an admirer."

The girl took a box from her bag. She opened it before offering it to Clara. On a bed of silver fabric lay a brooch in the shape of a moth, the wings fashioned from black lacquer. Clara had never seen a more beautiful thing. Before she knew it, she was holding the brooch in her hand. She could barely resist the temptation to pin it to her scrubs.

"What admirer?" she asked. Will would never buy her anything so expensive. They barely had enough money for their apartment. Will's mother had left it to her sons, but with a hefty unpaid mortgage.

The pin pricked her finger as she returned the brooch to its box. "I cannot accept this."

"Clara." The girl pronounced the name as though she was savoring its sound on her tongue. How did she know Clara's name? Of course. The name tag on her scrubs.

The girl took the brooch and, despite Clara's protests, pinned it on her. "I wish I had a name," she said. "Sixteen. But that's just for those who came before me."

What was she talking about? Clara saw a drop of blood on her finger. The needle had gone surprisingly deep. Heavens, she was suddenly so tired. Too many night shifts.

She looked up.

The girl had her face.

"It's just as beautiful as your name," she said. "I have many faces." She became the girl again. Yes, Clara remembered that face. It reminded her of a photograph Will had of his mother. She tried to get up, and her knee hit the desk.

Her legs buckled. Sleep. She just wanted to sleep.

"Spindles. Thorns." The girl sneered. "A brooch is so much better."

7

THE BLOODY CRIB

The woman was hysterical. Donnersmarck didn't understand a word she was muttering in her peasant dialect, her bloody hands stretched toward him. The two Goyl soldiers who'd found the screaming nursemaid in the corridor were visibly disgusted by so much human lack of restraint, yet even their faces showed some of the horror the woman was screaming into the palace.

"Where is the Empress?" Donnersmarck demanded.

"In her dressing room. Nobody dares to tell her." The soldier who'd answered had the same carnelian skin as his King. Amalie allowed only guards with her husband's skin to attend her.

"Nobody dares to tell her." And so they'd come to him. God knows, Donnersmarck would've rather delivered different news to his former employer's daughter, especially just after Her Imperial Majesty Amalie had taken him back into her service despite his weeks of unexplained absence. He'd told her about the Bluebeard but had kept all other details from her: the terrible wounds the

stag servant had inflicted on him, the weeks at the child-eater's. Leo von Donnersmarck, adjutant to the Empress—even the merchant's daughter whom he was hoping to make his wife this coming fall didn't know about the scars on his chest. He didn't want to explain why the fingerprints of a Witch were burned into the skin next to them. His chest looked like the churned mud of a battlefield, yet that wasn't the worst. In his dreams he changed into the stag who'd wounded him. Nearly every night found him pleading with the god protector of warriors and soldiers to let him keep the body his bride had fallen in love with.

The chambers of the Moonstone Prince lay far away from his mother's so the infant wouldn't disturb Amalie's sleep. That's why this morning's dark news had indeed not yet reached her.

The young Empress was sitting in front of her mirror, which supposedly had been crafted by the same glazier who'd made her grandmother's infamous speaking mirror. *"Mirror, Mirror on the wall, who is the fairest of them all?"* If Amalie's mirror answered such questions, it probably would've given her the answers she wanted to hear. The golden hair, the flawless skin, the violet eyes—there was but one woman whose beauty compared to that of Amalie of Austry, and she was not human. The day and the night. Since his wedding, Kami'en, the King of the Goyl, preferred the day, and his Fairy lover bore her own darkness like a veil, mourning the death of her love. It had to be bitter that the beauty that so enchanted Kami'en had been granted by a Fairy lily.

The lady's maid who daubed Amalie's hair every morning with naiad tears shot an irritated glance at Donnersmarck as he entered. It was too early. Her mistress was not yet ready to face the world.

"Your Highness?"

Amalie did not turn, but her eyes met his in the mirror. She'd celebrated her twenty-first birthday barely a month ago, but Donnersmarck still felt he was looking at a child who'd gotten lost in the woods. What good did the crown or the golden dress do if even her face had been bought by her mother because the one she'd entered the world with had not been pretty enough?

"It's about your son, Your Highness..."

The darkness of the world made no distinctions; it entered its palaces as it did its huts.

Amalie still hadn't turned around. She just looked at Donnersmarck in the glass of the mirror. There was something else in her face now beside the familiar lostness, and he couldn't tell what it was.

"The wet nurse was supposed to have brought him already. I should never have hired her. She's useless!" Amalie touched her golden hair as though it were that of a stranger. "My mother was right. These peasants are even dumber than their cattle, and servants are no smarter than the pots in my kitchens."

Donnersmarck avoided the maid's eyes, though she was probably used to her mistress's insults. He was tempted to ask, "What about the soldiers? Are they as dumb as their uniforms? And the workers in the factories? As dumb as the coal they shovel into the furnaces?" Amalie wouldn't even have noticed the irony. She had just sent her husband's troops to put an end to a workers' strike. Without Kami'en's approval. A child in the woods. A child with an army.

"I don't believe it was the nursemaid's fault. Your son was not in his crib this morning."

The violet eyes went wide. Amalie pushed away the maid's fingers. But she was still looking into the mirror as if she had to

49

read her own face to understand what she was feeling.

"What do you mean? Where is he?"

Donnersmarck lowered his head. The truth and nothing but the truth. No matter how dark.

"My men are searching for him right now. But the crib and the pillows were splattered with blood. Your Highness."

One of the maids began to sob. The others just stared at Donnersmarck with open mouths. And Amalie sat and stared at her reflection, until the silence grew louder than the nursemaid's screams.

"So he is dead." She was the first to say what everybody thought.

"We don't know that. Maybe—"

"He is dead!" she cut off Donnersmarck. "And you *know* who killed him. She's always been jealous of my son because she can't have one herself. But she only dared to do something about it once Kami'en was out of the city."

Amalie pressed her hand to her perfect mouth. The violet pupils swam in tears as she turned around.

"Bring her to me!" she ordered as she got to her feet. "To the throne room."

The maids stared at Donnersmarck with a mixture of horror and pity. They'd been told by the kitchen girls that the Dark Fairy had them boil snakes to give her skin the luster of their scales. The servants whispered that anyone whose shoes even so much as brushed the hem of her dress died immediately. The coachmen swore that anyone touched by her shadow died immediately. The gardeners insisted that anyone who stepped into the footprints she left on her nightly walks died immediately. And yet they were all still alive.

Why should she have done anything to that child? She was

the reason he'd been born at all.

"Your husband has many enemies. Maybe—"

"It was she! Bring her to me! She's murdered my son!" Her rage was different from her mother's. There was no logic in it.

Donnersmarck bowed his head in silence and turned around. Bring her to me. Amalie might as well have ordered him to bring her the oceans. For a moment he considered taking the entire palace guard with him, just to reinforce the invitation. But the more men he brought, the greater the affront would be, and the greater the temptation for the Dark Fairy to demonstrate how silly any threat of force was against her magic. The two soldiers who'd brought the nursemaid to him could not hide their terror when he told them that only they were to accompany him.

Donnersmarck had ordered the nursemaid to be locked in her room, but the bad news had already spread through the entire palace. The faces he passed showed not only shock but also relief. The Moonstone Prince had the face of an angel, but the child had seemed like a bad omen to many, Goyl as well as human. *Had, Leo? You're already thinking of him in the past tense*. Yes. Because he'd seen the crib.

After the announcement of Amalie's pregnancy, the Dark Fairy had moved into a pavilion in the palace gardens. The Fairy had supposedly picked the place herself, Kami'en had it remodeled for her, and it was guarded by Kami'en's personal guards. Nobody could tell who they were supposed to protect her from. The lovestruck men who kept falling under her spell after a fleeting glance as she drove through the city? The supporters of the old Empress, who kept smearing DEATH TO THE GOYL or DEATH TO THE FAIRY on the houses of Vena? Or the anarchists who painted their DEATH TO ALL RULERS on the same walls? "Nonsense! The Stone

51

King is not protecting the Fairy. He is protecting his subjects from his lover." So said the flyers that could be found on park benches and train platforms every morning. After all, nobody doubted that the Dark Fairy could have held her own against the combined armies of Lotharaine and Albion.

"Bring her to me."

As the glassy gables of the Fairy's pavilion appeared behind the trees, Donnersmarck caught himself hoping she might be out on one of her drives, which could sometimes last for days. The stable boys whispered that the horses pulling her carriage were actually enchanted toads and the coachman was a spider to whom she'd given human form. But the Dark Fairy was home — if that's what she called this place. Or any other place.

Kami'en's guards let Donnersmarck pass — a jasper and a moonstone Goyl. Unlike Amalie, the Fairy did not insist that all her guards have Kami'en's stone skin. The two soldiers with Donnersmarck, however, could not pass. Donnersmarck did not protest. If the Fairy wanted to kill him, then no human would stop her. So far he'd only ever seen her from afar, alone, or by Kami'en's side at balls, state receptions; the last time had been at the celebrations for the birth of the Moonstone Prince. She hadn't brought a present — her gift had been the skin that kept the child alive.

And there she was.

No servants, no maids, just her.

Her beauty took one's breath away, like a sudden pain. Unlike Amalie, there was nothing of the child in the Dark One. She'd never been a child.

Kami'en had put a glass roof on her pavilion to let in light for the trees that the Fairy had planted among the marble tiles. The saplings were only a few months old, but their branches already touched the glass roof, and the walls had disappeared under blossoming vines. The Fairy's presence made them grow as though she were the source of life itself. Even the bright green dress she wore looked like it had been sewn from their leaves.

"That is a very dark mark you have on your chest, Donnersmarck. Has the stag stirred yet?" She saw what he was trying to hide from everyone. Donnersmarck longed to hide between the trees. Her shadow tinged the marble as dark as the forest floor around the child-eater's hovel.

"The Empress wants to see you."

Do not look at her. But she held his glance with her eyes.

"Why?"

Donnersmarck felt her rage, like an animal stirring.

"I know her son is still alive. Tell her that. And tell her she will die if that changes. I will send her my moths until she has caterpillars hatching from her doll skin. Can you remember that? I want you to repeat it to her, word for word, but do it slowly. Her mind is as dull as her hatred. Now go."

The shadows formed wolves under the trees, unicorns behind the silk-upholstered chaise lounge Donnersmarck knew she never sat on, snakes on the rugs Kami'en had bought for her in Nagpur. She did not belong between these walls built by mortal hands. Beneath her rage, Donnersmarck could feel a pain that touched him more than her beauty. And he stood there and looked at her and could not understand how the King of the Goyl could be sleeping in Amalie's doll bed when he had this woman waiting for him here.

"What are you waiting for?" she asked. But this time her voice sounded softer. The tiles under Donnersmarck's feet bloomed into

53

flower.

He turned.

"Come to me when the stag stirs," she said. "I can show you how to tame him."

Kami'en's guards opened the doors, but Donnersmarck hardly saw them. He stumbled out into the wide courtyard, his hand on his mangled chest. His two soldiers eyed him quizzically. He could see their relief that he was alone.

8

SLEEPLESS

Four o'clock. For hours, Fox had been listening to the chimes of Schwanstein's market church tallying the night. She spent the night in Jacob's room, as she always did when he wasn't there. The bed smelled of him, though she probably only imagined that. Jacob hadn't been to Schwanstein in months. Beneath her window, a late patron of The Ogre stumbled drunkenly into the square. The clinking of glass told her Wenzel was clearing the tumblers from the tables in the taproom below. In the chamber next door, Albert Chanute was coughing himself in and out of sleep. Wenzel had told her the old man had been unwell for weeks, but Chanute had apparently threatened that anyone who told Jacob would be drowned in a vat of his most rancid wine. Jacob would have done the same. The two were so similar, and always so anxious not to show how much they meant to each other.

Just how unwell Chanute was had only become clear to Fox

when he'd asked her to fetch Alma Spitzweg. The old treasure hunter couldn't stand Witches, light or dark. They scared him, though he'd have chopped his remaining arm off rather than admit it. But after the new doctor from Vena had been unable to do anything for him (further confirming Chanute's opinion of city folk), there was only the old Witch left, who disliked him as much as he disliked her, and who had never forgiven him for taking Jacob as his treasure-hunting apprentice.

Alma had come to see Chanute tonight. Fox could smell thyme, fairy mint, and lungwort, and Chanute's cough had begun to sound slightly less labored. Alma usually mixed a few of her cat's hairs into her potions, but that was a detail Chanute didn't need to know. A dog barked outside, and Fox thought she could hear the scream of a Thumbling. She pushed her hand under the pillow until her fingers found the fur dress. She'd worn it only twice since her return, but the temptation to ignore that it kept stealing years off her was strong. In every library they visited for Jacob's treasure hunts, she would search for clues to some magic that might slow the premature aging of shape-shifters, but all she'd found so far were stories about those who had either died young or had ended up burning their other skin. So she now tried to spend most of her time being a human.

She'd been out with Ludovik Rensman, and with Gregor Fenton, who'd already asked her a dozen times to model for one of the photographs the people of Schwanstein always stopped to admire in his shop window. Both men knew nothing of the fur. Nobody in Schwanstein knew about it, except Wenzel and Chanute. When Ludovik had tried to kiss her, she'd pushed him away with some stammered excuse. Ludovik Rensman wouldn't even have dared to go within sight of the Black Forest, so how could she have explained the memories his shy kisses evoked — of another's kisses, of a dark carriage, a red chamber, the fear-milk she'd drunk. The Bluebeard's terrible parting gift had been to make desire rhyme with death and fear.

Definitely not the right thoughts to find sleep.

Fox pushed back the blanket under which Jacob had slept so many times. She reached for her clothes. The scents of another world clung to them. Clara had insisted on washing them. It was finally quiet behind Chanute's door, but now two Heinzel were squabbling over a rind of bread in front of it. Fox shooed them away before they could wake the old man. Just then, Alma stepped from the room. Her face seemed even more wrinkled by night. Like all Witches, Alma could look as young or as old as she wanted, but she mostly wore the face that gave evidence of her long life. "I prefer to look as old on the outside as I am on the inside," she said to anyone who was stupid enough to ask her about it.

The Witch gave Fox a tired smile, though she was used to long nights. People called her to tend to sick cattle and ill children, to help with aching souls and hurting bodies, or whenever there was reason to believe someone had been cursed. The women in particular trusted Alma more than they trusted the city doctor, and she was the only Witch within a hundred miles...except for the child-eater in the Black Forest, but she now lived out her days as a toad in a well.

"How is he?" Fox asked.

"How do you think? He quit the liquor too late for a quiet death of old age. I can ease his cough, that's all. If he wants stronger remedies, he'll have to go to a child-eater. But he's not at death's door yet, though that's what he'd want you to believe. Men! A few nights of coughing and they see the reaper standing by their bedside. And what about you? Why are you not sleeping?"

"It's nothing."

"In the beginning, Jacob couldn't sleep for weeks after coming through the mirror. Was this your first time?" Alma pinned up her gray hair. It was as thick as that of a young woman. "Yes, I know about the mirror, but don't tell Jacob. He's always worried someone might find out. Is he with his brother?"

Fox wasn't sure why she should even be surprised. Alma had already been alive before the ruin became a ruin.

"He wanted to be back days ago—"

"Which doesn't mean much when it comes to Jacob." Alma finished her sentence.

They exchanged a smile—one Jacob wouldn't have liked at all.

"If he doesn't come soon, maybe we should let him know about Chanute," Alma said. "The old drunkard would feed me to his horse if he knew I said that, but Jacob might do him good. I can't think of any man Albert Chanute's heart clings to like it does to Jacob. The only competition is probably that actress whose face he had that hack in Braunstein tattoo on his chest. The old fool was so embarrassed about it, he wouldn't open his shirt!"

Chanute started coughing again. Alma sighed.

"Why do I always feel sorry for them? I used to wish the spider's plague on Chanute every time he beat Jacob, and now I'm letting him keep me from my sleep. The child-eaters get rid of their compassion by eating the heart of a child. I wish there was a more appetizing method. Will you keep me company while I brew him a tea? Which he will again just spit all over my dress, because there won't be any liquor in it."

Fox knew Alma didn't need company. But the Witch could see Fox needed to be distracted from the thoughts that were keeping her awake. They went downstairs and found the taproom empty. Wenzel had gone to sleep. He rarely went to bed before daybreak. It was Chanute's firm rule that The Ogre closed only when the last guest went home. The dark kitchen smelled of the soup Wenzel had prepared for the next day. Tobias Wenzel was the first to admit he'd been a lousy soldier, but he was a very good cook. Fox warmed the soup while Alma brewed Chanute's tea.

"I've known about the mirror for a long time. Much longer than Jacob. He wasn't the first I ever saw come out of that tower."

The revelation came as such a surprise to Fox that she let Wenzel's soup go cold again. She'd never asked Jacob about the mirror. He didn't like to talk about it, maybe because it had been his secret for so long.

"I'm not talking about Jacob's father," Alma continued. "John lived in Schwanstein for a long time. I didn't like him, which is why I never told Jacob about him. No. The first one came nearly half a century before him. Back then Vena was still ruled by some Ludwig or Maximilian—the one who fed his youngest daughter to a Dragon. The ruin was still the prettiest hunting castle in Austry. Half of Schwanstein was out chasing a Giant who'd abducted a baker, probably to give him to his children to play with. They liked to play with humans."

Alma strained the tea through a sieve, which also caught a couple of cat hairs. "Erich Semmelweis. I'll never forget that name, because it reminded me of that abducted baker. Semmelweis is, as I later found out, also the maiden name of Jacob's mother. The Semmelweis I met must've been one of Jacob's ancestors. He was as pale as a grub, and he smelled like those alchemists over

59

in Himmelpfortgrund who're always trying to turn their hearts into gold. Semmelweis was a big success in Vena. For a while he even tutored the Emperor's son."

Alma turned to Fox. "You're probably wondering why I'm telling you all this in the middle of the night. Erich Semmelweis one day returned from Vena with a bride. He let it be known he was going to sail to the New World with her. The people believed him, just like they believe Jacob's Albion story. But a year later, I saw Semmelweis and his wife come out of the tower, and shortly afterward, Semmelweis summoned me because she couldn't sleep. Jacob does very well at covering up the strain caused by changing worlds, but even he used to get quite sick at the beginning. So be careful."

"What happened to Semmelweis's wife?"
Alma poured the hot tea into the mug that Chanute claimed he'd stolen from the King of Albion. "Someone stole her firstborn child. I always suspected the Stilt in the ruin. She had two more children. She brought them a couple of times to visit her parents, but eventually Semmelweis came out of that tower alone."

A bride from Vena. She stayed in the other world. With her children. Fox's weary mind took a while to grasp the meaning.

"You have to tell Jacob!"
Alma shook her head. "No. You can tell him I know about the mirror, but it's best he doesn't learn about the other things. For Jacob, everything was always about his father. Who knows. Maybe his yearning for this world has a lot more to do with his mother."

60

9

Over

Amalie's guards didn't keep the mob from climbing the walls separating the palace gardens from the streets. From up there, even the stones flung by the children reached all the way to the Dark Fairy's pavilion. That she had only to lift her hands to put the shattered windows back together just angered her attackers even more. But the Dark One enjoyed showing them how droll she thought their hatred was. If only she could've silenced their chants as easily. And still no word from Kami'en.

His subjects took Kami'en's silence to mean he believed Amalie's version of events. Excuses were easily found: He hadn't received the Fairy's letters, the rebels had intercepted them, his answer had been lost on the long way from Prusza to Vena. But the Fairy had given up deceiving herself. Kami'en's soldiers were still there, but they were no longer posted only for her protection. They neither drove away the stone throwers nor did anything about the insults

Amalie's subjects hurled over the walls every day and every night.

Water Witch, Demon Fairy... Those names were not new. Only one was: Child-Murderer.

Could Kami'en really believe she'd kill his only son, after all she'd done to keep the infant alive? Her efforts to save that baby had cost her so much strength she still felt weak. And now the pain from his silence...

Just as her sisters had foretold when she'd left their island, she'd become a shadow of herself. And she would have paid even that price for Kami'en's love, no matter how it shamed her to admit it, but maybe that's how it always was when the end began.

Her moths swarmed around her like smoke, winged shadows of a bygone love, the only helpers she had left. No, there was one more. Splintered glass crunched under Donnersmarck's boots as he approached her—the limping soldier who'd once served Amalie's mother. He was an outcast, forever different from all those who were screaming out there, though he might be able to hide that fact for a while longer.

"The rebellion is spreading through the north. Nobody knows when Kami'en might return to Vena."

The Fairy picked a piece of glass from her brown hair, which she was wearing down and loose again, like her sisters. For Kami'en she'd dressed like a human woman with her hair pinned up, had slept in their houses, and with the Man-Goyl she'd given him thousands of sons. How could he betray her so? Kami'en... Even his name tasted like poison now.

Donnersmarck listened. The screaming seemed even louder than it was yesterday. Above them another glass pane shattered. The Fairy raised a hand. She briefly imagined the glass turning into water and washing them away—all the screamers, Kami'en's soldiers, and his doll-wife. Her rage became ever harder to control.

"I can no longer guarantee your safety." Donnersmarck spoke without lowering his eyes. He was not afraid to look at her.

"I can look after my own safety."

"The whole city is in turmoil. Amalie had your carriage burned. She's spreading the word that everything you touch is cursed."

The Doll showed an impressive talent for intrigue. And what a chance to win her subjects' sympathy, after she'd lost their love on her wedding day. The mob had even forgotten how much they'd despised the Moonstone Prince. Now she was just the grieving mother.

"What about the baby?"

Donnersmarck shook his head. "Not a trace. I have three of my soldiers looking for him. The only ones I can still trust."

She herself had sent dozens of her moths to search for Kami'en's son, but so far none had returned. The Fairy looked at the broken glass around her feet. Her shattered cage. And the one who'd put her in it was far, far away. But, no, she had caged herself.

Donnersmarck was still standing there. Her knight. "What do you want to do?"

Yes, what? It was hard to let go of love. Once woven, its ribbon was hard to tear, and this one she'd woven quite firmly herself.

The Dark Fairy stepped under the trees she'd planted. These trees only grew at the shores of the lake that had borne her and her sisters. She picked two of the seedpods from the dense foliage. She broke the first one, and two tiny horses, both green like the pod itself, sprang into her hand. She set them on the tiles, and they began to grow. A carriage rolled from the second pod. It sprouted leaves and pale green blossoms as it grew. The wheels and axles were black, the coach box, the leather benches, all as

63

black as her pain, as black as her rage.

Donnersmarck's glance betrayed what all mortals felt when they witnessed magic: disbelief, yearning, jealousy... How they all wished for such powers.

Carriage. Horses. Now all she needed was a coachman. The Dark Fairy raised her hand. A moth settled on her fingers, its spread wings looking as though their black velvet had been sprinkled with gold dust. Head and body gleamed emerald green.

"Chithira, Chithira," the Dark One whispered to the moth. "You helped me find him. Now you have to take me away from him."

The moth lowered its wings until they brushed her hand, lightly, like a kiss. Then it fluttered down to her feet and changed into a young man. Like the moth's wings, his black clothes seemed to have been dusted with gold. His turban and his vest were of gleaming emerald green, and his pale face showed how long he hadn't been at home in this world. Chithira... His name was one of the few the Fairy remembered. A prince who'd fallen in love with her more than a century ago, and who'd stayed faithful even after death, like so many others who'd fallen for her or her sisters. They were accustomed to the everlasting love of mortals. How could she have known that Kami'en's affections would be so short-lived?

Chithira silently climbed up onto the coach box. Donnersmarck still stared at the horses and carriage like someone lost in a dream. But this dream was Kami'en's love. Time to wake up.

The Fairy gathered up her dress and looked around one last time. Splinters. They were all that was left. Dead, like solid water. What else but death could you hope to reap when you gave your heart to a mortal?

64

Donnersmarck opened the carriage door for her. The Dark One had known for a while—longer than he'd known himself—that Donnersmarck would come with her. He came to protect her, but also for her to protect him—from what was stirring in his chest.

Kami'en's guards moved to block the path of her green horses, but they were no match for Chithira, who'd already steered them past her sisters' unicorns. The guards in the courtyard scattered as soon as they saw his deathly-pale face. Donnersmarck opened the gate while the Fairy looked up at the balcony from which Therese of Austry had announced her daughter's engagement. Amalie didn't show. The Dark One probably would have let her live. Probably.

10

Too Many Dogs

Three attacks in as many days. Two on border posts and the third one a direct attempt on Kami'en's life. His bodyguards had acted so clumsily that Hentzau had to kill the assassin himself. Then he had the bodyguards executed, with a public threat to cut out the tongue of anyone who used this incident to lament the disappearance of the Jade Goyl. There would be whispers, of course. "First the Jade Goyl leaves him, then the Fairy. The King of the Goyl is as doomed as his moonstone son."

The assassin who'd managed to get into Kami'en's tent was not one of the human rebels who'd risen against the occupation. No. It was an onyx Goyl. Just weeks before, they'd crowned one of their own as rightful King of the Goyl. A shadow king, allied to Lotharaine and Albion. Traitors to their own people. Not surprising. The onyx had always been parasites, living off the blood and sweat of their subjects. Under their rule, only those born onyx could thrive. Hentzau had stuffed the assassin's head with stone maggots and had sent it to Nia'sny, the most powerful onyx lord, who now resided in Lotharaine, but his spies were everywhere.

Too many days… Hentzau put one of the pills, which Kami'en's personal physician had prescribed for his chest pains, under his tongue. They were as useless as the ones Amalie's human doctor had given him in Vena. So he'd sent one of his soldiers to the underground forest north of the royal palace, to where the Clay-Matrons lived. The potions they brewed could burn even Goyl tongues, but they had also helped Hentzau survive his wounds from the Blood Wedding.

Hentzau had to get back under the earth. Down there he needed neither pills nor the potions of the Clay-Matrons. And now that idiot of a quartermaster had assigned Hentzau a tower room as his office, with a window and so much light that he'd soon be blind in both eyes. Hentzau had asked for the window to be bricked up, but apparently the only soldiers with any bricklaying experience had died in the last skirmish with the rebels.

Kami'en loved taking up residence in human palaces, despite all the windows and towers. The one they were in now they'd taken from a Holstein cavalier who'd tried to avenge the theft of his property by releasing poisoned rats into the cellars. Thirty of Hentzau's men were in the sick ward after they'd slept down there to get away from the daylight. The longer they lived above ground, the more susceptible they became to human diseases. It was one of the facts the onyx Goyl used to support their argument that Goyl had no business being above ground. But like Kami'en, Hentzau hadn't forgotten what happened when the Goyl tried to stick to life under the earth. There was too much down there the humans wanted—not only silver, gold, and precious stones but ore, coal, gas, oil... All of which had grown more precious to them than what grew in their fields.

"Lieutenant Hentzau?" Nesser poked her head through the door.

"What?" He quickly dropped the pill bottle into his desk drawer. Nesser didn't deserve the harshness of his voice, but there were already too many whispers that the King's Bloodhound was old and sick—though only the Fairy had ever dared say it in front of Kami'en. By all the gods of the heart of the earth, Hentzau was so glad she was gone.

"New dispatches." Nesser positioned herself behind him before ushering in the courier. After an attack had left Hentzau lightly wounded, Kami'en had made Nesser Hentzau's personal bodyguard. Against his will, of course. The King's Bloodhound guarded by a soldier who could've been his daughter? It could hardly get any worse... Though, admittedly, Nesser was much smarter than the imbeciles who guarded the King.

The courier was one of the Man-Goyl who'd remained in the Goyl King's service, though his skin had in places already turned back to the snail-like softness of his birth. Hentzau would've had all Man-Goyl shot, but they'd proven to be very useful as scouts and spies. They hardly remembered their human lives. This one had been a ruby Goyl. The red stone was still on his brow and cheek, and there was a shimmer of gold in his brown eyes. Entire armies of them were now roaming as mercenaries, plundering above- and below ground.

The Dark Fairy's legacy. Yes, Hentzau was indeed glad she was gone, though he didn't dare contemplate how much damage she might do as their enemy. His spies reported she was traveling east. The Suleiman Empire? Unlikely. Its sultan believed magic should be the domain of men alone. But there were other rulers she could peddle her magic to: the Cossacks in Ukraina, the Tzars of Varangia, the Wolf-Lords in Kamchatka and Yukaghiria. For centuries, the Goyl had maintained lively trade relations with most of the rulers of the East, and some of their oldest underground cities lay in the East, but Hentzau had little doubt that most of their old allies would turn against them if the Fairy promised them her magic. His greatest concern used to be the Wolf-Lord who was married to Isolde of Austry. But the youngest sister of the deposed Empress had died a few weeks earlier. Poisoned by her husband, according to the whispers in Vena.

The dispatches the Man-Goyl delivered did little to improve Hentzau's mood: a fire in one of their airplane factories, a murdered Goyl ambassador in Bavaria, a suicide attack on one of their cave cities on the surface. Four hundred dead. The last dispatch was from Thierry Auger, one of their human spies in Lotharaine. He reported that Crookback had received an interesting visitor: Isambard Brunel — the human who built planes and ships but hated to travel. It was the first time Brunel had left Albion, and that he'd done so to pay his respects to the King of Lotharaine was the most alarming message of them all.

Nesser waved the Man-Goyl out of the room. As he left, he pressed his fist to his chest, saluting like a Goyl. Hentzau still couldn't get used to them. Nesser waited in the doorway. Hentzau had no children, but the feelings he had for Nesser probably came as close to being fatherly as he would ever experience. He even valued her weaknesses, the impetuousness, the youthful impatience, the need to see the world in black and white, all good on her side, all bad on the other. Enviable. Life is so simple when you're young, though of course that's not what it feels like to the young.

Brunel and Crookback. Maybe the bad news could be turned into good news. No, better, a present.

"Tell Kami'en's attaché I need to speak to the King. Right away."

As soon as Nesser had pulled the door shut behind her, Hentzau clutched his chest. The pain was brutal, but a soldier was used to living with pain.

* * *

Kami'en no longer had the windows of his rooms bricked up. He'd had his eyes hexed by a Witch, and he made fun of Hentzau for fearing that magic more than the milky white film that dulled his vision. When Hentzau entered his chamber, the King of the Goyl was standing by the window, and, yes, he was probably thinking of the Fairy.

Hentzau was sure Kami'en still loved her. But whether Kami'en believed she'd killed his son — there were things not even Hentzau knew about him. He turned around, and his face betrayed nothing. Carnelian. The Goyl called it fire-skin.

"Brunel in Lutis. I assume we're both thinking the same?" the King said after he'd scanned Thierry Auger's message. "The Walrus of Albion isn't quite as stupid as I thought. Have the troops along the Lotharainian border enforced, and make sure the crown prince doesn't run out of elven dust."

"That won't be enough." Hentzau rubbed his skin. The daylight coming through the high windows was granite gray, but it still hurt his eyes. "We need to sow unrest in their colonies so their troops can't join forces. Anarchists in their cities. And we have to make sure the East is on our side. I suggest a present to the Tzar of Varangia. A present that will give him the military confidence to challenge Albion and Lotharaine."

"And what present might have such a miraculous effect?"

...and be more enticing than what my lover could offer the Tzar? Neither of them would mention the Dark Fairy's disappearance, though it was all the world could speak of.

"The present just dropped in our laps, Your Majesty."

They both loved the game of reading their thoughts off each other's faces. So many wars fought together. So much shared: defeats, triumphs, fear, rage, despair, relief...and the rush brought by the proximity of death.

"Interesting." Kami'en looked out the window again. He pointed east. "How many men do you need?"

"Ten. More would be too conspicuous. I'd also like to take a few Man-Goyl."

"Indeed? Didn't you want me to shoot them all?"

"A good soldier adapts his strategy before the enemy expects him to."

Kami'en smiled.

So much shared. The King's Bloodhound would defend his King, let the pack tear him apart in the King's stead. But first he'd put a bear by his side.

11
ONCE UPON A TIME

Will was still awake when the phone rang. Two o'clock in the morning. Clara had put his mother's old alarm clock on his desk. Clara had kept many of his mother's things in the apartment, and she often asked Will about her, maybe because she'd never known her own mother.

He reached for his phone without wondering about the late hour. Clara had been working night shifts at the hospital for weeks, and Jacob was often out until dawn, and both of them knew Will rarely went to bed early. Even as a child, Will had feared his dreams, and since his time behind the mirror they'd turned into enemy territory.

"Will? Dr. Klinger. Clara works in my ward."

"Yes?"

Dr. Klinger kept talking. The sound of the physician's voice reminded Will of another call. The same mixture of soberness and empathy. *"Your mother is deteriorating. You should come."* That call had not been unexpected, but this time the words were making no sense to him. She'd only just gone to work!

Dr. Klinger's final words broke through his thoughts. "I'm sorry, that's all I can say right now."

Will left immediately. From the taxi, he desperately tried to reach Jacob.

Their mother hadn't died in the hospital where Clara worked, but the elevator was the same, reminding Will of the weeks he'd spent visiting her. The elevator, the corridors, the smells...

The doctor was waiting for him. Will remembered having met him at a party Clara's colleagues had organized for her when she published her first paper. "A sudden coma...Unconscious...One of the nurses found her." Words that only conveyed the doctor's helplessness. Will followed him into one of the rooms, and there she was. Sleeping.

Will had seen such a sleep before, but how could he ever explain to anyone in this world about the princess he'd found lying on a bed, covered in wilted roses? Clara's coat was on a chair by the bed. Pinned to it was a brooch he'd never seen before. It was shaped like a moth, with black wings and silver tentacles.

The wrong world.

The doctor was uttering more helpless phrases. "Rare infection... An injury on her finger...Blood tests." Will said nothing. What could he say? Had she been visited by a Fairy?

He asked Dr. Klinger to leave them alone. He approached her bed. No thorny brambles keeping him away, no tower. *It's so easy, Will. Kiss her.* But she looked so alien, just as his mother had. He tried to forget where he was and to remember how he'd first met Clara, but all he got were other images: the gingerbread house,

73

the cave, the disgust as she'd stroked his jade skin.

Just a kiss.

But all he did was stand there. Maybe his heart was still made of stone. How else could he have lost his love so easily? How could he betray her now? He just had to kiss her like he had then, remember that first time, in the hospital corridor, outside his mother's room. Why were love and death such close neighbors?

He leaned down. Clara's lips were so warm and familiar. But she didn't wake up. And all Will could see was the dead girl in the rose tower, with her parchment skin and hair like bleached straw.

Wake up, Clara. I love you!

He kissed her again, but all he felt was his own despair. *I love you*. She loved him more. Always had.

Dr. Klinger came back and told Will about some more tests they would run. Will signed the papers and tried again to reach Jacob. He tried and tried. No reply.

The doctor sent him home, promising to call if there was any change.

Will couldn't recall whether he'd taken the elevator or the stairs. He just found himself out on the street, waiting for the tears that wouldn't come, staring into headlights as if they could explain what had happened. Jacob. He had to talk to Jacob. His brother would know a way. Some spell. That did what? Replace true love? Whatever that was...

Will looked back at the hospital. He couldn't just leave Clara there. He had to take her with him. Jacob would find something to help her, she would wake up, and he'd love her the way she deserved to be loved.

"You always put all the blame on yourself, Will. Is it because

74

your brother takes his responsibilities so lightly?"

Will turned around. The strange man sitting on one of the benches in front of the hospital had used his name like he was an old acquaintance, but Will couldn't recall ever having seen him before. Clara called these benches the "pews of tears" because they were the first stop for people leaving the hospital who'd just had bad news.

"I'm sorry, do I know you?" It was the kind of question you asked when you wanted to be left alone but were still as helpless and polite as Will.

The stranger smiled. "Yes, but you were probably too young to remember. I was a close friend of your mother's."

An ambulance drove past. Someone bumped into Will. So much activity, so many people, especially at this time of day. But something about the stranger didn't belong here. Or was it that their surroundings didn't fit him? Maybe Will was just dreaming. He'd been thinking that a lot since he'd returned. How did Jacob do it, change worlds all the time? It made you lose your mind...

Why couldn't he wake her? If only he'd looked after her better. If only he hadn't stopped loving her.

The stranger watched Will with an amused expression, as though he was listening to Will's thoughts. He still hadn't introduced himself. Suddenly Will heard words in his head: *Woulda, coulda, shoulda...Always the good son, brother, friend, lover...Will Reckless, the canvas others paint on. What about you? Who do you want to be, Will?*

"Sit with me for a while." The stranger patted the bench next to him. Will hesitated. He had to go back. To Clara.

"Sit, Will." The stranger's voice caressed him like a warm breeze, but the invitation didn't sound like a request. "I have an offer for you."

75

A drunk man stumbled by. A couple kissed by a bus stop. True love...

"I'm sorry," said Will. "I have to go back." He gestured toward the revolving door of the hospital. "My girlfriend..."

"Yes, my offer is about her." The stranger again patted the bench. There was a hint of impatience in the gesture. The dirty curb, the tired faces, the coffee shop on the corner. The stranger made it all look so unreal. Will slowly sat down next to him. The man had a tiny ruby in his earlobe. What did that remind him of?

"I assume you've tried kissing her? Sadly, that only works in the rarest of cases." The man pulled a silver cigarette box from his pocket. "The spindle sleep is very old Fairy magic. Very effective, and very easy to use. I assumed your brother had warned you and your girlfriend. You rejected the Fairy's gift, the skin of sacred stone. Immortals take these things very personally. And since she can't do anything to you..."

He took a silver cigarette case and lighter from his pocket. That's when Will saw he had six fingers on each hand. The wrong world. This entire night belonged to the wrong world.

"Fairies love to play fate, Will, and that's not limited to their infamous love magic. We both know what I'm talking about: a different skin, a deadly sleep, a wooden prison..." He lit a cigarette as white and slender as his fingers. "But this time your brother won't bring everything back to the way it was. This time you will have to do it yourself. Isn't that your biggest wish? To have everything the way it was? Before you made the mistake of following your brother?" He exhaled smoke into the night and ignored the disapproving looks of the passersby. "Once upon a time...There's a reason all fairy tales begin like this. But the 'and they lived happily ever after' at the end? That has to be earned."

Will thought he could see the face of a woman in the wafts of smoke. Moths were fluttering around it.

"It's incredible, isn't it?" The stranger tucked the cigarette case and lighter back in his pocket and pulled out a pouch. "She made you immune even to her own magic, all to save her lover. Love makes fools, even of immortals." He dropped the pouch on Will's lap. Jacob had a similar one. "It all began with her. It can only end with her."

The pouch seemed empty, but when Will reached inside, he felt a wooden handle.

The stranger got up.

"Find her. Use my gift, and you have my promise everything will be just as it was meant to be." He leaned down. "I will show you who you are, Will Reckless. Your true self... Isn't that what you're looking for?"

He didn't wait for Will's answer. He turned and walked toward a car parked by the curb. A driver got out and opened the back door, and the stranger slipped inside. Will sat with the pouch in his hand and watched as the car merged into the pre-dawn traffic. Jacob still didn't answer his phone, and Clara's face was as pale as a corpse's. Will didn't have the courage to kiss her again, and the night nurse just shook her head when he asked whether he could take Clara home.

The apartment was so still, the rooms so empty. *Once upon a time*. Will sat at the kitchen table and took the pouch from his pocket. He carefully put his hand inside, and his eyes widened at the sight of the weapon that slid out. A crossbow. It was so beautiful and so terrible. The silver fittings were warm, as though the silver were melting under his touch. There were whispers lodged in the patterns etched into the precious metal. Will closed

77

his fingers around the hilt. He cocked the glass string, placed the silver arrow, and feared what he felt: the wish to let the arrow fly, into the heart of darkness, to where all magic came from. But that place has no heart.

12
In The Wrong Place

Fox had spent so many months waiting for Jacob in the past that it seemed absurd to be so worried after three days. But during the fourth night of being kept awake by Chanute's coughing, she found it easy to convince herself she had to find Jacob for the old man's sake. The idea of going through the mirror by herself was not very enticing, but her fear was one more reason for Fox to do it. Fear was like a beast that only grew fiercer when one gave in to it.

She took Chanute's horse. The old gelding was as ill-tempered as a stray dog, but he'd carried Jacob to and from the ruin so many times that Fox knew he'd be able to find his way back to the stable by himself. Chanute used to claim his gelding wasn't afraid even of wolves, but when Fox let him loose by the ruin, he seemed very keen to gallop straight back to Schwanstein. Horses didn't like the ruin. Alma thought it was because the place was haunted by the ghost of a stable boy who used to torment his master's horses. There was no sign of a ghost on this misty morning, but Fox did find boot prints in the damp ground by the tower. She'd also seen prints when she returned, on the broken steps leading to the old stables. Wenzel had told her the mayor of Schwanstein was trying to sell the ruin and put an end to the rumors that it was cursed. The charred walls had so far deterred any potential buyers, but maybe it was time to start thinking about a new hiding place for the mirror.

The heavy silence in the tower reminded Fox of the many days she'd spent by the door waiting for Jacob, every day filled with the dread of his not returning.

The mirror was clear this morning, as if someone had polished it. Fox had stood in front of it many times, but she'd always turned away again, preferring to wait for Jacob in her world. She'd never followed him; that was the rule. His paths, her paths. But whose rule was it? More hers than his, if she was honest. Jacob had always wanted her to come with him.

She reached out and pressed her hand against the glass.

It was dark. That was strange. The tower had been bright with morning sunshine, and time was supposed to be more or less the same in both worlds. Fox reached for the edge of the desk, the window through which she'd seen Jacob's city. Her eyes were already adjusting to the darkness, her fur sharpening her human senses even when she wasn't wearing it. But there was no desk, and there was no window. The room she was standing in looked and smelled like the old stone barns she used to hide in as a child to avoid having to mend her stepfather's fishing nets. In the murky light, she could just make out bricked-up windows and rows of crates along the walls, some of them as tall as a man, others small enough for her to carry.

What was the mirror doing *here*?

There were other mirrors leaning among the crates, most of them smaller than the one she'd come through, but of all shapes and sizes. The only thing they had in common was a silver frame. Fox felt like she'd strayed into a room with hundreds of glass doors, and now she had to figure out which one Jacob had disappeared through.

She put her ear to a wide gate that seemed to be the only exit. Voices. Car engines. Proof she was in Jacob's world.

He's fine.

The fur had taught Fox to ignore her fear, but it was harder when she feared for Jacob. She pulled the gate open, just wide enough so she could peer through.

It was as though she could see two places at once.

One place seemed deserted—a wide courtyard overgrown with thistles and nettles, a group of empty buildings surrounded by a dense forest. But superimposed on this place was a second place, blurred as though its reality was trying to push through to make itself invisible. Fox knew this kind of magic from her world: a place hidden to protect a secret. Bridges, castles, treasure caves ...sometimes they stayed invisible until they were touched, or until you spoke a magic formula, but they could never completely fool the shape-shifter. She was just surprised to find such magic in Jacob's world.

The buildings hidden among the empty houses had towers and gables like the ones Fox knew from home but also the high glass facades and iron beams she knew only from Jacob's world. Beyond them, among the trees, she could make out giant vats and silver chimneys. To the right of the overgrown courtyard were

81

two basins, plumes of shimmering smoke hovering above them.

Where was she? And who was hiding behind magic in Jacob's world?

No, Fox. This was not the time to find out.

Where was Jacob?

A van pulled into the courtyard. The two men who climbed out and started to unload were so unmistakably from this world that they made the glass buildings seem even more unreal. One of them had hold of a huge dog the size of a calf, and Fox was glad she hadn't shifted shape yet. Neither of the men looked in her direction as she squeezed through the gate. But the dog spotted her. "She's a fox!" his bark warned. The man holding the leash silenced the dog with a sharp command, but he looked around. Fox barely managed to find cover behind a few barrels. She scented water—maybe a river.

Fox shifted as soon as the dog and his master had disappeared into one of the abandoned buildings with the other man. As a vixen she could see even more clearly what the magic was trying to hide: plants that to the human eye were mere silvery shadows, swarms of Grass-Elves in bushes with blossoms that yielded elven dust. All of that didn't belong here. Who had brought it across? She rolled in the grass to mask her own scent. The vixen could smell that there was more than one dog.

Rotting crates, rusting barrels, mounds of broken glass between overgrown brick walls. A wretched smell surrounding the hidden buildings made the vixen's fur stand on end. She recognized it neither from this nor her own world. She avoided them, as she did the basins with the shimmering smoke.

He is fine.

Another building appeared between the trees. It was from this world and, at first glance, appeared to be empty, but the windows had bars that grew from the brickwork like silver vines. Jacob was behind those — the vixen knew it. Her instinctive knowledge rarely had an explanation, but Fox never had to regret relying on it.

He is fine. No. The vixen told her differently. Even if the scent of sickness and death around the building was so stale it only carried echoes of long-past misery, beneath it was the scent of life, weak, like from a wounded animal — or a wounded human.

The vixen couldn't reach up to the window, so Fox shifted again. But that brought her human fears back, with all those useless questions: *What's happening? How did the mirror get to this bewitched place?* She had no time to search for answers, lest there'd be only one question left: *Why didn't you save him, Fox?*

She'd pushed her way through nettles and dead wood to one of the barred windows when she heard steps behind her. She tried to call the fur, but it was too late, and she cursed her big human body while she sought cover behind a tree. Luckily, the man approaching the building with a plate of food was less vigilant than the dogs who were barking in the distance. He nearly stepped on Fox's hand as he walked past her. His face looked strange, as though someone had shaped it from clay and hadn't taken much care doing it. The sight made Fox's heart beat faster, but from relief rather than fear. Food was brought to the living. Now she could only hope it was for Jacob.

The man disappeared around the back of the building, and Fox heard him unlocking a door. It was hard to resist the temptation to follow him right away. She probably could've overpowered him easily, but she'd once thought the same thing about a servant of a Catalonian vampire who'd then turned into a bat and alerted his master with a bloodcurdling scream before she could grab hold of him.

It felt like days had passed before Clay-face appeared again. He was talking to someone, and when he turned the corner, Fox saw the phone in his hand. Another reminder of which world she was in.

The lock in the door was as strange as this world, but her fingers had opened the tombs of kings and the living strongbox of a Troll, and this lock proved no harder. As she squeezed through the door, she wondered whether the invisibility spell was to fool the two men unloading the van. Clay-face had to be part of it, or his first step would have triggered an alarm. In between the filthy floorboards were silver threads, which probably announced any uninvited guest who was clumsy enough to step on them.

Fox was also wary of the flowers growing from the cracked plaster. They looked too much like the ones on the frame of the mirror that had brought her here, and their scent filled the musty air like a lullaby. They, like the mirrors, the Grass-Elves, and the cloaked buildings, clearly did not belong in this world.

Everything around her seemed dangerously beautiful, like a Venus flytrap trying to snatch its prey amid mildewed stones and rat droppings. Every step increased her fear that Jacob had been caught by that very trap. But the first rooms she checked were empty. She followed footprints across the dusty floor to a staircase leading down into a basement. Fox listened, thought she could hear the scraping of shoes and then a suppressed curse. It wasn't Jacob's voice, but he was there. She could feel it like the touch of a familiar hand. She heard an engine in the distance, the slapping of water against wood or stone, voices and steps, worryingly clear. But they weren't coming closer.

The flowers also grew along the stairs. Fox carefully avoided touching them. The staircase ended in a wide cellar, from which a corridor with windowless rooms branched off. The mesh of wires in the doors was hard to spot, even for her eyes. Silver gratings. The cells behind them were empty, except the last one.

Fox recognized the lifeless body behind the grate, though Jacob had his back to her. She closed her hands around the bars. It felt like clutching air. The magic was so strong that not even touch revealed it. Fox pulled her hands back nevertheless. Her skin tightened as though it was turning into silver itself.

"Ah, *bonjour*! Or is it *bonsoir* out there?"

There was a man crouched on the floor behind Jacob, wearing clothes from this world. His back was against the cell wall as though he'd been sitting there for a long while. His dark hair was as curly as sheep's wool. "Your face is new. Whoever you stole it from!"

He got to his feet, his fists clenched like a boxer ready for the next round. "You come to invite me for another look in the mirror, *non? Sacrament*, you must really like my face. *Mais*, Sylvain Fowler will not come voluntarily, *ma puce*."

He raised his fists and boxed the air as though to prove how hard he'd make it for her.

Fox would have laughed if Jacob hadn't stirred.

"There's no reason to fight," she said. "I don't belong to them. I'm here for him." She nodded toward Jacob. "What did they do to him?"

The gloves she pulled from her pocket had saved her from many magical traps, but she couldn't be sure they'd work here. "*Ostie de moron*!" Sylvain let his fists drop. "You don't recognize your own kind anymore, Sylvain? She is human!" He leaned over

85

Jacob. "I think he's fine. Probably had too much of their dust. How did you find him? Love, and all that?" His sigh sounded jealous and understanding.

Fox started forward.

"Do not come in! There's something with the door." Sylvain pushed up his sleeve to show her his forearm. Next to a tattoo of a fiery maple leaf, a strip of his skin shimmered like metal. "This is what happens when you try to get through."

"It's a grille made invisible with camouflage magic." Fox cautiously closed a gloved hand around one of the bars. It was still an unpleasant feeling.

"With *what*?" Sylvain eyed her as though she weren't quite sane.

The lock, once visible, was easily picked. The gloves shimmered silver as Fox pulled them off. She ran to Jacob. His skin was warm and his breathing regular, like he was asleep. Fox couldn't see any wounds, but then her fingers found the head of a tiny needle in his dark hair. It was embedded in his left temple. They had a fairy tale in Lotharaine—her mother had told it often—in which the Devil held a prince captive for a hundred years by sticking a silver needle in his head. The prince woke as soon as his sister pulled the needle out. In Fox's world, it was often a good idea to follow the lessons of such tales, but this was Jacob's world.

"I can carry him if he can't walk," Sylvain whispered. "We have to cross the river. They control the entire island. Won't be easy, but we find a boat, maybe?"

Although Fox guessed Sylvain Fowler to be in his mid-forties, his lively eyes and wide mouth made him look like a handsome boy who'd aged only a little but had broken his nose a few times in the process.

86

"We don't need a boat. We'll take another way." *We? Fox!* She couldn't take a stranger through the mirror.

But Sylvain was right—she might need his help. First, though, she had to find out a bit more about him. "Why are you here?" She tried to make her question sound like little more than concerned curiosity.

"I worked for them."

"Them?"

Jacob shuddered as soon as Fox touched the needle.

"Immortal Glass and Silver. I delivered their mirrors."

Mirrors. *Pull it out, Fox.* Jacob groaned, but the needle slid out without resistance.

"My daughter's hair is as red as yours," Sylvain whispered. "I'm thinking of her all the time since I looked into that damned mirror. *Maude merde.* That devilish glass doesn't just steal your face—it brings up the memories, as though someone's stirred them around. All the filth I'd forgotten, but the good things are worse."

That didn't sound like the mirror that had brought her here. In Fox's world, there were mirrors that fulfilled wishes, gave aid, revealed the truth—they could be a promise or the perfect trap. Witches always spat on a mirror before looking into it to make sure it wasn't magic.

Jacob began to stir. Fox had to whisper his name a dozen times before he finally opened his eyes. They stared at her through silver.

"Fox?" His fingers sought her face. "I can't see."
She was glad to hear his voice, but there was no time for joy, nor for fear. Jacob groaned as he leaned on his right hand.

"What's happened to your arm, Jacob?"

87

"Long story."

Fox helped him to his feet. He was so weak he had to lean against the wall.

"We should wait for dark," said Sylvain.

"Who is that?" Jacob squinted. He seemed to at least be able to make out shapes.

Sylvain gave a bow. "Sylvain Caleb Fowler. It seems we have the same enemies. That's a beginning, *non*?"

He was right—they should wait for dark—but Fox wanted to get away. This place made her sick. "You can try finding a boat," she said to Sylvain as she dragged Jacob through the open door. "Good luck."

Sylvain cursed, then followed them. Fox only just managed to stop him before he stepped on one of the flowers at the bottom of the stairs.

"Sylvain! This place is cursed!" she hissed. "Your eyes are as useless as Jacob's. Stay where you are and place your feet only where I place mine."

She told them both to wait while she carefully broke the flowers growing along the steps. She could only hope her fingers wouldn't trigger any alarms. All seemed still. Nonetheless, Fox kept stopping to listen, and her mind pestered her about how she planned to take Jacob across the courtyard and to the mirror undetected. Even if he were able to see, he could barely stand. She could think of only one way, and for that she would need Sylvain.

It took endless patience to cross the room. Fox laid her coat over the floorboards so they didn't step on the silver threads.

"Do you know your way around here?" she asked Sylvain when they finally reached the door. A rat scampered away as Fox opened it, but apart from that, all was still. The voices she could hear were far enough away.

"Sure. I told you, I delivered their crates for months." Sylvain pointed in the direction from which Fox had come. "They keep the mirrors back there, and there"—he pointed north toward the silver chimneys—"is where they make the glass. These cursed islands in the East River. My wife warned me. Ex-wife. 'Sylvain,' June said, 'why do you think they pay you so well? Those islands are cursed. Find some decent work.' But how much can you make with decent work?"

Sylvain was talking himself into a rage. Fox put her hand over his mouth. "Not another word," she whispered. "Or you can try swimming across the river."

That helped. Sylvain was as quiet as a mouse as he tiptoed after her and Jacob. They reached the courtyard. The van was gone, but other visitors had apparently arrived. Neither Jacob nor Sylvain could see the three carriages, nor the building they were parked in front of. To Sylvain they probably looked like ordinary cars. Camouflage magic didn't just make things invisible; sometimes it gave a different appearance to them. Fox remembered a hazelnut shell she'd found in a cave. Jacob had seen only the shell, but to her it looked like a tiny silver cradle in her hands.

The guards waiting by the carriages had the same clay faces as the man who'd brought the food. Their weapons, however, looked very much of this world. Jacob, blind and lame as he was, would never get past them undetected, and if that wasn't enough, the huge dog and his master also appeared from behind one of the carriages. He was the only human Fox could see, if he really was human. He was very young for a guard.

"You have to make it to that building there," she whispered to Sylvain. "The one in front of the glass vat. Try to sneak around to the other side."

Sylvain stared at her blankly. *He can't see the vat, Fox.* She could only hope the flowering bushes were there to feed the Grass-Elves and not to trigger alarms.

"That building next to the rusty gas tank," she corrected herself. Sylvain nodded with relief, but Jacob closed his hand tightly around her arm.

"What are you planning?" As if he didn't know. He just didn't like it. Together in her world they'd gotten through situations that had looked much more hopeless. Now they just had to find out whether they could summon the same luck in this world.

The dogs lifted their heads. They could smell human sweat for miles, but Fox was planning to give them an even more enticing scent. She waited until Sylvain and Jacob had disappeared between the trees before she stepped out into the courtyard. One of the guards saw her and called out to the others. They all reached for their weapons as she shifted in front of their eyes.

And the vixen ran. Away from the building where the mirror was waiting.

13

A BROTHER'S DEBT

Schwanstein. As a child, Will had often gone to sleep with
the city's name on his lips. It had sounded like a magical place.
The darkness he'd since encountered in the Mirrorworld had
not changed that. The church towers were visible from the ruin.
They proved to be good guideposts, and as Will asked his way to
The Ogre (despite the puzzled looks his clothes attracted), every
street name reminded him of a story his brother had told him.
Jacob had so resented Will for following him through the mirror
without asking that he'd never taken his little brother into
Schwanstein. And then the jade had made it impossible. Jacob
had always been good at keeping a secret, even the existence of
a younger brother. Will had never been able to even keep a bad
grade from their mother. The only secret he'd ever kept from his
big brother was that he did actually remember some of what had
happened to him behind the mirror, even though those memories

felt like someone else's.

The smell of stale pipe smoke and spilled wine, the child-eater's oven door on the wall, the Ogre's arm above the bar... Jacob had described Albert Chanute's tavern so often Will felt like he'd walked into its taproom a hundred times. As a child he'd dreamed of seeing Chanute's trophies with his own eyes and sitting at one of the tables to plan treasure hunts with his brother.

"We're closed!" Flaxen hair, round glasses, crutch...Tobias Wenzel. Jacob had only mentioned him on one of his last visits. Chanute's cook had lost a leg in the Goyl war. Will was glad his skin no longer gave away that he'd been the Goyl King's bodyguard at one time.

"Is Fox here?" Will could never remember her human name. "I'm Jacob's brother, Will."

Wenzel hobbled toward the bar. His crutch was studded with the semiprecious stones Goyl officers wore to signify their rank. Moonstone, jasper, ruby. Memories...

"No, she's not here." Wenzel poured himself a shot of schnapps. The dirty tables spoke of a long night. "I didn't know Jacob has a brother."

The look he gave Will was wary as well as curious.

Fox was not there. What now? Will had not only wanted to tell her he hadn't heard from Jacob in days. He'd also hoped Fox would know where he could find the Dark Fairy. He was tempted to ask for Chanute, but if even half of what his brother had told him about the man was true, he'd be in an even worse mood than his cook was at this early hour of the morning.

"Can I leave a message for her?"

Wenzel downed his shot. "Sure."

The only piece of paper Will could find in his pockets was a flyer for a play he and Clara had seen a few weeks earlier.

He sat down at one of the tables. What should he write? Despite everything they'd been through together, he'd always felt shy toward Fox. Wenzel was looking at him. Will concealed the ballpoint pen. Maybe he could find some clothes in Jacob's room, something less conspicuous than what he was wearing now.

A girl carrying a pail stepped through a door by the bar. She was as scrawny as a bird and nine years old at the most. But it was obvious she was used to hard work. She stopped when she saw Will, but then she put down her pail of water next to one of the filthy tables. She went to the bar and let three Heinzel climb out of her apron pocket. The first time Will had heard about Heinzel was when Jacob had given him one of their tiny jackets for his sixth birthday. Jacob never forgot his little brother's birthday, and Will's fingers would tremble with anticipation when he opened his presents. The only one to whom he'd shown Jacob's presents was Clara.

"I assume you've tried kissing her?"

The Heinzel started washing the dirty glasses. Will put his pen to paper again. *Write.* What? That Clara was sleeping herself to death? That a stranger had promised to make everything all right again? He folded the paper and put it back in his pocket.

The Heinzel, though hardly bigger than the glasses, were surprisingly noisy. With all their splashing and spluttering, even Wenzel only noticed the Goyl when he reached the bar. The Heinzel gave the stranger just a quick glance, but the girl stumbled against her pail, and Wenzel's face froze with hatred.

"You're closed, I know," the Goyl forestalled him. "I just want some information."

Will had forgotten how rough Goyl voices were. The golden

93

eyes briefly met his. A jasper face, and a King with dull red skin... Lost images filled his head.

The Goyl was an onyx, the noblest skin to have, but the black was veined with green stone. The unwelcome stranger didn't wear a uniform like the Goyl Will had seen in Schwanstein's streets. His clothes were tailored from the speckled skin of saurians Will remembered seeing from the shore of an underground lake.

"I am obliged to serve your kind, but nobody says I have to speak to you." Wenzel struck the counter with his crutch so hard the Heinzel scampered behind a couple of empty bottles.

The Goyl gave Wenzel a wolfish smile. He wasn't as tall as most of them. "Have you forgotten who's in charge in your little backwater town now? That kind of attitude could easily cost you another leg."

The girl eyed the Goyl with a mixture of disgust and fascination, but Wenzel shot her a warning glance and she quickly resumed mopping up spilled water.

The Goyl looked up at the Ogre's arm above the bar. "I am looking for a man who frequently stays here. Even though"—he eyed his surroundings with disgust—"I would've thought he could afford better lodgings. Jacob Reckless?"

Wenzel acted as if he'd forgotten about Will. He shooed the Heinzel back to work. "He hasn't been here in months, and even if I knew where he was, why should I tell that to a stoneface?"

"Yes, why indeed?" The Goyl looked at his claws. "Even if you're as stupid as you appear, I'm sure you can come up with a reason or two. Tell him the Bastard was here and that I shall find him. I always find what I seek; nobody knows that better than Reckless."

"I will tell Jacob just one thing," Wenzel hissed back at him. "That a damned Goyl was asking for him and that he'd better look out for himself."

Will got up. The Goyl gave him a blank look. Will remembered the revulsion he himself had once felt at the sight of human skin. "What do you want with Jacob Reckless?" Will asked.

"I fail to see how that's any of your business, snail face." The Goyl reached into his pocket and put a moonstone on the counter. "He stole something from me. This could be yours if you tell me where he is. That one"—he nodded toward Wenzel—"hasn't earned a reward."

Will couldn't take his eyes off the gem. Red moonstone. Kami'en's bodyguards wore it on their collars.

"I've only heard of him," Will said. "Isn't he a famous treasure hunter? I didn't know he's also a thief."

Will kept his head down as he spoke. He also remembered how easy it was for a Goyl to read a human face.

"I've changed my mind about the message," Will said to Wenzel. "I have something for the Dark Fairy. Can you tell me where *she* is these days?"

Wenzel looked at the Goyl with triumph. "Nobody knows where she is. The Fairy left Kami'en. Soon we'll see whether the stonefaces can win their wars without her magic."

"The Dark Fairy," the Goyl growled. Will felt the Goyl's eyes like fingers on his skin. "Didn't your mother warn you about what Fairies do to little lovesick fools like you? She'll turn you into one of her moths before you can even lay your puppy eyes on her." He dropped the moonstone back into his pocket before one of the Heinzel could snatch it.

"You know where she is?" Will asked.

The Heinzel started squabbling. They sounded like angry crickets.

"Even if I knew, why should I tell a snail face? Read your newspapers. They've been full of nothing else since the Dark One left Vena."

"And her spells went with her!" Wenzel raised his empty glass to the Goyl. "The Man-Goyl are changing back. Your King will soon be out of soldiers."

The Bastard ran his claws across the counter. "There will be enough left. And who says the Man-Goyl will start fighting for *you* just because they have their soft skin back? Maybe they'd rather fight for a King who won't let his soldiers be captured like cattle and who doesn't send them to war in some faraway colony."

To die for a King. Will couldn't stop staring at the black claws. Claws like that, as sharp as steel, had torn into his neck. Time opened up like a well. He was back in the cathedral, shielding Kami'en with his own body.

The Goyl was watching him. "Well, good luck." He reached across the counter, and before Wenzel could stop him, he'd grabbed one of the schnapps bottles. "You'll have a lot of competition. Amalie has promised the rubies she wore at her wedding to anyone who catches the Fairy." The Bastard put the bottle in his knapsack and dropped a couple of coins on the bar. "Those stones are worth more than all of Austry. Her mother had them stolen from one of the onyx lords."

Two men stepped into the taproom.

They eyed the Goyl with the usual disgusted fear. The Bastard scowled at them as he pushed past them toward the door. He turned around once more and, with his eyes fixed on Will, slammed his fist to his chest.

Will quickly jammed his hands into his pockets as his fingers clenched in response. Behind him he heard Wenzel cursing the stonefaces to his new guests. The three men started to conjure a glorious future in which they'd drive the stonefaces back into the earth and let them suffocate like rats. One of the men, whose pale skin actually did make him look like a snail, was going on about how handy it was that the Goyl turned to stone after death so that their corpses could be mined for gems.

"I always find what I seek."

Will stepped outside. It was market day, and the farmers were putting up their stalls: fruits and vegetables, chickens and geese, but there were also Heinzel and—supposedly—talking donkeys for sale. Will looked around. He needed a horse. And supplies.

The Goyl was leaning in a doorway on the other side of the square. Above him, the head of a unicorn stared down on the people of Schwanstein, who were all giving the Bastard a wide berth. He seemed to be enjoying himself tremendously.

"What? I still can't tell you where the Fairy is," he said as Will approached him. Malachite—that's what was tainting his dark onyx skin. Will had no idea how he knew that.

"I am Jacob Reckless's brother."

"And I'm supposed to be surprised?" The Bastard winked. "He carries a picture of you. Touching. I admit, I've always been grateful that my mother spared me the competition of a brother."

"My brother is not a thief. Why do you say he stole from you?"

The Goyl gave him such a taunting look that Will thought he could feel it pierce his skin. To find what? Jade?

"I don't want to rob you of your illusions. I'm sure you're carrying a sack-load of them. But Jacob Reckless is a thief and a liar, though of course he wouldn't rub his little brother's nose in it."

Will turned his back on the Goyl. He preferred to hide his rage,

97

which was so like a scorpion crawling from the darkest recess of his heart that it frightened him. Nothing had made the stone more terrifying than the feeling that his rage and hatred had become uncontrollable. The Goyl savored both, like a rush.

"Well, by my heart of stone!" The Bastard laughed behind him. "You're much more sensitive than your brother. Shall I help you find the Dark Fairy?"

Will turned again.

"I have no money."

"I don't want your money. Only Kings can afford the services of Nerron the Bastard." He pushed himself off the wall. "I want what your brother stole from me. You think you can get that for me?"

"What is it?"

The Bastard looked at a passing girl. She quickened her steps when she noticed his golden stare. "A swindlesack. It looks empty, but what's inside it is mine."

Will suppressed the urge to feel for the sack under his shirt. "What's inside it?"

Two women walked past. They stared daggers at Will as if he were talking to the Devil himself, but the Bastard clicked his tongue at them and they quickly stalked away.

"A crossbow. Nothing special. A family heirloom." He wasn't a very good liar. Maybe he wasn't even trying. "I think I know what you want from the Dark Fairy," he whispered to Will. "I've heard a few interesting stories about the brother of Jacob Reckless. He supposedly gained the most sacred skin a Goyl can have, yet his brother purged him of it."

Will's heart began to beat at a ridiculous speed.

The Goyl pulled an amulet from under his lizard shirt. It was made of jade. "If I were you, I'd want it back as well. Who'd be so stupid to trade holy stone for a snail's skin?"

"Yes," Will managed to say. "You guessed it. The Fairy is the only one who can give my jade back to me."

Lies... He forced himself to look at the unicorn head. Jacob had told him so many lies about the scars on his back, until Will had finally found out that they'd come from unicorns. Would Jacob have believed that he wanted his jade skin back?

"I guess we have a deal." The Goyl dropped the amulet into his shirt again. "And to seal it, you will show me the mirror you came through." He smiled. "Let me guess. It's close by, isn't it? Look at your clothes. Nobody wears such things in Schwanstein."

Will stopped himself from looking toward the ruin on the hill. A Goyl in the other world...and then? A child-eating Witch? The Stilt who'd attacked him on his first trip through the mirror? He was—very briefly—tempted to ask the Bastard about the stranger who'd given him the sack with the crossbow. But he was afraid of the answer he might get.

"What mirror?" he said. "I have no idea what you're talking about. Do we have a deal?"

The Bastard looked toward The Ogre. "Sure," he said. "Why not?"

14

His Roads

Humans. They were everywhere. Like mosquito larvae on a pond. Mortality was so fertile. Fields, roads, cities... The world created anew according to their mortal tastes, groomed, straightened, pruned, and tamed. Had she always loathed humans like that, even before Kami'en discarded her for one of their women? The Dark One didn't want to remember. She wanted to give in to the hatred, the disgust, the rage. If only all that hadn't also washed away her love.

She didn't even try to avoid their settlements. Let them see she didn't fear them, though they'd throw rocks at her, burn her effigy in straw. She saw them peering nervously from behind their curtains as Chithira drove her carriage past their houses. "There she is, the Fairy Witch!" she heard them whisper. "She murdered the child of her unfaithful lover. She has no heart."

So many villages. So many cities. Like a fungus sprouting

mortal flesh. And they all had Amalie's face.

Initially, she'd let the moths weave the web under which she slept during the day in front of one of their churches or town halls, or next to one of their monuments. But after someone took a shot at Donnersmarck as he guarded her sleep, she'd begun to go into the forests for rest. There were at least some left that hadn't been fed into their factories' furnaces.

Donnersmarck would sometimes ride into the nearest town to find out how things were in Vena. He reported that the rubies Amalie had pledged to the Fairy's captor had already cost six women their lives just because they'd been mistaken for the Dark One. Crookback and the Walrus had declared that Lotharaine and Albion would grant her asylum. Asylum... How stupid did they think she was? Did they really believe she'd sell her magic to the highest bidder? Or that she was looking for another crowned lover? None of them could compare to the King of the Goyl. She'd loved the best of them, only to be betrayed.

Donnersmarck also gave her news of Kami'en. He tried to utter the name casually, as though the Goyl King was just any other man. The Dark One was touched that Donnersmarck was trying to protect her from the pain caused by her lover's betrayal, from the humiliation that was Kami'en's silence. The Goyl still hadn't said a word in her defense. He'd made peace with the rebels in the north, and he was negotiating with the renegade Man-Goyl. He was so much better than his enemies. Maybe because they only fought to enrich themselves. Soldiers didn't like to die for the gold in their officers' pockets. But revenge was something one could fight for with passion. Kami'en only ever went to war for revenge. He was the fox who'd turned on the hunters.

Yes. She was still on his side.

101

At night, Chithira steered the carriage over the roads built by Kami'en's soldiers, and in her heartless chest, sadness and rage rose and fell like tides. The memories followed her, no matter how hard her dead coachman drove the horses. Memories that were as alive as the present, more real than anything rushing past outside.

Would she ever be again what she'd been before Kami'en? Did she even want to be?

She traveled only at night, yet her carriage was often blocked by groups of men who'd drunk up enough courage in some tavern to try to earn Amalie's reward. In most cases Donnersmarck handled them, even when they'd armed themselves with scythes and axes or hid themselves behind barrels of burning tar. Sometimes Chithira's shifting in front of their eyes was enough to make them scatter. But one night there was a woman among the taunting masses, and the Fairy set her moths on her, imagining it was Amalie who was doubled up screaming on the muddy road.

Of course, she wondered whether Kami'en was also looking for her. Four days after her flight from Vena, six Goyl soldiers had blocked her carriage's path. They didn't answer when Donnersmarck asked them if they'd been sent by their kind, and they quickly looked down when the Dark One descended from the carriage. *"Don't look at the Fairy Witch."* That's what Hentzau had taught them. But the Dark Fairy forced them to look, and poisoned them with her beauty.

They stumbled after the carriage for miles. Chithira ignored them, but Donnersmarck kept looking back, and when they finally disappeared into the night, it was the first time the Fairy saw a hint of fear in the soldier's eyes, along with the stubborn warning not to try her magic on him.

15

BLIND

The dogs were barking. There was no sound Jacob feared as much now that the vixen's life meant more to him than his own. He wanted to stop, turn around, but Sylvain, who to Jacob's silvered eyes was barely more than a broad-shouldered shadow, dragged him on. The world consisted of shadows and silver, of what his fingers could feel, and of the barking of the dogs.

How many more times would she have to save him?...He should never have brought her into this world...Useless thoughts. Fox was so much better at suppressing those.

He stopped again.

Shots. The only sound worse than barking.

Sylvain pulled him along, uttering curses in French—no, Quebecois. Behind the mirror, that part of Canada still belonged to Lotharaine. Jacob had never been there.

Onward.

If Jacob hadn't known they were in his world, the dense undergrowth would have made him believe he was lost in the Black Forest again. Even the brick walls they were sneaking along felt like the weathered walls of a Witch's house. The Elf had brought these worlds too close together. It had all been so much easier when Jacob thought the mirror was all that connected them.

Sylvain opened a gate and quickly pushed him through. It was pitch-dark inside, and his unwilling helper stumbled around as blindly as Jacob. Jacob felt crates. And glass. He quickly pulled back his hand.

"Where are we?" he asked.

"Where I was told to bring you. It's one of their storage sheds. *Bout de charge.* Your pretty girlfriend, she is crazy. We should have tried our luck on the river."

"A storage shed for what?"

"Their mirrors. What else? *Maudit Tabarnak'Ostie d'Câlisse! Ciboire!*" The curses flowed as inexhaustibly as brackwater. Sylvain Caleb Fowler could have easily won one of the Dwarfs' infamous cursing competitions.

Jacob leaned against the crates. His head hurt a little less when he closed his eyes. If this blindness was permanent, his treasure-hunting days were over. His right arm, on the other hand, felt as good as new. Maybe that needle had some good effects. The man who'd rammed it into his temple had looked like he'd been formed from clay. Maybe a cheap version of Sixteen and Seventeen. Jacob could still see the Mirrorlings in his mind's eye: with his face, with Clara's, his father's. *"Your mother never noticed the difference."* The man who'd gone to the park with him and Will, the man who'd kissed his mother in the kitchen…how many of his memories were actually memories of Spieler? *"In this world, we can even have children with mortal women."* So often had he wished for a different father, but not like this one. *Stop it, Jacob. He's not your father, neither yours nor Will's.* Could he really be so sure, though?

The dogs were still barking, but at least nobody was shooting anymore. Maybe because the last bullet had hit its target.

"How did they catch you?" he asked Sylvain. He had to take his mind off things. Just listening for sounds from outside was going to drive him mad.

"My curiosity. And I couldn't keep my hands off their powder."

"Powder?"

"Yes. They give it to their best customers. A little envelope here, another there. It brings back the lust—for life, for love, everything. It lasts for days, but then you feel rotten. As though someone has torn out your heart."

That sounded like elven dust. How did they make it without Grass-Elves?

Maybe he has Grass-Elves, Jacob. Maybe he sends his clay faces through the mirror to catch them. Or Sixteen, or Seventeen, or the fifteen who came before them. But then why hadn't he ever heard about them behind the mirror? *Because they looked like humans, Jacob.* Maybe...

"I liked working for them. Not a bad job," Sylvain muttered. "Even though I hardly ever got to see anyone. And well paid. Maybe they could've forgiven me the powder stuff if I hadn't run into the Mirrorling. *Ciboire.* June told me a thousand times. My wife. Ex-wife. 'Sylvain, don't stick that flat nose of yours into things that aren't your business.' *Simonac!* I'm a curious person! Got me into a lot of trouble as a child."

"Who do they deliver these mirrors to?"

"Hotels, restaurants, shops, offices... They're very popular.

105

Nobody thinks twice about it. And why should they? I wanted to take a closer look once. After all, I'd been hauling those crates for months, and these sheds are rarely locked. Didn't feel good looking into them, though. I thought it must be my stupid visage. But no. The mirrors don't just steal your face. They also bring memories back, whether you want to remember or not. Everything you'd forgotten, especially the things you wanted to forget."

Yes. That made sense. Jacob had been wondering why he'd suddenly been thinking of long-forgotten teachers, neighbors, and friends. And his mother. "*Jacob, come here!*" The images were so clear he thought he could actually feel her kisses on his face. He'd been sure he'd banished the memories of her as thoroughly as those of his father. It had helped that she'd always preferred Will over him.

One of the dogs howled. Jacob leaped up.

"Where are you going?" Sylvain grabbed his arm.

"I can't be sitting here while she's out there. I have to look for her."

"Cocombre! You cannot see!" Sylvain dragged him back between the crates.

It was quiet again outside. Hideously quiet. What was taking Fox so long?

"Did you also see one of the Mirrorlings?" It was clear Sylvain hadn't enjoyed his encounter.

"Yes," Jacob answered. *But they don't frighten me half as much as their maker.*

"As I was standing between all the mirrors, I thought to myself: *Bring her one, Sylvain. June would like one of the smaller ones.* There were so many—I was sure they wouldn't notice. I was high on their powder. Thought the world was mine. And then I saw him lying

106

there. A man, just all silver. And suddenly there he was, standing behind me, as if he'd been there the entire time. Everything was reflected on his skin, and then he suddenly had a face. And then another face! *Simonac*! Sylvain, I'm thinking, *you were right. The aliens are already here.* I hit him. I used to be quite a decent boxer, you see — Canadian heavyweight champion. That trophy was the only one of my things June kept. But hitting is not a good idea, when — "

Jacob pressed his hand over Sylvain's mouth.

Someone had just shoved open the gate. The noise killed all hope it might be Fox. The men sounded as human as Sylvain, and luckily they didn't grab the crate the pair was hiding behind. The gate opened twice more, and both times Jacob and Sylvain stayed undetected. But Fox didn't come, and Jacob didn't care what he owed the Alderelf and what that meant for him and her. He didn't care if his eyes had to see silver for the rest of his life or whether Spieler kept walking around with his father's face. Didn't care. At all.

If only Fox came back...

Hours. And hours. And hours. While Sylvain told him about his Canadian cousins and the girl he'd moved to New York for. For the first time in years, Jacob thought about the only teacher who hadn't thought he was an idiot. And he thought about the night Albert Chanute had nearly shot him in a drunken rage.

And then, finally and barely audible, a sound.

The snap of a lock. Steps, so quiet. Jacob knew only one person who could walk so quietly.

"Jacob?" The voice was more familiar than his own. Her outline was unmistakable, even through the silver fog in his eyes. And this time he would have said it, right? *I love you. So much. Too*

107

much. But that was forbidden. For all time. The Elf would take his heart in payment.

"And what now?" Sylvain whispered. "Why did you want me to bring him here? *Maude merde*, we are sitting in a trap!"

Fox didn't pay any attention to him.

"The mirror from your father's study," she whispered to Jacob, "is *here*."

Here? Thoughts tumbled through his aching head. "What about Will? And Clara?"

Fox shook her head. "You two were the only prisoners." She took his hand. "We'll come back once you can see again."

Sylvain whimpered like a child when Fox told him he was going to have to step in front of a mirror once more. Finally Fox took his hand and pressed it against the glass. Sylvain Caleb Fowler disappeared, and the mirror was their secret no more.

It never had been. Spieler had probably always known where it was.

16
Like an Open Door

"Ayoye! Ta-bar-nak!"

A shrill scream. Sounds of a fight. Jacob thought he could make out the outlines of the tower's windows, and in front of them the figure of his cell mate, who seemed to be struggling with something. Whatever it was, Sylvain won.

"Saint ciboire!" Sylvain was leaning over something lying by his feet. "I swear it jumped me!" He sounded disgusted and fascinated.

"That, Sylvain, is a Stilt," Fox explained.

"A what? *Maude merde*, I think I broke its neck!" He didn't seem to relish the thought. It was good to know they hadn't brought a savage killer through the mirror. And he'd killed the Stilt! For years Jacob had tried to catch that old bloodsucker. The creature was a committed baby-snatcher, and its bite had been Jacob's first welcome to this world.

"What now?" Fox stood next to him.

109

To Jacob's silver-blind eyes, the mirror was just a shimmering blob. Hard to imagine his father's study was no longer waiting for him on the other side.

"Shall I go back and check on Will?" Fox took his hand.

"No. I'll go, as soon as I can see again." Jacob led her away from the mirror. He felt a brief fear that the Elf could be watching them through the glass. *"Your vixen will make beautiful children. I hope you don't take too long!"* Jacob let go of her hand, as though his very touch might deliver her to the Elf. And yet he desired her even more. Of course. That was the game, wasn't it? Forbidden desires...and always a price.

He wanted to smash the mirror, but then what? Everything seemed to indicate there were many more, but until he found the others, this was his only way back.

"Where are we?" Sylvain was standing by one of the windows. "Looks old. Really old."

Jacob was staring at the mirror, or at whatever he could see of it.

"Let them come!" Fox whispered. "We'll make it hard for them to find us."

What would he do without her? He couldn't give her up. *You don't have to give her up, Jacob. You just have to stop wanting her.* Forever. He hated that word.

She went ahead. Sylvain and Jacob followed. He nearly broke his neck following her through the hatch, but he managed to descend the rope without further incident. Fox barricaded the door to the tower with a few stones so she could check later if someone had come through.

"Zut alors!" There was a tiny man over there!" Sylvain shouted. He'd just seen his first Heinzel. "I know magicians can do wild

110

things with mirrors, but this is..."

All those years, and now a stranger knew about the mirror. He could tell about it, here and in the other world. Not a nice thought. Jacob hadn't even told Chanute about the mirror.

"*Bout ∂e charge!* And what is this?"

"That, Sylvain, is a Thumbling." Jacob could hear Fox having trouble maintaining a serious tone. "They're very skillful thieves, so always chase them away before they can get to your pockets."

"*Ta-bar-nak!*" The delight in Sylvain's voice was obvious.

It didn't sound as if Sylvain Caleb Fowler would want to go home anytime soon.

17

AN OLD ACQUAINTANCE

John Reckless couldn't wait to get back to Albion. The ferry crossing was certainly not an experience he was looking forward to, but the island had for a long time now been the only place he'd called home. Albion had given him protection when he'd been so broken he feared he'd never put the pieces together again. It had given him the appreciation he'd been thirsting for since his life in another world, and a wife who worshipped him. Who cared that she loved a fake face?

So many reasons to be perfectly happy. Why wasn't he? *Nobody is happy*. That answer usually silenced the inner voice that kept pestering him with such questions. John had always been good at ignoring it, anyway.

His return was going to be celebrated with elaborate pomp. After all, he was bringing the news Wilfred of Albion had been hoping for. John felt flattered to be the "great hope" for the King, and the uniformed protectors who came with that role might have been annoying at times, but they were also very comforting. One of them leaned in the carriage window to tell him they were three hours from Calias. His breath smelled so strongly of garlic that John had to struggle not to avert his face. There were more ferries from Dunkerk to Albion, but John had insisted on crossing from Calias because Dunkerk was in Flanders, which had been occupied by the Goyl two months earlier. The commanding officer of his guards tried to lecture him that even the Goyl had enough respect for international law not to attack an official convoy of the King of Albion. But what did John care whether a young upstart officer thought him a coward? He knew he was one, and four years locked in a dungeon was surely a good reason to be cautious. Flanders had been an easy prize, especially after Albion's shipment of weapons had ended up at the bottom of the sea. A strange situation, to have been the one who'd not only designed the flagship but the planes that had sunk it. As though he were playing war with himself.

Meadows and apple orchards drifted past the carriage window. John decided to forget politics for a while. Lotharaine was such an enchanting country, and they drank and ate so much better here than in Albion. Even the Walrus secretly employed a chef from Lutis, and his Lotharainian wine was as well guarded as his treasure chambers. John opened the basket Crookback's servants had packed for his journey: goose paté with just a hint of swan fat, stuffed Witch-frogs, leaf-gilded mille-feuilles. Opening a bottle of red wine in a jolting carriage was not an easy feat, but the first sip was going to make the effort worthwhile. They'd even wrapped a crystal goblet in Lotharainian linen for him. The only pity was he thought he saw Arsene Lelou's pointy-nosed face in the dark red wine. He downed the whole glass as though it could wash away the memory. *"The Albian secret service may not be as omniscient as its reputation suggests. Jacob Reckless survived the sinking of the fleet."*

So he still had two sons. Good. Granted, he hardly ever thought of Will. Jacob had always been his favorite. Will had been Rosamund's. He'd married her for her illustrious ancestors, and by the time he'd actually fallen in love with her, it had been too late. Not that she hadn't loved him still, but he couldn't bear the love he constantly betrayed. He'd disappointed her, and himself, time and time again. He was never the man she'd seen in him.

More wine. *Memories be gone.* Away with her face, which he still remembered all too well. He had a recurring dream in which they reconciled, and she always looked as young as on the day he'd met her.

Heavens, the bottle was already half empty. And? He was going to vomit it all over the ferry railing later anyway. John brushed a fly off his nose. His fingers still remembered the other nose, fleshier, straighter. Who would've thought his fake face could fool even his own son?

The carriage bounced and stopped abruptly. John's wine spilled over his tailored shirt. This was another thing he'd discussed with Crookback. Progress required good highways. John was picking some snail paté off his lap, when his hands went numb with fear. Shots.

John ducked under the window and peered outside. The soldier with the garlic breath was lying next to his horse, his face shot to pieces. There was no sign of the other soldiers. John's trembling fingers tried to pull the revolver from its holster. He'd improved the weapon in ways that weren't visible from the outside, but it still couldn't fire more than six shots.

114

The young man approaching the carriage wore a well-tailored greatcoat and didn't look like a highwayman, but maybe he was one of those who dressed like lords and pretended to be protectors of the poor. Travel in Albion was no safer than in Lotharaine, and John had fallen prey to robbers like him twice before. For years he'd been trying to convince the Walrus to raise a tax to finance armed patrols along the highways.

"Monsieur Brunel." The stranger greeted him with the hint of a bow while he trained his pistol on John's head. "Thierry Auger. My pleasure."

Monsieur Brunel...He knew who John was. That wasn't good. *Put the gun away, John!* He was a decent enough shot, but not very fast.

Ransom. Of course. That's what the stranger wanted. Money for the famous engineer who'd taken Albion to the pinnacle of modern times. John's mouth was as dry as parchment. He'd always had a very physical reaction to fear. John moved to open the carriage door, even though he could barely feel his own legs. But the young robber shook his head.

"Stay where you are, monsieur. Your destination has changed, but your mode of transport will remain the same." A highwayman who spoke fluent Albian, though with a heavy Lotharainian accent. Monsieur Auger was so young he probably hadn't been growing his beard for long, but his confidence spoke of some experience in highway robbery.

A man who suddenly appeared next to Auger was much older and less groomed, though just as well dressed. This was obviously a profitable trade.

"Get in there with him," he ordered Auger. "But watch out he doesn't try to jump."

Thierry Auger did as he was told. He picked up John's pistol from the floor of the carriage before taking the seat opposite. John could hear more voices outside, but he couldn't make out how many robbers there were. They'd picked their time and place well. Even the fields were deserted. Behind the fence, where the blood of the dead soldier had turned the grass red, a very disinterested cow was ruminating away, and in the distance, church bells had started chiming to complete the idyll.

The carriage turned around. Through the window, John could see two men dragging another of his uniformed guards off the road. He looked as dead as the first one.

"Where are you taking me?" Not only did fear make his body go numb—it also started producing embarrassing amounts of sweat. But his mind stayed surprisingly clear, as though disengaging from the sweating, trembling coward who was staring into the pistol of a boy.

Thierry Auger lit a cigarette. Crookback had made them fashionable, but this one smelled different from the ones the King smoked. Witch-leaves, if John's nose wasn't mistaken. They grew all over these woods.

"We're off to Flanders," Auger said. "I see you have some food. You'll need it. It's a long drive."

He wouldn't reveal more, no matter how much John asked. The voices outside didn't all speak with a Lotharainian accent. John thought he could make out some Lombardic sounds. The older man who seemed to be the leader sounded more Leonese.

They passed the Flandrian border at night. When John saw the Goyl at the tollgate, he nearly leaned out the window to beg the Lotharainian border guards for help. The Goyl had a garnet skin, considered to be volatile. One of John's prison guards had

116

been a garnet Goyl.

Stop it, John! Your kidnappers are humans.

But why were they taking him to Flanders?

The guard on the Lotharainian side cast a bored glance into the carriage and waved them on. Maybe John should've screamed, but Auger gave him a warning look. He'd draped his jacket over his pistol, but it didn't take too much imagination to assume it was pointed at his stomach. John had once seen a man die from a shot to the stomach, one of the prisoners of war who worked in the underground factories of the Goyl. No. He didn't scream for help. He even managed to look the garnet Goyl straight in the eye. *He's seeing the face of Isambard Brunel, John.*

As the Goyl receded into the darkness behind them, John breathed such a sigh of relief that Thierry Auger gave him a crooked smile and offered him a drag of his cigarette. And on they rolled through the night. They were headed northeast, if John was reading the constellations above the fields right. The stars were the same as in his world; they even had the same names. A mirror image, nothing more…How often he'd told himself that, despite the two moons, despite the Fairies and the Witches. He'd even wondered whether there were Goyl in his world and whether they just never came to the surface. Useless thoughts, but a welcome distraction from the fear that was growing with every mile.

John had no idea how long they'd been traveling. Auger had searched him for weapons and taken his pocket watch, together with his purse and the gold cuff links he'd been given by his lover, engraved with the initials he had stolen from another engineer. Who were they working for? What were they going to do to him? Torture? Execution? More time in a cell? All his carefully devised routines, the precious illusions of stability and safety—why did one begin to trust them if even the biggest fool would've realized by now that there was no such thing as constancy in life?

Auger nodded off once. John had his hand on the door handle instantly, though the carriage was going so fast that the jump would have certainly broken his neck. At that very moment, the leader rode up to the window and shouted Auger's name. Bad luck or not? John wasn't sure.

It was light again by the time they stopped in front of a house. The smashed windows and bullet holes in the whitewashed walls indicated it had been abandoned for a while. There were windmills in the distance, the same kind that dotted the Flandrian landscape in John's world, though on this side their wooden wings were painted in different colors: sky blue (though a blue sky was a rare sight in Flanders), green (like the vast, wet meadows), or red (like the fields of tulips that often surrounded the mills). There wasn't much in Flanders that could've protected the small country from the Goyl.

Impatiently, the leader waved John out of the carriage. His black beard and bushy eyebrows would've suited an anarchist. That's how anarchists were generally depicted on the posters, anyway. Auger pushed his pistol into John's back as he climbed out behind him.

They didn't walk to the house but toward a well.

And how John's heart began to race. Oh yes. There was always more fear to be felt. Those stories of people who died of fear—all nonsense. He'd be long dead.

As John figured, there was no water in the well. Instead, steel rungs led down into the deep, the kind of ladders the Goyl installed in wells and mine shafts to take them to where they'd come from: under the earth.

118

No. He was not going back down there. He was a fast runner. His running had saved him several times in underground tunnels, and not only from the Goyl but also from giant bats, calf-sized lizards, spiders that built their nests by the hundreds in every available crack and cranny...

John spun around. Auger would shoot him. And? He couldn't think. He knocked down one of the guards, but even before he could take a step, Thierry Auger had rammed his pistol into John's stomach so hard that John cried out and dropped to his knees.

"I wouldn't do that," Auger whispered to him. "Diego won't hesitate to shoot off all your fingers if you cause any more trouble. And in the end, you'll go into the well anyway."

Diego. John had been right about the leader's Leonian accent. How could he have fooled himself just because they were human? It was well known that the Goyl had human collaborators. They paid them in diamonds. And some even worked for free because they saw the stonefaces as their liberators from the rule of their despised kings.

The soldier who dragged John back to his feet also looked like a human, but the strip of moonstone on his forehead gave him away—together with the black claws. Man-Goyl. A new race. Ever since the Fairy had abandoned Kami'en, nobody could be sure which side they were on.

Diego was the first down the shaft. He had a pit lamp to light the way. The Man-Goyl, who'd taken over guarding John from Auger, didn't need a lamp.

The well led down into one of the tunnels the Goyl had dug everywhere. This one was just a footpath, but John had seen others big enough for mounted soldiers. Many had space for carriages and some even for trains. During his time with the Goyl, John had seen maps of these centuries-old tunnel networks. There was hardly a place on the surface that couldn't be reached through them. John even knew of plans for a tunnel to connect Albion with the mainland. Similar plans existed for Sveriga, but not even John had been able to solve the problem of ventilation in underwater tunnels. He'd been glad about this limit to his knowledge, for the Goyl would've found ways to make him help them.

John followed his captors along a roadway that looked as if it had been constructed only recently. It was paved with onyx — a nice way to mock the old ruling class. The tunnel led into a wide hall similar to train stations that were now being built all over the surface, only this one didn't need a glass roof against wind and rain. Two freight trains were waiting on the tracks. They'd probably come from one of the ports of Flanders to supply the Goyl's underground cities with all the goods that country's colonies supplied: sugar, coffee, cotton, silkworms. The slave trade, Albion's and Lotharaine's most profitable enterprise, was of no interest to the Goyl. They sympathized with peoples who were considered inferior, and preferred to use their prisoners of war as laborers. It was an attitude that had earned the Goyl some loyal allies even in those countries that were out of their reach – for now – because of their fear of the sea.

A third train was parked behind the others on a platform guarded by soldiers. Its cars were reinforced with steel plates, and the locomotive bore Kami'en's carnelian-red coat of arms, which, since his marriage to Amalie, now showed the imperial eagle of Austry instead of the Dark Fairy's moth.

The Goyl waiting for Jacob in the last car probably didn't feel at all comfortable between the forged walls. Hentzau hated everything these modern times had brought forth, and John was fairly certain that hadn't changed. Hentzau's left eye was now so clouded that Kami'en's Bloodhound would probably soon be blind. Fear, hatred, helplessness... Seeing Hentzau brought back memories that threatened to drown John's mind like water. Since his kidnappers had told him they were taking him to Flanders, John had feared that the jasper Goyl had sent them. He'd tried to dismiss the thought as paranoia, but reality had again outdone his worst nightmares.

Hentzau's skin was riddled with fine cracks. He was paying a high price for his loyalty. Few Goyl stayed above ground for more than one or two months, yet Hentzau was always up there for his King. The jasper face was as familiar to John as his own, or that of Kami'en. Had Hentzau's King aged as much as his Bloodhound? The portraits the papers printed of the King and his wife showed him unchanged. The King of the Goyl was an attractive man, younger and much better-looking than the human rulers he was waging war against. Hentzau would've said it was the humans who'd been waging war against the Goyl—and for a long time.

John felt his new face like a mask. Would it hold? He'd taught himself to speak with an Albian accent and had even learned to box to acquire a new body language. Nothing gave one away like a familiar gesture. The nervous tremor—the legacy of his years underground—still came back far too quickly. Hentzau would certainly recognize that. And more.

"May I ask what the purpose of this abduction is?" *Yes, John. That's the way. Isambard Brunel has no fear, and he knows nothing about the Goyl, only that they are the enemies of Albion and that they fear open water.*

"Abduction? It was certainly not my intent that my invitation

121

be interpreted that way. The Clifton Bridge, the rail line from Goldsmouth to Pendragon, the tunnel under Londra, the telegraph cable to New Amsterdam?" Hentzau rubbed his cracked skin. "Our King is a great admirer of your engineering skills, Mr. Brunel." Yes, the mask was holding even under the milky stare of the man who for years had taken every opportunity to rob John of any delusions about himself. But why should he be surprised?

"Too much honor. I am well aware that the Goyl have an engineer of at least similar accomplishments in their employ. It was his planes that sunk my best ship." Oh, his fake face made him reckless. *What are you doing, John? Still can't get enough praise for your genius?*

Hentzau smiled. If that's what one should call what was going on around that lipless mouth. "Oh yes, the planes..."

The female soldier behind him handed Hentzau a flat leather pouch. From it, Hentzau pulled a mirror with such a delicate silver handle it all but disappeared in his massive jasper hand. "The first time I heard of the engineer who'd given Wilfred of Albion his much-admired horseless carriage, I had my spies give me a description of that Isambard Brunel. What I got sounded like I'd been mistaken. But then I heard about Brunel's iron ship. Years ago, we had plans to build iron ships, but we lost our engineer before the construction drawings were completed."

Hentzau stepped to John's side and held the mirror so they both could look into it. John stared at the image on the glass.

He'd not seen his own face in over eight years.

"Fabulous, isn't it?" Hentzau put the mirror down. "The man whom I relieved of this magical device claimed he'd found it in one of the abandoned silver palaces. You've heard of them? Very unhealthy places to visit."

122

John looked around. The Man-Goyl was standing right behind him. Diego the Leonian was guarding the door. *Say good-bye to the sun, John, to strolls in the cold morning air, to restaurants and theaters. "Ah, Mr. Brunel! Always an honor! George, take the gentleman to our best table."* His lover's skin, as soft as the furs she so loved to wear. All for nothing. The endless weeks of hiding, sleepless in lightless tunnels, his skin scorched by fire-geckos, blistered by festering rat bites and poisonous spiders. He still washed himself obsessively, as if he could scrub the memories off his body. Where had he gotten the courage? He couldn't remember. The first time he'd been truly brave, and he couldn't tell anyone about it, for John Reckless had died in those tunnels.

"Why Albion, John Reckless?" Hentzau dropped the mirror back into the pouch and handed it to the soldier. Goyl women were beautiful, and this one was no exception.

"Albion was the second stop. First I made my way to Sveriga." John had tried to get some water—the only thing Goyl truly feared—between himself and the Goyl, but his ultimate goal had always been Albion, with the unlimited resources provided by its colonies, and the cheap labor they got from the slave trade. Both were indispensable for the inventions John wanted to sell there. It had taken him months to smuggle himself on to a freighter sailing from Birka to Goldsmouth.

"And the new face?"

"Tummetotts. They are quite generous with their magic if you're desperate." It had been November, deepest winter in Sveriga, and the gnomes were so shy he'd nearly died of cold trying to find them. He'd learned about them in the Goyl archives. There was some debate about whether Tummetotts were distant relatives of the Heinzel, Hobs, and follets or a separate species of Nordic

123

Dwarf. In Sveriga, they were also called *hjälpare i nöden* —helpers in need. They had to believe you were desperate, or else they wouldn't show themselves.

"So it's true they don't expect anything for their help?"

"Yes. It's true." It was bizarre to be having a conversation with a Goyl about Tummetotts, but John had accepted long ago that no word better described his life: bizarre. He tried to calculate the steps to the door of the car. And then what? Would he make it to the well shaft? No. The Man-Goyl might not be a good shot, but Hentzau could still shoot out the eyes of a Gold-Raven in flight, even though firearms just didn't gel with his sense of good soldiership. He preferred his saber to a pistol.

John felt a brief surge of homesickness for Albion, so strong it caused him a physical pain.

"You needn't have gone all the way to Sveriga to find selfless helpers," Hentzau said. "We have stories of eyeless salamanders who fulfill wishes for free. Wagi Aniotiy. Scaly Angels. They supposedly live in caves with phosphorous stalactites. I've never seen one, but maybe that's because I was just never desperate enough...or because I've never liked to ask for help."

"Can I, as a last request, get some fresh air? One final look at the sky?"

Hentzau looked at John with scorn in his milky eyes.

"Still that love for drama. I can assure you, you will be seeing the sky soon enough. Three, four days, and you'll be back with your kind."

His kind. That didn't necessarily make much of a difference, as his kidnappers had proven.

Hentzau smiled as if he'd heard John's thoughts. It had always been a myth that it was those who loved you who could see through

124

you. It was those you feared who could see through you most clearly.

"You should be grateful, John," he said. "You so love to play the prophet of the New Magic. I will take you to a land that is still full of its enemies. Albion is already converted."

The stomping of the locomotive trembled through the metal floor beneath John's feet. It was he who had shown them how to run trains underground.

"Oh, and before I forget," Hentzau continued while John wondered which land the Goyl could have meant, "I met your son."

And that.

"Yes, I heard he stole one of my planes." John tried valiantly to sound as casual as Hentzau. "He got his fearlessness from his mother's side." The stolen plane, Jacob's role in the Blood Wedding... There hadn't been much about all that in the *Londra Illustrated News*, but Albion's King of course knew more than could be read in the papers, and whatever the Walrus knew, his valued chief engineer was sure to find out.

The female soldier waved in a courier. The man handed a sealed message to the jasper Goyl. It did not contain good news. The years of imprisonment had taught John to read that stone face like his own.

"Bad news?"

The Goyl's glance was a warning. No familiarities. Kami'en's Bloodhound didn't like people forgetting they were at his mercy. Hentzau folded the paper carefully, as one did when lost in deep thought, and tucked it into his uniform.

"Bad news for which you're quite responsible," he replied. "You're here to make amends."

125

18

THE WARNING

Compresses and a bitter broth to fight poisons. Alma drove the silver from Jacob's eyes. He was mortified to learn from Fox that Alma had known about the mirror for a long time. But the old Witch just shrugged when he tried to apologize for all the years of lying. She listened in silence as he told her about Spieler, but when he asked whether she remembered the Alderelf, she shook her head and smiled. "Eight hundred years? You overestimate my age. Some of the child-eaters eat the mushrooms growing under the Silver-Alders to speak with Alderelves, but they give you a wooden tongue, quite literally, so I've never tried that."

Silver-Alders. The nearest one was barely a day's ride away. Jacob had always thought the custom of bribing a tree with coins, spoons, or rings to grant one's darkest wishes was based on superstition. He was just considering a visit to the Silver-Alder despite Alma's warnings, when Wenzel told Fox that Will had

126

been to The Ogre.

Will had come through the mirror? Why? To escape when Spieler took the mirror? But if so, where was Clara? Jacob couldn't even think her name without seeing Sixteen standing at the bottom of those museum steps. Fox promised to find out where Will had gone after leaving the tavern, and Jacob decided to speak with Chanute. He hoped that among Albert's endless trove of anecdotes was at least one about Alderelves, or about the child-eaters who communed with them.

The girl who helped Wenzel in the tavern had washed Jacob's clothes. He was embarrassed by how quickly he dropped the neatly folded shirt when he saw the card slip out from under the sleeve. The handwriting was all too familiar. At first he wanted to throw the card out the window, but then of course he read the words written in green ink:

I am sorry you didn't want to enjoy my hospitality any longer. Don't try to find your brother. He's delivering my present to the Dark Fairy. Call it a peace offering. She herself made sure she can't harm him, so there should be no reason for you to play his guardian. On the contrary, your brother shall be richly rewarded. But I should take it very personally if someone tried to hinder him in this mission. So, meanwhile, should you be feeling bored (and don't I know that feeling!), the hourglass you've been seeking for so long is in the country house of a Venetan count, not far from Calvino.

It was unsettling to have an enemy who could read your most

secret wishes, while you knew nothing about him. Jacob again wanted to dispose of the card, but then he tucked it into his pocket. He was sure Spieler had anticipated that as well.

Chanute had been coughing all night. When Jacob got to his chamber door, though, he heard loud laughter. Chanute was not alone. Sylvain immediately stopped laughing when he saw Jacob. He looked at him like a schoolboy caught telling a dirty joke. He was seated in the chair that some upholsterer had sold Chanute with the promise it could cure the worst hangovers by simply sitting in it. A half-empty bottle of barley grog stood between Sylvain and Chanute. No prize for guessing where the other half had gone.

"Grand!" Jacob said to Sylvain as he snatched the glass from Chanute's hand. "He hasn't drunk in years. Did he tell you how he lost his arm?"

"You mean your version or mine?" Chanute snatched the glass back and filled it to the brim. "Be nice to Sylvain. He's been through a lot. I was just telling him how I went looking for the magic lantern and caught borefleas. Before your time. My skin looked like I had woodworm!" Chanute's laugh turned into coughing.

But he still downed the liquor.

"The Witch comes every day," he slurred. "Every damn day. You think I don't know what that means? And when were you going to tell me about the mirror? Before or after I join Snow-White in her coffin?"

Sylvain tried hard to look as innocent as a doe, but his face was not the kind that let him do that.

"We should've left you at the Elf's until he'd put your face on all his golems!" Jacob barked at Sylvain. "Who *else* did you tell

128

about the mirror?"

Chanute spoke before his new friend could. "I'm from Albion—didn't I always say you have a strange accent? But you always were a better liar than me, and that's saying a lot. Shifty as a Greenstilt, aren't you? I showed you everything, and you? You hide an entire world from me! How's that for a thank-you? What were you thinking?"

Sylvain gave Jacob an accusatory look, as though he too was owed an explanation. But what should he say? That he forgot all about his own world when he was here? That over there Chanute would be nothing but a crazy cripple who blabbered about Ogres and Witches? That he never wanted his friend to be seen like that? Or that he was worried Chanute would tell everyone on Fifth Avenue about the mirror? The truth was probably a dangerous mix of all that.

"What?" Chanute persisted. "I'm waiting."

"You wouldn't like it there." That sounded feeble, even to Jacob's ears.

Chanute eyed him like a traitor. "I should damn well be allowed to decide that for myself, don't you think?"

Chanute was so hurt, his answer to Jacob's question about Alderelves was uncharacteristically terse and to the effect that they were nothing but ancient tales, kept alive by old shrews who bribed trees with silver spoons. And Sylvain didn't have anything to add beyond what he'd already told Jacob in Spieler's warehouse. Jacob decided to give up and come back when both men were sober. His secrecy over the mirror was not going to be forgiven for a long time to come.

"I'll have Sylvain show it to me," Chanute growled as Jacob went to the door. He was right to be offended.

"I will show it to you myself," Jacob replied. "But the mirror isn't safe anymore. Your new friend can explain it to you. Let me know if you remember anything else about the Elves."

And then he went to search for Wenzel.

❋ ❋ ❋

Chanute's cook was in the kitchen, chopping vegetables for The Ogre's lunchtime soup offering.

"Fox isn't back yet," he said when Jacob poked his head through the door. The previous night's excesses still clouded his pale brown eyes. "Did she tell you about the Goyl who came looking for you? Onyx skin, speckled green?"

Great! Jacob knew only one Goyl who matched that description, and that one had shot an arrow through his chest. Upon which, of course, Jacob had snatched one of the most precious pieces a treasure hunter could find. Of course the Bastard had not simply accepted this, and of course he'd managed to follow Jacob's trail to Schwanstein. Now all Jacob could hope was that nobody had told the Goyl that Jacob Reckless rode up to the old ruin all the time.

"You're quite in demand these days, you know?" Wenzel threw some celery into the soup, which already smelled so much more palatable than the meals Chanute used to cobble together. "A Dwarf came by here several times to ask after you. Evenaugh Valiant…He spelled his name so I wouldn't forget it. I'm supposed to tell you he plans to cut off your nose. And some other parts."

Valiant. The Alderelf. The Goyl. Two Fairies. The former Empress of Austry. And don't forget Louis, the crown prince of Lotharaine. *More enemies, more honor, Jacob.*

When Jacob asked whether Will had said anything beyond asking for him, Wenzel shrugged. "I was a bit distracted by the Goyl. No, wait. He wanted to know where he could find the Dark Fairy."

Jacob's stomach cramped tight.

"Call it a peace offering."

What could possibly inspire peace if the feud was as strong as the curse suggested? Spieler had never said why the Fairies had punished his kind. But he'd given away why Will was the perfect messenger. *"She herself made sure she can't harm him."* Whoever survived a Witch's curse was forever immune to their powers. Why shouldn't the same apply to Fairies? And, no, Jacob didn't want to think about any other reasons why the Elf used his brother: Spieler was not Will's father, just as he wasn't Jacob's. Both brothers were too human. He'd just have to keep repeating that to himself.

"Ludovik Rensman dropped off more flowers for Fox," Wenzel said. "He turns up with presents every time he hears she might be in town. Otherwise he just stands on the square and stares up at her window."

Ludovik Rensman. His father was one of the richest men in Schwanstein. *Jacob! Focus! What is Will taking to the Fairy?*

"Tell Ludovik that's *my* window he's staring at."

Wenzel didn't like that. "It's not right that she sleeps in your room," he said without looking up from his chopping board. "The whole town is bad-mouthing her. I know she doesn't care what people say, but you should protect her from all the gossip."

How? She was a shape-shifter. Sooner or later, all of Schwanstein was going to know about that as well. Definitely after Ludovik Rensman put a ring on her finger and discovered the fur dress she wore beneath her human clothes. *He's probably seen it already, Jacob.* Not a good thought for his aching head. He suddenly had a vision of Fox crossing the square with a child's hand in each of her own. No, that wasn't the life she wanted. Or was it? Maybe not, but what she definitely didn't want was her firstborn claimed by an Alderelf.

Wenzel stirred his soup in silence. He was probably as much in love with her as Rensman was. How could one *not* be in love with her?

"Your brother took the road to Hinterberg." Fox was standing in the kitchen doorway so suddenly Jacob felt caught.

"Was Clara with him?"

"No." She brushed the rain from her red hair. So beautiful. *Set her free! She is free!* No, she was not, they were just both quite good at pretending otherwise.

"But your brother wasn't alone. He rented a horse from the blacksmith. The stable boy says a Goyl was with him. The description sounded like the Bastard. They rode away together." The Bastard and his brother? This was getting better by the minute. At least this piece of news erased Jacob's last bit of doubt over whether he should follow Will, despite Spieler's threats. Hopefully, the Bastard hadn't yet dragged Will off to some Goyl fortress or sold him to an Ogre as revenge for Nerron's defeat in the Dead City. "I have horses and provisions." Fox dipped a spoon into Wenzel's soup. He blushed as she leaned over his cauldron. "Oh, and this..." She reached into her jacket. "An answer from Dunbar."

Reading was still hard on Jacob's eyes, so Fox read the telegram aloud:

```
Alderelves STOP What has Jacob stirred
up now? STOP Just arrived Tasmania STOP Long
story STOP Assume it's life or death again and
can't wait until I return STOP In admiration
Dunbar STOP Is he treating you well? STOP
```

The last words made Fox smile. "Answer him—it can't wait,"
she said.

What was Albion's most eminent historian doing in Tasmania?
The colony to which they shipped not only thieves and murderers
but also strike leaders and pacifists? It didn't have libraries like
Pendragon's. It wasn't often Jacob wished for an item from his
world, but Robert Dunbar would've appreciated the portable
knowledge of a computer. Though, of course, the secrets he was
after were so forgotten, they weren't even found on parchment
rolls.

The Bastard with Will? Wouldn't the Goyl regard it as
dishonorable to avenge the sins of the elder brother on his younger
sibling?

No.

19

REGARDLESS

Chanute was still upset when Jacob came to say good-bye. That he still got unusually sentimental just showed how miserable he really felt. Sylvain promised to look after Chanute. Jacob was still annoyed he'd told Chanute about the mirror, but it was good to know the old man wasn't going to be alone. Sylvain had offered to earn his keep by helping Wenzel—an offer Chanute had roundly rejected, stating that friends always stayed for free (which was news to Jacob). But after Sylvain ended a violent tavern fight by single-handedly throwing all eight brawlers into the street, Wenzel was convinced the man could be useful. It seemed Sylvain Caleb Fowler was settling to stay in Schwanstein, and he already fitted in like a piece of gingerbread on a Witch's house.

Jacob hadn't looked at Spieler's card since it dropped out of his clean clothes, but as he waited outside while Fox fetched the horses from the stable, he couldn't resist another look.

New words were waiting for him.

You're declaring war?

Jacob had told Fox about the last message. If he was going to endanger her by ignoring Spieler's warnings, she had a right to know.

"Didn't he say his name is also his trade?" she said as Jacob handed her the card. "He's distracting you from what you should be thinking about. What is his plan? Let's find out. Let's find Will."

The green ink was forming new words while the card was still in Fox's hand. Jacob already regretted showing it to her.

Did he tell you about my price?

Fox tucked the card into Jacob's jacket pocket. "His price for what?"

Jacob was sick with rage. To have to remind Fox of the Bluebeard was almost as vile as the Alderelf's price. The scars on her wrists already made it difficult to forget.

"Nothing. He helped me...once."

"When?" Her eyes warned him: *No lies*.

"In the labyrinth." He couldn't speak the name. Not the name, not the place. Of course, she didn't need to ask which labyrinth he meant.

"You made a magical trade for a way out?" Fox turned as pale as the forgetyourself blossoms the Bluebeard used on his victims. "Of course," she whispered. "What did I think? I didn't think anything."

And? Who could think in a Bluebeard's house? Jacob wanted to embrace her, but Fox evaded him.

"What was his price?"

"Nothing we should think about now. We should go."

135

"What was his price, Jacob?"

"It has nothing to do with you." He'd sworn to himself it would never have anything to do with her. Never. But it was the wrong answer.

"Everything that concerns you concerns me."

How right she was. *No lies, Jacob.*

"It's the usual price."

The Witches took it, Stilts, Sable-Fairies, Nightmares... Back in the labyrinth, it hadn't even occurred to him that the Alderelf might have the same price. He'd been too afraid for her, so terribly afraid.

" Today I bake, tomorrow brew, the next I'll have the young Queen's firstborn child." Fox recited the verse as though she were sleep-talking, caught in a very bad dream.

They were the same words in her world as in his, but here they were real. Fox turned her back to Jacob, but he'd already seen the despair on her face. They'd met women who'd made the trade and had tried to keep their firstborn children. Fox probably remembered, as he did, the lace-maker for whom they'd retrieved her daughter, only to witness the girl run away screaming. Or the child who'd turned out to be a changeling and had melted in the father's arms like wax.

Jacob touched Fox's arm until she turned around.

"It's *my* debt," he said. "Mine alone. And nobody else will pay, least of all you."

She wanted to say something, but he put his finger on her lips. "Friends. That is all we shall be. It's more than enough, is it not? It has been so far."

She shook her head, averted her face so he wouldn't see her tears.

136

"I want you to be happy," he said. "There's nothing I want more. I want you to hold a child in your arms one day without fear of losing it. Fox! He's an Alderelf. He is immortal. He can wait; you can't. Please. You will find someone else."

He wiped the tears from her eyes, from the face he so wanted to kiss, now more than ever. But he didn't, for her. He would do anything to save her, and nothing would ever be harder.

"I don't care," she said.

"No." He said for himself, and for her.

No, Jacob.

She was silent as she mounted her horse, and she was silent all the rest of the day.

20

A HEINZEL'S WOE

Alma rode to the ruin at daybreak, as she always did, to collect herbs. The morning mist covered Schwanstein's roofs, and the world looked deceptively young and untouched. Jacob and Fox had been gone for days. Chanute told her they were looking for Jacob's brother.

Alma had seen Will only briefly, after he'd followed his brother through the mirror. Jacob had always known Will was looking for something, but he had never really wanted to know what. Jacob didn't trust many people, but he trusted this world, like the twelve-year-old who'd looked under every stone and gone into every cave expecting to find treasure, even though he'd only found Ogres. Jacob never worried about whether what he found might surprise him. But Alma had gotten the impression Will Reckless knew exactly what he would find, and it scared him. If she'd known him better, she might've tried to explain to

Will that life never lets you hide. Plant, animal, or human—life forced them all to grow and learn. The more you tried to run, the harder your path got, and you'd still have to travel it.

The kitchen gardens were surrounded by walls, though the fire had collapsed most of the rest of the castle. Rusty hoes and shovels still lay on the paths, showing how the fire had surprised the gardeners as much as their lords. The trellises were brittle and the beds overgrown, but Alma found everything growing in this abandoned garden to be surprisingly potent, and she could even find herbs that usually only grew deep in the forest.

She was harvesting the leaves of a rare thistle when she heard the sobs. Kneeling among the herbs was a Heinzel woman. There were more than two hundred Heinzel living around the ruin. Alma often cared for them, splinting their broken limbs, administering to rat bites and bee stings, all of which could be very dangerous to their tiny bodies. The Heinzel trusted her more than their own doctor. They also had their own priest, mayor, and two teachers. Their houses were hidden among the crumbled walls of the ruin and in the cemetery behind the old castle chapel. They lived and dressed just like the people of Schwanstein, but the locals scorned the Heinzel who lived there among the humans, who let themselves be sold by them like chicken or geese, just to live under their protection.

Only a few weeks earlier, Alma had removed a thorn from the tiny foot of this Heinzel woman. She looked up, full of hope, when she noticed the Witch, but Alma shuddered when she saw the stiff body of a boy in her tiny arms. He looked like he'd been cast in silver. The Heinzel saw Alma's puzzled face and buried her face in her boy's chest. The first Gold-Raven of the morning had landed on the wall, and the first Thumblings would also be

139

there soon. It was not easy to convince the Heinzel mother that the body of her boy would be safer in a Witch's house, but finally she relented and let Alma take him away in her soft frock pocket.

The door to the tower was still barricaded with stones, but among Fox's and Jacob's familiar footprints Alma saw more tracks, every imprint as clear as if it had been stamped deliberately into the ground. Alma was relieved to see that the footprints didn't seem to have followed Jacob and Fox. They appeared to be following along another, older trail.

Alma pulled the body of the Heinzel boy from her pocket. She put her finger to the tiny lips and felt that he was still breathing. Silver. She'd dealt with the silver in Jacob's eyes by using a recipe against metal curses. Even her oldest books said nothing about silver eyes, let alone silver limbs.

Alma gently put the little body back in her pocket and leaned over the strange tracks again. The outline of each footprint was smooth and round, as though she'd pressed one of her herb jars into the damp earth. She rose and looked up at the tower. Before Jacob first arrived, Alma had often been tempted to smash the mirror. She regretted not having asked him more about who'd put the silver in his eyes, but there was already enough danger in this world: Stilts, Nightmares, child-eaters, Fairy curses. She hadn't really wanted to think about the vanished Alderelves as well. And she'd been worried about a sick child. While Jacob talked, all she'd seen was the child's flushed, feverish face. *You didn't listen, Alma. You're getting old, and tired.* Four hundred and twenty-three years were more than enough.

It started to rain, as though the skies wanted to recall those who'd waged war on the Alderelves. The water and the earth belonged to the Fairies. Which elements had belonged to the

140

others? Not hard to guess: fir and fire. According to the child-eaters, the reason nobody remembered the Elves was that the Fairies had their human lovers destroy all records of them. The Elves must have been very angry.

Alma ran her fingers along the earthen edge of the footprints. There were two of them, whoever they were. Something ancient was trying to return, but these here were young. What if Jacob's world had rejuvenated them? Changed, renewed...The Heinzel in her pocket suddenly felt heavy. If nobody remembered whoever was coming, who should recognize them or their messengers? How many had they sent? And what was their mission?

A copper beech swayed in the wind. The rusty leaves made the morning sun draw spots on the old Witch's skin, which reminded her of another tree, less than a day's ride from here.

A silver tree with a wooden tongue.

Maybe there was a less dangerous way. Eight hundred years in a tree... Surely that made one yearn for a good conversation, and Alma had even spoken with stones.

Still, she'd also take some silver spoons.

21

MIRROR, MIRROR

"She's traveling to Lotharaine!" "She cursed a village in Flanders." "She's gathering an army of Man-Goyl." "She's turned herself into poisonous fumes." "...into water."

"… into a swarm of moths."

The Dark Fairy didn't have to lay false trails. The whole world laid them for her: bored villagers, coachmen, village reporters... Every vagrant high on Elvendust had seen her! But Nerron had more reliable sources. Not only Kami'en's secret service but also the spies of the onyx lords still regarded him as one of theirs, despite the crossbow debacle (proof that his talents as a double agent were at least as remarkable as his treasure-hunting skills). A drayman who'd been spying for the Goyl for years knew about a carriage that had crossed the river fifty miles to the east by driving over the water. A Thumbling working for the onyx (the little thieves were excellent spies) reported that two guards on the western border of Ukraina were turned into hawthorn bushes after they tried to stop a carriage drawn by green horses. Yes, Nerron was certain that not only Kami'en's generals but also the Walrus and Crookback were having sleepless nights: The Dark Fairy was traveling east.

Why? Nerron didn't really care about the answer. He would leave that to the professional spies. What he wanted was his crossbow, the undoubtable proof that nobody hunted treasure like the Bastard. And by the looks of things, he could be giving Kami'en the Jade Goyl as a bonus. Who would've thought a trip to a sleepy Austrian town could yield such a rich return? But there was one fly in the golden chalice that fate was offering him: his revenge would have to wait. Revenge. It was all he could think about since Jacob Reckless had escaped through that mirror with the crossbow. All the scenarios he'd come up with while he'd searched for that sly swine... And then the Pup walks right into his path. In his darkest fantasies, Nerron could never have come up with a plan as gloriously vile as capturing Jacob Reckless's little brother!

As they rode side by side, Nerron almost thought he'd have to tie his own hands, so overwhelming was his urge to punch that innocent face and at least vent some of the rage that had been eating away at him like a poison since the Dead City. He wanted to tie up Will Reckless and drag him behind his horse, scratch a note to his brother on his bloody skin, and hand it to the one-legged cook in The Ogre. He wanted to bottle the boy's screams, pickle his soft flesh.

Oh, how cruel not to be able to do any of that but instead to have to ride next to the Pup and endure the friendliness with which he met every creature, the guilelessness with which he

143

moved in this world. If this little weakling hadn't confirmed that he'd once worn a jade skin, Nerron would've dismissed the rumors about Reckless's little brother having been the Jade Goyl as the senseless blubberings of imbeciles.

He still didn't quite believe it.

And he was still tempted to sell him to the nearest Ogre.

Damn.

He kept telling himself: one week, two at the most. By then they'd have found the Fairy. The Pup would lead him to his brother, and he'd get the crossbow back — and then he could kill them both. Or sell them.

Yes... *Patience, Nerron!*

Until then, he'd just have to keep imagining his revenge.

They spent their first nights in the woods, but after a Drekavac woke them with its horrifying screams, Nerron moved them to an abandoned logger's cabin. The Pup was too squeamish to skin the rabbits Nerron shot, but at least he could build a fire. Nerron caught him staring, but Will's face showed none of what Nerron had seen on his big brother's face: the revulsion over the stone skin, the "you" and "us," that unbridgeable chasm between humans and Goyl. Not surprising in one who'd once been a Goyl himself.

It really was hard to believe. The princes of this world must have all dreamed of having a face like Will's, while the princesses probably dreamed of seeing a face like that climb through their window. The fair hair, the blue eyes, the soft, almost girlish mouth. He even had long eyelashes like a girl's! And his gentleness could've filled a honey pot. All that niceness was enough to make one sick, and every "Thank you, Nerron," "Good morning, Nerron," and "Shall I keep watch, Nerron?" just made him want to pummel the boy until his face was blacker than onyx. By all the acid-spitting salamanders of his world, this one saved bugs from the fire! Will called for a rest as soon as the horses got tired, then unsaddled them before taking a sip of water himself. And every animal Nerron shot made Will look as though the bullet had gone straight into his own soft chest. And this same boy had defended Kami'en against dozens of imperial guards?

"Tell me about the Blood Wedding."

They'd lit a fire and were eating a hare Nerron had shot. Nerron's question made Will nearly drop the warm meat into the flames. Bull's-eye!

"Your brother is mighty proud that he turned you back into a human, am I right? He loves playing the noble hero, but he never anticipated just how badly the Fairy would take his interference. You should've heard him scream as the moth tore through his chest."

How Will looked at him.

Ah, so Jacob had never told Will about that. And still Will didn't ask Nerron to tell him more. Will Reckless kept his own counsel.

"Did you know Kami'en's bodyguards still talk about you? They admit the Jade Goyl could've taken on every one of them." Nerron thought he saw the briefest hint of a smile on that innocent face. "The stories are probably exaggerated," the Goyl added. "Or are they?"

Will looked at his hands. "I don't remember."

Liar. Human faces were so easy to read. Will had enjoyed the fighting. Maybe he was more like his brother than he cared to admit. Nerron had never understood the attraction of open battle. Of course, he knew how to defend his own speckled skin.

145

Nobody wanted to be ended by some idiot's bullet or spear. But Nerron preferred a well-planned ambush, just like the one he'd laid for Jacob Reckless, only then he'd been careless enough to leave him to the wolves.

"Have you ever seen her?" Will stared into the fire as he waited for Nerron's answer.

Her. The Dark One. The Fairy. The fairest of them all. Jacob Reckless knew too well how dangerous it was to know her true name.

"Yes, but only from afar."

And each time he'd thought the same: She was even more beautiful than everyone said, and Kami'en was a fool to have chosen the dollface over her.

"They say her moths are her dead lovers."

Heavens, he never knew.

After that, the boy just stared into the flames until Nerron finally sent him to bed. He could barely walk as he went into the hut. He was clearly not used to sitting in a saddle for hours. Where had his brother kept him?

In another world, Nerron.

When he wasn't dreaming of killing Jacob Reckless, Nerron tried to imagine what that other world looked like.

He made sure the Pup was asleep before he searched his backpack. The boy had a pouch with him, which he kept touching so often it had to contain something precious. Nerron supposed it held some trinket, a keepsake from his love, dried flowers, or a lock of hair. At first the Pup had kept the pouch under his shirt, but after the rain had soaked it a couple of times, he'd not quite so stealthily tucked it into his backpack.

The first things Nerron dug out were not very exciting: a

146

compass, a knife, a few gold coins, spare clothes. But then his fingers found the pouch. It was a swindlesack! Now, there was a surprise. Nerron reached inside. A wooden handle, metal fittings. A bowstring as smooth as glass.

Embarrassing how childishly fast his heart began to beat. Impossible. But the swindlesack gave up its contents, and there it was. In his lap. The most powerful weapon in this world.

Nerron closed his eyes for a while. All those months, the sleepless nights, the helpless fantasies of revenge, the vows to peel the skin off Jacob Reckless's double-crossing bones. Did the Pup steal the crossbow from his brother? *Who cares, Nerron?* The jeers he'd had to endure since his return from the Dead City... And how they were going to squirm before him. The onyx, Crookback, the Walrus, all the highborn thieves of this world. Even Hentzau would be on his knees. Oh, and the Bastard would make them beg. He would take their gold, their gifts, their castles, their daughters, and then he would give the crossbow to Kami'en so the King of the Goyl would never again have to worry about Albion or Crookback, or about the shadow King of the onyx. They'd be dead. All of them.

Nerron looked toward the hut.

Unbelievable. He had fallen for the boy's show of innocence. But that was over now. No more reprieve for Jacob Reckless's little brother. And as far as the Jade Goyl was concerned — to hell with him. Soon enough, Kami'en wouldn't need any bodyguards anymore.

Nerron pulled the swindlesack over the crossbow. Had he ever been happier? No, happy wasn't the right word. Exulted, yes, that was more like it. Rewarded. Triumphant. *Forget the Jade Goyl. Hail the Bastard. He is the best.* Soon every Goyl would be whispering it.

147

The story of how Nerron regained the crossbow would need some work, of course. How should he begin his revenge? He could lure the Drekavac into the hut with a trail of blood, then send the Pup's bones to the one-legged cook to give to his brother.

A breeze brushed through the clearing. Too warm for this cool night. Nerron felt it on his skin as though their fire had begun to breathe.

He tucked the swindlesack into his jacket and reached for his pistol.

There. Under those trees. Something was reflecting the fire like glass. The flickering light outlined two bodies, which even Nerron's sharp Goyl eyes could barely make out. Leaves and trees were mirrored on their limbs, the horses, the fire, the darkness of the night. But then they grew skin and hair.

What are you waiting for, Nerron? Take the crossbow and run. But he wasn't sure turning his back on these creatures was a good idea.

Whatever they were, they seemed uncertain which face to show to this world. They seemed to have many. How they stared at him with their mirror-eyes. As though it was he and not they who didn't belong here. Then the girl approached him. She was beautiful, like a wasp or a flesh-eating plant. Her hands were still glass, her fingernails silver.

Where is he?" she asked with a voice that sounded unsettlingly human.

Glass humans? Were they some kind of local phantom?
Nerron pointed to the hut. Whoever they were looking for, the Pup would hopefully distract them long enough to give the Bastard time to run. Though it was annoying that he'd again lose his shot at revenge. Nerron carefully took a step back. The horses were just a few yards away.

The girl disappeared into the hut.

To Nerron's dismay, the other one made no move to follow her. To the contrary. He suddenly seemed to have eyes only for Nerron. The Bastard had met many terrifying creatures in his life, but the glass boy, now walking calmly toward him as though he had all the time in the world, made him feel a new kind of fear. Maybe it was the eyes, which looked like colored glass. His clothes were also strange, like the Pup's when Nerron had first met him in Schwanstein, but then suddenly they were changing until they were an exact replica of Nerron's own clothes. Saurian leather, but made of glass.

Then Whatever-He-Was stopped, and Nerron could see his own face in the glass pupils.

"Give me the swindlesack."

Damn. What did this creature know about the crossbow? He held out a hand. The face he now wore was even more boyish than Will's. If it weren't for those eyes. And those hands of glass and silver.

"You can have the sack," Nerron replied. "But its content is mine."

The reply was a smile that was a dozen smiles.

Whatever-He-Was leaned forward until his cheek touched Nerron's face. His skin was warm, as smooth as glass. "I can turn your heart to silver," he whispered in Nerron's ear. "Or glass. Which would you prefer? I've done it with human skin, fur, even insects, but never with speckled stone. I can't wait."

He reached into Nerron's jacket and pulled out the swindlesack. The saurian leather became covered in silver, which disappeared like frost as soon as Whatever-He-Was pulled his hand away.

"What *are* you?" Nerron was surprised his tongue hadn't turned

149

to silver. And his heart was still beating, if a little too fast.

"You have to ask the one who made us. He calls me Seventeen."

"Made you?" Nerron couldn't take his eyes off the sack. He'd just been the king of the world, and now he was back to being the Bastard. He clenched his empty hands. He wanted to peel all the faces off Seventeen. Twice found, twice lost.

"He also made the crossbow," said Seventeen.

Nonsense. That was an Alderelf weapon. What next? The return of the Dragons? And the Giants?

To Nerron's surprise, Seventeen tucked the swindlesack back into Will's backpack. Then he eyed Nerron as though he wanted to copy his soul. "I'm thinking I should kill you. He doesn't like thieves."

He... What the lava?..Nerron stumbled away from the touch of the silver fingernails.

"Wait!" he panted. "The message for the Fairy. The Pup's delivering it for *him*, right? The one who made you? Tell him if he wants his message to reach her, he'll need the Bastard. Or do you really think the boy can find her on his own?"

Seventeen looked at Nerron's stone skin as though he was dying to find out what it would look like in silver. But then he lowered his hand.

Breathe, Nerron. He could still feel the glass fingers on his skin.

"Good. Why not?" Seventeen said. "I can always kill you later. But you make sure he finds her soon. This world's not good for us."

Nerron didn't have the slightest idea what he was talking about. He just knew he didn't want a silver heart, or a glass one.

Seventeen eyed his own fingers as though looking for traces of onyx. "None of my faces are like yours. Are you also different inside?"

Interesting question. Seventeen was intriguing. *As intriguing as a viper, Nerron.*

"Different from what? Different from the snail skins you pretend to be? Oh yes. Very different."

Seventeen changed his face. He seemed to do that a lot when he was thinking. He had quite an impressive collection. None of them appeared particularly happy as he looked up at the two moons.

"I don't understand why they want to go back."

They. Back. This really did sound like the lost Elves. The only thing Nerron knew about the Alderelves was that they supposedly once built their silver palaces at depths where even Goyl skin melted.

"Back from where?" *Stop it, Nerron.* But Seventeen hadn't heard him anyway. He was looking with disdain at the crumbling hut where Will was sleeping.

"Look at that. It's all so primitive. Nothing but dirt and decay. The other world is so much better."

"The other world?"

Nerron forgot about the crossbow. His revenge. The Pup.

"Yes. You've never been?" A fly was stupid enough to land on Seventeen's brow. His hand caught it as quickly as a toad's tongue.

"Show me how to get there and I'll find the Dark Fairy for you." Nerron hated the obvious longing in his voice. Another world. His greatest desire, for as long as he could remember. And the reason why Jacob Reckless had been able to steal from him. Because of his silly boyhood dream.

Seventeen had noticed. *Pull yourself together, Nerron.*

"It's behind the mirror, right?" At least he had his voice under control again.

"Yes." Seventeen opened his hand. The fly was now silver. "You said you're different on the inside. What about your soul? Sixteen is worried she doesn't have one. Do you have one?"

This was getting better and better.

"Admit it, you don't know." Seventeen dropped the fly in the grass. "Because there's no such thing as a soul. I keep telling her, but she won't believe me."

He listened into the night as though the wind were whispering a message. Then he turned to black glass.

"I'll be back soon," he said. "*Watch out for Sixteen. She has quite a temper.*"

Then he was gone. Or was he? Nerron couldn't be sure. He stared into the night, but his eyes found nothing. He bent down and picked up the silver fly. The frozen insect was so perfect it would have made any silversmith give up his trade in shame. Nerron threw it in the dwindling fire.

"*Watch out for Sixteen.*"

He hesitated, but then he went to the hut.

❊ ❊ ❊

Nerron was used to his skin making him invisible, but Sixteen immediately looked up as he stepped through the door. She was kneeling next to Will.

"I thought my brother killed you. He likes to kill."

Brother. Nerron doubted very much that these two had come from a mother's womb.

Sixteen's silver fingernails were sheathed in leather gloves. She

152

touched Will's face.

Eyes of glass.

"Your...brother and I have an arrangement."

She just looked at him. Nerron felt like he was talking to a knife. A perfectly wrought dagger in a scabbard of colored glass. She leaned over Will. She eyed him like a cat eyes a bowl of milk. "It's too bad. I'm supposed to show him only *her* face. But I have so many that are much prettier."

The face she was wearing now was so beautiful it made him forget her silver fingernails.

"Go," she said. "I want to be alone with him."

Nerron decided to heed Seventeen's warning. He turned around in the doorway and, out of the corner of his eye, saw Sixteen lean down to kiss Will. The Pup was going to have pleasant dreams.

22

WAR

Three days. The mountains on the horizon were already part of Ukraina, and Fox and Jacob still hadn't caught up with Will. Fox had found what she suspected were Will's and the Bastard's tracks, hidden among many others on the unpaved road, and they'd been less than twenty-four hours old.

The Goyl had halted their conquest on the Ukrainian border, but that didn't mean the lands beyond were at peace. The Cossack lords who ruled this country were fighting over the throne. Right behind the border, Fox and Jacob got caught in an exchange of fire, and for a moment Jacob felt relief that Nerron was riding with Will—even though he still couldn't figure out why.

Snow-covered hills in June. Mountain gorges so dark they were still filled with fog at mid-afternoon. The Karpathy mountains guarded Ukraina's fertile lands like a thick wall, and they were so untamed that even Jacob could barely name half the land's magical inhabitants. Not that knowing their names would've made them any friendlier. Crouching among the trees were Lidercs, ghostlike creatures who appeared suddenly, as though formed of the fog itself. Then there were the pit traps concealed under branches that had been dug by cat-sized gnomes whom the people of these mountains referred to as Manoks. Tiny, Heinzel-like men pelted them with raven droppings. And the bumblebee-sized cousins of the Grass-Elves swarmed them so closely that Fox and Jacob were still picking them from their clothes even hours later.

In this kind of terrain, the vixen was a much better guide than the Bastard, and by the end of the third day, the tracks they were following were barely two hours old.

Fox was still very taciturn. Instead of talking about what preoccupied her, however, she quarreled with Jacob about the tiniest things. It didn't feel good, this sudden strangeness, and it made him so miserable he didn't pay attention to the path, let alone to the very out-of-place warm wind brushing his face.

Fox had dismounted. Her horse had a stone in its hoof. She unwittingly turned her back to the figure who was standing all but invisibly between the nearby rocks. Seventeen's clothes were as gray as the rock surrounding him, and his face reflected the leaves and branches, until it changed into the one he'd last shown to Jacob. Jacob yelled a warning, but it was too late. Seventeen looked steadily at him while he grabbed Fox. His lips silently mouthed one word: *war*. He pressed his hand against Fox's face, and when he let go, it had turned to silver.

Jacob stumbled toward the Mirrorling. He drew his pistol and shot, helpless and desperate. What did he expect? That Spieler had neglected to protect his creatures against bullets? Seventeen's skin swallowed the bullets like liquid glass.

155

Fox was no longer moving. Jacob stopped, his limbs as frozen as hers.

Seventeen let go of her still body and walked toward Jacob.

"So we meet again." He put his hand on Jacob's chest. "He warned you, didn't he?"

Jacob felt the very air in his lungs turn to silver. It froze his blood, and his last thought was of Fox and that he hadn't protected her. It broke his heart — into a thousand silver splinters.

23
SOON

War. Yes. Spieler wiped the mirror in his medallion. He liked
to call it his glass eye. The images were brought by Heinzel, birds,
insects…Some swallowed the glass unknowingly or carried it as
jewelry or an amulet, and some had to be bribed with a few silver
baubles. The system had become a little unreliable during the
Elves' extended exile, but right now it showed him exactly what
he wanted to see. The two silver bodies were a beautiful sight. All
those attempts to cross him! He'd forgiven Jacob before, because
he was Rosamund's elder son. But that was over. Spieler snapped
the medallion shut. Eight hundred years was long enough to make
even an immortal a little impatient.

Her younger son was doing just what they'd hoped for. Krieger
had suggested years ago that they make Jacob complicit in their
plans so that one day he might go on the mission Will was now
performing. Spieler had always objected to that plan. Rosamund's

elder was a born rebel, unwilling to follow any advice, let alone instructions. Jacob had been used without his knowing it. That's how he'd brought them the crossbow. Will, in contrast, was as easily impressed as he was manipulated. He wanted to believe, to trust, to serve.

Good. It hadn't been easy to get him to go through the mirror the first time. Of course he'd wanted to know where his precious big brother disappeared to all the time, but he never would have abandoned his mother. Only after Rosamund's death had the temptation become too strong, and then they could only hope that the Goyl would infect him with the curse of the Dark Fairy, thus making him immune to her magic. A game of roulette, as they would say in this world. Spieler had to admit he'd never, not in his wildest dreams, imagined Will as the embodiment of a Goyl legend. Of course, Seer claimed he'd seen the jade in the innards of some raven years ago, but after all Seer claimed to have seen in disemboweled animals or some filthy crystal, he'd never foretold the curse of the Fairies. *Nyet. Nada.*

Spieler closed his eyes and searched his memory for Rosamund's face. Will looked so much like her. She'd never understood who and what she was and why she'd felt that longing all her life. Maybe she shouldn't have asked her elder son to find the answer for her. Too late. Mortality was such a strange fate. At least Spieler had managed to steal her face before it became tired and wilted. He'd already put it on three of his creatures.

His creatures...Thanks to Fabbro's help, the Mirrorlings were slowly coming close to what he'd hoped for. Glass had always obeyed Spieler's command, but Fabbro could make it sing. He was the only one of them who liked to show himself deformed. A hunched back. A missing eye. He could never be ugly enough.

158

Fabbro had convinced the other Elves not to steal only the pretty faces. Hundreds of faces were needed to make the creatures Elven-wise. Another thing they'd learned only slowly. For the golems you needed only three, but golems didn't need to be smart. Breathing clay was easy, but glass and silver could only be awoken by the Alderelves' greatest secret: their true face. Not many had volunteered, especially after it became clear that the Mirrorlings were not immune to the curse. The first ones had barely lasted more than a day behind the mirror. By now they managed weeks. Sixteen and Seventeen hid their Elf faces, the ones that gave them life, behind two hundred human faces. After all, their job was not to catch a few Grass-Elves or to pick some of Krieger's favorite flowers. They were guarding the weapon that would end the Alderelves' exile—and the one who would deliver their revenge.

All those human helpers who had betrayed them—Guismond, Robespierre, Stone, Semmelweis…a long list. Only Dee had honestly tried to complete his mission. No, the one they were now placing all their hopes on would be under glass guard.

Spieler stepped closer to the statue. He'd commissioned it from a famous sculptor three hundred years ago, to commemorate all those who hadn't managed to escape. The artist had given impressive shape to the curse. As a model for the changing Alderelf, Spieler had given the artist a description of an old friend. Now every time he looked at the statue, he wondered whether he'd ever see him again. Him and all the others. There had been suggestions to divide the world among those who hadn't been stupid enough to get caught. Krieger even wanted to chop down all the Silver-Alders instead of liberating those held prisoner inside. Spieler wasn't sure what to think about such plans. More than eight hundred years of shared exile had not made the closest friends out of him and the twenty-three others. Maybe one day it would prove useful to have allies among those who'd underestimated the fury of the Fairies.

One of the golems announced a visitor. Who was it this time? Letterman? Krieger? They couldn't keep still now that they knew another hopeful was on his way. Their constant visits were going to raise suspicion and give away the island. Spieler had lived in many places in this world, but he'd liked none of them as much as North Brother Island. He had a weakness for the New World, maybe because he so clearly came from the old one. The others still arrived by carriage. Ridiculous. They'd never understood this world as the opportunity it was.

Sometimes he dreamed he was the only one who'd managed to escape. An enticing fantasy.

24

Her Mortal Play

The Dark Fairy had heard many stories about the river she now saw meandering southward through the damp meadows. The Goyl called it Gleboki, the Deep River, because it was fed by some of their underground waterways. They feared it, as they did all water. Just a bit north of here, Kami'en had nearly drowned in this river.

She was going to have to travel much farther to truly escape his name.

The morning sun, as pale as a moon, shimmered on the water. The Dark One stood on the bank and listened to what the river had to tell her. It remembered everything its waters had seen—so much life in every drop, so many forgotten stories. The Fairy filled her heartless chest with the rush of them all, just so she wouldn't have to feel the bitterness love had sown there.

She slipped off the shoes she wore when she traveled their

161

roads, and she waded into the cool waters until they soaked her dress with the light of the new day.

The embrace was cold, but the water caressed her without demanding she forget herself in its arms. It recalled to her who she'd been before Kami'en. *Do it like me,* the river roared. *Roll on and on, until the bond breaks.* Yes. Maybe it would break without her having to pay the price.

Chithira unhitched the horses. Before he let them go, he whispered the names he'd given them. They disappeared into the meadows as though the Fairy had made them of grass. The world was so still, so quiet in these lands. Just a lark was singing as though it alone had the task of singing the day into existence. As she waded back to the shore, she saw Donnersmarck standing next to the carriage. He still had no fear of looking her straight in the eye. Of course, he desired her, but that didn't scare him. She liked that. And he didn't have the wish to control her. He sprinkled ground deer horn on his food, and his arms were covered in cuts. He hid them under the coat he now wore instead of Amalie's guard uniform, but the Fairy saw them. He inflicted pain on himself whenever the stag stirred, to remind his body of its human flesh. How could a soldier comprehend that sometimes surrender was better than resistance?

"He is getting stronger. You promised to help."

The Fairy raised a hand, and Donnersmarck's shadow became that of a stag. "You misunderstood. I can help you be both, but you have to stop fearing him."

She left him with the shadow he tried to flee. And she resisted the temptation to show herself the shadow she was running from. Her moths had spread their night-catching net between the only trees standing near the riverbank. They were young willows, reminders of when, thanks to her red sister, she herself had nearly been turned into one. That night she'd felt the cruelty of the punishment suffered by those who'd misused the Fairy lake's water for their mirrors.

Chithira had laid a pattern of blossoms on her pallet, a greeting from a faraway land she'd seen only in his eyes. Donnersmarck felt very uncomfortable in his presence. The soldier liked to separate life and death as carefully as man and beast. Sometimes Chithira amused himself by walking through Donnersmarck, as if by chance, to enjoy the confusion on his face when his mind and heart were suddenly flooded with memories of a royal childhood in Bengalian palaces. The Fairy had forbidden Chithira to do that, but princes, even dead ones, did not do well with orders.

Outside, Chithira was talking to some Rusalkas. The Dark One could hear them laugh. It really did sound like tinkling water. Rusalkas were much less aggressive than the naiads who lived in the river next to the royal fortress of the Goyl. There was no place Kami'en loved more, and yet he hadn't been there in months. Kami'en didn't live for love alone. There was much that was more important—another thing she'd learned only very late.

The Dark One kneeled on Chithira's carpet of flowers and swiped away the moth that wanted to settle on her chest. The red wings betrayed the sender. Her sister had been sending her fluttering messengers for weeks. Fear. Her sisters were always afraid. A wilted leaf, a card floating in their lake, the crossbow of a dead King...as though she hadn't seen all those as well. *"Come to us. You'll only be safe on our island. You're putting us all in danger!"* Maybe. But she wasn't going to hide. She wanted to be free. Kami'en had nearly made her forget that, but she wasn't going to forget again.

The Fairy crushed the moth, and her sisters' cries and clamors stuck to her fingers. *"You'll only be safe on our island."* Safe from what? Not from the pain of betrayed love. Was she supposed to sit with her sister under the willows, pitying herself, or maybe send death to Kami'en, as the Red One would have done with an unfaithful lover?

Outside, a Rusalka laughed again. But then she heard some less peaceful sounds through the moth's net: hooves thumping on the damp grass, voices, louder than the lark that was still greeting the day.

She stepped through the net, and for one absurd moment she expected to see Kami'en surrounded by his guards—even though she knew how he hated to sit on a horse. One of the many fears he hid so well. The strength of that hope made her feel ashamed, and yet, through that shame, she felt the old longing she'd tried to suppress since her flight.

The riders approaching through the meadows were not Goyl. There were around fifty of them, all wearing the same colorful dress their ancestors had worn when they rode into battle. Cossacks. Hentzau liked to joke that the day he'd start being afraid of Cossacks was the day they realized that a uniform was more practical than their flapping wide pants. The Cossacks, in contrast to the Goyl, did not think much of modern times, though they were also warriors. The elected their leaders, did not tolerate women in their ranks, kept their chins clean-shaved to distinguish themselves from their hairy enemies in Varangia, and preferred to be paid in horses rather than gold for the rich harvests of their fertile fields. Their leader's gelding was probably worth more than that entire train Kami'en so liked to ride in. And the horse was definitely more beautiful. His rider sat as proudly as a young cockerel claiming the morning, the river, and the land the Fairy had so recklessly entered as his own.

Reckless? No. He took her to be stupid, like all women. The discarded mistress of a King.

Love had made her so small.

His men stared at her with the usual mixture of fear and longing. Men liked to claim how different they were, yet they were all so alike.

Riding next to the cockerel was one of the blind minstrels without whom no Cossack ever rode into battle. Their musical craft was reserved for the blind, as though the past they sang about could be seen only if one were blind to the present. Most traveled through the lands begging for their meals, but some had the fortune of falling in with a band of soldiers—if fortune is what you'd call it. Cossacks loved to have their feats praised in song, but the wrong verse could easily get the minstrel shot.

The leader would, of course, not stoop so low as to address the Fairy himself. The man who spurred his horse to approach her was smart enough to fear her magic, though he was ashamed of that fear. His skull was bare except for the chupryna, the long lock of hair only experienced Cossack warriors were permitted to wear. This man's story was known even at Amalie's court: Demian Razin's escape from the dungeons of the sultan of Turkmara, his courage under torture. Just a year ago, Razin had tried to buy weapons from the Goyl. Kami'en had sent him home with a polite refusal. The Goyl respected the Cossacks for their bravery, but they were not half as powerful as their eastern neighbors, the Tzar, the Wolf-Lords, or the Mongolian Hun Khans. Maybe the young cockerel saw an opportunity to change that with this early-morning visit.

165

Razin nervously wiped his mustache before he swung himself out of the saddle. The Cossacks pampered their hairy lip ornaments with the same dedication Kami'en's doll-wife spent on her golden hair.

He did not dare look at her.

Donnersmarck eyed him with open disdain, but the Fairy felt for the old warrior. There was nothing soldiers feared more than what they couldn't fight with their weapons.

"My lord, the most noble Prince Yemelyan Timofeyevich welcomes you to his father's kingdom."

Ah, yes, she'd heard Kami'en's generals mention that name. The Dark One used to regularly attend their briefings, as did Amalie—to the generals' great discomfort.

Razin waited for a reply. He stared at the grass in front of his feet, his hand on the hilt of his saber. The Cossacks shared the Goyl's love for this weapon, but their saber had a double-edged tip. They called it a szabla. Kami'en owned a very nice specimen. How her mind kept finding excuses to think of him!

"The most noble Yemelyan Timofeyevich..." Razin actually dared a quick glance. The desire flushed his face like a rash. Desire— and shame. "...conveys his father's greetings and welcomes you to his kingdom." His kingdom? As far as she knew, Yemelyan's father was fighting a whole horde of lords for the throne. "Prince Yemelyan is offering you his protection. His warriors are yours. These woods and rivers are yours, every animal, every flower..."

Donnersmarck shot her a quizzical look. Yes, let him talk to them. All that pride, the hunger for power, the unending urge to fight one another, and their unquenchable thirst for conquest. Mortals. She was so sick of them.

"In exchange for what?" Donnersmarck's voice was so cool it

166

made not only the messenger frown but also the prince himself. The Cossacks were better riders than the Goyl, but their bravery made them careless. Donnersmarck had been a soldier long enough to know that. Kami'en was going to have no problem with them, should he ever decide to fight them. The Cossacks would, of course, never surrender, but instead would fight him from their dark woods, from the fog that perpetually hung between their mountains. They all feared death. Why were humans constantly seeking it?

The prince was growing tired of letting the old warrior speak for him. He spurred his gelding forward and stopped it only a few feet from her.

"We have come to escort you to my father's castle." He spoke in the language of the Goyl. The East had always found it easier to coexist with their stone-skinned neighbors. Kami'en had told her about the old Goyl cities, underground fortresses of amber, malachite, and jade that lay even farther east and had been depopulated by disease. He had promised to take her there.

"We have come to escort you to my father's castle."

What had become of her that the spawn of some local strongman dared to speak to her like that? His glance was even more insulting than his words. He eyed her like one of his father's concubines. *"Look at the Dark Fairy. She'll do anything for the man she loves. And now that her lover has discarded her, she must be looking for a new one."* Yes. That's what they were thinking. She had turned herself into an accessory, had misused her magic to fulfill the wishes of mortals. So small. And the fault was all hers.

"What a generous offer." She answered the prince in his own tongue.

The young fool smiled. He missed her sarcasm as he missed

167

her rage. The old warrior was less blind. Razin drove his horse to his master's side, but he wasn't going to protect him. The Fairy easily read the young prince's ambitious thoughts: Why should he stop at Ukraina's throne? With a Fairy by his side, he'd be as powerful as the Goyl King. No, even more powerful. Because he wasn't going to be so stupid as to let her go.

The Fairy looked around. The magic of this land was as green and golden as its wheat fields, but it wasn't strong enough to break her bond with Kami'en. There was only one who could do that, and there was a long way to travel.

"Ride home!" she said to the fool. "While I still let you."

She was tired of their words. All the noise. Their mortal limitations. Flies dressed up in satin, dreaming of power and eternity.

So tired.

Of course, the young cockerel's reply was to reach for his saber. He was scared she might give to the Tzar or the Wolf-Lords what she had denied him. As though that could be any more dangerous than trying to stand in her way. But all he saw was a woman with only two men to protect her, one of whom was as pale as death and unarmed.

"You will come, or you will turn around."

Razin drew his saber hesitantly, as though he knew he was sealing his fate. The other Cossacks followed his example.

The Fairy felt her fury rise. Night had returned.

She knew this was not about the riders in front of her. All the pain of the past months, the jealousy, the loneliness, the betrayal... It made her fury darker than anything she'd ever felt before. The rain she summoned turned into diamonds as it fell from the clouds. The gems pierced their skins, shaved the desire off their faces, and were red from their blood by the time they hit the ground. She spared the horses as well as the old warrior and the minstrel. Let the blind man someday sing about how those fared who thought they could command her. Then she let the river wash away the dead.

Donnersmarck watched in silence as the water turned red, washing away her fury until she felt nothing but emptiness.

What had become of her?

"They will hunt you," said Donnersmarck.

"I'm sure you've seen worse," she replied.

"Yes, but when we mortals do it to each other, we find it easier to forgive."

Chithira stood in the water, watching the bodies float past. It was so strange that they had died. Aging and dying. The Dark One had promised Kami'en to never let him die. She wondered if he thought that promise still stood. He was not afraid of death, or if he was, he didn't show it.

Chithira picked black blossoms from the water and carried them ashore.

"I gave you the wrong name, Devi," he said, scattering the flowers around her feet.

"What is the right one?"

"Kali."

The Fairy knew nothing of his gods, as little as of Kami'en's, but she'd liked the old name better. She looked at the black petals. Was that all she could sow? Flowers of death? Darkness?

She brushed her fingers through her hair until dozens of her moths swarmed around her. From now on she'd travel unseen, invisible to human eyes and to her sisters, or else she risked choking on her own darkness. She whispered words to the moths, which

169

they would weave into the gossip of the markets, onto the tongues of coachmen and soldiers. Words that would be believed as truth, because they spoke to the fears of the East and the wants of the West.

25
LIKE OLD TIMES

Jacob's flesh was melting, and every breath was as hard as a new skill to be learned. Fire. He was aflame. But it felt good, as though the flames were melting the silver in his veins. If only they weren't so hot.

The silver was also in his eyes again. But he could still recognize the face that was staring at him. For many years, it had been the first face he saw every morning.

"There you go!" Chanute's voice was hoarse with relief.

The liquid he poured into Jacob's mouth tasted salty, but at least it wasn't liquor, which he used to force on him in the past. And another face drifted into his silvery field of vision.

"*Voilà! Salut!*" said Sylvain.

Jacob tried to sit up, but Chanute pressed a hand on his chest. "Stay down! There's still enough silver in you to make a dozen candlesticks."

Seventeen.

Jacob turned his head. Fox's hair shimmered faint red, but it was still silver.

He pushed Chanute's hand away. His body was as heavy as if every limb were made of silver, but he managed to get to his knees and crawl to Fox's side. Her face felt like warm silver picked up from a fireside.

"She got it worse than you." Chanute threw a few branches into the fire. It burned very high and made the night air smell sharply of singed leaves.

"You have to thank the old Witch for making us go after you. She found a silver Heinzel up by the ruin and thought something must've come out of the tower. She got the recipe for this concoction from a Silver-Alder, but she said we'd best not try it."

"When did you find us?"

"Two days ago."

Two days. Will could be anywhere by now. Seventeen had done his work. But what did it matter? The firelight flickered on Fox's frozen face as on a mirror. Her hair was curled as though shaped by a silversmith. Jacob put a finger to her lips. She was still breathing, but barely.

"Why did Alma's recipe not work on her?"

"Can't you see? Her lips have turned so thoroughly to silver we can't get the potion into her." Chanute avoided looking at Fox. She was almost as much a daughter to him as Jacob was a son.

"How did you find us?"

"Has there ever been anything Albert Chanute could not find?" The old man coughed some slime into his handkerchief. Jacob saw blood in it. "Don't you look at me like that!" Chanute growled. "Alma wanted to send young Bachmann, the one who helped her

172

get rid of the Stilt in the White Brook, but what does he know about following a trail? I know you so well I could find you with my eyes closed!" Chanute stopped coughing, but he looked bad, as though he'd crawled fresh out of his own grave.

"You should've seen how angry she got when Bachmann told her Sylvain and I were going." He laughed, which brought on another coughing fit. "I thought she was going to hex me into my bed."

"Pity she didn't."

"Really? Then why don't you learn to take care of yourself?"

Just like old times. They were both so good at hiding what they felt for each other.

"Albert's taking something the Witch called grave-bitters," Sylvain said to Jacob. "It didn't sound as though she thought much of it."

"And that's how you thank me for taking you along?" Chanute barked at him.

"Grave-bitters? Are you trying to kill yourself?" Jacob managed to get to his feet. Every movement felt like Seventeen had poured lead into his limbs. *Not lead, Jacob. Silver.* The fire seemed to have melted it so it could now course through his veins. The shimmering film on his skin meant he must've sweated out at least some of it.

Chanute spat. "What's left to kill? I just wish we'd gotten here in time for Fox as well."

Sylvain stroked Fox's hair. "*Ciboire.* I will kill him," he muttered. "I swear, I will kill them all!"

Jacob didn't ask him how he planned to accomplish that. Instead, he had the same futile thought in his head. *I will kill him. All of them.* Even the girl with Clara's face.

"Was that one of the Mirrorlings Sylvain met?" Chanute threw

173

some fresh wood on the fire. Even the warmth reminded Jacob of Seventeen.

"Yes." Jacob didn't want to talk about him. Not about Seventeen or about the Elf. He took the card from his pocket. It was blank.

"What've you got there?" Chanute asked him.

Jacob turned away from Chanute, staring at the empty card. *Give her back to me. Give her back and I will turn around. I promise.* He could no longer think clearly.

"*Ta-bar-nak*! I haven't been in a forest like this for years!" Sylvain muttered behind them.

Because where Sylvain came from, there hadn't been forests like this for centuries.

What else could Jacob offer? Anything—it didn't matter. *I will find you. I will find something that will destroy you more thoroughly than anything the Fairies can do to you. Give her back!*

Then the words came.

Everything has a price, Jacob. And War means War.

War. He looked down, then up at the trees, anywhere, just not at Fox. *Fine. I'll pay your price. I promise. Stop it, Jacob!* But he would've offered Spieler his beating heart on a plate not to have to see her lying there any more.

"*Câlisse*, I'd forgotten how good it feels. I've been stuck in the city for too long." Sylvain stroked the bark of a pine tree as though it were a dog. "Damn cities. Spreading like a stone fungus. *Accouche qu'on baptise*, Albert. We have to go to Canada! What's it like on this side? The rainbow fish, the leaves of gold..."

"Canada? What's that supposed to be?" Chanute asked.

"He means l'Arcadie," Jacob said. "Ontario. It's many countries here. The West is the land of tribes." *Yes, keep talking about Canadian provinces. That way maybe you won't lose your mind.*

174

"Really? *Tabarnak*!"

"The last time Crookback sent troops over there, they were all turned into seals." Chanute didn't know how much he liked that kind of warfare. "The savages there know more about magic than our Witches do."

The savages. Jacob looked at his card. *Say something. Anything.* The letters formed slowly, in perfect green curlicues, every letter written with joyful relish.

Take her to Schwanstein. Maybe then I'll tell you how you can get her back.

He's trying to distract you from what you should really be thinking about. And he still wanted Jacob to turn around to look at Fox. But Fox wouldn't want him to. Jacob bent down and picked a small flower growing between the roots of a pine tree. Everlasting dock. Sylvain was right: This forest really was old. Old enough for someone found only in this part of the world? Maybe. But he was going to have to search farther down, where the pines gave way to beeches, oaks, and hawthorns. They, like Witches, preferred deciduous trees.

"What are you thinking? I don't like that look on your face." Chanute knew him as well as Fox did.

"Do you have your bluepowder?"

"Why do you ask?"

"Do you have it?"

"First you tell me what you want with it."

"You know exactly what I want with it."

Chanute took a worn leather pouch from his belt. "Even if you find one... Look at yourself. You can hardly stand! Since when are you the suicidal type? And she won't give you what you need, even if you offer your soul."

175

"I know." Jacob took the pouch from the calloused hand. "You're forgetting who taught me."

Seventeen hadn't touched their horses. Jacob felt like a traitor as he pulled Fox's fur dress from her saddlebag. Chanute, however, uttered an admiring grunt.

"Not bad. Just a pity that Fox will shoot you if she ever wakes up."

Jacob's fingers could hardly tie up his backpack. And that's how he was going to challenge someone even Alma could stand up to only on a good day?

Chanute stood in his way. "I'm coming with you."

"No. You make the sure the fire doesn't go out. And you keep the Klads off her."

Klads were the most dangerous treasure-wraiths in this world, and a whole silver body was a very tempting loot. Jacob didn't have to tell Chanute who else might be attracted by such a prize. "Fine!" he growled. "Then at least take Sylvain with you."

"So that I can look after him? No."

Behind them Sylvain was giving quite an impressive imitation of a raven's caw. Obviously, Chanute hadn't yet explained to him how dangerous that could be in this world.

Jacob looked at Fox.

"Why am I even trying to argue with you?" Chanute shouted after him as Jacob stepped under the trees. "Even as a child you were more stubborn than a gold-donkey. Did I come after you all this damn way so you could go and kill yourself? You're no faster than Wenzel on his crutch."

The concern in his voice was very touching, particularly from the man who used to send Jacob into Witches' houses and Ogres' caves without a second thought. Maybe old age did soften the heart. Jacob wasn't sure if that was a good thing for Albert Chanute.

26

THE WRONG FACE

Amalie always made Kami'en wait. Not on purpose, as he did with visitors and supplicants. No. Amalie's unpunctuality was caused by a last-minute change of dress, or having to powder the face she still wore like a mask. She never lost her fear that she could lose her beauty as suddenly as the Fairy lily had granted it.

The room where she received Kami'en had been her mother's favorite room. Amalie had redecorated it, like she had most of the palace. She bought furniture, rugs, paintings, as though she were decorating a dollhouse. And the results looked like it as well: too much gold, the kitsch of a past that existed only in her decorator's mind. Her mother would have hated it. And Kami'en didn't like it any better.

The Goyl King was about to send one of his adjutants to get her when her favorite maid announced the Empress. Amalie loved rituals. She walked in a little too erectly, as usual—her feeble attempt to imitate the Fairy—and she was again a little breathless, as though she always had too much to do, despite all her servants and maids. Her dress was white. The color of innocence. Surely not a coincidence. Amalie spent hours planning what to wear. She could be very calculating in a very childish way. She had her mother's intelligence but not her self-assurance. It was never good for children when parents felt they had to buy them a new face because the one they'd been born with wasn't good enough.

He had, of course, known all this before he married her. His spies had told him things about Amalie that not even her mother knew. But he'd still underestimated her cruelty, her helpless selfishness, and her impressive talent for seeing herself as the victim and everyone else as guilty. She despised, and still loved, nobody more than herself. Maybe she felt some love for him, but he'd also believed she loved their infant son. Kami'en didn't really like Amalie, but he still desired her, like a sweet fruit he was forbidden to eat.

Niomee had always understood this. She'd told him her name only after a whole year. If that was her name. In her language, it meant "green".

"I am so glad you're here!" Amalie's violet eyes swam in tears. It had taken Kami'en a while to understand that she only ever shed tears for herself.

She wrapped her arms around him and offered her lips for a kiss. Such perfect lips. Yet all he wanted to do was hit her for the game she was trying to play with him, for the pain her lies had caused him. Niomee had understood the rage that lived in Kami'en's stone flesh, just as she'd understood his impatience and his urge to break rules, and his preference for attack over defense. Not as gently as he'd intended, he freed himself from her embrace.

The teary eyes became alert.

"Kami'en? My love? What is it?"

"You hid my son at your godfather's? How stupid do you think I am?"

Through all the powder, Amalie blushed like a child caught lying. Like a child? Like a human child. Goyl learned early to hide their feelings. Stone skin came with a lot of benefits.

"I just wanted him safe. I was afraid she might do something to him."

Ah, she'd planned exactly what to say in case he found out.

"And the charade with the bloody crib?"

Kami'en turned his back on her. He wasn't sure his face didn't still show some of the despair he'd felt when he heard the news. For a few hours he'd believed her. His son…What did he care if he had a moonstone skin? He was born to a human woman; that was all that mattered.

His revenge for all the years that humans had hunted him like vermin. For the way they still stared when they thought he wasn't looking.

"You gave him to a hunter who couldn't even read!"

The alertness in her eyes turned to fear as she realized he was speaking of the hunter in the past tense.

"I was going to tell you."

Kami'en went to the window. Behind the stables, he could see the glass roof of the pavilion where the Fairy had lived. Amalie was stuttering excuses, explanations, accusations against the Other One, as she liked to call the Fairy.

"The child is no longer at your godfather's."

That made her shut up. Never had her perfect face looked more like a mask.

"I had the castle and the grounds searched by a hundred men. They just showed the torture instruments to your godfather and he confessed." Kami'en imitated the heavy Austrian accent: "'It vaz Amalie's plan, ja! She sent for zee tshild as soon as the Fairy vaz gone.'"

Amalie's face turned whiter than the lilies that had made it beautiful. "That's a lie!"

"I don't care. Where is my son?"

She shook her head, again and again. "He promised to protect him like his own son until you..." She fell silent, like someone who suddenly realized she was standing in quicksand.

Until you cast out your mistress. Until you've forgotten her. Until you love no one but me.

"Where is my son?" he repeated.

Had he actually taken her to be intelligent? She was stupid. How could she expect love if she made him lose what he loved more than anything? And that was? The Fairy? Or his son? Who cared. They were both gone.

He so wanted to hit her.

"This palace is now your prison. Your subjects need not know. I can't afford any more unrest. I give you one month. If by then my son is not returned to me unharmed, you will be executed, together with your godfather."

He went to the door.

Amalie stood there trembling in her white dress. Kami'en still remembered the other one, the wedding dress covered in blood. A marriage born out of betrayal could not end well.

His adjutant opened the door. He turned around once more.

"Wasn't it one of your great-aunts who got her head chopped off in Lotharaine? Goyl are less savage. I will have you shot."

180

"I don't know where he is. Please! You have to find him. He is my son as well. I never wanted to lose him."

Kami'en was already out of the door when she asked, "Will you get the Fairy back?"

"Why should I? She betrayed me just like you did."

He had decided to see it that way—it made it easier to forget that he had betrayed her first.

27

A Thousand Steps East

Walking was so hard. The body his legs had to carry seemed to be three times its usual weight. *Pockets full of silver, Jacob.* No, not the pockets—his bones, his skin, his flesh.

A thousand steps eastward. That's how one was supposed to find the skulls of the Baba Yaga.

He'd barely walked a hundred steps when he had to lean against a beech tree. His breath came as a silver mist. At least it was a beech. There were now more leaves than needles around him.

Did her house really stand on chicken legs?

The fairy tales of his world sometimes gave surprisingly accurate descriptions of things behind the mirror.

A thousand steps...

Every tree trunk seemed to make faces at him. Elf faces everywhere.

"War is war."

A hundred and fifty steps. Two hundred. Compass in hand, through shoulder-high ferns, through undergrowth furry with moss and flowering lichen. A young wolf ran away only after Jacob pointed his pistol. He could barely bend his finger around the trigger.

Three hundred. The next hundred felt like a thousand, and breathing became as hard as if he were carrying Fox's silver body on his shoulders. He was such a lousy savior.

Four hundred. Five hundred. Six hundred.

Seven hundred. Eight hundred.

Jacob rubbed the bluepowder on his scorched skin. It masked his smell. The skulls had fine noses, and meeting them unprepared could make the difference between life and death.

Nine hundred and fifty.

A thousand.

And there they were. So far, the fairy tales were right. Fence posts with skulls on top appeared between the trees.

The fence surrounded a hut adorned with carvings: leaves, flowers, animals, human faces. They reminded Jacob of the woodcuts found in old fairy-tale books. Or maybe those woodcuts were reminiscent of this hut.

He stopped, waiting for his breathing to slow and the weariness to leave his poisoned limbs. In his first years with Chanute, he'd dreamed of finding one of the famous glowing skulls of the Baba Yaga all by himself. He'd wanted to give it to Chanute as a night-light. Fool. Back then he'd been always on the lookout for ways to prove his courage to himself and the world. That had changed. *"Has it?"* he could hear Fox jeer.

A gold bunting in a nearby oak stopped its song. A brittle branch snapped under Jacob's boots. The air was heavy with

183

the scent of woodruff and damp wood.

A toad sat between the fence posts, peering at him through golden eyes. A short croak and the hut began to rise from the wet grass, exposing two spindly, leathery legs. The fairy tales of his world were true, though Jacob doubted they'd gotten the animal right. Chicken legs? Those blood red legs looked more like a lizard's.

The hut slowly turned around a few times. Then it settled back into the grass, now with the door facing Jacob. The toad hopped away, but its mistress took her time. Maybe she wanted to give the skulls enough time to take a good look at him.

But then the Baba Yaga appeared out of the wood next to the door. A bony face. Flowers became a patterned dress; carved branches turned into arms and legs. The dress gained color as she moved toward Jacob, dozens of colors in embroideries depicting the magic of the world and the Baba Yaga. The dress was not clean. Its owner obviously liked to rub forest earth on her skin, but the colors still would have put the most precious royal robes to shame. Ukrainian villagers traditionally imitated the dresses of the Baba Yaga, embroidering patterned blankets that were passed from generation to generation to wrap their newborns and their dead. There were as many stories about the Baba Yagas here and in Varangia as there were carvings on their huts. It was said that their noses sometimes grew all the way into their attics, and their fingers ended in raven claws. They could probably make these stories all true, if they felt like it. Like all Witches, Baba Yagas could make themselves look any way they liked.

On this young morning, this one showed herself to Jacob as old as she was, older than the forest she lived in, older than the house that had been her home for centuries. Her skin was as furrowed as the walls of her hut, her hair as gray as the smoke drifting out of its chimney, and her eyes as red as the wild poppies growing behind the skull-fence.

"Look at what you're bringing me." She snapped her fingers, and the silver evaporated off Jacob's skin like steaming sweat. "I thought Alderelves had all been caught! Incarcerated in bark, silent and blind, smothered with leaves, their fleet feet tied by roots." She made the silver dance in the air until it settled on her skulls. "Did one of them escape? And you made him your enemy? That's not good. Not even I can take them on."

Jacob approached the fence, but he stopped one step short. Beyond it all time and memory would cease. They said the Baba Yaga ate time like bread.

"I will not tell them that you helped me. I have brought you something very precious to trade for one of your *rushnyky*."

Witches appreciated it when you got straight down to business. The smile spreading on the haggard face confirmed that Baba Yagas were no exception to the rule.

"Ah. A trade. Why don't you come in?"

"You know why."

The smile now spread through all her wrinkles.

"Too bad," she purred. "Your face would make a wonderful addition to my wall."

Jacob counted more than a dozen faces among the carved flowers and birds. One of them looked familiar. It looked like a treasure hunter he'd known, a greedy fool who'd enjoyed feeding Heinzel to his wolfhound. What had he tried to steal from the Baba Yaga? One of her magic eggs? The hen that laid them? Or had he been after the same woven magic Jacob had come for?

The Baba Yaga raised a bony arm, and one of the carved birds

185

flew off the wall. It was a raven. Its feathers turned black in flight. It dug its claws into Jacob's head and began to pick at his skull as if it wanted to drive out his thoughts. Not a pleasant feeling. Then the raven flew to its mistress' shoulder and pushed its beak into her ear. Its caws sounded like an old man's whispers.

"So you don't want the *rushnyk* for yourself?"

The rustling through the surrounding woods sounded as though the trees themselves were impressed by such selflessness.

"No. I need it for a friend."

The Baba Yaga squinted as if to see more clearly. "So show me what you have."

The red eyes widened with desire as Jacob pulled the fur dress from his backpack.

"Oh yes," she whispered. "Now, there is one dress that could compete even with mine."

She leaned over the fence and held out a hand. "You smell strange," she said. "As though you've come from far away."

"Very far." Jacob dodged the outstretched hand. "You know what happens if you take this dress by force."

"You're right. That would indeed be a pity. I will be right back." The Baba Yaga turned and went to her house. She used the door this time, and was humming to herself as she stepped inside.

She stayed for an eternity.

All the while, the raven kept staring at Jacob from the roof.

When its mistress finally appeared in the doorway again, she was holding a cloth that was even more richly embroidered than her dress.

"It will hide you from your enemies, did you know?" she asked as she approached the fence. "Even from those ancient ones the Fairies banished into trees. My cloth makes them all blind."

186

With his right hand Jacob reached for the *rushnyk* while his left lifted the fur dress across the fence. He had to recall Fox's silver face to stop himself from pulling back at the last moment. As the Baba Yaga tucked the dress under her thin arm and hobbled back to her house, Jacob felt as if he'd sold Fox's soul. *There is no other way.* He repeated it to himself, again and again, as he retraced his steps back to the clearing where Chanute and Sylvain were waiting. It seemed forever before he finally saw the flickering of their fire between the trees.

28

The Colors of the Baba Yaga

Fox was lying as if she hadn't moved at all, trapped in her own flesh. Chanute had cut open her silvered clothes so the warmth of the fire could reach her skin, and he'd covered her with the old blanket he took on his travels. (Jacob had always suspected it was the gift of some long-lost love.)

"Go on, turn around!" Chanute barked at Sylvain before Jacob wrapped Fox's silver body in the Baba Yaga's cloth. Sylvain obeyed silently. He had tears in his eyes and seemed to have run out of expletives.

Please! Jacob wasn't sure whom he was appealing to. He didn't believe in the ghosts and gods to whom the people behind the mirror addressed their pleas. But Fox did. He stroked her hardened hair.

Please!

And, yes, she was going to shoot him when she found out what he'd traded for the *rushnyk*. Or even worse — she was never going to look at him again.

Chanute knelt down next to him.

"If she wakes up —" He cleared his throat. "I mean, watching you two is such torture. You should stop fooling yourselves. Damn, even that beardless girl-face Ludovik Rensman has shown more nerve than you."

"What's that got to do with nerve?" Jacob hissed back. "I have my reasons. We are friends — isn't that enough? And now mind your own business. Did I ever say you should've proposed to that actress instead of having her face tattooed on your chest?"

Chanute rubbed his ugly face. "Oh, I *did* propose. Many times. She didn't want me." Her photograph was still in his room. Eleonora Dunsteadt. Not a particularly gifted actress — Jacob had seen her onstage in Albion — but she had an army of admirers.

The Baba Yaga's patterns were beginning to stitch themselves into Fox's silver brow.

She would find another. Or he would find someone for her. *Another... As if the very thought doesn't make you sick, Jacob.* Still, it was good to speak of her as though she could answer them, frown at them like she did when she was angry with them.

If she wakes up.

She had to wake up.

"You're made for each other! Even Sylvain says so." Once Chanute got to talking, you'd have more luck trying to silence a Gold-Raven.

"Leave it! It is impossible!" Jacob didn't want to talk about Spieler's price, or about the fight he and Fox had over it.

"I see. Jacob Reckless is being his mysterious self again!" Chanute sulked and went to Sylvain, who was crouched despondently under

189

a tree.

The hours went by, and the Baba Yaga's embroidery danced over the Alderelf's silver. Flowers, trees, mountains, moons, and stars... Jacob lost himself in the *rushnyk's* images until a sigh made him look up. Fox's lips had opened a little, like a blossom greeting the morning dew.

"Chanute!"

The old man nearly stumbled over his own feet as he rushed to Fox's side. Sylvain looked after him in disbelief.

Chanute poured Alma's potion into Fox's mouth with unexpected tenderness.

Jacob got up, his limbs still stiff and heavy. He looked up at the trees. It was getting dark. The best time to visit a Witch's house, in the East just like in the West. Witches were rarely at home while the moon was high.

"When she wakes up, tell her something," he said to Chanute. "Tell her I'm following Will's trail, tell her I'm—tell her anything, but don't let her follow me."

Chanute lumbered to his feet. "You can't get the dress back!" He knew Jacob too well. "It's suicide. Fox will get over it."

No, she would not. Ever. He had given away her soul. How could she live without it?

29

THE FORGOTTEN MOTH

The river was so wide! Nerron felt like vomiting. The wheels of the carriage had carved deep ruts into the damp earth, and they led straight into the water. Nothing proved Kami'en's fearlessness like his choice of lover. He'd brought the Goyl's greatest fear into his bed: a woman born of water.

The Fairy had left more than the tracks and the remnants of her moths' web in those young willow trees. There were corpses spread along the river for miles. Men with slashed skins and faces, as if a terrible hailstorm had sliced them up. A very precious hailstorm...Nerron leaned over one of the dead bodies and picked a couple of diamonds from his wet hair.

"Are you still sure you want me to find the Fairy for you?"

Will looked at the corpses and nodded. Maybe the sight reminded him of the massacre in the cathedral. He'd heard the Fairy's moths had killed more than three hundred humans there.

Nerron carefully scanned the area, but he couldn't see their travel companions. Which was not to say they weren't there. Nerron was certain Will had no idea of their existence. But Nerron had the dubious privilege of Seventeen showing himself to him regularly. Things were going too slowly for the Mirrorling; Will and Nerron kept eating and resting too much, which were clearly needs Seventeen did not have. But the Fairy was traveling fast. They weren't gaining on her at all, and Nerron didn't need some mirrored face to tell him how sluggishly this hunt was progressing.

He would have loved to ask the Pup about Seventeen's maker. Nerron would've bet his speckled skin that Will had met him and was here at his behest. But Seventeen wouldn't like such questions, and Nerron didn't feel any desire to end like that silvered fly. So he kept on playing the part of the obedient stoneface, following wheel tracks, and daydreaming about melting Sixteen and Seventeen into a set of goblets in which he'd serve Goyl wine. Yesterday the milk-faced Pup had interrupted one of these fantasies by asking Nerron whether he believed in true love. *"What's that glass girl doing to you at night?"* Nerron had wanted to reply. *"Is she making you dream of a different one each time? She's got enough faces for it."*

True love. The Pup looked as guilty as if he'd robbed at least three princesses of their virtue. Nerron couldn't make sense of him.

But each time the temptation to ask Will more about his mission became almost too strong to resist, Nerron would feel the air around him warm and he believed he could feel Seventeen's silver fingers around his neck.

He was wasting too much thought on Milk-face. He'd get used to him, like he'd gotten used to the tame salamander he'd once owned. Those puppy eyes were not going to make him forget

192

whose brother he was.

Damn.

It didn't matter what Milk-face was taking to the Fairy. It didn't matter why the Mirrorlings were watching over him. His brother had stolen from Nerron, and the Bastard wanted his revenge. He played the guide because eventually he'd guide Milk-face to the slaughter, just as he'd done before with magic calves, enchanted doves, and speaking fish. Who cared if his clients had cut their hearts out, or their speaking tongues? Nerron would've taken any bet that Sixteen and Seventeen had similarly gruesome plans for the boy. Revenge. Fame. Wealth. That's what kept the Bastard going. In that order. And to top it all off, a brand-new world.

The only thing Nerron found disquieting was how often he had to repeat that to himself.

Maybe it helped to picture it. Every time the Pup annoyed him with his kindness, Nerron imagined how much he could make off him at one of the illegal Ogre markets, or how he would throw him into one of the lava traps the onyx used to roast their enemies alive.

"How do you think she crossed the river?"

Just as well the little choirboy wasn't half as good at reading stone faces as Nerron was at reading his.

"She drove over the water, how else? Did she never do that when you were guarding her lover? While you had a decent skin on you?"

How the Pup looked at him every time Nerron stopped coddling him. As though the boy thought he'd turned into an Ogre.

Lava traps, Nerron, meat markets.

"Do you know where the nearest bridge is?"

"Bridge? Goyl don't need bridges."

The Pup didn't seem to remember the Goyl's fear of water. Nerron sometimes thought he was like a grub who'd forgotten he'd once been a butterfly.

Something glinted in the sunlight by the riverbank. Ah. There they were. Half mud, half river, the sky in their many faces. Nerron was getting better at spotting the Mirrorlings. Sometimes they mirrored what was behind them, sometimes what was in front, and sometimes the images were as haphazard as their faces. They kept away not only from the willows and the remnants of the Fairy's net but also from the river. Nerron suspected they disliked the water as much as he.

He would show them why they needed a Goyl.

He found the nearest tunnel barely a mile south from where the Fairy had killed the Cossacks. Mosaics by the entrance showed lizards and bats. Their style indicated that the tunnel was close to a thousand years old. The Goyl's fear of the water was older than most human bridges, and in this area, their tunnel networks were particularly dense because their lost cities lay east of here. The largest one was supposedly built entirely of malachite. Nerron's mother had told him about it whenever he'd felt ashamed of the speckles in his onyx skin. She'd described it in such detail that he'd begun to believe he'd seen it with his own eyes. One day...

Most humans hesitated before entering a tunnel, especially one as steep as this one. But not Will Reckless. He disappeared into it without even waiting for Nerron. Maybe he hadn't forgotten everything after all.

The Mirrorlings probably needed neither tunnels nor bridges.

30
All Lost

She was made all of colors. They patterned her skin, her bones. Red. Green. Yellow. Blue. Fox opened her eyes. The fabric on her skin felt almost as warm as her fur.

Someone was leaning over her.

Chanute. What was he doing here? Where was she?

Sylvain was standing next to Chanute. "Your servant, *ma jolie.*"

...her thoughts took strange paths, as though they weren't her own.

"Welcome back!" Chanute stroked her face so gently that for a moment she felt like a child again. He had tears in his eyes, which was a very unusual sight. What had happened? She felt like she'd been sleeping for a hundred years.

"Bring her clothes, Sylvain!" said Chanute. "There are some in her saddlebag."

Her clothes... Only now did Fox realize she was naked beneath the colorful cloth. She drew it closer around her and sat up. Sylvain looked very embarrassed and averted his eyes as he handed her the spare clothes. What had happened to her normal ones? And where was Jacob? She looked around. He'd been with her, hadn't he? And then the images came. Terrible images: a figure, human and not, beautiful and terrible, the hand on her face, like hot metal, Jacob's scream.

Where was he?

"Albert,where's Jacob?"

Chanute grunted and began to load his revolver. Not an easy task with just one hand.

"Accouche qu'on baptise!" Sylvain grabbed the weapon and the bullets. "Tell her already. She's going to find out. She's smarter than the three of us combined."

Fox looked down at the cloth. She saw the birds, the flowers. The magic embroidery of a *rushnyk*. Hard to find, and even harder to afford.

"Where is he, Albert?"

Chanute always looked like a schoolboy when he was called by his first name.

"Albert!"

"Yes, yes, fine," he grumbled, taking the loaded pistol from Sylvain. "I'll go and look. But you wait here."

Sylvain shot a glance at Fox's horse. Fox knew, even before she reached into the saddlebag. The fur dress and Jacob... The two things in her life she could never lose. Gone. The woods surrounding her seemed like the darkest place she'd ever seen.

"He went *back* to her?" There it was, that familiar fear, love's terrible price. "How could you let him go?" she screeched at Chanute.

196

"And how should we have stopped him?" he barked back. Sylvain looked like a whipped dog. Like someone who knew how it felt to lose his most precious possession.

✼ ✼ ✼

Jacob had covered his tracks so they couldn't follow him. But Fox had watched him do it often enough. She no longer felt any of the silver inside her. To the contrary, she felt reborn, which she probably owed to the cloth. The slope soon became so steep that the horses refused to go on. They let the horses go, for they couldn't be certain they'd be coming back the same way. The carpet of pine needles made way to rotting leaves and black earth. Fox was following Jacob's trail so swiftly she soon heard Chanute panting behind her. Sylvain, however, kept up easily, as though he'd known these woods since childhood.

"Ah, *merveilleuse*!" Fox heard him whisper. Even she'd never seen woods older than this one. Some of the trees could've housed whole villages in their crowns, and it soon grew so dark under the leafy canopy that Chanute and Sylvain had to follow their ears more than their eyes.

A scream.

Fox stopped. She couldn't be sure if it came from a woman or a bird.

"Ah, she's angry!" Chanute whispered behind her. "That is good. Or very bad."

When Fox asked him whether he'd ever met a Baba Yaga, he spat. "A Witch is a Witch," he growled. "I know how to handle them."

But Fox had heard differently. If Jacob was to be believed,

whenever they'd had to deal with a Witch, Chanute had sent Jacob on ahead.

The fence of skulls appeared behind the trees. They were glowing like lanterns.

"*Tabarnak*! Like pumpkins on Halloween!" Sylvain looked enchanted, as though he'd never seen anything more beautiful.

No, Jacob's skull was not among them. These skulls were weathered and probably many years old. "Hundreds of years," the vixen whispered. It was a comfort to still hear her voice. When would she leave if the dress was lost? Who would she be without her voice, her cunning, her daring? Celeste. Just Celeste.

The hut behind the fence looked menacing and beautiful. Fox had heard that birds that were foolish enough to land on its roof in search of insects immediately turned to wood. Judging from the faces in the walls, humans met a similar fate if they came too close. Fox didn't see Jacob's face among the carvings, but that didn't mean anything. She was only looking at the front of the hut, which also meant the Baba Yaga must have noticed them coming.

Chanute signaled to Sylvain. Fox shook her head, but of course Chanute took no notice. The skulls spewed flames from their eyes and mouths as soon as the two men approached the fence. All Witches were sisters of fire. Chanute stumbled back, cursing. He shot the skull next to the gate to pieces. Sylvain smashed another with a branch. The skull set his shirt on fire as it shattered, but Chanute smothered the flames with his jacket and dragged Sylvain back under the cover of the trees.

Fools! Fox cursed them both, though she knew it was only fear for Jacob that had made Chanute act so carelessly. "Well done!" she hissed. "If Jacob's still alive, then you've just given the Baba

Yaga a reason to change that. I'm going in alone, and don't you dare follow me."

She ignored Chanute's appalled glance as she handed him her knife and weapons belt. These were useless against a Baba Yaga. All she carried was the embroidered cloth that had saved her. The skulls speckled her clothes with fiery light, but they didn't attack her as she walked up to the fence. She reached out, and the gate opened by itself.

Was this good or bad? *Don't get caught in your own thoughts, Fox.* They would make her deaf and blind.

The wooden faces stared down at her, and, no, Jacob was not among them. What difference did that make? He could be in the smoke rising from the chimney, or the black earth beneath her boots. Flowers blossomed wherever she stepped. Fox avoided stepping on them. She also avoided the snails dragging their mottled houses through the Witch's garden, as well as the grubs, the millipedes, and anything else in her path.

"Bring death to the Baba Yagas's house, and death is what you shall receive," the birds were singing. The vixen understood them, but human ears wouldn't have heard the warning. She didn't want to become that deaf again. She wanted her dress. And Jacob.

The carved flowers on the door closed their blossoms as soon as she knocked. She was tempted to try the handle, but she waited. Finally, the door opened.

A child stood in front of her. It was a girl, maybe eight or nine years old (if her age could be counted in human years). Her dress was as colorful as the cloth in Fox's arms. Witches could take any form they wanted.

"If you're looking for my grandmother," the child said, as if she'd heard Fox's thoughts, "she's not here. Oh, she was angry.

199

He tricked her, and that does not happen often."

The child's bright laughter was in stark contrast to the gloomy hut.

She reached into the air, and her fingers caught a thread of golden yarn, not as fine as a spider's silk, but strong, like wool. The child traced it with her fingers until it led her to Fox's heart. "I knew it." The thread vanished as soon as she dropped her hand. "He's yours."

She took the *rushnyk* from Fox and pulled her across the threshold into the hut. The room beyond was dark, but the girl clapped her hands.

"What are you waiting for?" she called. "We have a visitor. Make light!"

A dozen candles flared up, as if lit by invisible hands.

"Bring milk and bread!" the girl called. The invisible servants obeyed. Fox sat on the chair that had been moved toward her. "*Where is Jacob?*" her tongue wanted to ask. "*What have you done to him?*" Instead, she drank the milk and ate the sweet bread that appeared before her. All the while, the girl was watching her through eyes as green as a cat's. She waited until Fox had drunk the last drop and eaten the last crumb. Then she took her hand again.

She led her to a chamber even darker than the rest of the hut. The wooden chains that fettered Jacob to the wall were wrapped around his arms, his neck, his legs. His face was bloody, and he was unconscious. The wounds on his cheeks and brow were deep.

"She set her ravens on him," the girl said, "but he didn't tell where your dress is. He just made it vanish, in front of her eyes!"

The chains tightened as Fox tried to pull them off Jacob, but when the child touched them, they fell to the ground. Fox caught

200

Jacob in her arms. He came to, but he was dazed. She wasn't sure he recognized her.

"Quick, take him," the girl urged. "Before my grandmother comes back."

Fox needed all her strength to support Jacob. She didn't ask him about the dress. She could see he barely remembered where or who he was.

"Why are you helping us?" she asked the child at the doorway.

The girl held out her hand until the shimmering golden thread again appeared in her fingers.

"Even my grandmother has to heed the Golden Yarn. But she *so* wanted your dress."

Jacob leaned his head against Fox's shoulder. He could barely stand.

"Give him time," the girl said. "His soul had to go into hiding, or the ravens would've picked it apart."

She plucked a thistle growing next to the door and filled Fox's hand with its prickly harvest. Then she pulled a handkerchief from her sleeve. "Scatter the thistle seeds behind you when you hear the raven's scream. If the raven keeps following you, spit into the handkerchief and throw it behind you. And now go! You have to reach the gate by yourself. She knows when I leave the hut."

The fence with the skulls looked so close, but Fox could barely hold on to Jacob, and every step made the gate seem more distant. She kept whispering his name for fear he might leave it behind. Chanute was waiting with Sylvain under the trees. "*Stay where you are*," Fox pleaded with her eyes. The vixen often had to speak without words. Chanute took Sylvain's arm and pulled him back.

Just a few more steps.

201

Fox looked over her shoulder.

The Baba Yaga's granddaughter was standing in the doorway, looking at the surrounding trees as though she could hear her grandmother's approach.

One more step. *Just one more, Jacob.* But he was so far away, and Fox was worried he'd never find his way out of that dark hut even if they managed to escape the Baba Yaga.

Her fingers found the gate. She kicked it open, wrapping her arms so tightly around Jacob she could feel his heartbeat.

The girl was still standing in the doorway, but when Fox pulled the gate shut behind her, the child vanished into the carvings as if she'd never been anything but a slender figure between a carved old woman and a carved raven.

Chanute's brow was damp with sweat, but he waited until Fox reached the trees. Without a word, Sylvain lifted Jacob onto his shoulders.

They turned northeast, toward where the woods thinned out. Soon enough, they heard the raven. Fox scattered the thistle seeds behind her, and they instantly grew into a thorny hedge as tall as the trees. They could hear the Baba Yaga's angry screams. They pushed on, through creeks and morass, across meadows where lush green circles marked the dancing grounds of the Rusalkas. Fox had once seen one of those creatures at a village fair in Lotharaine. Its captor had put a bucket of water in the cage, but the naiad's green skin had been brittle like wilted leaves. Fox's stepfather had poked a stick through the bars, but Fox had torn it from his hand and run away, away from the caged naiads, *matagots*, Woodmen, and the half-starved follets.

Onward. Through the strange forest, pursued by the angry screams of the Baba Yaga.

Jacob was still unconscious. Fox couldn't shake the terrible thought that she'd left his soul in the hut and Sylvain was carrying nothing but an empty shell.

The raven found them a second time, just as the Baba Yaga's granddaughter had foretold. Fox spat into the handkerchief and threw it behind her, and it turned into a vast lake. The raven tried to fly over it, but its mistress called it back. The Baba Yaga was standing on the shore in a dress as colorful as the *rushnyk* that had saved Fox's life. She looked at them, then turned away, the raven on her shoulder, and disappeared into the trees. Maybe she'd seen her granddaughter in that lake, and the reproach on her little face.

Fox kept going until they'd left the woods well behind. Only when there was nothing but fields and meadows around them did she let them stop. Chanute was coughing so badly, he dropped on his back like a bug. And Jacob slept. And slept. And slept, while around them the farmers came and went. Fox sat next to him, wondering whether that forest had taken everything from her.

The fields lay deserted in the moonlight. Sylvain was cursing in his sleep when Jacob finally opened his eyes. At first Fox didn't dare look him in the eyes, fearing she might find nothing there. But they'd brought him back. Maybe his eyes now contained a little more understanding of the darkness of this world. Maybe the Baba Yaga had kept a few years of his life, but she hadn't kept his soul, as she supposedly so often did.

With trembling fingers, Jacob pulled a feather from his jacket. Fox recognized it, though the white down was covered in blood: It was a Man-Swan feather. She herself had stolen it from its nest a few months back. And had paid for it with a scar on her shoulder.

Jacob put the feather in her lap.

The fur dress appeared as though conjured by her deepest wish. With one hand, Fox stroked the fur that felt so much more familiar than her own skin; the other hand wiped the tears from her face.

All lost. And all gained.

"You never should have gone back," she said. "It's just a dress." Jacob rubbed the cuts on his cheek.

"Sure!" he said. "Just a dress."

Fox could've kissed him on the mouth just to taste the smile on his lips. Forbidden. She'd almost forgotten.

31

GONE

The Dark One was gone. Without a trace. As though swallowed by the river she'd just filled with dead Cossacks. It was like she'd never crossed the border to Varangia! But after two days of fruitless searching for her trail, a stagecoachman whom Nerron asked swore, just like the blacksmith in the last village and the river boatmen they'd met that morning, that the Dark One was on her way to Moskva to give the Tzar an army of bears—and Wolfmen. Varangia was going to defeat the Goyl, and greedy Albion, and the crooked King of Lotharaine. Oh, golden times! The gout-ridden coachman turned into a happily babbling child as he described it. Even the boatmen, squatting by the river with their shoulders scraped raw, half dead from the strenuous work of dragging barges across the sluggish waters, looked rapturous as the coachman described the glory the Dark Fairy would bring to their motherland.

*They said...One heard...Supposedly...*Nerron would've preferred actual evidence that the Fairy was indeed on her way to Moskva, but Seventeen was getting more and more impatient, waking him every damn morning before sunrise. Nerron's shoulders already had permanent silver spots from the Mirrorling's fingers.

The stagecoach disappeared between the trees. Will was staring down the empty road. The Pup was very quiet this morning, even more so than usual. He must've been having hot dreams. Sixteen still sat with him every night. One could've almost felt jealous. He was again carrying the sack with the crossbow under his shirt sometimes, and sometimes in his jacket pocket. His brother had obviously not told him about the devious temperament of magic weapons. An onyx lord had once stabbed his two children with a magic dagger. But Nerron didn't tell that to the Pup, nor did he talk about the magic sword that had quartered the wife of an Albian count. He was trying to stick to his own resolution not to get too soft toward Milk-face. Instead, he amused himself by picturing how he'd tell Jacob Reckless that, thanks to the Bastard, his brother was back in his jade skin. It was quickly becoming his favorite daydream. Closely followed by the one where he presented the brother as a silver statue.

"I don't think she's going to Moskva," the Pup finally said. This was a surprise.

"Indeed? She told you that herself? Or did you hear it in a dream?"

Jacob would've parried his sarcasm with some of his own, but his younger brother was so serious! It really took all the fun out of it.

"I can feel her, just like one feels the sun even if you can't see it." The Pup actually put his hand over his heart. "Maybe she's closer than we think."

That would be too good to be true. Nerron didn't want to know what Seventeen was like when he really got impatient. He thought he'd spotted the Mirrorling among the trees. The light there was producing some suspicious glints.

"Water the horses. I'll shoot us some dinner."

Will nodded. He kept looking down the empty road as though he could see the Fairy. "Have you ever heard of the Long Sleep?"

"Have I ever seen a Thumbling?" Nerron retorted. "Sure. The Fairies like to use it."

"And only true love can wake you. Did you ever hear of it not working?"

What the devil..?

"There's no true love. How old are you? It's what we call our lust when we explain it to children." Nerron put the reins in Will's hands. "I'll be back soon."

Will looked after him as though he hadn't said all he wanted to say. He stood there looking so lost that Nerron wanted to go back and ply him with the Goyl wine he always carried for such occasions. Did Milk-face really feel the location of the Fairy?

Nerron went to the trees and stopped when he was sure he couldn't be seen from the road.

"Seventeen!"

It got warm, pleasantly warm for his Goyl skin, but the ferns around him began to wilt as leaves and shadows turned into clothes and faces. How the devil did that work? Mirrors that chose which image to show. Did they collect the pictures? Like memories?

Seventeen's face was younger than any he'd shown before, but he changed it as he stepped out from the ferns. Seventeen what? Faces? He had more. The Knife, as Nerron had secretly named Sixteen, eyed him as though her stare alone could turn him into precious metal. Maybe she'd gotten over the fact that he'd seen how much she liked the Pup. She had a bark-like spot on her cheek, which she quickly hid with her gloved hand. Bark. Seventeen had a similar spot on his forehead. The curse… They were not immune! No wonder they were in a hurry.

"Not a trace of the Fairy. Rumor has it she's headed to Moskva, but the Pup says he knows better."

"You should believe him." Seventeen picked a caterpillar from the tree next to him. "The Fairy did put a spell on him. There's a connection." He changed his face again. This new one looked eerily familiar.

"Where did you get that face?"

Seventeen looked at the silver caterpillar in his palm. "From his brother. Why?"

"When did you meet him?"

"He was following us. Very careless."

Jacob Reckless had followed them? "And? Where is he now?" Seventeen held up the silver caterpillar.

What a stew of emotions! Nerron felt surprise, and glee, and — sharp and painful — disappointment. What about his revenge plans?

"You killed him?"

Seventeen dropped the caterpillar with a sigh. "That was the plan, but he survived. Some Witch magic. This world is irritating. Too much magic. Too much dirt. Pathetic roads. And trees everywhere." He eyed the oak next to him with obvious loathing. "Don't worry. He's lost your trail."

Oh, but you always had to worry when Jacob Reckless was on

208

your trail. Still, Nerron was glad his foe had survived Seventeen's silver fingers. He was fond of his revenge fantasies. Maybe Jacob just wanted the crossbow back. But the possibility that he might be fooling them because he knew exactly who his brother's guide was? Well, that was very satisfying.

Oh, life was beautiful.

Unfortunately, high spirits always made Nerron reckless.

"You don't like trees?" he said, pointing at Seventeen's brow. The bark even stained Jacob Reckless's stolen face.

"Looks like you'll be one yourself soon enough. Your mirror-sister is also looking a little...bark-y?"

The fingers that gripped his arm felt like blades slicing into his stone skin.

"Careful," Seventeen whispered. "If Milk-face knows where the Fairy is, what do we need you for, Stone-man?"

Yes, he'd been aware they might be having that thought. But offense was still his best defense.

"What do you need the Bastard for? To keep your precious messenger alive! Or are you going to turn everything into silver that stands in his way? That could attract quite a bit of attention." Nerron picked up the silver caterpillar Seventeen had dropped. "You can't leave these things lying around. You're right. This world is full of irritating things, and something so irresistibly shiny could attract a number of them."

Seventeen took the caterpillar from Nerron. He studied it as though he'd only now realized how perfect it was. "You're right. I shall start collecting them." The belt pouch into which he dropped the dead grub showed a perfect reflection of Nerron's lizard-skin shirt.

"Why do you show yourselves to me but not to him?" Nerron

209

asked.

"The Fairy cannot see us!" Sixteen replied curtly. She really didn't like him. *Don't worry, my pretty one, the feeling is entirely mutual.* It seemed like she was going to melt every time she looked at Will. Actually melt. Was that how they reacted to their own feelings? An interesting thought...

※ ※ ※

When Nerron returned with a bloody rabbit, he found Will rubbing down the horses. They should've had one of those newfangled photographs made before they left: the Pup and the Bastard. He could've left a print at The Ogre for Jacob.

"So, where do you think the Fairy is really headed?"

Will hesitated, as though he wasn't convinced Nerron believed him. Then he pointed southeast.

That wasn't very precise.

But it was definitely not where Moskva was.

32

THE OTHER SISTER

The silver days, running from the Baba Yaga... Jacob couldn't remember ever having been more tired. He felt as though he'd left the best of himself in that dark hut. But Fox was alive, and he'd gotten her fur dress back. Why did he still feel defeated? Of course, he knew the answer. They'd lost Will's trail, and he had no idea how he was going to find his brother and the Bastard again.

"I don't know," Chanute grumbled as they were purchasing new horses in a village across the Varangian border. "Maybe we're in over our heads. Challenging an immortal never gets you anywhere, and your brother is grown up enough to look after himself. How about we show Sylvain l'Arcadie and Ontario? Manitoba and Saskatchewan also sound nice. I've heard they're full of treasure, and I'd rather be turned into a bug by some savage than die in my bed in Schwanstein."

Give up?

Chanute had never had a problem with quitting. A hunt became too dangerous, or it took them to a place the old hunter didn't like? For Albert, there was *always* a point of return.

Jacob looked at Fox. Sylvain was having her explain the carvings on the houses in the village. Almost all of Varangia's magic creatures were represented there: Wolflings, Bearskins, the Birds of Pain and Pleasure, Flying Horses, Dragons (long gone here, like everywhere else), Baba Yagas, and Rusalkas.

Sylvain whispered something to Fox, and she responded with the sort of carefree laugh Jacob hadn't heard from her in a long time. It had been close, oh so close. Without the Baba Yaga's *rushnyk*, Jacob would've lost her, despite all his oaths to never let happen again what had almost happened in the Bluebeard's castle.

He'd telegraphed Robert Dunbar from the border station. *A phone, a kingdom for a phone!* His father had brought iron ships and airplanes to this world; why not phones? While he'd waited at the telegraph office, he suddenly remembered events he'd forgotten about for years: an evening in which he and his father (if it had in fact been his father) had taken apart a plane engine; a fight with his mother after she'd caught him in his room with torn clothes. She'd never suspected anything about the mirror—or had she?

Jacob guessed it was still the Elf mirror that was washing up these memories. Did Seventeen remember them when he wore his face? Did Sixteen know about the Larks' Water when she wore Clara's face? So many questions...and not a single answer.

Chanute had arranged for a room in the village's only tavern. In return, he'd promised the landlord to take care of his cellar sprites. But the interval with the Baba Yaga had taken its toll

212

on Chanute more than he cared to admit, and when Jacob saw how much fun Fox was having with Sylvain, he decided to take care of the cellar sprites himself. Fox had even stopped being annoyed by Sylvain's attempts to act as her protector. Just that morning, the old Canadian had picked a fight with a Troll who'd accidentally bumped into Fox. Trolls were infamous for their tempers and violence, but that Troll had ended up apologizing to Fox and offering her a wooden flower he'd carved himself.

To the left of the unpaved road leading to the tavern was a meadow with a wide pond. A few willows brushed their summer-green branches across the water, and from the opposite shore, a swan and a couple of ducks were launching into the pale blue afternoon sky. Varangia's Tzars supposedly had tiny spies, Bolysoj, who rode on eagles and wild geese.

Jacob decided the cellar sprites could wait, and he walked over to sit down on the damp grass between the willows. He felt so tired and worn that he probably couldn't have handled a sprite right then, anyway. Sprites dwelled in cellars all over this world, just like mice, and were of similar size. Jacob had once given Will one of the tiny pickaxes the sprites used to dig through cellar walls to build their rooms and larders.

Where was Will?

As children, the brothers had been convinced each could sense whether the other was all right. Maybe Jacob still believed that, but no matter how hard he listened, his heart wouldn't tell him how Will was, where he was, or what he was doing. Something seemed to have separated them, even though they were in the same world. A wall of silver and glass. Or was this one made of jade?

Normally, Jacob would've been embarrassed by the speed with

which he spun around when he heard something rustling behind him. But there was nothing coming through the willow branches. Only the wind was swaying the slender leaves, and he was about to turn around in relief when he saw the card in the grass.

I am impressed. Too bad the vixen had to return the rushnyk. I have to say, the silver skin made her even more beautiful, though that would have deprived me of my prize. How are you going to save her next time? You don't always have a Baba Yaga nearby.

Jacob didn't know what was worse, his helplessness or his rage. He was a fish on a silver hook. What fun it must be to watch him wriggle. Yes, if only he could've held on to that magic cloth, but he'd been stupid enough to get caught. *Turn around, Jacob. Do it for her. Take her to safety, take her away, far from here, where he can't find her.*

Fox was still talking with Sylvain. He could see them through the branches. *For her. Give up, Jacob. L'Arcadie…*Why not? Surely nobody had heard of Alderelves there. Or what about Aotearoa, Tehuelcha, Oyo... So many places they hadn't seen.

The card filled with new words. What? Was he being congratulated on his decision? No, it was more. It was his reward. The green letters formed from such slender lines, it looked as though a spider was threading them with its silk.

In Nihon is a tree where the caterpillar of an invisible butterfly goes to pupate. Shape-shifters who carry one of the empty cocoons will not age faster than a normal human.

Spieler? Oh no, he was the Devil. *"Do what I tell you and I give you what you desire most."* And then he sank his hook in even deeper.

214

They pupate only every ten years.

Jacob flung the card as far as his weary arm would let him. But the wind carried it back to him.

"Can't get rid of it that easily. You have to bury it in damp earth."

The speaker was standing by the edge of the pond. Her face was hidden behind a veil as red as her dress, which looked like it belonged in a palace, not a Varangian village.

Jacob rose to his feet.

Looking for one Fairy but finding another. His deadly mistress, so beautiful and so unchanged. Without thinking, he reached for the amulet that had hidden him from her for so long, but he hadn't worn it in a while. Careless. Was she getting tired of waiting for her sister to finally kill him for her? After all, she had tried twice. He attempted to feel proud that she'd come herself. In contrast to her dark sister, the Red Fairy hardly ever left her island. Do not look at her, Jacob. But it was hard not to look at so much beauty.

"Challenging an immortal never gets you anywhere." No.

She lifted her veil. Eyes that were darker in the daylight. And he'd so hoped she might have forgotten him.

"Like you forgot me?" She could still read his thoughts.

She gave him a smile that had cost many men their lives — or their sanity. Miranda. Jacob was the only mortal to know her name. She didn't hate him for that, at least not as much as her dark sister did, but she would never forgive him for leaving her.

"Yes, all you think of is the vixen," she said, coming closer. "And she's not even half as beautiful as I."

The setting sun turned the horizon behind her as red as her dress.

He didn't dare scream for fear Fox might hear him.

The farmer who was trundling his cart past them probably took them to be young lovers. He would never know he'd been looking at a Fairy.

Jacob backed away from her. He felt the willow branches in his back. They let him through like a curtain, but the Red Fairy followed. The light of the setting sun filtered through the leaves, and Jacob felt like he was back on the island. With her.

"You're as white as snow." She stroked his face. "You think I'm here to kill you. You are right. I've wished for this every day. I should not have saved you after the Goyl shot through your faithless heart, but it seemed too quick and easy a death for all the pain you've caused me." She put her six-fingered hand on his chest, and Jacob felt his heart slowing.

Look at me! her eyes commanded. *How can you prefer a human woman over me?*

He wanted to say, "*Get on with it. Do it already.*" Sylvain would hopefully keep Fox away from her. That was all he could think about. *Please, Sylvain!* Fairies liked to turn their rivals into flowers, which they wore in their hair until they wilted.

"You have to find my sister."

Jacob's brain was too numb with fear and exhaustion to comprehend what she'd just said.

"She's hiding, even from us. She is putting us all in danger. Not that she ever really cared. She knew some of the Alderelves had gotten away, even when she went off to find the Goyl. She knew there was only one way for them to break the spell. Why could you not leave the crossbow where you found it?"

There was something in her face, something Jacob had never seen there before. Fear. It didn't seem to go well with immortality.

216

What did *she* have to fear? But the Red Fairy was afraid. And she had not come to kill him.

"What do you want from me?"

"To find my sister before your brother kills her."

"*Will?* My brother couldn't even kill one of your moths."

"Nonsense. I have seen it. In my dreams. In the lake water. He *will* kill her, and we will all die with her. Because you brought them the crossbow."

Oh, she so wanted to kill him.

But she did not.

"Do you understand how desperate I have to be to have come here?" She pulled the veil over her face. "It is a terrible curse. Terrible and foolish. But we can't undo it. Please. Find her."

A dog barked in the distance. Magic and reality—the mix that made this world.

Will. Jacob didn't want to see them, but the images came: his brother in a bloodstained uniform shielding Kami'en with his body, a dozen corpses at his feet. If his brother really had the crossbow, then he must've gotten it from Spieler. What had the Elf told him? Why should Will want to kill the Dark Fairy? It was she who had let him go.

"Jacob?"

Fox. She was coming down the road. He could see her through the leaves. The Red Fairy raised her six-fingered hand. Jacob grabbed her arm.

"You touch one hair on her," he whispered, "and I myself will put that arrow through your sister's heart."

"Jacob!" Fox's voice sounded worried. And too close.

"You will forget her like you've forgotten me!" Miranda whispered back. "And she will hate you for it as much as I do."

But she did not drop her hand.

"Rumor has it my sister is on her way to Moskva," she said. "She probably wants to offer her magic to the Tzar. She'll never learn." With that, she stepped through the willow's veil of branches and approached the pond.

Jacob followed her. She looked around before wading into the water. There was much in her glance: regret, longing, anger. And maybe the plea not to forget her.

Fox saw the Red Fairy and stopped abruptly.

"Stay where you are!" Jacob shouted at her. Of course, she didn't listen.

"Watch your heart, Fox-sister," Miranda called to her. "I don't have one, and he still managed to break it."

Sylvain had followed Fox.

"Do not look at her!" Fox warned him, but it was too late. His eyes went as wide as a child's. Miranda smiled at him. Her hands caressed the water. Her red dress floated around her like a blossom. It turned darker as the water soaked into the fabric.

"You're afraid of them. Why?" she called out to Jacob as she waded deeper into the pond. "You brought them the crossbow. What else could they want from you? The usual price? You'll have to pay it, should they manage to come back."

The water closed over her shoulders, swallowed her dark hair, the red dress.

"Where did she go?" Sylvain's face showed his longing, but at least he still had his voice. Some men were turned deaf and mute by the sight of a Fairy. Or they lost their minds. Fox looked quickly at Jacob and Sylvain, as though making sure they'd both survived the Fairy's visit unscathed. She had good reason to be worried. The first time Jacob met the Red Fairy, Fox had waited a whole year for his return.

"You heard what she said about her sister?" Jacob asked.

Fox nodded. She'd heard everything.

"We're traveling to Moskva, Sylvain," she said. "L'Arcadie and Ontario will have to wait."

33

CITY OF GOLD

A hundred golden domes and a Tzar who owned more magical objects than the Kings of Lotharaine and Albion combined.

They reached Moskva on a cool July afternoon. There were more wolf and mink pelts on display than in Schwanstein in winter, but the golden towers seemed to warm even the north wind, and the mustard-yellow and mint-green facades reminded visitors from the West that Varangia was closer to the Orient than to their home countries.

Jacob had first visited Moskva as Chanute's apprentice. They'd been on the hunt for a magic doll that had once belonged to Wassilissa the Beautiful. Chanute had started his days with a breakfast of Varangian potato liquor, and Jacob had mostly been left to roam the streets on his own. He'd never seen a city like Moskva on either side of the mirror. Varangia's capital was a combination of North and East and West, and though the

220

September air had already smelled of snow, the South was still present in its streets. One of its recent Tzars, Vladimir Bear-Friend, had been so captivated by the architecture of Venetia he'd had entire streets torn down and replaced with the designs of an Lombardian architect. Still, Moskva's heart was beating to the east. The carved Dragons on the roofs looked like they'd flown in from Drukhul, and the golden horses spreading their wings on the pediments of the palaces recalled the wide steppes of Tangut. So what did it matter that even in the midst of spring, you'd find frozen Malen'ky on the cobblestoned streets? (That's what Varangia's Heinzel were called.) The burghers of Moskva weathered the rough climate in the countless steam baths while they dreamed of Constantinople and the beaches of the White Sea.

Jacob remembered how much he'd wanted to stay back then, but Chanute had heard in one of the taverns he frequented about a magic hammer in Suoma, which immediately redirected their hunt, as such news so often had before. They'd found the hammer and sold it to a count in Hostein—and Jacob had not returned to Moskva until now.

Before they boarded the train, Chanute had wired one of his old friends about accommodations. "Aleksei Fyodorovich Baryatinsky owes me his life," he replied (loudly enough for the entire train to hear) to Sylvain's question about who exactly that friend was. "It's time to settle that old debt. I saved him from being torn to pieces by a Wolfling. Back then he was just the lost son of some bankrupt local nobleman, but now he supplies weapons to the Varangian army. The war in Circassia has made him filthy rich, so I'm counting on first-class accommodations."

Jacob had met some of Chanute's old friends over the years,

and those encounters had rarely gone well. But unless they found a way to earn money, they couldn't afford a hotel. Jacob had tried to fix the handkerchief that for years had faithfully filled his pockets with gold coins, but even Ukraina's seamstresses, so famous for their dexterity, had shaken their heads with regret. He was going to have to find a new one, though he still had horrible memories of the kiss he'd had to plant on some Witch's hot lips for it.

Chanute's message had reached Baryatinsky. As they disembarked in Moskva's extravagant railway station, they were greeted on the platform by a liveried footman. When Jacob asked him whether the Dark Fairy had arrived, he made the sign of the cross three times and voiced his hope that she'd turned herself into a swarm of moths and flown south to Constantinople. Moskva's newspapers were all putting out their own predictions about when she would present herself to the Tzar. Chanute knew some Varangian, and he could read enough Cyrillic to decipher the headlines: "Dark Fairy Expected at Tzar's Ball." "Dark One Less Than a Day Away." "She Has Arrived and Is Hiding in the Tzar's Palace."

Jacob caught himself scanning the crowds for Will and the Bastard as they pushed toward Baryatinsky's carriage, which was drawn by a silver horse. Trying to protect Will from the Goyl still sounded much more feasible than saving the Dark Fairy from Will. But her red sister's fear had been all too real. The Elf's card had stayed blank since her visit, but Jacob had yet to follow her advice to bury it. He had to admit he was afraid to cut his only connection to the Alderelf. *"But how will you save him next time?"* He had no idea. Maybe he was going to have to beg for mercy, though he was clueless as to what gave him any hope it might be granted.

He'd told Fox about the invisible butterfly cocoons. "If they exist, we will find them" had been her reply. "But first we find your brother." She'd kept quiet for a long time after he told her what the Red One had said about Will. "Do you believe her?" he'd finally asked her. "Yes" was all she'd said. Then she'd gone back to looking out the train window, as if trying to imagine her world without Fairies.

They had not spoken again about Spieler's price, but Jacob was reminded of it by every touch he avoided, and every time Fox looked at other men. He just had to look at her to know she was feeling the same about him as he did about her. She didn't care about the Fairy, and, like Chanute, she believed Will should look after himself. She was still on this hunt because it was the only way to get back at the Alderelf for what he was stealing from her. But all Jacob could think was that he'd been unable to protect her, and even the rare silver gelding pulling the carriage reminded him of Seventeen.

Love makes cowards of us all. He'd never really understood what that meant.

❊ ❊ ❊

Chanute had been right to promise them princely accommodations. Aleksei Fyodorovich Baryatinsky resided in the best part of the city, just a few blocks from the Kremlin, the medieval fortress that the current Tzar, much against the protests of his nobility, had turned into his residence and seat of government. His predecessors had ruled from St. Vladisburg, the port city built in the Western style, but Nicolaij the Third wanted to remind Varangia that its roots lay in the East.

223

Aleksei Fyodorovich Baryatinsky's city palace lay behind a gate plastered with more gold than the one in front of the imperial palace in Vena. The dogs that were paired with the guards were as rare as the geldings that had brought them here: Barsoi, Yakutian windhounds. Despite their size, they were as slender as if the wind had shaped them, but that wasn't what had given them their name. Their fur changed color when the wind brushed through it. The most valuable ones turned light blue, the others more silver, as though their short-haired coats caught the starlight. This trait had nearly caused the Barsoi's extinction, until the Varangian nobility began to use them as guard dogs instead of for their coats. A Barsoi would attack without warning, and it did so quickly and silently, as if by magic.

They raised their heads, catching Fox's scent as she stepped out of the carriage. The palace was quite typical for Moskva, where all people, rich and poor, dreamed of country life. Peacocks and turkeys were pecking the ground between the many vegetable beds in the wide courtyard. There was a shed for firewood, and a greenhouse where orange trees thrived, despite the biting cold. The palace's roof was as colorful as an Oriental rug, and its towers pushed their gilded roofs into the sky like golden bulbs.

They were made to wait for the man whom Chanute had saved from the fangs of a Wolfling. Chanute's face turned darker with every minute he had to sit idly on a leather sofa that was probably worth more than the entire furnishings of The Ogre, and watch Sylvain down one glass after another of the potato liquor the servants offered on Parsian silver trays. Jacob was glad Chanute was staying away from drink, though he knew the only reason was the grave-bitters he was taking.

Fox stood by one of the fur-draped windows (even summer

nights could be bitter-cold in Moskva) and looked down at the city's skyline, spread out like layers of colored paper. Jacob knew that silent look on her. She could stand like that for hours. Images, sounds, scents... Even years from now, she'd remember every detail. Jacob loved watching her face when she was so absorbed, so in the moment. *Not allowed, Jacob.* Chanute was telling them for the third time how he'd earned the eternal gratitude of Aleksei Fyodorovich Baryatinsky, and Jacob longed for what couldn't be, a longing more painful than Seventeen's fingers or the ravens of the Baba Yaga.

An elaborately carved clock ticked on the mantelpiece. On the hour, a golden bear would come out of the large dial and dance to the tune of the chimes. When the bear appeared for a second time since they'd arrived, Chanute rose with a curse he'd picked up from Sylvain. At that very moment, the servants pulled open the doors as though Aleksei Fyodorovich Baryatinsky had only been waiting for this vulgar cue. He was the most corpulent man Jacob had ever seen. Even the Olchs from Fron, who fended off the cold of their icy homeland with six layers of fat, would have bowed with respect. Hard to believe Chanute's story that Baryatinsky was a highly decorated officer who'd fought in two wars. His first glance at Fox, however, did confirm what Chanute had said about his fondness for beautiful women. Their host was also a passionate dueler. The following morning, one of the servants would tell them his master had just shot one of Varangia's most famous pianists in the left arm because he'd suspected the musician of having an affair with his wife.

Baryatinsky shot a quick look at Jacob, and he commented on Sylvain's tattooed neck: "Not bad. Yakutia or Constantinople?" But he didn't wait for a reply before burying Chanute in a bear hug that was probably meant to compensate for the long wait.

"An unexpected invitation...the ambassador of Louisiana. Always good for a card game, but I lost a fortune!" Baryatinsky's voice sounded like that of an opera singer—not surprising, considering his girth—and at the same time as soft as the bear fur he wore around his wide neck.

"What did you do to your arm, old friend?" he called out, poking a heavily ringed finger at Chanute's chest. "Look at you—you've grown old. Weren't you looking for the fountain of youth at some point?"

"Didn't find it," Chanute replied crankily. "What about you? Did you get bitten by a Kyrgyz flesh-fly? Hope it was worth it. Did it at least make you shit gold?"

Baryatinsky stroked his belly with a smug smile. "Interesting. But, no, I blame my new incisors. You wouldn't believe it, but they make me hungry." He bared them like a dog: four teeth made of pale red carnelian. "A wager. I had to get them after the Goyl sank Albion's fleet. And you know what? I enjoyed doing it! I made so much off the war against these island dogs, and it was about time someone showed them they aren't the masters of all seas. Nothing personal," he looked at Jacob. "You're from Albion, aren't you? One of my dearest friends is from there. He even spies for your King. He denies it, though all of Moskva knows. Too bad. A fantastic drinking companion. I tried to convince him once to work for me, but he wouldn't have it. Patriotism. How you can love any country but Varangia is beyond me."

Chanute joined his laughter, but the look he gave Jacob was controlled and cool.

"And so what? I'm sure you have better spies than him in your employ," Chanute said, wrapping his arm around Baryatinsky's massive shoulders. "Now tell us, is the Dark Fairy already in Moskva?"

Baryatinsky tugged angrily at his golden cuff links. He suddenly looked like a schoolboy who'd been caught bragging.

"The Fairy! The Fairy! Who cares where she is?" he replied with a dismissive gesture that nearly took out his servant's eye. "Varangia needs no magic to defeat its enemies. Not to mention our Tzar would never be so foolish to attack the Goyl for their King's discarded mistress. But enough of that. You are in Moskva, the best city in the world. How about a new arm? I know a smith who makes artificial limbs for all the officers who sacrificed theirs in the war in Circassia. His steel arms are much more appropriate for Albert Chanute than that pitiful piece of wood you're wearing. He can make moving fingers! And if you pay him enough, he'll even make them in gold!"

Chanute looked at Baryatinsky as though his friend had just claimed he could grow arms in his hothouses.

"Nonsense..." he grumbled, stroking the wood that had been his hand for years. "This pitiful piece has served me well. But who is that friend from Albion you were talking about? The spy? Maybe I know him." Albert Chanute never gave up easily.

"They call him the Barsoi." Baryatinsky pulled a watch from his embroidered waistcoat and looked at it. "He convinced the Tzar that he has Varangian ancestors. He's a shameless liar. I have it on good authority he's from Caledonia."

"The Barsoi? I once knew a man called the Windhound," Jacob interjected. "He was Albion's best spy in Leon."

"Same man, probably." Baryatinsky patted his carefully curled hair and put his watch away. "Excuse me. The Tzar is hosting a ball tonight. I have to change, and I still have to discuss next

week's menu with the cook. Food is very important in this palace."
He gave Fox a carnelian smile. "I could do with some female
company at this ball. My wife went to the country with our
daughters. She finds Moskva tiring."

Fox shot Jacob a quizzical look.

"I am sorry, Aleksei Fyodorovich," Jacob replied for her. "But
Mademoiselle Auger will be accompanying me to the ball."

"Is that so?" For the first time, Baryatinsky looked more
closely at Jacob. "Why should the Tzar honor some recent arrival
with an invitation for which even the most prominent citizens of
Moskva had waited in vain? I mean, no hard feelings, but even
my coachmen are better dressed than you."

"He will have an invite, Aleksei," Chanute replied. "Maybe you
have heard of him? Jacob Reckless? He is a treasure hunter of
some renown. And no wonder. He was my apprentice, after all."

"Reckless? But, yes, of course!" Baryatinsky took a stuffed fig
from a servant's tray and popped it into his mouth. "You found
the glass slipper for Therese of Austry. But she's supposedly
not that fond of you anymore. And didn't the crown prince of
Lotharaine put a bounty on your head?" He smiled at Fox as
though apologizing for her unworthy companion.

Fox smiled back, and with a squeeze of her hand, she reminded
Jacob of their empty pockets and stopped him from giving an
answer that might cost them Baryatinsky's hospitality.

"I had my best rooms made ready for you," he said. "My palace
is a hospitable place…even if the guests are from Albion," he
added with a look at Jacob. "Every noon I fly my flag to show
all of Moskva that my cook has done his work. The whole city
is invited to taste for themselves that there's no better food in all
Moskva. Sometimes I don't know anyone at my table, but life is

short and winters are cold. Where are you from?" he asked Sylvain, who was helping himself to one of the stuffed figs. "I hope not from Albion as well?"

Sylvain nearly choked on his fig. He looked at Chanute for help.

"Oh no, Sylvain is from L'Arcadie," Chanute answered for him.

Baryatinsky gave Sylvain a sympathetic look. "So barbarous, these colonies. Crookback is not having much joy with them. Varangia would love to relieve him of that burden."

He smiled at his own joke—and gave Fox a bow as one of his servants reminded him of the time.

"Do svidaniya, mademoiselle," he said, kissing her hand. "For the pleasure of having you under my roof, I might even forgive Chanute for bringing an Albian into my house. There are many balls in Moskva, and I am an excellent dancer. I shall not give up hope."

Chanute barely noticed that his old friend was again leaving them alone with his servants. He was staring at his wooden hand. "Metal fingers," he mumbled. "Wouldn't they rust?"

Jacob noticed Fox looking disdainfully at her filthy clothes. Yes, how would they pay for an expensive ball gown? He wished he could've pocketed all the silver Seventeen had poured into their bodies. Chanute was eyeing the clock on the mantelpiece, probably estimating its value on the Moskva black market. But Fox pulled a ring from her finger.

"Here," she said, dropping it into Jacob's hand. "I am sure its previous owner wouldn't mind us trading it for a ball gown and a suit."

She'd found the ring in a cave. The Ogre she'd killed there had just been polishing his victim's jewels.

229

34

THE TZAR'S BALL

Voices filled the great hall like the hum of wild bees. Even the thick gold covering the walls looked like honey. And the music! As a child, twirling through the forest with closed eyes, the birds and the wind as her orchestra, Fox had dreamed of dancing in a hall like this. She could hardly wait to do the same here, between the malachite columns that had supposedly been a Witch's gift to the Tzar of Varangia.

The huge hall seemed not big enough to hold the crowd of people streaming through the high doors. Many of the men were in uniform, and it was impossible to count all the countries and their colors. Fox saw the black uniforms of Varangia, the blue of Albion, Lotharaine's red, the peacock green of the Suleiman Empire. The women wore naiad tears and nets of gold in their hair, veils of Lotharainian lace, dresses sewn from Zhonghua silk, all shades of night blue, violet, emerald green, hemmed with elven glass and diamonds. And yet it was Fox who attracted the most looks as she made her way through the crowd on Jacob's arm. Her dress was vermillion red.

"I stick out like blood on snow," she whispered to Jacob.

"More like a wild poppy in a bunch of fake flowers," he whispered back. He picked two glasses of champagne off a servant's tray. "Are you sure you can look after yourself while I offer our services to the Tzar? Baryatinsky will hone in on you as soon as I leave."

"As long as he's a good dancer. If not, I'll just step on his toes," Fox whispered back. "Our host is probably very particular about his shoes."

She'd danced with Jacob only once, during a village fair in Albion. They'd barely taken a couple of turns when a bunch of drunken soldiers set fire to Jacob's friend Dunbar's rat tail.

She would have so loved to dance with Jacob right now in this hall, in this dress, but the Alderelf had taken what she'd just begun to hope was hers. The last few months, the signs of tenderness they'd begun to show each other. And now they avoided even touching hands. Fox knew Jacob well enough not to hope that would change again. Not as long as he felt it was the only way he could protect her.

The Tzar had been very pleased to receive the news that the West's most famous treasure hunter had come to Moskva. He'd not only extended Jacob an invitation to the ball but also offered him a tour of his Magic Collection, which, in contrast to Vena's Chambers of Miracles, was not open to the public. Fox had a bet with Sylvain that the Tzar would ask them to find a firebird, while Chanute believed he was after the feather-dress of Vasilisa the Wise, the legendary daughter of the Sea King, whom many Tzars had tried to lure to their court. Whatever the job would

231

be, the down payment was going to fill their empty pockets, and the protection of the Tzar would allow them to travel freely throughout Varangia in case Will and the Fairy were not coming to Moskva.

A Varangian officer tried to push past Fox, nearly knocking the glass out of her hand. His smile was part apology, part compliment. Baryatinsky's doorman, who spent most of his time playing cards with the errand boys, had told Fox that Varangia's officers were as proud of their dancing skills as they were of their marksmanship. Most of them went to at least one ball every night. When she asked him whether they also dueled at least once every night, he'd replied with a proud nod.

So many men.

Look at them, Fox. There are more fish in the sea.

But her eyes wandered back to Jacob. He seemed to have seen something he didn't like. Fox followed his eyes. Five gray uniforms. Goyl. Baryatinsky had told Chanute that Kami'en was in Moskva. Not, as his aides never forgot to stress, because his former lover was expected to come here but to forge an alliance with the Tzar.

Three of the Goyl were unknown to Fox, but two of them were old acquaintances. Hentzau's presence was not surprising. Kami'en never went on a state visit without his Jasper Bloodhound. And the soldier at Hentzau's side—Fox had last met her in a Goyl dungeon. Not a pleasant memory.

Hentzau had also noticed Jacob. He stared at him as though he couldn't believe his eyes, the left of which was already as white as snow, blinded by the sunlight. Hentzau said something to the other soldiers, then came toward them. His female shadow followed him.

232

Fox saw Jacob's shoulders tighten. Not many men got the chance to meet their murderer. Hentzau smiled as he approached Jacob, as though savoring the memory of his well-aimed shot through his heart. Jacob had nearly killed Hentzau's uniformed shadow in the valley of the Fairies, for which she had put scorpions on his chest. But Nesser's face showed no emotions. Fox sensed the effort she was putting into concealing them.

Memories. Jacob's show of calmness seemed as effortless as the Goyl's, but he couldn't fool Fox. Hentzau had delivered Will to the Dark Fairy, and he had humiliated him, tried to break him. Jacob's response to such offenses was belligerence, arrogance, and the coldness Fox used to fear so much before she got to know him well enough to see the vulnerability it meant to conceal.

"Ah, the plane thief. Or should I say the man who simply refuses to die?" Hentzau greeted Jacob in Goyl-fashion, with his fist pressed to his chest. Or maybe he wanted to remind him of the bullet he'd once put there. "And I had already toasted to your drowning in the Channel with the Albian fleet. The Bastard swears he saw it with his own eyes, but I always knew he was a liar."

"Ah, yes, the Bastard. How is he?" Jacob's voice expressed nothing but politely masked boredom.

"How would I know? He comes and goes. I don't trust him. Too much onyx blood in his veins."

It sounded to Fox as though Hentzau really didn't know who the Bastard had with him. The Goyl had been searching for the Jade Goyl since the Blood Wedding. Nerron hadn't delivered Will, which could mean many things. Had the Bastard recognized him? Did he have his own plans for revenge? Or was Hentzau just a good actor? Fox wasn't sure which would be more comforting.

233

She just knew that even the vixen found it hard to read Goyl faces.

The quick glance Hentzau shot at her confirmed he hadn't recognized her. She had looked very different the last time they met: younger, filthy, tear-stained, convinced that the Goyl had shot Jacob dead. She would never forgive Hentzau for that pain. "And?" He scanned the crowd of guests. "What brings Jacob Reckless to Moskva?"

"I haven't changed my trade," Jacob replied. "Just like you. But I see you now have a bodyguard. All that time in the sun is taking its toll, I assume. And you're no spring chicken."

Oh, how they would've loved to jump at each other's throats, like two dogs who still hadn't established which was the stronger one. Nesser stared at Jacob with such hatred that Fox was tempted to place herself between them.

"Gospodin Reckless?" The officer who snapped to attention behind them had pronounced his last name with barely an accent. "His Highness, Nicolaij the Third, Tzar of all Varangians, would like to talk with you about the limitless magic of our land."

Hentzau looked after Jacob as he walked off with the officer. The Goyl had forgotten Fox. The memories Jacob had brought back to him were almost as humiliating as the one he'd just given Jacob: escaped prisoners; a stolen plane; the Blood Wedding, which he'd barely survived...

The orchestra began to play a waltz. Hentzau turned around abruptly, without another glance at Fox, and disappeared into the crowd with his female shadow. Fox was glad not to have to see him—or Nesser—anymore.

Jacob was already standing next to Tzar Nicolaij, who was holding court on a garlanded gallery at one end of the hall. With him was his current favorite. The rumor around the capital was that she had Rusalka blood in her veins. The slight green tinge of her hair made that seem probable. She was laughing with a man whom Fox had never before seen out of uniform: Kami'en, first King of the Goyl. He'd undoubtedly chosen the dress coat to stress his peaceful intentions. His carnelian skin shimmered like copper in the candlelight. Fox would so have loved to hear what he was saying. The Goyl's bodyguards seemed a little nervous about the crowds at the bottom of the gallery. The onyx lords had just recently made another attempt to kill Kami'en but had only managed to kill three of his protectors instead. Whether he really had come here to forge an alliance with Varangia, or whether he feared his former mistress might make Varangia an offer the Tzar couldn't refuse, Kami'en didn't really know the meaning of fear. Even his enemies said that about him. But what about love? Jealousy? Anger toward the murderess of his son? If she was the murderess. Jacob doubted it, and he wasn't alone—though, of course, in just these past weeks, many men had paid with their lives for running into her.

Moskva seemed to be expecting the Dark One with bated breath, even that night, even in this hall. And what would have given her a better entrance than the Tzar's ball? Every time the master of ceremonies banged his staff on the floor, all eyes went to the door, even Kami'en's.

The Varangian officer bowing and proffering his hand in front of Fox was picture-perfect beautiful. *More fish in the sea, Fox*. She placed her hand on his proffered arm. Maybe she'd learn more about the Fairy on the dance floor than Jacob could from a Tzar who only wanted to speak about magical treasures. It wouldn't have been the first time truth left its trail in a most unexpected

235

place.

The orchestra started again, and music filled the hall like an enchanting scent neither Celeste nor the vixen could resist. The officer spoke neither her mother tongue nor the language of Austry or Albion. No answers from him, just smiles and the kind of silences that reminded Fox she was in a faraway and strange land. He didn't dance as well as Ludovik Rensman, who'd shown her the latest dance steps from Vena at his father's ball, so it was all Fox could do to try and keep her feet and the hem of her dress out from under his shiny boots. And Jacob was still standing between Kami'en and the Tzar...

The minister who asked Fox for the next dance was a much better dancer than the officer, and he spoke fluent Lotharainian, but he had nothing more to offer than court gossip: the Tzar's newest mistress (apparently not the woman next to him), the best tailor in Moskva, the most in-demand hatmaker...He was clearly convinced the topics of interest to women were very few and limited. Fox wished the orchestra would play louder and drown out the nullities pouring from his mouth. His voice was like a badly tuned instrument among the strings and clarinets.

Her third suitor was an admiral whose sweaty hands left damp imprints on the red silk of her dress. After he pressed a moist kiss on her hand and asked for her address, Fox truly regretted she couldn't have left the dancing to Jacob and instead conversed with the Tzar about treasures.

Someone next to her cleared his throat.

"I shall not presume that my dancing skills do justice to the dress or the lady wearing it, but I promise I will give it my utmost."

The Windhound had barely changed. He still didn't look like a spy. The Barsoi—Fox definitely preferred his Russian nickname.

He'd addressed her in her own language, the Lotharainian rolling off his tongue quite naturally (Fox recalled that he spoke more than a dozen languages fluently), though he tinted every word in Caledonian colors: gray and green, stony mountains, oxblood housefronts, valleys scarred with the footprints of Giants, and salty lakes that blurred the reflections of crumbled castles and in which monsters with iron scales prowled for fish. Nowhere else were the beaches as white from naiad tears, and nowhere else could one find valleys where the fog created rain warriors. Fox loved Caledonia. And she liked the Windhound. She'd been looking forward to meeting him again.

He was good-looking and yet not quite so, as slender as a reed (which gave rise to the misunderstanding that his figure had something to do with his nickname), with stubborn ash-blond hair that he had to keep brushing away from his eyes as he spoke. His eyes were brown, unusual for Caledonia, and they were almost as disconcertingly bright and as fearless as Jacob's.

"Pray, what name goes with such a beautiful face and that wonderful dress?"

Fox had expected him not to recognize her.

"Celeste Auger. And yours?"

His smile showed how pleased he was with himself. He had addressed her in the right language.

He gave the hint of a bow, which showed that he did not like to curtsy. "Tennant. Orlando Tennant."

Fox was surprised. She had expected a false name. Or...maybe it was false.

"Mademoiselle Auger." He offered his arm.

"Under one condition."

He smiled. Fox suspected everything was a game to the Barsoi, maybe even more than to Jacob.

"Which is?"

Fox cast a furtive glance toward Jacob. He was still talking to the Tzar. The Tzar's companion, however, had eyes only for Kami'en.

"I decide the topic of conversation," she said. "I cannot bear another dance spent talking about the newest hat fashions."

The Barsoi laughed. "Pity! My favorite topic. But I shall do my best to find another."

This time Fox accepted the arm.

"Is it more enjoyable to serve Wilfred of Albion in Moskva or in Metagirta?"

Ah, his eyes said, you know more about me than I about you. That needs to change. "To serve is never enjoyable."

She liked the answer. The vixen caught the scent of duplicity, but no deviousness. Still, her senses hadn't warned her of the Bluebeard, had they? The memory briefly made Fox pull back her hand as Orlando Tennant reached for it, but she caught herself. She did sometimes fear she might never again completely trust the touch or the smile of a man. Even Jacob's face was forever linked to the Bluebeard's blood chamber.

The dance floor gleamed in the light of the chandeliers like a frozen lake. The orchestra was playing a polka. Fox felt the music like a second heartbeat.

"Is it true the Tzar has made the daughter of a serf his lover?"

"Oh yes. He's even had a palace built for her, where he keeps her hidden. She has a beautiful voice, but she may sing only for him. All his other lovers are just to show his nobles he doesn't prefer a serf's daughter to theirs."

The Barsoi was a good dancer, a very good one. Fox had rarely enjoyed her human body more.

"Would you like such a life? The lover of a Tzar, your own palace, as a prisoner of love?"

"Love is always a prison." The words came easily, as though Fox had spoken them many times, yet she hadn't even known she felt that way until this very moment.

"Interesting. What makes you say that? Experience?"

"I decide the topic, remember?"

"Touché. The men we serve, the women we love... What shall we speak of next?"

"Will the Dark Fairy bring her magic to Moskva?"

It's hard to hide your surprise when you're dancing, even for a spy. But the Barsoi only skipped one beat.

"I'm afraid I don't know the answer, and neither does the Tzar's secret service." He leaned forward until his lips nearly touched her ear. "I promised Wilfred the Walrus to telegraph an answer within a week, but I promise you will have it even before him."

Now it was her turn to smile. She felt light in his arms. *You're dizzy from the dance, Fox. That's all.*

She kept asking questions so the Windhound wouldn't notice she'd only been after one answer. "What is the most precious item among the Tzar's magic treasures?" "Is it true the Tzar exiled two of his half brothers to Yakutia because they were after the throne?"

They danced. And danced. And the Barsoi told Fox about an iron wolf and the flying carpets in the Tzar's Magic Collection. He talked about the ice palaces of Yakutia, which the banished half brothers had built, and how the streets of Moskva had recently quaked, causing the Tzar to organize a search for a possible surviving Dragon under the city. Fox loved the disappointment

239

in his voice when he added that they'd found nothing but rats and an anarchist's bomb.

When the musicians lowered their instruments, the world suddenly felt very still. And much cooler without the Barsoi's arm around her waist.

"Three days," Orlando Tennant whispered as he led her off the dance floor. "Give me three days for your answer. Though I still don't understand why you'd want to know."

Fox sensed the Bluebeard's shadow as Orlando kissed her on the cheek, but she sent the shadow back to its bloody mansion and forced herself to forget that he'd made desire rhyme with fear.

"Well, I never! Orlando Tennant." Jacob was next to her so suddenly that Fox gave a start, as though a stranger had grabbed her arm. "Got tired of the hot summers in Metagirta?"

"Jacob." So the Barsoi remembered him. He frowned and eyed Fox from head to toe. "No. Impossible."

"I know. This one still wears her fur too often. Tell her! She won't listen to me anymore."

Fox couldn't read Orlando's look. Maybe there was some understanding in it. How often had he changed his name, invented a new life in a new place, changed his appearance?

"It's not something one can just stop doing," he said. "Please forgive me for monopolizing her. I truly had no idea that I was dancing with the girl who is so inseparably linked to Jacob Reckless."

"Oh no, Fox belongs only to herself." Pride and tenderness weren't the only feelings she heard in Jacob's voice. Something else had come into it. Pain. Regret. Fear. *Go! You are free. Save me from causing you more pain.*

240

The Tzar was moving to leave the ball. The musicians quickly picked up their instruments. The crowd parted like a flock of birds for the hawk while the orchestra intoned Varangia's anthem. The Tzar nodded at Jacob as he walked past. Nicolaij was taller than most of his officers, with dark, curly hair and a profile that matched that of Varangia's heraldic animal, the double-headed eagle. Women looked at him as longingly as the men did. "He will return Varangia to greatness." "He will remind our nobles that our roots are in the East." "He will reconcile the rich and the poor." "He will free the serfs." Fox had not heard a single bad word about him that night, but this was, after all, his palace and his ball.

Besides his mistress, the Tzar was accompanied by a dozen officers. And Kami'en. Hentzau, Nesser, and the other Goyl joined them as they reached the door.

"So, Varangia and the Goyl are now officially allies?" Jacob asked. "Your master won't like that."

"No," Tennant replied. "The Goyl supposedly made Nicolaij a gift that's more useful than the jeweled swords he usually receives. But what that gift was is Moskva's best-kept secret. What are you here for? A firebird? Golden apples? Baba Yaga skulls? Or has it to do with your companion's questions?"

He didn't wait for Jacob's reply.

"I hope the Dark Fairy doesn't arrive for a while," he whispered to Fox, "if that will keep you in Moskva."

Then he disappeared into the throng.

241

35

CONNECTED

Flowers blossomed wherever the Dark One stepped in the sharp-bladed grass. The rain kissed her skin, the trees whispered her name, but all she saw was the yarn. It was a noose since Kami'en had come to Moskva, a noose of golden yarn.

So close.

Why had he come? So strong was the temptation to have Chithira turn the carriage around and make her own lies come true by driving her to Moskva after all. Drive on! she tried to command herself while the rain soaked through her hair and clothes. It kept pouring down as though trying to turn the whole world into a lake, a lake like the one that had spawned her. *Away from him!* Instead, she stood under the wide and alien sky and wondered what Kami'en was thinking, whether he missed her... Whether he really believed she'd killed his son.

He was so close.

"We have to move." Donnersmarck wiped the rain from his face. "I have a feeling we're being followed."

As though she didn't know that. Her dreams were of glass and jade. But what did it matter? Kami'en was the one she was running from. Her sisters would never understand that, just as they'd never understood her leaving them for him.

To be free. Free of them, free of him, free of herself. That's what had made her get into her carriage. The boy who was following her had followed her into her dreams for as long as she could remember. Maybe to be truly free she had to let him catch up to her. She'd always known he would one day. As for those who watched over him…the Dark One's dreams only showed hazy images, two blurry outlines of glass and silver barely visible behind the dark figure of a Goyl. As though they had a way to hide themselves from her. She knew who'd sent them, even though neither she nor her red sister had ever encountered the vanished Alderelves. Years ago, she'd come upon one of the Silver-Alders near a castle she and Kami'en were staying in. Despite the thick snow all around it, the air under the Alder's crown had been as hot and humid as a summer night. A voice had whispered through the rustling leaves. She'd liked that voice, just as she liked many of the things her sisters were afraid of.

Why had Kami'en come to the East?

Not for her.

No.

And even if he had, he would never admit it, not even to himself.

The Dark Fairy kept standing there, despite Donnersmarck's obvious impatience. She reached out, with the heart she did not possess, to the one she'd fled from. Kami'en had given her a heart. She'd always felt it when she was with him.

243

Dusk was falling when she finally climbed back into the carriage. Chithira urged the horses on. The Golden Yarn tightened like a string, and it sang and sighed.

The Dark One ordered her coachman to go faster.

Not because of the silver.

Or the jade.

Because of him.

36
She Belongs Only to Herself

They returned from the ball shortly after midnight. Their host spent the rest of the night playing cards with the Lotharainian ambassador. Jacob lay in a bed made of singing wood, which Baryatinsky must have gotten from Suoma, and despite the beautiful sounds, he could not find sleep. The Fairy had not come to the ball. There was no sign of her, let alone of Will. Dunbar had not sent word, and the Tzar would only meet him in two days' time to tell him whether and what for he might need the services of a treasure hunter. Waiting. He'd never been good at waiting. He should've done as Fox did and dance himself weary. With her...

Dawn was breaking (Moskva's summer nights were short) when he finally gave up and put on his old clothes. Baryatinsky's servants had cleaned and mended them, but that hadn't made them any more presentable, not even the waistcoat that had been a gift from an Empress. Fox liked to tease him about his weakness for good tailors, and he always retorted it was her world's fault for still making him feel he was playing masquerades. Of course, he knew that was not the whole truth.

This time the card fell from his waistcoat pocket. The green words appeared as soon as Jacob picked it from the floor.

I see you have competition now. Which was only to be expected, right?

Jealousy. Of course. The perfect means for the Elf to drown Jacob's sanity. He should have followed the Red One's advice and buried the card.

She's probably tired of this never-ending journey. But you'd rather take the advice of a former lover instead of thinking of her for once. Your brother. The Fairy. Clara. Others are always more important. You really only have yourself to blame. She could not take her eyes off the Windhound.

Every word like a drop of poison, and knowing who was writing them was no antidote.

Jacob stepped out of his room. Baryatinsky's palace was still steeped in early-morning silence. The only sounds were the muffled steps of the servants who were placing bowls of honey in the windows for the Kikimoras, or sweeping out the Malenk'y who'd sought refuge from the cold overnight. All was quiet behind Fox's door. Jacob didn't wake her, though he would've liked to talk to her. The sleepless night had given him an idea, but his tired mind couldn't decide whether it was a good one.

Jacob didn't really believe in soothsayers and prophets — he'd never wanted to know the future, neither his nor anybody else's — but it was said that the glass-sayers of Moskva could see what was happening at any moment in any place in the world. It could be worth asking them about his brother instead of sitting around waiting for the Fairy or news from the Tzar. Moskva's glass-sayers came from all corners of the East: Mongol, Kazakh, Zhonghua. Most were of the Sintisa, as traveling folk called themselves on this side of the mirror. "Their home is any place and no place, so their time is any time" was how Alma explained their gift. "Of course, that scares the settled people, who also envy them their freedom." Enough reason to set their colorful caravans on fire from time to time.

Jacob found Baryatinsky's kitchen by following the scent of freshly baked bread. The cook was nearly as fat as her master, and after she'd recovered from the shock of one of her master's fancy guests having found his way into the palace's deep bowels, she poured Jacob a cup of tea from the samovar and served him a bowl of wheat porridge with cinnamon.

"I hear their spot is behind the slaughterhouses" was her answer to where he might find the glass-sayers. "But they'll tell you nothing but lies. They keep the truth for their own kind."

And yet even the Tzar went to them, and he was not the only one.

It was still early when Jacob left the palace. Peddlers were sleeping on the curb in front of the gate. The only ones up were a couple of officers returning from a late party and the men who collected horse manure from the cobbled streets. Jacob only noticed the Goyl because he caught a glimpse of him in a shop window. He turned around quickly, but the Goyl had disappeared. He again caught a glimpse at the next corner. A moonstone Goyl, like most of their spies. Their pale complexion was most easily mistaken for human skin.

Jacob stopped at the window of a furrier, though the fox pelts made him nauseous. At first he thought he should simply ignore the Goyl. What was he going to report to Hentzau, anyway? That Reckless had consulted a glass-sayer? On the other hand, if Hentzau's shadow found out who he was inquiring after... No.

He decided to change direction. For a while he pretended to be strolling the streets. The Goyl was good, but Jacob had shaken better tails.

The beggars' square was busy even at this early hour. Its church was one of the prettiest in Moskva. The steps were crowded with men, women, and children, standing, sitting, crawling, trying to attract the pity of the more fortunate. Some managed by playing instruments; others displayed their scars and wounds or some other stigma of misfortune. Cripples, lepers, veterans of Varangia's wars...They all filled the square with what was only a semblance of equality in wretchedness. The hierarchy among the beggars of Moskva was as strict as at the Tzar's court. They had their own lords and serfs, their rebels and lickspittles. The rag-clad bodies came from all corners of Varangia's domain. Trained monkeys and small children grabbed at his legs as Jacob tried to wade through their masses. He looked around and noticed with satisfaction that the Goyl had stopped because a leper was trying to touch his face. Jacob intended to make it even harder for him.

He reached into his pocket and grabbed a handful of the coins he had left from selling Fox's ring. He didn't wait for the beggar lords up by the church columns to notice him. He needed their masses who filled the square like a carpet of bodies. Jacob threw the coins into the crowd, and the carpet turned into a raging sea.

The Goyl sank without a trace. Jacob nearly felt sorry for him. He was not going to have an easy time reporting to Hentzau how he lost his prey in a swarm of beggars.

※ ※ ※

An abandoned abbey on one side, the stables of two slaughterhouses on the other... The Sintisa had not gotten the best place to make camp. And still it was not a sad sight. The carts and tents were colorful enough to compete with any *rushnyky* woven by a Baba Yaga. A viola and an accordion sowed wanderlust into the fresh morning air. The music was a reliable source of income for the traveling folk. The rich liked to pay to have their salons filled with dreams of freedom and adventure. The Tzar himself could only breakfast to the sound of a Sintisa viola.

A tame bear, whose nose ring still showed that his taming had not been entirely voluntary, was yawning in front of one of the wagons. Chickens were pecking at the ground between the tentpoles, and a one-eyed cat was watching a fight between two amber-eyed dogs. It was as though a long-lost past had snuck into the modern era.

A man whom Jacob asked for directions to the glass-sayers had a Malen'ky hanging from his beard.

The man pointed at some tents by the walls of the abbey. According to legend, the monks there had worshipped the Devil. Jacob didn't allow himself to wonder whether the Alderelves had been behind that as well. He hadn't touched Spieler's card since the Elf had so successfully stoked his jealousy.

"Please. You will find someone else." His own words. So why

249

shouldn't that someone be the Windhound? Because he wasn't good enough for her. *Really, Jacob? And who is?*

The woman in the first tent was so old she looked like her own mummy. When she saw Jacob, she spat three times and screeched through toothless gums, *"Серебко!"* —the Varangian word for silver.

The woman in the second tent quickly gave back his coins when her crystal ball filled with black moths. Did that mean Will had already found the Dark Fairy? Jacob didn't wait to find out.

The next tent appeared to be empty. He was about to back out of it when a young woman emerged from behind a curtain. Her clothes were a mix of Mongolian and Anamian fabrics, and the butterfly-like veil over her jet-black hair was probably from Prambanan.

"We rarely have clients this early in the morning," she said with a shy smile as she pulled the curtain over the entrance. "The glasses of others are better in the dark."

She didn't need glass. The third eye above her nose was like those on certain kinds of Nymphs. Even some Ogres had them, but the almost invisible eyelid and the high cheekbones made clear that the girl was the daughter of a Bamboo Woman.

"What images do you seek?" She pulled the veils over her forehead until they covered the third eye, a gesture she must have practiced since her childhood. A third eye was considered bad luck.

"I'm looking for my brother. He's disappeared, and I would like to know where he is."

Jacob had shown Will's photograph in so many places that it was worn and creased. At least it made it less obvious that the picture was in color. Photographs in this world were still black and white.

The Bamboo Girl looked at the photo and returned it to Jacob. Then she closed her eyes. The eye on her forehead, however, widened. Jacob could see it even through the veils.

Outside, the whinny of a horse.

The cries of a child.

The Bamboo Girl suddenly gasped for air. "He tricked your brother... Oh, he is devious. He promised he could make everything right."

"Make right? What?" Jacob took her hands. They were soft, like a child's. "Can you see where my brother is? Is he alone?"

She shook her head and shuddered.

"Is the Goyl with him?"

She didn't hear him. "They are silver and glass," she whispered, "and so empty, despite all their faces." She pressed her hand to her forehead and looked around as though the images she'd just seen had entered the dark tent. "He has a skin of stone," she whispered. "And he will kill her. She always knew he would."

Then she dropped to her knees and pressed her head to the floor. Jacob knelt down next to her, but he couldn't understand what she was muttering. It was not a language he understood. The girl rocked back and forth like a child. She began to hum a melody, a lullaby, as though she were trying to put herself to sleep.

A man entered the tent. Jacob had seen him outside, juggling with Thumblings. "She'll now sit like that for hours," he said. "I hope you paid her well?"

"Certainly," Jacob lied.

He left the tent. Two men, probably casting agents for one of Moskva's theaters, were watching a hair-raising performance in

251

which six children were contorting themselves to form an almost real-looking Dragon.

"*He promised he could make everything right.*" What? Jacob couldn't even be sure it was Will she was speaking about. It had been a stupid idea to come here.

Jacob stood and watched as the "Dragon" unformed to become six children, who bowed and nervously awaited the verdict of their audience. They hadn't learned yet that these spectators never showed their enthusiasm, in order to keep the price low.

"*They are silver and glass.*" Good. And bad. If Seventeen and his sister were Will's bodyguards, that explained why Jacob hadn't seen them since the attack. "*He has a skin of stone.*" That was the worst sentence. Had the girl seen the present or the past?

No. This couldn't have been for nothing. All the pain and the fear... Almost having died. *You did die, Jacob.*

The Thumbling-juggler was standing once more in front of the Bamboo Girl's tent. His face said it clearly: He wasn't letting anyone in anytime soon.

"*But you'd rather take the advice of a former lover.*" Spieler was right. Who cared if Will killed the Dark Fairy? She more than deserved it. And if she'd turned Will into a Goyl again, Jacob too wanted to see her dead, together with all her sisters.

"*He has a skin of stone.*"

Jacob had never more felt the need to speak to Fox. Nobody could sort his thoughts better; nobody had better advice. The walk back to Baryatinsky's palace seemed to take forever. His relief when he finally saw the gilded gates was almost comical. But Fox was not in her room, and the maid making her bed only mumbled in broken Varangian that Mademoiselle Auger had gone out.

Jacob didn't ask the girl whether Mademoiselle Auger had been alone.

"She's probably tired of this never-ending journey."

Poison.

Jacob went to his room, looked down through the window at Baryatinsky's busy courtyard, and wished he could be one of the stable hands who were brushing down the horses by the stables, or the messenger who was running down the street as though there could be nothing more important than the message he was carrying. Jacob had never wanted a normal life. The same routines, the same people, places, tasks. But after these past few days—*Days, Jacob? Weeks. Months*—a normal life suddenly didn't sound so bad anymore. No dangers beyond a runaway horse on the street, no life-or-death decisions, no immortals, no two worlds... Just one thing to hold on to: her.

He was just trying to write down what the Bamboo Girl had said before he forgot the exact words when a servant brought him a telegram. His mood brightened a little on seeing Dunbar's name, but what he read was very sobering:

```
Libraries in Albion's penal colonies rare STOP
as expected STOP more silver encounters? STOP any
sign of Dark One? STOP Papers here say Walrus
sick? STOP not sure if good or bad STOP Dunbar
```

Even at the end of the world, Dunbar kept an eye on politics. Good or bad news... Dunbar's first question for the Alderelf would probably be whether Arthur of Albion had indeed been the son of an Alderelf and a Fairy.

Jacob pushed aside the paper on which he'd noted the Bamboo Girl's words. Instead, he started writing a reply to Dunbar:

Keep looking. Will probably encounter Mirrorlings if we find Will. Need to know of all weaknesses. Would caustic soda and saltpeter work on breathing glass? Still believe have to tackle the spell and not the manifestation. No sign of Dark One, but sister tried to recruit me. To hell with all immortals. J.

Dunbar would not have to read between these lines to know how Jacob was feeling.

Jacob asked one of Baryatinsky's errand boys to send the telegram. Then he fetched some of their host's wine to help him stop wondering where Fox had gone to. He managed to convince himself for a while that he was worried about Seventeen, but then his jealousy reared its green face even in the glass he'd already refilled too many times.

Shortly before lunchtime, Chanute and Sylvain joined him, providing a welcome distraction. Sylvain told him they'd gone to visit the limb maker Baryatinsky had praised so much. His account was laced with admiring invectives. The idea for the visit had apparently been Sylvain's. Chanute chuckled over Sylvain's enthusiasm, but Jacob could see that the steel limbs had made an impression on Chanute, too. When Sylvain said how much such a limb would cost, Chanute again became the sickly old man who'd crawled away into his bedchamber in Schwanstein. Jacob inadvertently patted his empty pockets, though he knew their contents wouldn't even pay for one artificial finger. To cheer his old teacher, he told him about his audience with the Tzar scheduled for the next day and that he had high hopes for a good advance payment. Advance for what? Jacob had no idea, but Chanute's face lit up again, and an hour later he and Sylvain were already back to planning new treasure hunts.

Fox was gone for another two hours. Jacob only had to look

at her to know whom she'd been with. The Barsoi had given her the tour: the golden churches, the Dragon's gate, the horses that carried the Tzar's couriers to Yakutia and Zhonghua, and the bakers by the Kremlin walls who baked the singing bread. Jacob hadn't seen her this carefree since the Bluebeard.

"I see you have competition now. Which was only to be expected, right?"

Jacob felt his jealousy like a sickness. *Just what the Elf wants you to feel, Jacob.* But not even that helped. He told her he was finally going to meet the Tzar and see his Magic Collection. She looked distracted, as though she hadn't really returned. "Tomorrow Orlando is meeting some of his contacts to see whether they have news about the Fairy. He's offered to take me along."

Orlando. She'd never mentioned anyone's name in that tone. *What tone, Jacob?* Heavens, he was dying of jealousy. The words were already on his lips: *Come with me. What should I do all alone in the Magic Collection? What should I do with the Tzar?*

She looked so happy. And why not? The Barsoi had no debt with an Alderelf.

He showed her Dunbar's telegram and told her about the Bamboo Girl, but he tried to play down how much the glass-sayer's words worried him. All the questions he wanted to ask Fox... He just couldn't get them out.

"Your brother. The Fairy. Clara. Others are always more important."

It was the terrible truth: The Alderelf's poison was nothing but the terrible truth.

She looked happy.

"I thought you don't believe in soothsaying?" She studied his face the way she always did when she sensed he wasn't telling her what he really felt or thought.

And what had he expected, after all he'd told her in Schwanstein?

255

Not that it would happen so quickly. *Damn*. He couldn't even imagine not seeing her for more than a few hours at a stretch. *Better start imagining it now, Jacob.*

"Even if she was right about everything else...Will is alive, Jacob," she said.

"Yes, but what if..." He couldn't even say it. He didn't have to. She knew what he meant.

Fox took his hand. Jacob didn't pull it away as he'd done so often in the past days. It felt good.

"Remember what Alma says about prophecies? That they're always misunderstood? The future doesn't speak our language. Let's see what Orlando finds out tomorrow."

Orlando. Tomorrow. He pictured how....*Stop it*!

"Did she see the Goyl with Will?"

"She didn't say anything about him." And even if she had, the Bastard couldn't give Will his stone skin back. That would have been a neat revenge, but at least that was past, since the Fairy was gone."*He has a skin of stone.*" No, only the Dark One could bring the jade back.

And all these months he'd believed Will had forgotten the stone. *All these months? How often did you see him, Jacob?* The things we keep from others. What if Will didn't even want to be found? Just like before?

"You look tired," Fox said. "Why don't you go and sleep?"

She felt safe. Jacob could hear it. She liked being in Moskva. Or maybe she was just thinking of the other one.

37

THINGS WE DESIRE

A human dagger with a mother-of-pearl handle. Kami'en's brother Skala had found it in one of the caves where they built their surface cities. Yes. That dagger had been the first thing Kami'en had truly desired. The desire had been so strong that he'd stolen the dagger from his brother. Skala had broken two of Kami'en's fingers for that. Four years later, Kami'en had killed him in battle and buried him with the dagger. The two fingers still ached in cold weather.

Things we desire...

The palace where the Tzar was putting him up was full of things that woke desire. To Goyl eyes, the rooms seemed overloaded with pomp, all those golden tendrils and flowers, the paintings teeming with human gods and heroes. But Kami'en couldn't help admiring the craft in all those things. His weakness for human things—where did it come from?

The feet of his bed were formed like lion paws, which didn't help his sleep. The onyx lords kept black lions in their palaces. Kami'en had fed the last assassin they'd sent to a lion.

And, of course, there was a mirror. Humans were so obsessed with their reflections. Nowhere in their palaces could you ever escape your own face. Kami'en briefly eyed himself in the polished glass. A Goyl face gave nothing away — not the rage they felt so quickly, nor the love that came and went so quickly, nor the pride that ruled them all, nor the determination to retaliate for all the humiliations that were as familiar to them as the heat beneath the earth.

He turned away from the mirror.

Was she coming to Moskva?

He poured himself a glass of water, ignoring the brief hope to see her face in it. He'd never loved like this, and yet he'd betrayed her for things he desired even more: power, a son with human flesh, the throne of his enemy... All this he'd always wanted more than love. Love scared him. It was soft. And vulnerable.

One of his guards announced Hentzau. Kami'en had posted the Goyl soldiers by his door only as a courtesy to his Bloodhound, who saw spies even among the Tzar's guards. As usual, Hentzau's face didn't reveal whether he was bringing good or bad news. The past days had brought mainly good news. The rebels in the North were ready to compromise; the Man-Goyl were rejoining his army in droves; Wilfred of Albion was seriously ill, which put his alliance with Lotharaine in jeopardy; and the onyx were divided. Three of the black lords had crowned themselves King of the Goyl. But Hentzau was not bearing political news.

"We have proof Amalie's godfather handed your son to his grandmother's people."

The throne of his enemy. The Goyl were holding Therese of Austry two miles beneath the earth, but Hentzau had been suspicious for months that she was somehow managing to communicate with the surface.

"And? Where is he?"

"We can't find any trace of him."

Hentzau delivered bad news with refreshing neutrality. Kami'en appreciated that.

The Moonstone Prince was Kami'en's fifth child. None of the others had been as wanted by their father as this one. Kami'en suspected he knew why that was. The prince had also been her son for him. He'd made it official that the Fairy was not the child's murderess, but that hadn't brought her back to him. He wanted her back.

"Not a trace? The prisoners won't speak? Have you lost your touch?"

Hentzau straightened his back, though it obviously caused him pain. There was no part of the jasper Bloodhound's body that didn't cause him pain—all for his King. No, still for the old friend. Kami'en was aware that Hentzau's loyalty was not to the crown but to their shared past. He would have loved to reward him by giving him back his youth. He'd even asked Niomee, but she had claimed that kind of magic was not hers to dispense. Kami'en was sure that was a lie.

"I could not make them speak because they don't know where the infant is." Hentzau sounded brusque. Kami'en quietly reproached himself, as he always did when he'd offended his old friend. "Three of Therese's former court Dwarfs came to fetch your son. We found two, but the third is still at large. We reckon it's Auberon, Therese's old favorite. The others were obviously supposed to lead us off his track. They have no idea where Auberon was taking the child, and neither does Amalie's godfather."

Rage. His old foe. Kami'en felt it searing away all reason and political calculations. He went to the window so Hentzau wouldn't see how irritated he was, about Therese's cunning and his own foolishness. He should've anticipated that Amalie would do anything to drive away the Fairy. She hated her as much as she feared her. But he had to admit he'd never expected Amalie to make her own son a tool in her plans. He didn't know her. He had married a stranger, and a stranger she had remained.

The Tzar's troops were parading on the courtyard beneath the window. His allies. Kami'en and Nicolaij had signed the accord that morning. Varangia was a powerful ally in the East, and it was satisfying to know Albion had paid for this alliance, though he'd again had to give up the engineer who'd built his planes and underground railroads. But the Goyl had learned a lot from him before he ran to become Isambard Brunel.

"Was Therese questioned about the whereabouts of my son?"

"Yes. She claims she has nothing to do with the prince's disappearance. I think she was smart enough to make sure not even she knows his location, just in case we'd question her more... intensely."

"Did you let her know I will have her daughter executed if I don't get him back?"

"Yes. She wants you to know that you're a monster."

Coming from Therese, that sounded almost like a compliment. It takes one to know one. Inside him, his rage was whispering: *Have them both shot. Have their corpses mounted and put on display, like they used to do with your ancestors*. But Kami'en knew his greatest successes had been fueled not by his rage but by his ability to control it.

"Spread the word we're closing in on the Dwarf. And make sure Amalie knows what game her mother is playing."

Hentzau thumped his fist to his chest. He'd rather have received the order to execute both women, but he was smart enough to know that would've meant the death of the prince. And, of course, Therese of Austry knew that as well.

"You should return to Vena, Your Majesty. Albion may soon have a new king. Two more Man-Goyl commanders are offering to return to your banner, and the anarchists in Lotharaine want to cooperate with us. The wind is turning in our favor." *Despite what your Fairy lover is up to.* Kami'en knew Hentzau was adding that in his thoughts.

Kami'en looked over the roofs of Moskva.

Why hadn't she come? Because she knew he was here?

He felt a brief sharp pain—as though he'd lost something he desired more than the soldiers in the courtyard or the son who was alive because of her. But he was afraid to name that something.

38

RIDICULOUS

Ever onward, following a trail only the Pup could read. Nerron had followed many trails, but this was the first time he'd had to rely on the eyes of another. *Eyes, Nerron*? No. Will Reckless was tracking the Dark Fairy without ever looking at the ground. Maybe she was washing away her tracks with the rain that had been falling for days from the endless gray skies. However she was doing it, she wasn't leaving a single sign, neither on the ground nor in the grass that grew like shaggy hair all over this infernal country. But she couldn't hide from the boy in whose body her magic had lived.

If it hadn't been for the occasional lone spire or the outline of a village on the horizon, Nerron would've thought she was luring them into a land that belonged only to animals. They were everywhere—deer, boars, beavers, martens, hares, snakes, and toads, as though it were they who were covering the Dark One's tracks. Nerron and Will's own trail, in contrast, was very visible

262

and obviously also quite enticing. A pack of wolves, a black bear, and finally a rather oversize Ogre—all had made the mistake of taking Will to be easy prey. But the glassy guardians took care of them so silently that the Pup didn't even look around. Nerron's treasure-hunting heart ached from having to leave all that precious metal in the Varangian taiga, but Seventeen had taken his advice to hide at least his larger victims. Nerron marked the places on a map. His personal stash of silver... Not bad. The bear and the Ogre were worth a fortune, for they were still alive. Nerron had reached into one of the wolves' frozen jaws and had felt warm breath. For how long, who could say?

Will once nearly saw his guardians. Sixteen was getting sloppy. The bark was now all over her body, and at one point she forgot her camouflage when she scraped the wood off her arms. Nerron only just managed to distract the Pup by throwing a stone at his horse. Will's ignorance gave Nerron confidence that things were still moving according to his plan, but he did feel a little uneasy about how much he was beginning to enjoy the Pup's company.

The Bastard was a maverick. The last companion he'd grudgingly accepted had been a Waterman, and Nerron had been only too happy to be rid of him again. He definitely hadn't missed having someone by his side who stopped his horse for every nightingale and who thought it wrong to shoot a deer when it looked at you. Yet he felt he was getting used to Milk-face. Maybe it was the way the Pup asked him about Goyl history. Nerron was the first to admit he loved holding forth about the lost cities and the forgotten wars, about the settling of the Deadly Caves or the expeditions to the Shoreless Lake. He'd never found anyone who would actually listen to his long lectures. He'd even caught himself thinking that he'd like to show it all to Milk-face one day. What was the matter

263

with him? Was he not eating enough? Was it the cold? The rain? Some human virus eating away at his stone heart?

Will turned to him as though he'd heard Nerron's internal curses.

Yes, the Bastard curses you, Milk-face. And he will sell you. Steal from you. Betray you. It is his nature. You can't expect the wolf to turn vegetarian because of one Pup.

He gave Will his most devious smile.

And the Pup smiled back with his princeling face. No, his was the face of the poor, noble shepherd boy who, despite being slightly dim, always got the princess in the end. Oh, that sweet icing of innocence—it still made Nerron nauseous. But something in his heart, a tiny, barely nut-sized spot, turned as soft as snail skin when Will asked him when he'd met his first human, or at what age Goyl usually came to the surface. Milk-face seemed to remember more every day—the King's palace, the Boulevard of the Dead, the Bridge of the Guardians. And he took Nerron with him into his memories, back under the earth, home. In return, Nerron told Milk-face about the things that he hadn't seen: the living stalactites, the Mirror Caves, the Blue Meadows...and the Pup listened like a child.

Ridiculous.

Dangerous.

"You talk too much. Do I have to remind you we're in a rush?" Seventeen, wearing his angriest face, had hissed to him last night.

No. Nerron had not forgotten. And yes, this excursion couldn't be over soon enough. Not just because of the bark that was eating their shimmering companions.

The Bastard liked his stone heart. He had used every blow,

264

every pain and injury, to harden it. Every humiliation, every defeat, and every betrayal life had dealt him—and there had been many. Even a nut-sized soft-spot was more than he could afford.

39

A Part of Her

The moth fluttered into the carriage like a shred of night. Absurd, how her sister dressed them in red. Black was so much more appropriate for the souls of men who'd chosen this shadow of an existence in the name of love. The Dark One wondered who this one had once been. There were so many who'd drowned themselves for her and her sisters in village ponds or castle fountains. It seemed only just that she was now feeling the same pain she'd inflicted so often. Just...The Dark One wasn't sure she'd ever used that word before.

Pain bore interesting fruit.

Just like love.

Why did she still need to know what had become of the infant? She wanted to swat the moth away, since it might be bringing her images of the boy. She'd visited the baby a few times in secret, at night, when only the wet nurse was sleeping next to the crib.

She'd gently pushed her finger into the tiny fists, and she'd touched his brow to give him the protection of her magic. And she'd been scared of what moved inside her. It would stop as soon as she severed the bond connecting her to the father. Wouldn't it?

The Dark One caught the moth, and the images came.

A river surrounded by steep and densely wooded slopes. A building, big, old, with whitewashed walls. The Fairy heard the chime of a bell. And the cry of a child. She heard it so clearly, as if it were calling her. A woman stepped out of the gate in front of the building. She was wearing the black habit of a nun. A convent? In contrast to her mother, Amalie despised churches. Therese of Austry still prostrated herself every morning in the underground cell where the Goyl were keeping her prisoner. She worshipped her god like she treated her servants: *"Look, I am lighting candles for you. Protect me. Grant all my wishes. Destroy my enemies."* Why a convent? Maybe because of the superstition that Fairies dissolved into water if they ever crossed the threshold of a church. Had Amalie forgotten that a Fairy had attended her wedding in the cathedral?

The building had many windows, but the moth took the Fairy to the one from where the cries were coming. And there was the infant. Wrapped in layers of pale blue cloth and white lace, he was barely visible in the arms of the young nun. But the tiny hand grabbing the black habit was the pale color of red moonstone.

Though dawn was still hours away, the Dark One had Chithira stop the carriage. She didn't want to feel what she was feeling. Relief, as though she'd recovered a piece of herself.

She stepped down from the carriage. The countryside around her was very different from the wooded riverbank she'd just seen through the moth. Lotharaine? No. The convents there looked different.

She was still holding the moth between her hands. What should she do? She'd kept that child alive. She owed him her protection, even if what she felt for him scared her.

She let the moth fly.

She told it to find Kami'en and to show him the images she'd just seen. He loved the child. He loved him so much. He would find him.

The night was lit brightly by the two moons. They both hung in the sky so large they looked as though they might descend to earth at any moment. Donnersmarck was looking up at them. *He's getting stronger*, his eyes said when they met hers. *Please! Protect me!* She should've also protected the child that lived only through her. Instead, she'd sat in a glass cage and bemoaned her lost love.

Should she tell Donnersmarck that nothing he'd learned as a soldier was going to help him in this fight with the stag, nothing he knew about himself or this world? He probably sensed it. His fear looked so alien on his face, as alien as what was stirring inside him.

She went to his horse, took the reins, and looked up at him.

"What exactly are you afraid of?" she asked. "That he'll make you forget who you are? And? Look at your memories. Most of them are of pain, struggle, fear. He won't take your joy or your love or your strength. He won't let you forget to eat, sleep, or breathe. True, he knows nothing of yesterday or tomorrow, but might that not be a good thing? You'll see, he knows much more about the now."

Donnersmarck didn't understand what she was saying, but soon he would.

"Stay with him," she said to Chithira. The dead, she'd learned,

268

knew much more about this world than the living.

Donnersmarck peered after her as she stepped into the night.

If she wanted to find the strength they all needed of her, she would have to be alone. The wide countryside around her seemed to know nothing of time. It made her feel young again. And the Dark Fairy let herself grow until she could feel the clouds in her hair. For far too long she'd made herself small, made herself fit into their world.

40

THERE ARE OTHERS

The Goyl was hiding behind an advertising column on the other side of the street. Jacob had told Fox that Hentzau was having them followed, but this Goyl was new. His skin was pale yellow citrine.

Fox hadn't asked Jacob how he'd lost the Goyl who'd been tailing him—they each had their very different methods—but while she was waiting for the guards to open the gate, Sylvain suddenly stood behind her.

"I'm coming with you," he whispered, "because of that one."

He pointed not very inconspicuously at the Goyl. Nothing Sylvain did was inconspicuous, even when he tried to be. Fox was touched that he'd gotten it into his head to protect her, but she had no idea how to deal with such attention. She wasn't used to someone looking out for her. Jacob rarely did it because he knew she could very well take care of herself, and he knew how it irritated her when someone doubted that.

"Sylvain," she said, "I am grown up. I don't need a father." *The father I needed is long dead.*

Sylvain sheepishly rubbed his perpetually unshaved chin. The dark stubble sprouting barely an hour after he'd scraped his skin, the curly hair, and even the bushy eyebrows—he really did look like a faun with his soft lips and brown eyes. Even his ears were a little pointy at the top, not to mention his insatiable appetite for good food and any kind of alcohol. Sylvain was such a strange mix of strength and vulnerability, of grown-up man and naughty boy. Sometimes Fox thought all the men she knew had the dreams and wishes of nine-year-old boys—at least all the men she liked.

"I apologize. It's the red hair." The sinister look he shot across the street was probably meant for the Goyl. "Reminds me of my daughter. One of them. I have three. *Tabarnak*—I've told you, *non?*" His eyes followed a taxi, as though he wanted it to drive him away from his memories. Sylvain had something on his mind, that much was very clear.

The guard gave her an irritated look when she stopped in the middle of the open gate.

"Is there something else, Sylvain?"

He studied the knuckles of his right hand. "I don't know how to say... You and Jacob, you know about all these magic treasures. Do you know, maybe, of a magic something that brings back love?"

He was trying really hard to sound nonchalant, but Fox heard the yearning through his words, of many sad days filled with longing. She would've loved to answer yes, but she knew of no such magic.

"You should ask Chanute," she said. "He knows more about

271

magic than me and Jacob combined."

But Sylvain shook his head. *"Non!"* he muttered. "That would be too embarrassing. Albert would make fun of me."

"Nonsense! When it comes to love, Albert Chanute is much more sentimental than you think. He'll probably go off to find something for you right away. Ask him!"

Sylvain looked dubious as he glanced up at the window of Chanute's bedroom. He was still standing there when the guard closed the gate behind Fox. *"A magic something that brings back love."* As she crossed the street, Fox wondered about the love Sylvain had lost. And how it must be not to feel it anymore. She'd felt the same love for so long now...

Fox shook off the Goyl by shape-shifting behind a flower stall. Before he realized the woman he'd been shadowing had shifted, the vixen was long gone.

❊ ❊ ❊

The church where Orlando was expecting to meet Fox looked rather plain compared with the gold-encrusted churches around the Tzar's palace. And Orlando himself also looked much more sensible and harmless in his gray suit than he had in his black tailcoat. But the eyes still gave him away. Fox could almost hear those eyes filing their report: dress from a Lotharainian tailor, not cheap but well worn...hair naturally red...two rings, one probably magical...concealed knife in coat sleeve...

She still liked the Barsoi. Maybe she liked him even better in gray.

Like so many churches she'd seen on her way to Moskva, this church was built of wood. The view from its tower was worth

272

all the steps she'd had to climb for it. The roofs of Moskva surrounded her like a landscape of shingles, towers, and mythical stone creatures. But Orlando hadn't asked her here to admire the view.

The eagle sitting on the tower's balustrade had two heads, like the one on Varangia's crest. On his back sat a Bolysoj. Apart from the hat and the tiny deer-leather coat, the only thing distinguishing him from the Thumblings of Austry was the color of his hair. He wore a gold tooth on a cord around his neck, and he accepted an Albian coin as payment. Even before Orlando had translated the tiny spy's words, his face had told Fox they weren't getting much for their money. There were just the usual rumors: The Dark One was on her way to Moskva in the shape of a black horse; she was already there and had fluttered into the Kremlin as a moth; she was in the Tzar's palace and was conjuring an army of bears...

Fox could see that Orlando didn't believe a word of it, and so could the Bolysoj, who quickly flew off on his eagle before Orlando could ask for his money back.

"I hope my next source is a little more productive," Orlando said as he flagged down a taxi in front of the church. "Ludmilla Akhmatova is one of the best spies in Moskva. We're meeting at my apartment. There were some other things she was looking into for me, but I will also ask her about the Dark Fairy. Do you want to be there, or shall I ask the driver to drop you at Baryatinsky's?"

Fox hesitated. It was still early, and she'd just be sitting in Baryatinsky's salon waiting for Jacob and listening to Sylvain and Chanute debate whether wine or potato liquor gave you the better buzz.

"I'd like to be there," she said.

Orlando tried to hide how much her answer pleased him.

273

Fox enjoyed his company very much, but when he opened the taxi door, her mind was flooded with the memory of a different face, one so beautiful that it could hide all the darkness of the world. She felt ashamed for her racing heart as she stepped away from the taxi, but those memories were so much stronger than anything her mind could set against them. The last man (were Bluebeards really men?) she'd followed home had filled a carafe with her fear.

Orlando signaled the driver to drive on without them.

"Why don't we walk?" he said. "It's such a beautiful day, and those are so much rarer here than in Metagirta."

Fox was grateful to him for pretending nothing had happened. They walked in silence for a while, past houses and palaces, churches and shops. Even silence was easy with Orlando.

"How often do you shift shape?"

The question came so out of the blue that Fox was unsure whether she should answer it truthfully. She never talked with Jacob about how often she missed the fur. It felt like treason to be talking about it with someone else. But something in her wanted to answer, to give voice to her yearning to be *both*.

"Not often enough." She'd expected her answer to trigger curiosity, the flood of questions every shape-shifter knew so well, the lack of understanding, the fear, all too often mixed with disgust or disdain.

Orlando's face showed none of these.

"It's never enough, is it?" he said, pulling a comb from his pocket. At first glance, it looked like one of those ivory combs for which elephants or saber-toothed tigers had to give their lives, but the decorations on the handle indicated this comb had been carved by a Witch from human bones.

Orlando ran his thumb over the fine teeth. "I found this on the forbidden market in Din Eidyn. Cost me a whole year's earnings, but it has proven very useful in my line of work. Though I admit that was just the pretext under which I bought it."

Fox hadn't met many other shape-shifters who, like her, had been born as ordinary humans. She avoided those who made a spectacle of themselves, and the others kept their double life as hidden as she did.

"Does the comb make you age faster?"

"I don't know. Do birds age faster than humans? Do foxes?" His smile was gleeful, like that of a boy. And he did look like a boy, though he was older than Jacob.

Jacob once had a Witch's comb. He said he'd stolen it from a gingerbread house when he was a boy, but Fox knew he'd never used it. Jacob didn't want to be anyone or anything else; the very idea scared him. He'd later traded the comb for a horse.

Orlando cast a quick glance into the next archway and then pulled Fox through with him. Just like Baryatinsky's yard, the backyard they entered belied the fact they were in a large city. An old beech stood among beds of vegetables and pens for livestock. The tree's branches hid them from any curious eyes. Orlando looked around cautiously before he pulled the comb through his white-blond hair. Then he took off his jacket and pushed up his shirtsleeves. Feathers were sprouting from his arms like grass.

Fox touched the sharp quills. "Does it hurt?"

"Yes."

The feathers were as gray as a winter morning.

"A wild goose!" Fox whispered.

"I beg your pardon? A *gander*!" Orlando snapped his fingers, and the feathers dropped from his skin, making the cobblestones

275

at his feet look as though a cat had just made a kill. Or a fox.

Orlando pulled his shirtsleeves down over his reddened skin. The next time you hunt a goose, think of me."

"Why not a raven?" Fox picked an icy-gray feather from the ground.

"I didn't want to develop a taste for the eyes of the hanged. The man who sold me the comb told me I could wish what bird I wanted to turn into. When I was a child, my favorite book was about a boy who was turned into a wild gander by a Wizard."

Fox liked his choice. The vixen was going to have to take wild geese off her menu.

Orlando put his jacket back on and tucked the comb into his pocket. "Is it as easy to call the fur?"

Fox again hesitated. She was used to keeping the fur secret. *But he understands, Fox.*

"It's getting harder." It used to come almost by itself. That hadn't happened in a long time.

The house where Orlando rented his apartment was painted the same green as many of Moskva's housefronts. It was a beautiful house, with tall windows, stone friezes, and wrought-iron balconies. It reminded Fox of Lutis, though the plaster was stained from the rain.

"As you can see, the King of Albion doesn't pay enough for a palace," Orlando said. "But there's not a single Kikimora in this house, which is rare in Moskva. I know they're useful, but I can't stand them. The one next door leaves dead cats for those who don't leave a bowl of milk for her, and many of the cats have been dead a while."

An old woman walked past, eyeing Fox as though she reminded her of her own younger days. What was she imagining? *What are you imagining, Fox?*

A small painted statuette stood in a nook by the entrance. Someone had left flowers at its feet.

"This is Vasilisa the Wise," Orlando whispered. "You see the bowl next to the flowers? That's salt water. Vasilisa is the daughter of the Sea King. She protects many houses in Moskva."

He placed a feather at Vasilisa's carved feet before he unlocked the door. His hand was so warm as he brushed Fox's arm. Maybe he could wipe the Bluebeard's caresses off her skin. Maybe Orlando could make her forget the one she'd longed for all these years. The Bluebeard's forgetyourself had managed only for a very short while.

A few Malenk'y scattered as she followed him up the stairs. In Baryatinsky's palace, they always stole the sugar from the breakfast table.

Orlando's apartment was on the second floor. It was bare, as if its inhabitant feared any objects might give away too much about who he really was. The walls were as gray as the feathers the comb had sprouted. A plain desk in front of one of the three high windows. Three chairs, a couch, a chest with a samovar. Fox found the plain interior very soothing after Baryatinsky's overstuffed rooms. Two of the windows were open, flooding the room with the scents of a cool, foreign summer. For an instant the vixen stirred inside her; she wanted to be off, into the woods she could smell through the smells of the city. But Celeste wanted to stay.

There had been other men before the Bluebeard: the son of a wood trader during one of the times Jacob was gone for weeks, and a young soldier who'd nearly caught her shifting shape in the woods. Both had just made her miss Jacob even more.

The maid who took Fox's coat spoke only Varangian. Orlando spoke to her as if he'd spoken it since birth. Shape-shifters. The girl poured some tea from the Samovar while Orlando went to look out the window.

"She should be here soon," he said. "When Ludmilla is late, it's time to start worrying."

A strange house, strange rooms... And they came again, the memories of another strange house, empty except for a few corpses. Fox shook her head a little too abruptly when the girl offered her a cup of tea. Who did she think she was fooling? She would never be free of the memories. They would stay with her like the scars on her wrists. The air suddenly smelled of small white flowers, sweet and alluring.

"I have to go." She could hear the servant with the bloody antlers behind the door. Someone touched her arm. She slapped the hand away and spun around. Orlando gently took her arm and stroked the scars left by the Bluebeard's chains.

"Sometimes we think we know people at first sight," he said. "As though we'd met them a hundred times before, in another life, in another world. And then we realize that we know nothing. How did they look as children? What dreams startle them from their sleep?" He let go of her arm as if he were returning it to her together with the memories still caught in her skin.

The girl was still standing there, holding the cup. She nearly dropped it when the doorbell rang.

"And there she is," Orlando said. "The best spy in all of Varangia."

The Dwarf woman who was being led into the room was dressed in the newest fashion, which was quite unusual for one of her people. Dwarfs generally preferred old-fashioned garments, to show how much older their traditions were. They also aged more slowly. Orlando's visitor could've easily been over seventy, though Ludmilla Akhmatova's face was that of a young and beautiful woman. An untrained eye probably would've missed the fact that she was carrying a gun under her coat, but Fox was used to spotting such little secrets.

"May I introduce you?" Orlando said. "Ludmilla Akhmatova... Celeste Auger."

The eyes that took in Fox's face were so large and expressive that there seemed hardly enough space for them in the beautiful face. They were almost as black as Ludmilla Akhmatova's hair.

"Ah, the vixen," she said with the surprisingly deep voice of a Dwarf woman. She offered a delicate hand to Fox. "What an honor. I've been following your career with keen interest. Women treasure hunters are even rarer than women spies."

"Fox was trained by a man," Orlando interjected.

"Who, according to what I've heard, would be long dead if it weren't for her." Ludmilla Akhmatova gave Fox a smile as she sat down on the couch. "Can she hear what I have to tell you?"

The maid brought in a plate with honey cakes.

Orlando gave the Dwarf an apologetic smile. "No, I'm afraid that is top secret, but maybe you know something about the Dark Fairy's plans? Mademoiselle Auger is looking for her."

Ludmilla Akhmatova took a cake and sipped some of the tea the maid had placed in front of her. "Did you hear what the Tzar's spies told him about her? It's too piquant—and he's said to have believed them."

Orlando offered Fox a chair.

"I would love to hear it, Ludmilla Akhmatova," she said.

The Dwarf flicked a few crumbs from her collar. "They told

279

him the Dark Fairy is on her way to Kamchatka to offer her magic to the Peasant Prince. One of the Wolf-Lords or the Khan probably spread that information, hoping Nikolaij would kill the prince before his rebellious farmer boys ransack their palaces. We really do live in interesting times."

Another sip of tea.

"But you don't believe that story." Orlando looked unsure what to think.

"Of course not. No *woman* would ever believe it." Ludmilla winked at Fox.

"What are you trying to say? That the Dark Fairy has had enough of all crowned men? Except for her rival in Austry, there's only one woman ruler, and that is the Empress of Nihon. A very long journey."

Fox exchanged a look with Ludmilla Akhmatova. Orlando knew how it felt to shift shape, but maybe the difference between man and woman was even more fundamental than that between human and animal.

"I think Ludmilla means something else," Fox said. "The Dark Fairy didn't help Kami'en because of his crown. So why should she offer herself to one now?"

"Indeed." Ludmilla dunked her cake in the tea, which was strong and dark. "The Dark Fairy loved the Goyl King, Orlando. They say it was a great love. Maybe even a Fairy feels pain when such a love is betrayed. She's not traveling east to find an ally against her lover. She is seeking the one who can sever the inseverable bond."

Fox gave Orlando a puzzled look.

He took her hand.

"Excuse us, Ludmilla," he said. "I'll have Olga bring you some of the Albian cake you like so much. And I'll be back before your next tea is cold. Then we can discuss that other matter."

He pulled Fox into a room that seemed far too small for all the books and papers in it. They were piled high, even on the bed beneath the window. Behind the door was a cabinet. Orlando opened one of the drawers and picked out a glove covered in scales.

"A present from my homeland," he said, pulling the glove over his hand. "The Walrus wanted me to find out if his foreign secretary had been with a naiad in his youth. The secretary's daughter was living proof of that affair, but I didn't tell on her or her father. This glove was a gift to show his gratitude. He said it could show true love. May I?"

Orlando reached into the air in front of Fox's face, and his gloved fingers grasped the same golden thread the Baba Yaga's granddaughter had shown her.

"True love, selfless and deep as the oceans in their most fathomless depths." Orlando let the glove run along the thread, which glistened like a ray of sunlight. "But I fear this one is not meant for me. This kind of thread is not spun in mere days."

He let his hand drop, and the gold disappeared as though it really had been nothing but a ray of sunlight. "The Golden Yarn... or the inseverable bond, as it is also called. As inseverable as the threads of fate. And there is only one who can spin them and who can cut them."

"*La Tisseuse de la mort et l'amour.*" Fox whispered the name as she did as a child. In Austry she was called the Weaver.

Fox never imagined she'd feel pity for the Dark Fairy, but Orlando's words reminded her of the Blood Wedding and the pain she'd seen on the other's face. His words reminded her of

281

the days when all her unrequited love for Jacob had made her feel so raw that she'd nearly set off in search of *la Tisseuse* herself. Orlando gently stroked her cheek. His touch felt good to the vixen and to Celeste.

"Yes, Takushy, *la Tisseuse*. The Weaver. *La Hilandera*. She goes by many names and has many stories. Some claim they are three sisters. But all agree on one thing: it's very dangerous for a mortal to ask for her help because she may sever not just the bond of love but also the threads of life." Orlando plucked the glove off his fingers. "But the Dark One won't have to worry about that. She is, after all, immortal."

And more powerful than the kings and emperors of this world.

"I can't believe she can't sever the bond herself."

"Yes, not even she. We've all tried, haven't we? It is somehow comforting that even immortal Fairies are powerless against the Golden Yarn. Don't you think?"

Maybe.

"But what happens when she has it severed?" She was speaking of the Fairy, only the Fairy.

"I suppose the love disappears. Like the pain of a wound of which only a scar remains."

Yes. A scar. Nothing more.

Orlando returned the glove to the drawer and shut the cabinet. Fox loved his face. It was like a promise that wishes could come true, that desire might lead to more than yearning.

Before she knew what she was doing, she kissed his mouth. The Golden Yarn. There had to be other colors.

Red. The Bluebeard's chamber became a bed of flowers as Orlando's lips kissed her back. The shadows of her heart grew gray feathers. Every kiss made her breath lighter, and her fingers sought Orlando's skin as though they sought her own. Celeste. For the first time only Celeste. And she didn't have to hide the vixen from him; he knew about her longing for the other body. He met hers with skin and feathers and followed her into the woods that spread inside her, where so far she'd met only Jacob. They lost themselves until he found her heart, beating so fast in his hands, and still he held on to it, weaving red and gray into the golden thread.

Minutes. Hours. Time transformed into touch. No more words on her lips, not even Jacob's name. Just the kisses she now gave to another.

Fox. He called her Fox. He whispered it over and over, as though to remind her he also loved the vixen even as he kissed Celeste's human skin. They forgot the Dwarf and whatever information she'd gathered for Orlando. They forgot the maid who was serving her Albian cake.

Fox had no idea how late it was when she remembered it all. Orlando was so fast asleep that she managed to wriggle out of his embrace without waking him. Much harder was to stop herself from looking at his sleeping face, as if something inside her was afraid of forgetting it. She pushed the warm blanket off her skin. The cool air made her shiver, feeling the sweat on herself. She stroked her naked arms. So soft. So warm. Was she happy? Yes. And no. Because now the words were back, and with them the name that had spun gold around her heart for so long she hardly remembered how things had felt before him.

She looked back at Orlando's sleeping face.

Gold and gray.

She wanted both, and peace between the two.

She picked up her clothes off the woven flowers of the carpet.

She'd never dropped her fur dress so carelessly and was relieved when she found it among the discarded human clothes.

Ludmilla Akhmatova was gone. She'd left a note for Orlando. Secrets. Fox didn't read it.

Baryatinsky's palace was far, but she walked. She took her time, looking at her reflection in shop windows as if looking at a stranger, not sure whether she should laugh or cry, and doing neither. She left someone behind on Moskva's streets: the Celeste who'd sat at the Bluebeard's table, but also the girl who'd followed Jacob all those years like a child. She couldn't yet tell who'd taken their place. When she passed the entrance to a park, she called the fur. It came more easily than it had in a long time. The gate scraped the vixen's back as she squeezed under it, but it felt good to break away from all human memory. If only the sun hadn't been spinning golden threads between the trees.

The guard at Baryatinsky's gates opened them without question. He lowered his eyes as she stepped past him, but she'd already seen the desire in his eyes. Like an echo of before.

Jacob was not back yet.

Fox was glad.

41

The Bear in the East

Wladimir Molotov was not just the curator of the Tzar's Magic Collection; he also taught Varangian history at the university of Moskva, as he proudly informed Jacob before he began the tour. Ten minutes later, Jacob already pitied every student who had to attend Molotov's lectures. The collection was indeed as unique as people claimed, and Molotov's Austrian was almost flawless, but his speech was slower than the gait of his gout-bowed legs, and even the famous magic eggs lost all their mystery under his dusty explanations.

Armor to make one invulnerable, ovens that gave a bear's strength to anyone who slept on their warm tiles, two rooms filled with invisible-making mushrooms, magic nuts, magic rose hips, and Baba Yaga bark. Three rooms full of carved figurines from all around the world to summon the old gods: a god of thunder from Fon, a snake goddess from Bengal, the Fire Dancer from Savai'is...

And there was no end in sight. Molotov's dull monologue gave Jacob much time to wonder what Fox was doing with Orlando. Ridiculous how persistently his thoughts drifted back to her. No matter how much he tried to force himself to pay attention to his guide, it was too obvious whom his mind tried to follow as naturally as she'd followed him all these years.

The seventh room into which he followed Molotov was filled from floor to ceiling with magical books. Jacob had only seen comparable collections in Pendragon's university library and in a Ligurian monastery. One of the books was bound in silver, which of course made him think of the Alderelves. Molotov explained how that book, should one be foolish enough to open it, gave the power to read things and creatures out of any book in the world. Jacob had never heard of such magic and was just about to ask Molotov about the silversmith who'd created the book's covers, but then he saw what was in the next room.

They flowed down the walls like woven water, and their patterns conjured a thousand and one faraway places. Flying carpets. Jacob's heart began to beat faster. There it was, the magic that could help him find Will. How could he have forgotten that the Tzar's collection was famous for its flying carpets? *Because your jealousy won't let you think straight, Jacob.* Most flying carpets would take the rider to a place, but a few could also be steered toward a person. The pattern for that rare kind of magic was so complex that even the most talented weavers rarely managed it without flaw.

The first carpets Molotov limped past were woven and could at best be used for short trips. Then came carpets with knotted patterns that indicated they could fly neither very fast nor very high, let alone do any other magic. But Molotov had much to say about each one, and Jacob had to restrain himself not to leave the old man standing there to go off in search of the right carpet.

The patterns became more complex. Knotted thickets of flowers and animals, abstracts, celestial constellations.

"This carpet brings love if you ride it with the lady of your dreams during a full moon."

Yes, yes, fine. Next.

"This specimen will throw off everything if one shouts the words hidden in its pattern. It was used to eliminate enemies."

Great. And next?

Carpets that could serve sumptuous meals in flight, carpets that would float like canopies over crowned heads, carpets that could act as bodyguards. Carpets that could steal, kidnap... He'd probably fooled himself. There couldn't be more than a dozen carpets in existence that did what he was looking for, and none of them had probably ever left their homelands, but were all tucked away in the treasure chambers of sultans and suleimans.

"Now this specimen" — Molotov had stopped in front of a carpet hung over a rod with golden Dragon heads at each end — "is the most precious in this collection, not only because of its size." He mumbled his words as if he were talking about a bath mat. "It can carry six men and their horses, and it will find any destination desired."

The carpet was bluish-green and not only covered the very high wall but spilled onto the floor in so many folds that Jacob estimated it to be at least fifty feet long. But size wasn't important. The magic was in the pattern. This one was so convoluted that the words were all but invisible to even the most experienced eye. They were written in Lahkmid, the secret language of carpet weavers. Every treasure hunter worth his mettle knew at least the most important words, as well as how to pronounce the ones he didn't know. Jacob found the words he'd been hoping for, in the very center, hidden among blossoms and fabulous birds:

I SHALL FIND THE ONE YOU SPEAK OF.

It became almost impossible to listen to Molotov with a calm expression, but Jacob reminded himself that he'd never again get the opportunity to see this collection — and that he'd look rather stupid at his next audience with the Tzar if he offered to find a treasure Nikolaij already possessed.

He would find Will.

But what for? Because the Alderelf was trying to stop him? Was that enough?

What did his brother want?

"And now...erm..." Another staircase, another floor. Molotov was so winded, every step they climbed made Jacob fear for the old man's life. "...we come to the final room of the collection."

There — an end in sight.

I SHALL FIND THE ONE YOU SPEAK OF.

Molotov stopped in front of the portal at the top of the stairs and wiped the sweat off his parchment-skinned face. The locks were secured with flame-wires and Pashtun copper, promising extraordinary treasures.

"He has a skin of stone."

What did his brother want? But when had Jacob last been able to answer that question with any certainty? A long time ago.

Molotov instructed Jacob to turn around while he unlocked the portal. Jacob always carried a pocket mirror for such situations, but he didn't bother. All this treasure made him think of the presents he used to bring back from this world for Will, the delight on his brother's face, the absorbed wonder. Will had once been as enchanted by this world as he. *Even more so, Jacob. She gave him*

288

a different skin. What if he liked it?

Yes, what then?

Did Spieler understand his brother better than he did? *"Oh, please! You're talking to an Elf. I know your most intimate wishes. It's my business to fulfill them."*

The smell that assaulted them as Molotov pushed open the heavy portal made it very clear what kind of room they were about to enter. The despair of magical creatures smells just as sharply as that of ordinary animals. Therese of Austry had never been interested in collecting living creatures, which was why Vena's Chambers of Miracles only contained stuffed and mounted specimens. All living creatures had been processed into tinctures or had met their ends in the imperial kitchens. The creatures in the cages Molotov was now leading him past would've probably preferred such a death to an imprisonment that, thanks to their long life spans, might have already lasted centuries.

A golden egg-laying goose, a blinded basilisk... What good did it do that their cages had gold bars and the landscapes of their native lands were painted on the walls? A Rusalka had to share the murky waters of her tank with a couple of water gnomes, while next to her two magic ravens were pecking at the hexed glass that kept their curses from reaching human ears. Jacob was glad Fox hadn't come with him.

A buck with silver hooves (*No, Jacob, it has nothing to do with the Elf*), three bees of Vasilisa the Wise, and the Gray Wolf, savior of three Tzars. The third Tzar had shown his gratitude by locking up the poor immortal creature. The golden eyes lost some of their dull indifference as Jacob stepped closer to the bars. The wolf was almost as big as a pony, and even after decades of captivity, its fur still shimmered like moonlight. The wolf's cage was the last one. There was a door beyond it, but Molotov bowed like an actor going offstage and gave Jacob a dusty smile.

"I hope you've enjoyed the tour, Mr. Reckless. The Tzar's chauffeur will now take you to your audience with His Majesty. Please convey my utmost regard. As a young man, I served his father as a soldier."

Jacob had one trait that was as uncontrollable as his impatience: his curiosity. He pointed at the door Molotov was studiously ignoring.

"What's in there? As far as I know, the Tzar wanted me to see *all* his treasures."

Leave it, Jacob! But there'd never been a closed door he didn't want to open.

"That is the secret wing of the collection." A note of disapproval dampened Molotov's voice. "Its contents are known only to the Tzar and his closest advisors — for reasons of state security."

See, Jacob? Leave the stupid questions. Every treasure hunter had heard about the secret wing of the Tzar's collection. Varangia's most famous treasure hunter (who, some said, was an illegitimate son of the Tzar) had once tried to enter it as part of a wager. He was now living out his days in a prison camp on Sakha.

The portal had a magic combination lock — that much Jacob could see, even though Molotov was trying to block his view. He'd once cracked a lock just like it in Pombal. *Stop it, Jacob!*

His careless question cost him dearly. Molotov never took his eyes off him, so as they made their way back, Jacob couldn't even get a closer look at how the doors to the hall of carpets were secured.

The Tzar's chauffeur was waiting in the courtyard, next to a highly-polished car. Even a hardened enemy of modern times as Nikolaij the Third couldn't resist the horseless carriages. Varangia's double eagle spread his wings over the hood. Jacob had seen too many horses whipped half to death to find anything romantic about horse-drawn carriages, but the clatter of hooves still sounded better than a sputtering engine. Fox would've laughed and reminded him that the horses probably didn't enjoy wearing iron on their feet. Where was she? He forbade himself to think about that.

❋ ❋ ❋

Throne rooms, army tents, stables, carriages, and trains — Jacob had met the rulers of this world in all sorts of places, but until now, none had asked him to take off his clothes and share wafting steam and tubs of icy water.

The steam smelled of fresh birch leaves, pushkin-herbs, and charred wood. The white vapors revealed his royal host only after a couple of enormous servants had fanned them away with birch branches.

Nikolaij, as naked as the day he was born, emerged from a pool tiled with mosaics depicting the diversity of Varangian mythical wildlife: Rusalkas, kraken, river sprites... The movements of the water gave them an illusion of life. The Tzar reached for the towel offered by one of the servants and wrapped it around his waist. His usually quite pale skin was now the color of amber. When the Tzars indulged in the Varangian passion for steam baths, they protected themselves with a salve supposedly derived from a Goyl recipe. Rumor had it the salve could deflect bullets. The sabers carried by the servants made Jacob even more aware of his own nakedness. Maybe the baths were the safest place for a

291

Tzar to receive his guests.

"Gospodin Reckless!" Nikolaij was handed a bowl of raw meat. "I hope my collection managed to impress the West's most famous treasure hunter?"

A bear suddenly emerged through the wafting steam, sniffing the air, wearing an embroidered waistcoat over his black fur. The Tzar was hardly ever seen without the animal by his side. On official occasions, the bear was dressed in a cavalry uniform, a sight Jacob had hoped to see at the ball, but Ivanuska-Dyracok had been indisposed due to a swallowed fish bone. The Tzar's tame bears were always christened after the hero of many Russian fairy tales, who, though he spent most of his life sleeping behind an oven, always ended up saving the world. With his massive paw, Ivanuska caught the meat his master threw at him, and Nikolaij handed the empty bowl back to the servant while his eyes stared at Jacob's naked chest.

"The Goyl claim that one of them shot Jacob Reckless through the heart. But I can't see a scar. So it's a lie?"

"No. The Goyl aimed well and his bullet hit its mark, but there's no longer a scar."

"And how does one survive something like that?"

"I *didn't* survive."

Jacob Reckless and his heart... The Tzar didn't look surprised. His spies had probably told him every version of that story. There were quite a few. Jacob's favorite was the one in which the Red Fairy planted the heart of a moth in his chest.

"How does death feel?"

"I wasn't dead long enough to answer that question."

The servants brought embroidered cushions as colorful as the *rushnyky* of the Baba Yaga. Varangia and Ukraina not only had

292

the same Witches; the two countries had so much in common that the larger neighbor kept swallowing the smaller one.

His royal host settled on one of the cushions and nodded at Jacob to do the same.

"The Magic Collection is much larger than what you saw today," he began. "It fills two more palaces, and their locations have been kept secret for centuries. My father had both of them searched for decades for two enamel eggs containing the waters of life and death. One of our ancestors supposedly lived for a hundred and ninety-eight years thanks to those eggs. But they are untraceable."

He spoke Albian with a Lotharainian accent. Varangian nobles traditionally had their children educated by Lotharainian teachers, but Nikolaij's two wars with Lotharaine had put an end to that. The East now looked to the East. What was it going to mean for Albion and Lotharaine if Varangia forged an alliance with the Goyl? Jacob would've liked to talk to Orlando Tennant about that, but... *Yes, Jacob, Fox is with him.* He should've stolen one of the nuts that made a person fall in love with the first woman he met. Though, as he recalled, that had been an old beggar who'd shoved her plate at him. The sight of his own naked skin confused his thoughts. *Damn it, Jacob, remember where you are.*

"Your collection is truly remarkable, Your Majesty," he said, "but there is plenty I could still find for you."

Ivanuska-Dyracok rested his muzzle on the Tzar's naked shoulder. The bear's eyes were almost the same color as his master's salved skin. There was a story that during a particularly harsh winter that took the lives of thousands of subjects, one of Nikolaij's ancestors offered himself to his bear to keep him from starving to death, but the bear took only the Tzar's left hand. Maybe that

293

was why they made such exquisite artificial limbs in Moskva.

"Magic objects only rarely help with political goals, don't they?" Nikolaij patted the bear's head. "Has any country ever been conquered by seven-league boots or by a Witch's brew?"

My brother is just now carrying something through your lands that already destroyed three armies. The words were on Jacob's tongue, but of course he didn't say them aloud. Nikolaij was right. Most magical objects fulfilled very private wishes—beauty, eternal youth, everlasting love...

He knew a woman in Caledonia who'd had a long affair with Orlando. She'd even followed the Windhound to Leon. *Stop it, Jacob.*

The Tzar nudged the bear's muzzle off his shoulder. No matter what fancy clothes the bears wore, their breath still reeked like that of any wild animal.

"I want you to find a bell."

The servant gave the bear a fistful of leaves to eat. Jacob smelled mint.

"Its sound is supposed to bring back the dead. I assume you've heard of it? And who better to find it than a treasure hunter who's already been in the Land of Shadows?"

No, Jacob had never heard of such a bell, but he knew better than to admit it.

"Sure," he lied. "It's supposed to be in a church in the Jamantau Mountains. But its magic only works if its tongue is sprayed with seawater. The bell once belonged to a Mer-king."

Not bad, Jacob. He nearly believed it himself. The bear kept his eyes on Jacob, who hoped it was just a rumor that the creature could smell a lie.

The bear's master, however, looked impressed. "I didn't know

294

about that part. Good. When can you leave? You shall have my swiftest horse."

Even easier than he'd thought—hopefully, the next step would prove just as simple.

"The Jamantau Mountains are difficult terrain for a horse, Your Majesty. One of your flying carpets would provide a much more reliable mode of travel." Oh, he was such a fabulous liar. After all, he'd already lied his way out of the oven of a Lotharainian Witch and the coffin of a Catalunian vampire. Practice a master does make.

Nikolaij frowned. The sweat formed glassy pearls on his amber skin. "I don't know. Those carpets are alien magic. Are you sure? I have very good horses."

Alien magic. The Tzar expressed a fear shared by many behind the mirror. But even if the carpets came from Fars, Pashtun, or Almohad, that made them no more fickle than the magic objects of his own country.

"Don't worry," Jacob said. "I'm used to handling magical objects from all sorts of lands. It's part of my trade. You just have to take your time to understand their magic."

Nikolaij reached for the glass one of his servants was offering. "Good. If you think so. Truth be told, I'd much rather part with one of those flying rugs than one of my horses."

The servant also offered a glass to Jacob. Spiced wine. Water would've been more welcome in this heat.

"Forgive the question, Your Majesty? Who is it you want to call back with the bell?"

Nikolaij threw his empty glass against the tiled wall. The servants quickly began picking up the pieces from the blue glazed stones. It was a Varangian superstition that broken glass drove away the shadows of past woes.

"My son Maksim."

"How long has he been dead?"

"Three hundred days, five hours, and a few minutes. Bring me the bell and you shall be a very rich man."

The Tzar rose from his cushion, a signal for Jacob to do the same.

"I shall bring you the bell." A difficult lie. Jacob was about to make an enemy of the Tzar of Varangia, and he felt sorry for him. He'd never had such scruples with the Empress of Austry or the crown prince of Lotharaine.

The servants sprinkled rose water on the oven. The vapors turned thick and white, as though they were suddenly in the clouds.

"I shall have the carpet delivered to you. Did Molotov show you one you'd prefer?"

"Yes, but it's the most precious one you own."

The carpet weaver had to trace the pattern with his bare feet for ten days and ten nights—that's what put the magic in the knots. "That, and the skills of his trade," Robert Dunbar would have added. "I keep telling you, Jacob. Every man can become a magician if only he raises himself to become a master at his craft."

The coat that was now being put on the Tzar had clearly been designed by such a master. Firebirds spread their flame-red wings over matte-golden silk. What magic had created such skill? Or was it the other way around? And did the coat make its wearer happy?

Nikolaij beckoned the bear to his side. "I shall have the carpet brought to you tomorrow. You are still staying with Baryatinsky?"

"Yes." So easy.

The servants rinsed the sweat off Jacob's skin before they took him back to the room where he'd left his clothes.

"How old was the Tzar's son when he died?" Jacob asked one of them.

"Six years, sir. Typhoid fever."

He felt very guilty.

He would have to find the bell, make up for the lies he'd told the Tzar. One day, with Fox's help. No Fairies, no Elves, just him and her searching for the lost things of this world.

He reached for his shirt.

The card dropped from it.

She was with him for quite a while. Who knew a vixen and a Windhound could make such a good couple?

Straight into the heart.

The Tzar did pay an advance. After Jacob received the coins, he asked the chauffeur to wait while he approached a boy begging by the palace gate. "Bury this by the river," he said, pressing the card and a shiny silver ruble into the boy's grubby hands. "But I'm warning you, if you just throw the card away, or if you try to keep it for yourself, it'll bring you bad luck for a hundred times a hundred days."

He hadn't curbed his jealousy, but Jacob felt better as he settled into the Tzar's automobile.

42

THE ROBBERS IN THE TREES

Should he have been more careful? *Yes, Nerron.* After every rain, Sixteen could barely move until she'd scraped the bark from her joints, and Seventeen kept growing roots he had to cut off with his own fingers. Each misty morning made it worse, the moonlight, the damp shadows beneath the trees. It was obvious Fairy magic was winning the battle against glass and silver, but—*A curse on you, Nerron, and on your speckled bastard skin*—he had relied on the vigilance of the Mirrorlings while he'd daydreamed of treasures in the lost cities, of the brand-new world that was going to be his reward. He'd stuffed his good senses into a saddlebag!

When something stirred in the oak tree above, he thought it was just the wind bringing more of the rain that seemed to have been following the Fairy like a damp veil. But then there was the shrill whistle, and bandits started dropping from the trees like wingless birds.

Old stories. This country was infested with them. Solovei the Brigand, who changed into a bird to evade his hunters. Years ago, Nerron had exposed another treasure hunter who bragged he'd found the flute with which that legendary bandit was said to have laid waste to entire regions. But the men surrounding them now were not the kind of bandits who inspired legends. They were so filthy he should've smelled them from miles away. One was missing an eye, the other an ear, and the feathers on their clothes had certainly not grown from their own bodies. They weren't even from the right bird! The legend was of Solovei the Nightingale, but these idiots had adorned themselves with the feathers of crows and finches.

There were twelve of them. The Jade Goyl had dealt with more during the Blood Wedding, but Will was wearing human skin now. The Pup did draw his saber, though. Nerron and Will had killed three before the others brought them to the ground. Nerron screamed for Sixteen and Seventeen as the bandits pulled the noose over his head. They'd knotted it so it wouldn't immediately break his neck. Nice! They wanted to see them wriggle. Nerron cracked one more nose before they pulled him up. Will smashed another's hand, but he was soon dangling next to Nerron. The Bastard's Goyl skin offered more resistance to the rope, but the Pup was writhing like a fish on a hook, and soon enough his body went slack. He was going to be dead in minutes. Beneath them, the robbers made off with their horses. They looked so dumb they probably weren't going to find the crossbow in the swindlesack. Even before they were out of sight, Nerron's fingers started feeling for the blade in his sleeve. *Hurry, Nerron!* Milk-face had softer skin. He already looked quite dead.

Nerron's hands were soon free, but the rope around his neck

was tougher, and when it finally snapped, the fall nearly broke his neck. Will's face was as blue as lapis lazuli, and he slumped to the ground like shot venison, but he was still breathing. Nerron cut the rope and grabbed the nearest stone as he heard steps behind him. But it was only Seventeen. The Mirrorling wasn't even trying to look like a human, or maybe it was no longer as easy for him. His face mirrored the forest, and his left arm was as stiff as a branch. Sixteen was in no better shape. She was all shadows and leaves, and it was hard to tell what was mirrored and what was actual growth. She knelt next to Will and reached out to stroke his face, but she stopped herself when she realized she wasn't wearing her gloves.

"Is he dead?" Seventeen was scraping bark off his stiff arm.

"No, but that's no thanks to you." Nerron's voice was hoarse, like a toad's. He was surprised his burning throat managed to utter any words at all. "Remember this the next time you wonder whether you need me."

Will stirred.

"Really? Then why haven't we caught up with the Fairy yet?" Seventeen's voice sounded metallic when he got angry. "You're a lousy guide! Look at my sister."

Sister? Since when did mirrors have sisters?

Nerron leaned over Will and immediately forgot his own aching neck. Will's skin was turning pale green where the rope had chafed it.

Jade. More pure than the most precious amulet you could buy in the King's capital.

Nerron jumped back as Will sat up and coughed. The fingers touching his abraded skin were made of green stone. It was quickly spreading through his forehead and streaking down his

300

neck. Sixteen stared at Nerron, but Seventeen waved her away impatiently.

Nerron hardly noticed them disappearing among the trees.

He believed neither in the lava-spurting god the onyx worshipped in their black grottoes nor in his mother's malachite goddess. When he entered a church, he felt nothing, no matter which god was worshipped there. Even the sinister places of sacrifice found beneath Silver-Alders or by the ponds of Watermen made no impression on the Bastard. But the sight of jade in Will Reckless's skin gave him that shudder of reverence he'd only heard others describe. Jade Goyl. A good feeling when fairy tales came true. That was why he hunted treasure—for this very feeling. Wasn't it?

Will's eyes sought his. Eyes speckled with gold. The Pup—no longer a Pup—moved differently as he rose to his feet. Smooth, like a Goyl. One of them.

What now, Nerron? But he didn't want to think. He just wanted to look at him.

"They have the crossbow," Nerron said, though he no longer knew whether that was important.

"Do you know where they went?"

Nerron nodded.

The jade was still spreading. Will touched the stone glossing his cheek.

"I called it," he said. "And it came."

"Good," Nerron replied hoarsely.

It was all good.

301

43

LOST STORIES

For someone who didn't like to travel, Robert Dunbar had
packed his suitcase far too many times these past months. Lectures
in Bengal, Nihon, and now Tasmania. He doubted it made any
sense to be lecturing Albian history in a land where at least half
the people were force-shipped convicts. But Dunbar had accepted
the invitation in the hope he'd find a place here, at the end of the
world, where his father could live out the rest of his days in peace,
without being harassed and beaten for his Fir Darrig tail.

But his first days here had already made Dunbar doubtful
whether Tasmania was that place. They didn't even treat their own
Aboriginal people with much respect. He liked the weather (the fur
he'd inherited from his father's side bristled most uncomfortably
in Albion's damp climate), and it was good to be away from all the
things that were taken so seriously in Londra and Pendragon. But
he missed his books, Pendragon's libraries, the countless sources

of knowledge left there over the centuries for thirsty minds like his. Jacob's telegram had been a most painful reminder of that.

Alderelves. Even in Pendragon, Dunbar wouldn't have been sure where to start looking for their long-lost trails. Most of his fellow historians would have ridiculed him for even trying. It was like looking in earnest for forgotten gods: Zeus, Apollo, Odin, and Freya... Had they actually existed? Dunbar's answer was yes, most definitely, but he'd long stopped voicing such opinions. The odds of finding something about the Mirrorlings were certainly better. Jacob's description sounded as though Isambard Brunel had gotten the idea to create humans, and that he'd joined forces with the Alderelves to achieve that goal. That they called themselves Sixteen and Seventeen was encouraging. After all, that could mean there were at least fifteen more of them who may have left traces somewhere.

Back in Albion, Dunbar would've started his search for traces of the vanished Alderelves in Tintagel and Camelot. Those places housed the most comprehensive collection of literature on Arthur of Albion and the legends surrounding his life. Those stories were the only sources Dunbar knew of that mentioned Alderelves. Still, every historian who publicly believed the legendary King of Albion had actually been the son of a Fairy and an Elf made himself impossible among his peers. Most of them didn't even know Alderelves had been a very special kind of Elf. And as far as the mirror creatures were concerned, the librarian at the history department in Pendragon, who looked as though it had been decades since he'd last seen a ray of sunlight, would've pointed him toward the travel journal of a writer who had, almost a century ago, seen a silver woman in a field in Austry. And Dunbar could've recruited one of his botanical colleagues to examine the Alder that grew not far from the city wall and that was hung with centuries' worth of jewelry and trinkets. But... he was not in Albion. He was in Tasmania, and the library of the very new university of Parramatta was a thin and feeble offshoot of the repositories of printed treasures in Pendragon.

If only Jacob's latest telegram hadn't sounded so worried. Not like Jacob at all. Some of that worry must've shown on Dunbar's face as he stood among the sparsely stocked shelves of the university library.

"May I ask what you're looking for? You seem not to have found it." The librarian in front of him was holding an enormous pile of books between her arms and her chin. Her hair was gray (and looked as though she'd pinned it up rather hastily), but the smile she managed despite her heavy load would've been perfectly at home on the face of a twelve-year-old.

"No, but I admit the information I'm looking for would be hard to find even in the libraries back home. From your accent, I'm guessing you're also from Albion? Robert Dunbar."

She unloaded the books on a table to shake his hand, even though it was covered in gray fur.

"Jocelyn Bagenal. And, yes, I was born in Albion. I was brought here years ago by a ship. May I ask what you're looking for?"
"Reports of creatures made of mirrored glass, silver animals and people... Alderelves?" Dunbar added the last word very hesitantly. Most humans thought of Elves only as the finger-sized Grass Elves and Sand Elves, and his list already sounded silly enough.

"Ah-ha. Lost stories." Jocelyn Bagenal began sorting the pile of books onto nearby shelves: Albian colonial policy, the history of the Koori and Anangy, the mines of New-Cymru. A librarian. Or, as Dunbar liked to call members of her profession, a book

304

priestess. Miss Bagenal—Dunbar saw no wedding band on her finger—pushed the last book onto a shelf. "Fir Darrig?"

She'd even pronounced it right.

"Indeed."

"A distant relative of mine has some drops of Fir Darrig blood, but only enough to make his beard more pronounced." She pushed a strand of hair behind her ear. The pearl on her earring was, if Dunbar wasn't mistaken, a Caledonian naiad tear. "Maybe I can help. I collect lost stories. Lost, forgotten, misplaced…whichever. Whether from Albion or Immrama, from Nam Viet, Aotearoa, or Alberica. Everyone in Parramatta knows about Jocelyn Bagenal's strange books. And people keep bringing me more. Soon I'll have to limit myself to Dwarf editions. I have barely enough space left for my bed."

She scribbled an address on a piece of paper and offered it to Dunbar.

"After five and before ten."

Then she disappeared between the shelves, as though she'd only emerged from one of the books to offer him help.

She even moved like a twelve-year-old girl. Maybe even younger than that.

Dunbar looked at the paper.

Jocelyn Topanga Bagenal.

Maybe Parramatta was the right place after all.

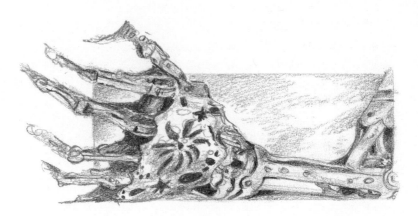

44

A New Hand

Chanute was in heaven. Age, death, all forgotten. He sat on Aleksei Baryatinsky's leather sofa practicing loading a pistol. With an arm and hand moved by sinews and joints of steel.

When Fox asked Sylvain how Chanute had paid for the new arm, he grinned like a child who'd executed a well-planned prank. "Sold my wristwatch. You should have seen the watchmaker's face. *Tabarnak*, I thought he was going to drop dead! And it was nothing but a cheap Rolex rip-off, but over here nobody would know that."

Jacob was going to kill him. No, he was going to quarter him first. Fox asked whether all his senses had gone the way of Baryatinsky's liquor. Sylvain replied with an injured frown and whispered that Albert Chanute needed a new hand, and to him, Sylvain Caleb Fowler, friendship was more important than any talk of two worlds that were best kept apart.

Maybe he was right.

Chanute laughed like a child when his new fingers managed to put the pistol back in its holster. It had been eight years since the Ogre had taken his arm.

"Look, *ma puce.*" Sylvain pulled a gilded medallion from his pocket. "The shop owner swore I just had to put a lock of my ex-wife's hair in it."

And then what? Fox took the medallion from Sylvain and held it to her nose. Always the vixen. And the vixen couldn't smell the faintest trace of magic. Sylvain watched her like a worried dog who'd just dropped his quarry at his master's feet. Then he took the medallion back, opened the window, and threw it into Baryatinsky's vegetable beds. The curses following it were elaborate enough to fill the entire palace to the rafters with Canadian obscenities. That done, Sylvain filled a water glass with the cinnamon-infused gorzalka that seemed to be everywhere in their host's palace and proceeded to immerse himself in the three-day-old copy of the *Londra Illustrated News* Chanute had found somewhere. The curlicued type gave him some trouble, but Sylvain read through every small item as though all the treasures of this world were to be found in that newspaper. Fox didn't have the heart to rob him of that illusion as well.

Outside, the lights of Moskva gave the night sky a grubby glow, and even the moons wore veils of human haze. But Fox didn't long to be elsewhere. The feelings flooding her heart had pushed aside the forests and the stars. She didn't want to know how long that would last. She didn't even want to give a name to the feelings.

"'The opening of the Londra Tunnel was marked without its builder, '" Sylvain read aloud. "'Isambard Brunel's illness seems

307

to be worse than the court will have us know.' Londra? Sounds like London. Is that what's it's called here?"

Fox shot him a warning glance.

She filled a glass with Baryatinsky's sweet port wine, though she'd already drunk too much of it, and reached for the book she'd been reading for a couple of hours without remembering a single word. It felt as if Orlando's touch had left a mark on her skin as clear as pollen dust on the vixen's fur. She was so happy. And so unhappy. It didn't help to remind herself of all the times she'd dusted some woman's talcum powder off Jacob's clothes or the times her nose had picked up strange perfumes on him.

Where was he?

When Chanute asked her for the third time to admire his new arm, Fox snapped at him so sharply that Sylvain shot her a nasty look over the top of his paper. Oh, to the Stilt with the both of them. To the Stilt with her. She wished she were back in Orlando's bed. She wished she'd never gone with him.

Sylvain was asking Chanute what a Man-Goyl was. Outside, a carriage was approaching. Fox heard the guards open the gate. How her heart pounded as she approached the window. Yet it wasn't Jacob climbing out of the carriage but Baryatinsky. Fox had given the perfume their host left in her room to her maid.

Sylvain got up for a refill, but Chanute's new hand was quicker on the bottle's neck. He gave Sylvain a triumphant smile, only to mutter a disappointed curse when the glass crushed between his steel fingers. Two servants immediately appeared to pick up the pieces, Sylvain blurted out an *"Oupelay!"* that made them flinch almost as much as Chanute's laughter, and the younger of the servants cut himself on the shards.

"Ayoye tabarnak!" Sylvain grunted as he dropped onto the sofa

308

next to Fox, sighing as though he'd just saved the world. "Nothing better could've ever happened to me than to end up in a cell with Jacob Reckless. To imagine I could've spent my entire life living in only one world."

Fox shot him another warning glance, and Sylvain pressed his hand over his mouth like a schoolboy caught in a lie, but that didn't dent his mood. Nothing in this or the other world could ever dent Sylvain's mood. Or at least he was good at giving that impression.

"Shall I tell you a secret?" he whispered to Fox.

She wasn't sure, but Sylvain didn't wait for her answer.

"Chanute and I will go to l'Arcadie! He's already bought maps and explained the route to me. It's a long journey, first on one of the river barges that take the pelt-hunters to Kamchatka, and then by ship to Alaska. Here they call it Alyeska. We're still arguing over how to continue from there. Chanute says we have to cross native territory and that they'll turn us both into marmots."

Fox looked across at Chanute. As far as she knew, he hadn't told Jacob about this plan.

"And when is this going to happen?"

Sylvain gave her a conspiratorial smile. "As soon as Jacob leaves Moskva. Chanute says you don't need him and he'd only be a third wheel. Well, he probably means fifth. He's not too good with numbers. If you ask me, I think he wishes you'd cancel the whole thing. He says that the Mirrorlings have only left you in peace because you've lost Jacob's brother and that Jacob won't admit even to himself how dangerous the whole thing is. And that everyone has to find their own path, even brothers. Well, you know Chanute better than I do—he doesn't really hold back his opinions."

309

And maybe he's even hoping his expedition might get Jacob to turn back. No, he knew his apprentice better than that. But Fox could already see Jacob's face when Chanute told him about his plans.

"When will he tell Jacob?"

Sylvain shrugged. "When the opportunity arises."

Chanute had the servant bring a new bottle of gorzalka. His eyes gleamed at Sylvain as his new fingers closed around its neck and lifted it without breaking it.

45

FROM HER

The moth settled on Kami'en's chest as he was reviewing a military parade with the Tzar—surrounded by Varangian generals and a bear wearing the same uniform as the soldiers marching below. Of course, he immediately recognized who'd sent the moth, but the images it brought only really registered when he heard the child's cry. Why had Niomee sent the moth? To take revenge on Amalie? To prove he'd suspected and betrayed her unjustly? All he could think was that maybe he hadn't lost her completely. And that his infant son was still alive.

After the parade, he immediately had a draftsman sketch what the moth had shown him: the river, the abbey, the nun holding the child. One of his officers thought he'd seen that building in Lotharaine, another in Lombardia, but Hentzau, after one quick look, shook his head.

"Bavaria."

It made sense. Bavaria was allied to Lotharaine, and its young King was related to Crookback. (They were all related to each other.) Not a stupid choice for a hiding place, but then again, nobody had ever called Therese of Austry stupid.

It couldn't be too hard to locate the abbey, but whom could he send to retrieve the child? Bavaria was enemy territory; even a unicorn would be less conspicuous than a Goyl. Hentzau's human spies thought the Moonstone Prince was a monster, a freak that should've never seen the light of day. Even his own officers shared this view.

Whom could he send?

There was only one answer.

Hentzau tried to argue him out of it. He reminded the Goyl King that Bavaria had given shelter to organizations calling for the complete eradication of all Goyl and Man-Goyl. But this just confirmed Kami'en's decision. Only one man would have a chance at retrieving the child unharmed. The King of the Goyl would have to bring his son home himself.

"What if it's a trap?" Hentzau asked. "It's her moth! Why should she care about the child except as an opportunity for revenge?"

Yes, why? Kami'en had no answer to that, not one Hentzau would have accepted.

He gave orders to prepare for his departure.

46
THE WRONG QUESTIONS

At night, Baryatinsky's palace looked even more enchanted than during the day. It would've been perfect for one of those glass globes that children shake to stir up a flurry of snow. There was no sign of Jacob's Goyl shadow when the Tzar's chauffeur dropped him by the gate. Wladimir Molotov had kept him for three hours, signing papers and reviewing the care instructions for the flying carpet. The curator had made no secret of how much he disapproved of the Tzar's decision to hand such a precious object to some dubious stranger who spoke with an Albian accent. Stealing the carpet would definitely have been more fun.

The gaslights patterned Baryatinsky's courtyard with the shadows of Dragons and Flying Horses, and for the first time since their arrival in Moskva, there was some real hope of finding Will. But Jacob was tired and in a foul mood. He was about to make an enemy of the Tzar, and then there was that promise he'd made so nobly in Schwanstein. What a fool he'd been! Such a damn fool. What had he been thinking? That he could just give her up, selflessly and virtuously... Was that at all like him?

"Jacob?" A figure came out of the shadows by the stairs that Baryatinsky had designed based on the heavenly steps depicted on Varangian icons.

Orlando Tennant.

Of all people.

"Oh no, Fox belongs only to herself." He'd as good as *invited* him to steal her. *Here, take my heart, I no longer need it.*

"Can I have a word?"

What about? Did the Windhound want to know whether he minded that Fox looked so happy? That she never missed an opportunity to savor the other man's name on her tongue?

Had he slept with her? *Stop it, Jacob.* But he could think of nothing else as he looked at Tennant's face. All the thoughts he hadn't allowed himself to think now smothered every last glimmer of reason.

"I assume you've heard of the present the Goyl have given the Tzar?"

There was a surprise. The Windhound hadn't come to discuss Fox.

"Heard, yes, but if you're hoping I'll tell you what it is..."

"I *know* what it is," Tennant interrupted him. "I'm supposed to steal it. But that means I've got to get into the secret wing of the Magic Collection. You were there today, weren't you?"

The Windhound. There was a reason Orlando Tennant had a reputation for being even crazier than Jacob.

"I only saw the doors. Forget it. Poisoned lacquer. Glass teeth. Knife-wire."

314

There was light in Fox's window, and the only thing Jacob wanted to discuss with Tennant was whether she'd spent the last night in his bed. He nearly asked him.

"I can handle knife-wire and glass teeth. But how do I get past the poisoned lacquer?"

"The Dwarfs have an explosive that can disable it. Officially they deny it, but if you offer them enough, they'll sell you some."

And the Windhound wouldn't be the first to kill himself with it. The stuff was more volatile than nitroglycerin. Jacob caught himself thinking Orlando Tennant was about to die young.

"Forget it!" Jacob said, as though that compensated for the satisfaction the thought of Tennant's death had given him.

"I can't forget it. The King's command. What about you?"

"We're leaving soon. I have an assignment from the Tzar." What was he doing now? Was he trying to brag to his rival? At least it wasn't a lie.

Tennant looked up at Fox's window. "I assume she's going with you? Jacob Reckless's loyal companion."

His tone answered the question Jacob had not dared to ask. Behind them, the guards were arguing with a deliveryman who'd come to the main gate instead of the servants' entrance.

"I would never have touched her if you yourself hadn't told me she was free."

The deliveryman was getting louder.

"It is as I told you. She *is* free."

Tennant eyed Jacob as if he'd lost his mind. "I'm very good at lying to other people," he said, "but not as good at lying to myself. A problem you very obviously don't have. I'm not sure I envy you that."

He looked over Jacob's shoulder.

315

Fox was standing at the top of the steps. She was smiling at the Windhound. Jacob had always thought that smile belonged to him alone.

"Chanute was about to go searching for you," she called to Jacob.

"He had a good reason for his long absence," Orlando replied. "I just learned you're going on a treasure hunt for the Tzar. Will you still have breakfast with me? There's a café on Woslki Square where they drizzle the pancakes with edible gold."

"Sure." Fox avoided looking at Jacob.

Gone. It didn't matter that he'd done it to protect her. Not a bit. She belonged to him. Why did such truths only reveal themselves after they'd become lies?

The guards called Orlando a taxi. The dogs licked his hands while he waited for it. The Barsoi. Fox stood and looked after the taxi, and with every step they then climbed together, Jacob remembered something he could've said or done that would've prevented the look she'd given Orlando. Oh yes, he was an idiot. He'd always been frightened by how much he needed her. And now it was too late.

Do you love him more than me? Jacob would rather have swallowed his tongue than actually asked that question, but he would've given his right hand for an answer.

"Have you ever heard of the Golden Yarn?" Fox asked.

"What's that supposed to be?"
She again looked out beyond the gate, as though she hadn't heard his question.

"The Tzar's giving us his most precious flying carpet. Maybe we can still find Will. We can leave soon." *In three days, at the earliest, Jacob.* It would take him at least that long to walk the spells into the carpet. Why did he not tell her? Because he wanted to see how much she minded leaving Moskva. He'd never hurt her willingly; this was the first time. Love didn't deserve the nice reputation it had.

"Good," said Fox. But she didn't mean it. She sounded sad. And guilty.

"Are you sure you want to come? He's *my* brother after all, not yours."

There was a moment when he thought she might actually say no. She stayed silent for a long while.

"So I can go retrieve your silver statue from some treasure chamber?" she finally said. It wasn't what she'd wanted to say.

She turned around.

"Let's find Will," she said over her shoulder. "What happens after that, we'll see."

47

A MESSAGE FOR CELEST AUGER

The carpet was delivered the next morning, as promised. Even though Baryatinsky's guest bedrooms were at least as big as The Ogre's taproom, Jacob still had to move some furniture to be able to unroll it even partway. Before locking himself away with the carpet for three days and three nights, he treated himself to a sumptuous breakfast in their host's dining hall. The portraits on the walls showed men in bearskin coats and turbans of embroidered silk, some faces as pale as Dragon bone and some as dark as night-wood. Baryatinsky's ancestors (if that's who they were) showed the diversity of Varangia. And its enormous size. It was better to philosophize about that than stare at the empty chair where Fox usually sat at breakfast. Pancakes with edible gold...

Jacob was sipping his third cup of mocha when Chanute and Sylvain joined him. But he didn't feel like talking, and the way the other two looked at the empty chair was too much. Every thought of Will or the Alderelf seemed to fade against the smile Fox had given the Windhound. *"What happens after that, we'll see."* He kept hearing her say it all the way back to his room. *"What happens after that, we'll see."*

He bolted his door and sat down on the carpet. Time to leave the present behind. Only the past could induce the carpet to carry him to Will. The past was not a place to which Jacob liked to return, but on this morning, it was a refuge from the thoughts and feelings he didn't want to think or feel.

Once upon a time, Jacob...

Memories. How did they get stored in the mind? Why did he remember that particular day with Will in the park, when there'd been so many more? Why did he remember that one quarrel or that one laugh as though it had happened yesterday, but other moments eluded him, even though he could recall their emotions? So little was left of all the weeks, months, years. *"My brother likes to fight."* Some things were preserved in the words used to frame them. Or in a touch. Will's hand in his, when they were both younger; the knock on his bedroom door when Will couldn't sleep; the jealousy, the rage, when he had to let him tag along; the impatience with the younger one...

Remember, Jacob.

But what came were the wrong images. The first traces of jade, their fight in the cage, their struggle in the palace in Vena, the Blood Wedding, Will at Kami'en's side, Man-Goyl.

"He has a skin of stone."

No. Jacob forced himself to go back further. He needed images from the other world, of the Will he'd known better than himself. Jacob closed his eyes. He found the way back through the mirror, saw Will in a room full of plush animals and toys. Brothers together in the school yard. In the corner store, where the owner sold cigarettes to a twelve-year-old Jacob if he promised to send his regards to their mother. Will had always tried to keep him out of that store.

Then.

Will looked so much like her. They were so similar. No, that wasn't true. The images came faster, and again they were images he hadn't wanted to recall. They wove themselves into the carpet's fibers until Jacob was sitting on his childhood. And then there was an image that made his heart stumble. He had no idea where it had come from, but it was as clear as the others: Spieler in their living room, with the same face Jacob had seen when he'd come to on the Alderelf's island. His mother was standing next to the Elf, close, like how one stood with good friends. The image came so suddenly, Jacob involuntarily looked around. Could Spieler put fake memories in his mind? But if it was real, why hadn't he recognized the face when Spieler had shown it to him? Because for all these years it hadn't meant anything, one face of many, his mother's friends—did a child really study them? Because Spieler only ever visited when he and Will were not at home?

Jacob got up and pushed open the window.

Sylvain was standing by the stables. Fox was with him.

She was back.

How long had he been sitting on the carpet? No matter. Orlando wasn't with her. Ridiculous how relieved that made him feel.

He had enough memories of Fox to feed all the flying carpets in the world. *Your brother, Jacob. Think of Will. Or do you want the carpet to take you to Fox?*

He closed the window, and the scents of the past again flooded the room, like a bunch of wilted flowers.

320

He sat on the carpet.

Closed his eyes. And remembered the night when the Goyl injured Will. No!

Someone knocked on his door.

Jacob had told the servants he didn't want to be disturbed. Was it Chanute wanting to show him a trick with his new hand? Had Sylvain again bought some fake magic? Or was it Fox?

He opened the door, hoping to see her face.

The corridor was empty.

"Too high!" a woman's voice said.

The Dwarf looking up at him was as beautiful as the dolls in Amalie's collection. No, she was more beautiful.

"Jacob Reckless?" she asked. "Ludmilla Akhmatova. May I speak with you in private? I have a request from a friend, and I'd rather explain that request behind closed doors."

Fox had told Jacob about the Dwarf spy, but the image he'd had in his mind didn't do her justice. Ludmilla Akhmatova looked as though she had a world of memories to feed to the flying carpet. She waved Jacob into the salon where Baryatinsky's servants served afternoon tea. There was a salon for every meal, as there was for each of Baryatinsky's countless hobbies, as well as three music salons, one each for his butterfly and weapons collections, and five (Sylvain had counted them) containing mementos of lost loves.

Ludmilla Akhmatova waited until Jacob had closed the door behind them.

"I come at the request of Orlando Tennant," she said, plucking the leather gloves off her fingers. "He wanted me to ask you to deliver a certain message. He's probably hoping you can find a way to make it sound less upsetting than it unquestionably is."

"And who is the message for?"

"Mademoiselle Celeste Auger. Orlando is asking you to tell her he can't take her to the ballet tonight."

Messenger boy for Fox's lover. Jacob had no idea the Windhound had such a vicious sense of humor.

"Orlando suggests urgent matters of state as an excuse," Ludmilla Akhmatova continued. "He believes it best if Mademoiselle Auger only learns the true reason once she no longer has occasion to do anything rash."

"Rash? That doesn't sound like Mademoiselle Auger. May I know what the true reason is?"

The Dwarf smiled a sad smile.

"Orlando's been arrested. The Tzar has decreed he shall face a firing squad at dawn." Her composure was a front. It was obvious Ludmilla Akhmatova had done a lot of crying, though she'd tried to hide it behind her makeup.

Jacob wasn't sure what he was feeling, and maybe he didn't really want to know.

"I warned him," he said. "But I admit I myself am not very good at heeding the warnings of others."

Ludmilla Akhmatova took a handkerchief from her bag. It was barely bigger than a calling card. "The man Orlando was trying to free—Isambard Brunel—is invaluable to Albion's interests, and Orlando had little time. Our informants had told us the Tzar wasn't going to use his precious prisoner to further Varangian progress, as the Goyl had expected, but instead was going to have him executed. And it's quite understandable. Brunel's "gift" was responsible for Varangia's defeat by Albion."

The gift of the Goyl . . .

That's what happened when minds got muddled by Alderelves

and jealousy. How often had Jacob heard in the past few days that Isambard Brunel's failure to appear in public was due to some illness, and he still hadn't managed to put two and two together?

"Where are they holding Orlando?"

"The same place from which he tried to free Brunel. In the secret wing of the Magic Collection." Ludmilla blew her nose, the only expression of emotion she allowed herself. "Orlando managed to open the door—I procured some explosive for the poison lacquer—but it closed behind him and raised the alarm."

The knife-wire. Obviously, Orlando hadn't quite known how to handle it.

"I'll miss him." Ludmilla dabbed a speck of mascara off her cheek. The women of this world still mixed their own beauty products. Some lamp soot, a few drops of elder juice... And there was, of course, the option to have a Witch conjure thicker lashes.

"There's never been a better spy than Orlando Tennant," Ludmilla Akhmatova continued. "Or a better dancer. It's only fitting he'll be executed together with the best engineer of this world. But I'm sorely disappointed in our Tzar. I thought he had more respect for talent."

The painting next to the door depicted a naval battle. Like many of Baryatinsky's paintings, it was fine enough that it could've been part of any museum's collection. It reminded Jacob of another sea battle. Only a few months earlier, the Goyl's airplanes had sunk this world's first iron ship into the Great Channel, yet in the shipyards of Goldsmouth, they were already building three new ones, all designed by Isambard Brunel. Thanks to Brunel, Londra had underground trains, and its iron bridges were wider and more graceful than any other city's. Nobody stood for the New Magic more than the man who called himself Isambard Christophorus

Brunel. He had proven himself worthy of his name, which was like an echo of Jacob's world.

Ludmilla Akhmatova had herself under control again.

Jacob wondered why she still spied for Albion. Madame Akhmatova didn't seem like someone who did things for reasons other than her convictions.

She glanced at the closed door and whispered, "We shall, of course, try to free Orlando and Brunel. If we succeed, we'll hide them in the Volodj Quarter until things settle down. A lot of Wolflings live there, so not even the secret police dare to search the houses. We have a trash collector who'll get them there unnoticed. Trash collectors are everywhere after nightfall."

Why did she tell him all this? After nightfall...

"You're trying *tonight*?"

"When else? Orlando will be dead tomorrow morning. And Brunel probably, too."

"How many helpers do you have?"

"Two."

Two? To break into the secret wing of the Magic Collection? Impossible!

"I assume at least one of them knows how to handle protective spells?"

Ludmilla Akhmatova looked up and smiled. Ah, yes. A message for Celeste Auger. Maybe Orlando really had sent the Dwarf, but that wasn't the only reason she'd come.

"No." Jacob raised his hands. "Orlando and I are just acquaintances." And these past few days he'd wished him worse than a cell, but that was none of her business.

"Then help us for Albion. It is your home, isn't it?"

"Even so. Do I look like someone who'd happily die for King

and country?"

Yet if he helped Ludmilla, it would prove to Fox he didn't wish Orlando dead. *You do wish him dead, Jacob.*

The Dwarf smiled again.

"Thank you," she said, pulling the gloves over her tiny fingers. "I was certain you'd help us. And that you wouldn't do it for King and country. One o'clock, in front of the Academy. It's right behind the Magic Collection."

Jacob opened the door.

And looked at Sylvain.

"It was Chanute's idea!" Sylvain defended himself. "He knew the two of you were having an interesting conversation. *Et voilà!* You will need a diversion."

48

THE DRESS OF WAR

The rhythm of his heartbeat had changed. Will felt it as clearly as the pain on his neck. The daylight stung his eyes. Just like it used to. Why was he less afraid now? Because he'd been through it before? No. This was different. *He* was different. He didn't fight it. He let it happen.

He had called the stone. Out of fear or rage, it didn't matter. He.

The robbers hadn't even tried to cover their tracks. Why should they? They thought he and the Bastard were dead. They followed the bandits' trail deeper into the forest, until they came upon a house. Its pale blue paint was weathered; moss and rot had settled into the wood carvings around the roof and windows. A wooden pavilion stood among overgrown flower beds like a skeleton of pleasures long past. The empty bottles and gnawed bones were probably from the new owners, just like the bear's head with bared fangs that hung above the door. The paws were nailed to the doorposts.

"Oh my, ghost guardians, how touching!" Nerron whispered to Will. "They probably buried the heart under the threshold. If the bear appears, don't worry—he can't do anything. In Lotharaine, they do the same with cats and dogs. I've never understood it. If I were a ghost, why would I guard the ones who'd killed me?"

Something moved behind one of the windows. They heard screams. One of the grimy windowpanes exploded, and a bullet struck the fence post next to them. The robbers had taken their guns, but Nerron still had his knife, and Will discovered a rusty hatchet in the grass.

They entered through a back door into a filthy kitchen. The robbers never got to the weapons on the table. Will and Nerron found them in the next room, six silver corpses on a moth-eaten rug. Will stared at them in disbelief. The same ragged men who'd tied the ropes around their necks were now shimmering sculptures, every hair frozen in precious metal. He looked at Nerron, who didn't seem very surprised.

Outside, a horse whinnied. It sounded shrill, frightened. Will went to one of the grimy windows. Next to the five frantic horses were three more corpses. There were two shapes leaning over them that mirrored the overgrown garden and the weathered house. Will flinched when one of them looked over at the window. It was a girl with eyes of glass; her face was a reflection of the sky above her, but as she approached the house, the gray clouds turned to skin.

"Ah, so now you've finally seen them." Nerron cut some silver hair off one of the dead bodies and tucked it in his pocket. "In case they fail to introduce themselves properly—the boy calls

327

himself Seventeen, but Sixteen may look a little more familiar."

Yes, she did. The girl who appeared in the smashed-down doorway looked so human she could've been the one living in this house. And Will knew her face from his dreams. Except for the rash on her left cheek. Sixteen hid it with her hand when she noticed him looking at it.

"What are you doing?" The boy who appeared next to her in the doorway was still a moving mirror. He pulled Sixteen aside and whispered something to her, but she didn't take her eyes off Will. Her glass eyes.

The boy was carrying the crossbow. He approached Will and placed it in front of his feet. Seventeen. His arms were sprouting leaves. He plucked them off with his fingers.

"You have to forget you ever saw us," he said to Will. "Sixteen isn't supposed to show herself to you. We are here for your protection, nothing else. We make sure you can do what you came here to do."

"Really? Well, I have to say, you're not doing it very well." Nerron picked up the crossbow and handed it to Will. "Who cut him off that rope? You?"

Seventeen's face turned silver. Nerron groaned with pain as the blades on the Mirrorling's fingers poked into his chest. "You promised to find the Fairy. What about that? You'd better find her soon, Stone-skin, you hear? Very soon."

Silver turned to glass again. "He can make himself completely invisible. Am I right, Seventeen?" Nerron reached out and waved through the air. "You can't even feel them. They're an idea, nothing else. A dark thought."

Sixteen was still standing in the doorway, her hand on her cheek. "He's gone, Stoneface," she said.

Then she turned into glass, like her brother. If that's what he was.

Nerron took a silver piece of bread off one of the dead and threw it through the window, cursing. He seemed only a little reassured that there was no reaction.

Will climbed over the solidified corpses and went to stand where Sixteen had just been. Why had she been in his dreams? He forced himself to think of another face. Clara. But he could only picture her in the hospital bed, so alien and still. He pulled the swindlesack from under one of the bodies—and stared at his own hand. Skin. He touched his bruised neck. The stone was gone. The disappointment was so strong that the Goyl could read it on his face.

"'And he wore the jade only as his war dress.' That's how my mother always ended her stories of the Jade Goyl," Nerron said. "I always wondered what that meant. I'm sure the skin will return when you need it."

Will stroked his soft hand. He wanted the stone back, but he hated himself for wanting it. Was he betraying her again? *Clara. Think her name, Will. Clara.* When had he last thought of her? He no longer even dreamed of her. He was forgetting her, like he had before.

"Everything will be just as it was meant to be."

"Let's turn around," the Goyl said behind him. "Who cares about the Fairy? The Jade Goyl is back! We'll wait for the next rain, lose your guards, and disappear. A few more wet days and you won't be able to pick those two from a row of trees. No loss, if you ask me."

Turn around? No.

Will shook his head. "I have to find the Fairy. I promised."

329

"Promised? Shall I remind you of another promise? You swore an oath to Kami'en, and Kami'en is in Moskva, barely three days' ride from here."

"The crossbow doesn't belong to Kami'en."

"Really. And to whom does it belong?"

"The one who made it."

"Is that so? You seem to know him quite well. What do they look like, the lost Elves?"

Elves? Was that what he was, the stranger from the hospital? Will pulled the swindlesack over the crossbow.

"I don't know him. I've only seen him once. You think he sent those two?"

"Who? Our silver friends?" The Goyl rubbed his chest. "I don't want to talk about them. You never know where they are. And they're quite spiteful." Nerron's lizard jacket had turned silver where Seventeen had poked his chest. There was also a damp spot. Will remembered Goyl blood had no color.

"Hey, you filthy, glassy brood!" Nerron shouted. "Soulless Mirrorlings!" He looked around and spat. "Looks like they're really not here. Probably scraping some bark off their limbs."

Silver. Silver and glass. *What does that remind you of, Will?*

Nerron planted himself in front of Will. He grabbed the boy's chin to keep him from averting his face. "Stop that. I want to see your eyes. What did they promise you? Why are you playing errand boy for them?"

Will shoved him away and reached for—what? He could almost feel the hilt of the saber between his fingers. His shoulder remembered the thrust.

The Bastard flinched.

His eyes told Will the jade was back even before he could see

330

it on his own hands. The Goyl smiled.

"What about the girl?" Will tucked the swindlesack under his shirt. "Sixteen... She looks sick."

"Her?" Nerron laughed. "Sounds like she showed you the right face. The Fairy curse? The Silver-Alders? You've got no idea what I'm talking about, do you? Just forget about it. I'll let them explain, or else they'll turn me into one of these." He nudged one of the dead robbers with his boot. Then he turned his back on Will and carried on plundering the corpses.

"*I'll let them explain.*"

Will stepped outside.

The overgrown garden was filled with the stillness of death. He touched his face and found stone and skin. The jade was fading again. It was coming and going like a fever. His war dress. The daylight still hurt his eyes, and he could sense the depths beneath the damp grass. The womb of the earth. He'd missed that knowledge.

No.

He must forget again. Just like he'd forgotten before. For Clara, for himself. The jade wasn't a part of him, no matter how much it felt like it was, even more so than before. It was a curse. A curse. A curse. *You've been hexed, Will.* That word had scared him so much as a child. Hexed.

He felt a warm breeze even though the sun was little more than a pale coin behind gray clouds.

Sixteen was standing at the bottom of the brittle steps, barely visible, just the outline of a body.

"You'll never find the Fairy, will you?"

The bark was already growing on her arm. Will remembered the day he'd found the first traces of stone on his skin, the horror, the disgust. It had passed. Maybe that was the worst thing about

331

it.

"Look how ugly she's making me." Sixteen peeled the bark from her arm. Blood, like liquid glass, ran down her hand. "But her magic makes *you* just more beautiful. Why?"

"Sixteen."

She turned around.

For a brief moment, Will thought he saw Jacob's face on Seventeen.

"Leave him be." The bird in Seventeen's hand was as silver as the corpses. "We have to move. You're just holding him back."

Sixteen hesitated. Will felt she wanted to protest. Her face flushed with silver as if in anger. But then she stepped back and became the grass and the sky, the weathered pavilion, the overgrown garden.

Will saw her again in his dreams the next night. And the night after that. But now she also showed herself to him during the day. Whenever he turned, she was there, like a flower of glass and silver. But there was more bark, and more colorless blood on her skin.

And Will rode faster.

"You'll never find the Fairy, will you?"

He had to find her.

As though only now did he really know why.

No, Will.

For Clara. He still did it only for Clara. He repeated it to himself, over and over, but Clara's face had turned into silver and glass.

49

HOME

CAUTION! DOGS!

When he saw the sign on the fence on the northern edge of Parramatta, Robert Dunbar was tempted to order the taxi driver to turn around. Beyond the fence, he could see the kind of house found all over Tasmania, an adventurous mix of wood, stone, and wrought iron. The white struts of the terrace and the iron borders under the roof reminded Dunbar of the sugar icing on the houses of Witches. The houses were shipped as kits from Albion, halfway around the world, to make a strange land feel like home. Under the wide blue sky and surrounded by eucalyptus trees, they'd quickly become part of that strange land.

Dunbar cursed his myopic eyes as he tried to see whether there were indeed dogs lurking under the flowering bushes in front of the house. Too many evenings spent reading in dim light... Soon enough he'd be as blind as a bat (of which there were irritatingly

333

many in Tasmania). Fir Darrig didn't get along too well with dogs, but Dunbar reminded himself of how much Jacob had risked when he'd rescued him from the drunken sailors. He opened the gate. The barks and yelps that greeted him as he climbed the steps to the front door almost made him turn around after all, but then he lifted his hand and knocked. There were four dogs, ranging in size from sand-mouse to brown wolf, and they painted their excitement in streaks of drool on his clothes. Their mistress called them off. Dunbar had to admit that none of them seemed particularly frightening.

Jocelyn Bagenal seemed not to be as tidy as librarians usually were, at least in Dunbar's experience. The room he entered resembled the lab of the archaeological institute in Pendragon, where the staff kept all the pieces of pottery, crafted objects, and strange weapons they'd stolen from all over the world. (Dunbar didn't have a high opinion of archaeologists.) Jocelyn Bagenal's collection was at least as diverse. Dunbar spotted a bran-kettel from Eire (which Miss Bagenal had clearly used for cooking—the archaeologists would have crucified her for that), Stilt-spindles from Bavaria, bufana-pots from Lombardia (here used as flowerpots), a Varangian Dragon-samovar, and a spear from Tilafegia.

"I know," Jocelyn Bagenal said, frowning at her treasures. "Travel mementos, terrible dust traps, but I simply can't get myself to lock them behind glass. I don't want to just look at them. How can you understand something without touching it every now and then?"

An interesting theory. Dunbar wasn't sure he agreed. He remembered a snapping box from Caledonia that had nearly taken off one of his hands when he'd given in to the temptation to touch it. Dunbar was curious to see how Jocelyn Bagenal kept her books. The long corridor down which she now led him was filled with hot and stuffy Tasmanian air, and the door at the end was decorated with a thief-deterring mask from Nihon.

Home... There was no place in the world Dunbar really considered home, but whenever he stepped into a room full of books, that word did come to mind. Jocelyn Bagenal's collection of lost stories was one of the most wondrous book places Robert Dunbar had ever entered. In the center of the room stood a weathered wooden signpost with countless arms. It looked as though she'd stolen it from a highway crossing, but the inscriptions seemed to be hers. Dunbar saw the names of existing lands and places, but also those of mythical cities, sunken islands, forgotten oceans. Many of the names were also written on the shelves, so that the reading traveler wouldn't get lost, because Jocelyn Bagenal's collection was sorted by country.

Oh, the temptation to spend a few days in this treasure chamber! Dunbar found it hard to remember he'd come here with a mission. With a heavy heart, he ignored the yellow shelf for Tasmania and the blue-green planks from which Aotearoa whispered its stories. The information he was after was probably hidden in the stories of the Old World. Albion was fittingly stored on a bright green shelf. The green for Caledonia was a little darker. Helvetia was on pale gray, Bolanda on blue. Dunbar found fairy tales from Leon, legends from Sveriga and Norga, folk tales from Hellas, but there were also travel journals, newspapers, biographies of explorers and adventurers, diaries, illuminated atlases, and nature guides. Many of the books looked well read, some little more than a collection of loose pages, but the breadth of the collection was as impressive as its order. Dunbar found the system much more stimulating than that of the historic library of Pendragon.

335

"I like that expression on your face!" Jocelyn Bagenal straightened a few stray spines. "A little better organized than the rest of the house, isn't it? Remind me—what are we looking for?"

One of the dogs snuck through the door, but not even that could dampen Dunbar's joy.

"Creatures of mirrored glass who can turn things and beings into silver with their touch. And how to protect yourself from them. A friend of mine had a very unpleasant encounter with such creatures."

"Encounter? Intriguing." Dunbar thought he detected a trace of sadness in Jocelyn Bagenal's voice, perhaps because she'd never had such an encounter.

"Mirror, mirror on the wall," she mumbled. "No, probably not. But I think I know where we should look. Didn't you mention something else? Alderelves?"

Dunbar nodded. Librarians. He'd never met one with a bad memory. He had a theory that words stuck to their minds like flies to flypaper.

"King Arthur's father... That kind of Elf?"

"Exactly."

Jocelyn Bagenal cast a doubtful glance along her shelves. "That is the most lost of all stories. I fear my books may not be old enough for that. But...let's try."

50

The Gift of the Goyl

No lies. Jacob hadn't forgotten his promise to Fox, nor the night on which he'd made it. But he also remembered the Bluebeard's blood chamber and her silver face. The Magic Collection was not the hut of a Baba Yaga, but it was still a dangerous place, and he couldn't bear the thought of having to be afraid for her, even if it was her lover he was risking his own skin for.

He mixed the sleeping powder into the pea puree Baryatinsky's cook had prepared to go with the stuffed pheasant. The apothecary had assured him the powder would make a person sleep for at least twenty hours without feeling any after effects. If that was true, then the Windhound would be free by the time Fox woke up — or Jacob would be in prison with him, or dead. To Jacob, the latter seemed the most likely scenario.

Chanute and Sylvain were so enthusiastically preparing for their roles in the nocturnal rescue mission that it was almost worrying. Just a few blocks from the Magic Collection was a park with a music pavilion and a stage for concerts for Moskva's high society—a credible target for one of the anarchist arson attacks that happened all the time all over town. And the pavilion was in the center of the park, so the fire would, hopefully, be controlled before it could spread to any of the surrounding residences.

Sylvain was so excited by the idea of playing an anarchist that he had Baryatinsky's stable boys write down every slogan they'd ever seen smeared on a wall in Moskva. Jacob even caught him painting one of those slogans across the wall of their host's pigsty, after which Sylvain proudly recounted all the buildings in New York City on which he'd left his mark. Sylvain Caleb Fowler was full of surprises.

He and Chanute had agreed that Chanute should be the arsonist while Sylvain would smear his slogans on the statues in the park as well as on some of the surrounding buildings. Jacob had to listen as Chanute recounted in great detail how a drunk patron once set fire to his wooden prosthesis and how much safer a metal arm was for such tasks. They could only hope they'd all survive the night. While they waited for nightfall, Jacob wished he and Fox had left with the carpet before the Windhound managed to get himself caught.

It wasn't the first time Jacob had broken into a magical collection. The invisibility slime of a snail had gotten him into the Chambers of Miracles in Vena. He'd asked Ludmilla whether there were such snails to be had in Moskva, but she'd just given him a pitying smile and whispered, "I'll bring something better." The Dwarf had also promised to take care of the Goyl shadow who was still keeping vigil outside Baryatinsky's palace.

Fox had gone to bed hours earlier (the powder worked very

quickly), but the sky was still summer-night bright when a very apologetic servant brought Jacob a telegram that had arrived earlier that morning.

It was from Dunbar.

```
Mention of silvered animals in lotharainian travel
journal STOP More than 130 years old STOP Glass
assassins with many faces in tales from Cymru
and Helvetia STOP Turn to trees in moonlight STOP
Weapons useless STOP Invulnerable STOP Cymru hero
finds safety on damp earth STOP Helvetia hero
escapes into water STOP No mention of Alderelves
but stories of human emissaries from immortals
STOP Remember I'm quoting fairy tales and dubious
travel journals STOP Best advice stay clear of
mirrorlings STOP Don't want you and vixen silver
statues STOP Regards from other side of earth
```

"Stay clear." Jacob wished he could follow Dunbar's advice.

Moskva's many church bells were chiming midnight when Jacob entered Fox's room to make sure she was still asleep. The apothecary had not promised too much. Outside, Chanute and Sylvain were sneaking through the gate like two boys planning a nighttime prank. Seeing Chanute like that felt good after the old man had asked Jacob to proofread the inscription for his tombstone: *Albert Chanute. Treasure Hunter. Still Hunting.* This night could earn Chanute a grave in Moskva, but if it came to that, it'd be a death much more to the old hunter's liking than dying in a bed in Schwanstein.

The feather on Fox's nightstand was not the one Jacob had used to trick the Baba Yaga. It was a quill feather from a wild goose. Fox turned her head in her sleep, and Jacob wished he could see who she was dreaming of.

339

Really, Jacob?

He stroked her sleeping face. Why couldn't he just leave the Windhound where he was? Even Fox would never have asked Jacob to risk his neck for Orlando. But she would also never forgive him if he let the other man die without giving her the chance to save him. And if the Barsoi died, Jacob would spend the rest of his life wondering whether Fox could've been happy with Orlando.

Ludmilla Akhmatova kept her promise. No Goyl shadow in front of Baryatinsky's gate. Beggars, drunks, flower girls, crowds of nobles and officers on their way to balls or nightly card games, or to one of the city's countless pleasure houses. Peddlers on every street corner, bear tamers, soothsayers, but the closer Jacob got to the Magic Collection, the quieter the streets became. There'd been some talk of moving the Collection inside the walls of the Kremlin; luckily, that had not yet happened. It would've made their nightly venture even more hopeless.

The palace that housed Varangia's magic treasures was surrounded by government buildings and schools, all of which were completely dark at this hour. Jacob climbed out of his taxi. Ludmilla Akhmatova was waiting in a side street. She was almost invisible in her black dress. The Dwarf by her side introduced himself, whispering a name that was familiar to Jacob, as was his bearded face. Basil Sokolsky… an artist who performed in Moskva's biggest circus. Jacob had admired Sokolsky's daredevil acrobatics when the circus had toured Albion. In the circus tent, Sokolsky called himself the Fly, and it was not hard to guess what task Ludmilla had in mind for him that night.

"Reckless?" he repeated after she'd introduced Jacob. "You are the treasure hunter for whom that Dwarf trader in Terpevas

340

has offered one kilo of gold."

One kilo? Anyone who knew Evenaugh Valiant knew he would never pay out such a reward, but Jacob still felt flattered. His old enemy-turned-friend-turned-enemy was obviously still bitter about how Jacob had tricked him in the Dead City.

Ludmilla listened to the night.

The bells of the fire brigade echoed through the empty streets.

She gave Jacob an appreciative smile. "Your friends are very punctual."

"And where is your second helper?" Jacob whispered back. Not that one more would make their venture any more likely to succeed.

At that moment, the answer came ambling down the street. A man revealed what he was not only by his size but by his gait. A Wolfling. Some very successful treasure and bounty hunters were Wolflings. Jacob had met a number of them. They could call their fur like Fox, but Wolflings were shape-shifters by birth, and unlike Fox, they had to shift every day to keep control over the Wolf. Wolflings who didn't shift regularly ended up as werewolves, forever howling at the moon. Ludmilla hadn't mentioned a Wolfling as part of her plan, and Jacob was especially glad Fox wasn't with them. She'd killed a Wolfling some years ago. They could supposedly scent that.

The Wolfling didn't introduce himself. In that respect, his kind were like Fairies and Witches—they liked to keep their names secret. He greeted the Dwarfs with a silent nod, and then his pale yellow eyes rested on Jacob. In some countries, mothers drowned their babies if they were born with wolf eyes. But in Varangia, they were treated with respect. After all, even the Tzars claimed to have descended from wolves and bears.

341

"It's working. The guards wouldn't notice if an army marched through their gate," the Wolfling whispered. His voice was so rough it was easy to imagine it turning into a wolf's growl. "You should see them. They're craning their necks as though they're trying to look over the roofs. Now we can only hope our heroic firefighters are not too quick about fighting that fire."

Ludmilla Akhmatova reached into her coat pocket and handed each of them something that looked like a dusty ball of wool.

Sokolsky looked at it with incredulous awe. "A night skin," he whispered. "Woven from the spiderwebs on a Baba Yaga's fence."

"And as hard to find as a three-headed eagle," the Wolfling murmured. "How did you get four of them?"

"I once had an admirer who traded in these," Ludmilla answered. She began to pluck hers apart. The cloak she unfurled made her invisible. A strange sight, how they disappeared one by one into the night. Only the Fly tucked his night skin into his pocket. He said it would just hinder him, and his small size made him almost invisible anyway.

"Forgive the question, but did you give one of these to Orlando?" Sokolsky asked.

"Yes, and it got him past the guards," Ludmilla replied, "but it couldn't help him with the door to the secret wing. Gospodin Reckless is here so we won't run into the same problem."

Jacob could only hope he wouldn't disappoint her trust.

The plan was to scale the rear of the palace. Hopefully, the noise from the fire brigades would keep the guards from doing their rounds for a while. The rope used to climb up to the second floor would not be invisible. It was not the first time Jacob was grateful that alarm systems were still a far-off idea in this world. The walls surrounding the palace were secured with iron spikes.

342

Sokolsky plucked them from the stone like flowers. The only metal stronger than a Dwarf was silver, and most builders were careless enough to skimp on that expense.

Chanute and Sylvain had done a thorough job. The guards didn't even look around when the Fly landed in the courtyard. The night was filled with the noise of carriages and excited voices. Jacob hoped Chanute wasn't enjoying himself so much that he'd land in prison. One nighttime rescue mission was enough.

Sokolsky truly lived up to his stage name. Seeing the Fly climb up a wall really was like watching an insect. The barred windows on the second floor were as little an obstacle to his Dwarf hands as the spikes in the walls. The others were hidden so perfectly by their night skins that they had to keep whispering to each other to avoid grabbing the rope at the same time. The Wolfling was just starting to climb when one of the guards recalled his duties. He nearly ran into Jacob, who was waiting at the bottom of the wall, but thanks to the night skin, the guard noticed neither him nor the rope he was hiding with his body. Invisible. Jacob had never liked the feeling, even though he'd experienced it often enough in his line of work.

Ludmilla's spies had discovered that since Tennant had so easily reached the door to the secret wing, the Tzar had put greyhounds on guard in the collection. The dogs pricked their ears as Jacob climbed through the window, but the Wolfling just had to shed his night skin and they immediately came to him like lapdogs.

They were now in the hall with the magic eggs. Jacob appreciated getting a second look at them without Molotov's dusty voice in his ear. Some were barely bigger than chicken's eggs; others would've made an ostrich proud. The shells were made of gold enamel, and, depending on their size, they contained gardens,

343

forests, or entire exotic islands. The goldsmith who'd created these eggs, Hiskias Augustus Jacobs, had reputedly learned his craft from mine sprites, and his descendants were still the exclusive goldsmiths to the Tzar. Jacob was sorely tempted to steal one of these masterpieces for Fox—she would love having a forest to carry in her pocket—but the eggs were so famous they'd always be recognized as stolen.

The next room contained the item Jacob needed to disable the knife-wire: a melting ax from Nihon, forged to the same perfection as the swords from that country. Molotov had gone into great detail about how the ax had come to be in the Tzar's possession, but he'd had no idea of its power.

Jacob only paid attention to the external safeguards of the glass case. His mind was too preoccupied with the thoughts it was trying not to think. He himself had often advised archivists about the tiny Hemlock-Flies who liked to bore into the wooden parts of magical objects. He felt the first sting as soon as he reached into the case. The effects were loss of balance and even unconsciousness. *Well done, Jacob!* The hand holding the ax was already swelling. He could only hope his body would resist the poison until they were done.

The others were already in the room with the magical creatures. The Wolfling was staring at the cage with the Gray Wolf.

"Once we have the prisoners, we should free him," Jacob whispered. "We should free them all. They'll distract the guards and help us get away."

Ludmilla didn't like the idea. Jacob could see her fear of the growling and screeching creatures. But she was smart enough to know the Wolfling would never leave without the Gray Wolf—and Jacob owed it to Fox to free the others.

The doors where Molotov's tour had ended still showed signs of the explosives Ludmilla had procured for Orlando. Jacob wondered what Orlando had used to disable the knife-wire. The ax melted it without triggering the alarm, and the rest was easy, as the explosives had damaged the other safeguards. Jacob tucked the ax into his backpack before opening the door. If they got caught, the theft of a magical ax would be the least of their problems.

There were many in Varangia who were wary of all progress and who demanded a return to the good old times. The Tzar was a moderate among that group. The secret wing of his Magic Collection was a reminder that those old times had not been all good. Its windowless walls hoarded the past like dirt, and the cages didn't hide their purpose behind gilded decor. The greyhounds tucked their tails between their legs as Ludmilla's gas lantern revealed the spiked cages. The floor tiles showed traces of illustrious prisoners — claws, horned tails, feet that could melt stone.

The prisoner in the first cage had the face and breasts of a human woman but the body of a bird whose pale blue feathers had lost their luster decades earlier: Sirin, the bird of pain. Varangian lore had more stories about her than she had feathers. The Tzar's ancestor had captured her in an attempt to exterminate pain itself, but barely a week later, Sirin's sister Alkonost, the bird of pleasure, had been found dead in their forest. The egg they'd found in Alkonost's dead body was stored in the next room. The Tzar had once tried to have it hatched, but whatever was hidden inside the egg either was as dead as Alkonost or was still biding its time inside the blue shell.

Sirin flapped her wings as the Greyhounds slunk past her cage.

345

The golden quills of her feathers made the cage bars ring out like bells, and the scream she uttered was so shrill even the Wolfling had to cover his ears. The voice of a bird from the mouth of a woman. Ludmilla extinguished her lantern in case the guards came to check out what had made Sirin scream. But nobody came. All they could hear was Sirin's claws scraping her perch — back and forth, back and forth, more than a century of back and forth.

Ludmilla turned up the flame of her lantern again. Jacob forgot his swollen hand and his increasing dizziness as the light illuminated the next prisoner. This cage was almost as big as a railway carriage and still too small for the creature huddled inside. There'd always been stories that the last Dragons, before vanishing forever, had interbred with other animals. The creature in front of them had the body of a Dragon, but the heads at the end of two scaly necks looked like the giant bucks found in the mountains of Varangia. Whatever the ancestry of this scaled creature, being caged up had done it as little good as the bird of pain. Yet the sight made Jacob's heart beat faster. Dragons... He'd never stopped dreaming of seeing one. The creature staring at him through empty eyes had as much to do with his dream as a donkey had with a horse, but it was enough to rekindle that dream.

The next cages had walls of solid iron and only a peephole to look at the captives. This was how Witches and Wizards were held. The first cell was empty, but through the next peephole, Jacob saw two men sleeping on an iron grate.

Brunel seemed unharmed, but Orlando had been badly knocked about.

The lock was tricky, so Ludmilla pushed in the door with her elbow. The strength of the Dwarfs was not limited to their men.

Sokolsky helped to wrench the torn metal farther apart. Orlando barely managed to get to his knees, but Brunel crawled so quickly through the opening that it was clear this wasn't his first time escaping from captivity. When he saw Jacob, Brunel stared at him with such surprise he even forgot to stand up straight. Jacob had not expected Brunel to remember him. The officer who'd introduced them in Goldsmouth must've really sung his praises.

Orlando just gave Jacob a nod as he struggled to his feet. He didn't look like he had strength for any more than that. The Wolfling had to support him. As they all left the chamber, they opened the other cages only a little and managed to get back to the window before all the captives noticed they were free. They could hear scraping and fluttering as they quickly pulled the night skins back on. Ludmilla had brought two more for Orlando and Brunel.

Orlando was too weak to climb, so they secured him with a rope. Ludmilla was probably wondering whether he'd given her name to his torturers. The sky above the park was bright red. Jacob worried that Chanute had blown himself up, together with the music pavilion.

The Wolfling had just reached the ground when the one of the guards spotted the rope. The soldier managed a couple of steps and fired off one shot before the Wolf buried him beneath his body. Jacob had grabbed the pistol by the time the other guards appeared, but Sirin spared him from shooting anyone. The guards writhed on the ground in pain as Sirin launched herself out the window with an angry screech. The Grey Wolf flew after her as Jacob jumped off the wall and down into the street. The useless guards had lost all sense of who they were or why they were in uniform as they stared like children after the rescuers and the

347

rescued. Circling among the stars above them were the stories of every Varangian's childhood.

The trash cart was waiting, as planned, behind the Magic Collection. The night skins were becoming as see-through as the spiderwebs they'd been woven from. They quickly shed the skins before they climbed into the cart. Despite the hideous stench that greeted them, Brunel clambered aboard their clunky escape vehicle as fast as he'd crawled out of his cell. In light of all Brunel's inventions, Jacob would've imagined him to be a braver man, though his cowardice was probably a good motivator for the invention of weapons and armor plates.

Orlando and Sokolsky were sitting in the trash cart when a huge semi-invisible wolf leaped over the wall as though gravity did not apply to him. He shifted back to his human form more slowly than Fox. The fur on his face only vanished as he strode across the street. He was hobbling, but the blood on his hands was definitely not only his own. One of the guards had taken his attention off the magic in the sky and had trained his gun on the Wolfling. Ludmilla had shot the guard down. She dropped her pistol into her bag like someone who'd killed many times before. That morning, Molotov had briefly chatted with one of the guards about his sick sister. They'd all been about Will's age. Jacob had also killed many times, but he was glad it still made him queasy.

Jacob could feel the Hemlock-Fly's poison working on his body, and when Ludmilla asked him where they should drop him off, he couldn't even answer. The Wolfling and Sokolsky caught him as his knees buckled. Jacob wanted to show them the sting on his hand, but he couldn't even do that. They lifted him into the foul-smelling vehicle, and the last thing he saw was Brunel's anxious face.

348

51

A Fairy Tale

Seventeen raged against the rain like an enemy. Nerron had watched him ram his silver fingers deep into the trunks of trees to make them suffer for what the curse of the Fairies was doing to him. And he kept squabbling with Sixteen. He didn't like that she was no longer hiding from Will. He should have been grateful!

The Pup was ever more restless in his pursuit of the Dark Fairy, and Nerron knew that Sixteen was the reason. Will's eyes kept searching for her. Nerron pictured her turning the Pup to silver with a kiss, but the thought of melting Sixteen and Seventeen down to make silver chamber pots was much more satisfying.

The jade.

It was the jade.

Nerron couldn't shake the sight. He still felt some awe, even though the Jade Goyl he'd dreamed of as a child bore very little resemblance to the innocent baby face riding in front of him.

The Jade Goyl of his fantasies had drowned the onyx in their underground lake, just like they used to do with their bastards. As a child, Nerron had gotten so lost in these dreams that he used to search his own face for traces of jade. Children were such sentimental idiots. Life had woken him from such dreams; it had taught him to despise his own skin and his own heart, and it had taught him not to trust stories with happy endings and heroes who would save him or the world. Yet what he felt stirring inside himself since he'd seen the jade were exactly those awe-drenched delusions. Too bad this Goyl-forsaken land had no child-eaters. They would have cleansed his head with a cup of blood.

They stopped at a river to water the horses—the only thing for which the Pup stopped. Nerron led his horse to the water, and he saw Will pull the swindlesack off the crossbow. The Pup now did this every time they stopped. He cocked the string quite easily. Then he aimed at a tree more than a hundred yards away—and shot. Strike. Incredible. A crossbow was not an easy weapon to master, but the Pup handled it as though it had been made for him.

Of course!

Nerron's horse lifted its dripping muzzle from the river as he began to berate himself with every invective ever hurled at bastards above or below the earth.

A message for the Fairy...

And he thought Milk-face was naive?

He looked around, but what the devil! Why shouldn't those Mirrorlings hear that he'd seen through their lies. Embarrassing enough how long it had taken him. He dragged his horse away from the water.

Will was cutting the bolt from the tree trunk.

"You're supposed to kill her, am I right?" Nerron grabbed Will's shoulders and shoved him against the tree. "You're not after the jade!"

Will's eyes showed golden speckles.

Nerron grabbed Will's hand that held the bolt. "I assume her immortality is not a problem for this crossbow. But have you forgotten the Cossacks? And even if you manage to kill her before she kills you,what if she takes the jade with her?"

The Pup tore himself free.

"I hope she takes it with her. I never wanted it, or have you forgotten that?"

"The jade is the best thing that's ever happened to you!" Nerron wanted to smash Will's soft face, make the stone come back, but there they were already. His glassy guard dogs. They didn't look too good. The bark was growing faster than they could peel it off. "Let him go." Sixteen. Sixteen times ten faces, and all of them wanted the Pup. How did she like the jade? Or was she more into the soft human flesh?

Seventeen went to Nerron. He had blood (if it was blood) stuck to his skin like colorless oil. He'd been a little too thorough peeling off the bark.

"Get out of here, Stoneface. He'll find the Fairy without you. You said it yourself. He doesn't need you anymore."

Really? The Pup had never needed him more. Will was still holding the bolt. The crossbow was silvering his mind. The crossbow and Sixteen.

"Is that so? And who kept him from becoming raven fodder?" Nerron stood so close to Seventeen he could see himself in his eyes. "Let me think. That may have been me. I'm not going anywhere. We had a deal."

351

Nerron wondered whether the coldness in Seventeen's smile was stolen, like the smile itself, or whether that was his own metal ingredient.

"Ah, the mirrors. Believe me, you'll never see them, or those who are waiting on the other side."

Seventeen wore his human face like a badly fitting mask. "We haven't killed you yet, Stoneface. That is payment enough." Sixteen went to stand by her brother's side, to reinforce his threats. "And did you find the Fairy? No. So what should you be rewarded for?"

Filthy mirror-brood.

The Bastard was sick of being cheated. Lied to. Robbed. If anybody did the cheating and robbing and lying, it should be him. "I will find her," he said. "And a deal is a deal."

Sixteen's finger was growing silver claws.

Get out of here, Nerron, before your legs turn to silver.

But he couldn't. He was too angry. That damned rage. And his pride. Broken too many times. Far too many.

Sixteen was really looking forward to turning him into a hunk of precious metal. She was almost as keen as she was on the Pup. A silver Goyl. *Probably a first, Nerron.* Not the kind of precedent he wanted to set.

"You are so ugly." Sixteen stared hard at Nerron as though she wanted him to see it in her mirror-eyes. "This whole world is so ugly. I hope they make it prettier when they come back."

She put her hand on Nerron's chest. Oh damn, that hurt. He shoved her back, but she grabbed his arm, and his skin erupted in silver blisters.

"What are you doing? Let him go!" The Pup grabbed her by her shoulders. Sixteen looked at him like a chastised child.

352

Seventeen stared at Nerron's arm. He seemed surprised that he hadn't turned all silver. *Ha! Goyl skin, you mirror-spawn!*

Nerron didn't turn his back on them until he reached his horse.

Yes, go, Stoneface, Seventeen's eyes teased him. *Before I do a better job than my sister. Milk-face won't be able to protect you.*

No. But he'd tried.

And the rain would keep falling, and soon the Bastard would be feeding them to his cooking fire.

Nerron kept his eyes on the Mirrorlings as he swung himself up into the saddle.

The Pup didn't try to hold him back, but when Nerron looked around, Will was still staring after him.

They soon moved on. Nerron followed them as soon as they were out of sight. The Pup was leaving a clear enough trail.

Yes, he'd tried to protect the boy, but he'd also let the boy's guardians chase him off like a mangy dog. He would have to remind himself of that the next time the jade threatened to make him all sentimental again.

52

FORGOTTEN

Why had Donnersmarck assumed it would happen at night? The sun was high in the sky when the stag came. The Fairy was asleep under her web, the horses were grazing under the trees, and the coach box was empty. Chithira preferred his moth guise during the day.

He would not let it happen. That had been Donnersmarck's mantra since the child-eater had let him go. He would defeat it. After all, he was used to fighting, and it wasn't even the first time his enemy was inside him. Every soldier had to battle his weaker self. His weaker self had brought Donnersmarck to his knees, trembling. He had screamed it away, he had outrun it, he had drowned it in the blood of others. And he had always defeated it. But what had come with him from the Bluebeard's house did not leave any time for screaming.

The stag surged forth with the same violence with which it

had been planted into him. Even the pain was similar. It felt as if the antlers that had torn into his chest were now breaking out from inside him, and before Donnersmarck knew what he was doing, he was bellowing into the forest while his name became as meaningless as the uniform he'd once worn.

He scraped the skin off his new antlers and looked at the dark web that hung between the trees as though the night had dropped its dress. The stag who'd once had a name knew who was sleeping beneath it, though he'd forgotten everything else. She was the thread that connected him to everything he'd once been. He took that one memory of her with him as he disappeared between the trees.

53

THE LOST SON

Why did their hideout have to be a basement? John tried to manage the panic he still felt underground by reminding himself of the iron cell he'd spent the past week in. Or had it been two? Time escaped so quickly.

The barred window let in some daylight, but the rooms reeked of turpentine and oil paints. Their hideout was the workshop of an icon painter. Probably not a very successful one, if he had to work in a cellar on artwork that required light.

Their liberators were again discussing possible escape routes from the city. John didn't speak Varangian, but they kept switching to Albian, since one of them seemed to be from there. What John gleaned from these bits of conversation didn't really help alleviate his nausea caused by being underground and breathing turpentine. The Tzar had apparently put the entire city on high alert, and without a special permit there was no way in or out of

Moskva. There were searches, roadblocks...

They were going to shoot him!

No matter how many times he'd thought it and no matter that he'd always gotten away alive, John quickly felt the usual symptoms setting in: shortness of breath, racing heart, cold sweats. The Dwarf doctor who'd been brought in to check on his cellmate made no secret of what he thought of his "symptoms." The looks he gave him made John wish the Thumbling-blight on his stubby neck. Dwarfs... The Goyl had procured most of the raw materials for his weapons from Dwarfs. Even in Albion, Dwarfs were the most important suppliers of such materials, and John had spent endless hours haggling over prices and delivery schedules. Dwarfs ran more mines than Lotharaine and Albion combined, and they had a network of trading posts in even the most remote colonies. "Rich as a Dwarf" was a well-used phrase in this world. The Dwarfs liked to point out that, unlike the riches of humans, their wealth was not based on the slave trade. Still, John didn't like them, even if two of them *had* just helped to free him.

John was very flattered that the Walrus had risked his best spy in his first attempt to rescue him. Orlando Tennant had been mostly unconscious after they'd thrown him in the cell, but John had at least learned his name. Tennant's Caledonian accent had made him very homesick. He wanted to go home.

There's a loaded word, John!

He snuck a glance at the straw mattresses strewn across the paint-splattered floor. Yes, there he was. The Dwarf doctor's other patient.

Say it, John. Your son.

Jacob was conscious and very impatient with the doctor,

just the way he'd been as a child. The urge to stare at him was so strong, but John was worried the Wolfling might notice his unusual interest. The shifter hadn't been too happy about saving a man who'd brought about Albion's victory over Varangia. In this country, even the traitors were patriots. On the other hand, Wolflings always looked like they were about to devour you.

Jacob could barely stay upright, but he tried. Slapped away the hand that tried to keep him on the mattress. Squabbled with the Wolfling, who wouldn't let him leave. After all these years, why did it still feel to John as though he'd held his son in his arms only days before?

John's stash of frost-fern seeds, which he'd sewn into the hem of his shirt, was running out. He'd tried in vain to create a chemical substitute. His fake face held for now, saving him from having to reveal himself to his older son. And what would have been the point? There was nothing to say. His reasons for leaving Jacob's mother were not really valid: ambition, selfishness, the look of disappointment in Rosamund's eyes.

"Brunel!" Their icon-painting host was offering him a bowl of borscht. Maybe his art wasn't popular because he was still painting the old gods. John looked at the pictures leaning against the walls: Vasilisa the Wise, the Weaver, Kolya the Undead. No, that wasn't it. Their host was simply a bad painter.

John took the soup, though he was not hungry.

How did an icon painter end up harboring spies and escaped prisoners of the Tzar?

Jacob was still arguing with the Wolfling. *Stop staring at him, John.*

The presence of his long-lost son left little room for the relief he should've felt over his rescue. During their encounter in

358

Goldsmouth, he'd already noticed with more than a little shock but also some relief how the grown-up Jacob looked more and more like him. But Rosamund's face was still there. She hadn't been the first to make John doubt his ability to ever really feel love. His son, who was shouting at the Wolfling only an arm's reach away, was the only person for whom he'd ever felt something close to love.

Did he love him now? No, his guilty conscience had swallowed all else. And this adult Jacob was a stranger. John longed for the child, the boy who'd listened with rapt attention to every one of his words, who'd thought everything his father did was wonderful. The man that child had grown into was definitely not going to have such feelings for him. Still, John wished he had the courage to tell Jacob exactly whom he'd saved from the firing squad the night before. But courage was something John Reckless only ever wished he had. Courage was not a given; it was acquired, earned. You had to take the difficult paths, and John had always picked the easy ones.

Jacob was looking at him. What did he think of the man who called himself Isambard Brunel? Even his name was stolen from a better man. The Wolfling pointed at Tennant, and John thought he heard Jacob say something about his brother. Will. Always his mother's son, never John's. The Dwarf doctor gave Jacob some pills. The Witches in Albion sold an herb that erased memories as completely as waves washed footprints from the sand. The problem was that it also erased feelings, and the love for the son who didn't know who he was, was still too precious to him. Losing that love would've removed the last barriers to the ever-growing emptiness inside him.

359

For a brief moment, John wished Jacob would see through his fake face, as Hentzau had. After all, his son had a reputation for revealing hidden things. But Jacob turned away and went to the mattress where Tennant was lying.

So many years. At least his son had followed him into this world.

54

HIDDEN WORDS

The midday bells woke Fox. She couldn't remember ever having slept so long. Baryatinsky's palace was humming with excitement. Something had happened during the night, but Fox couldn't make any sense of her maid's very excited Varangian. The only thing she learned was that all three, Jacob, Sylvain, and Chanute had not spent last night in their beds.

She went to Jacob's room to search for a message from him, but she only found the rolled-up flying carpet. For a few unreal moments, she imagined not leaving with Jacob, but moving into Orlando's apartment, calling a place home. Did Orlando want such a life? The gander and the vixen? There was no message from him, either. The last she'd heard, he was off on some secret mission for a few days.

She couldn't take her eyes off the carpet. Onward. And onward with Jacob, on that endless, aimless journey they'd been on for so many years. *It's the life you wanted, Fox*. Really? She had always been so certain, but something in her felt tired now. Jacob had been her beacon for so long, the one she followed without wondering where other paths might lead, whether there was something somewhere worth staying for. Until now.

When lunchtime came and went without the others having returned, Fox decided to look at the church Orlando had told her about. Better than just sitting and waiting for a message from Jacob. Moskva's churches were so different from the sparse stone chapels of her native country. The god living here seemed as warm as the gold that surrounded him, even though his saints stared down from the walls with dark and serious eyes. A god who liked gold had to have a heart for treasure hunters. But when she stepped outside to hail a taxi, she found the streets clogged and people everywhere staring up at the sky. She approached a group of Lotharainian tourists, who became quite talkative when she greeted them in their native tongue. A governess from Lutis had seen a flying wolf above the city, and a tax collector from Calias advised her to cover her ears should she hear the cries of a bird with the head of a woman.

What the devil had happened while she slept?

She went back to ask the boys in the stables, but the porter approached her with a letter. The envelope was small, Dwarf-sized, but the handwriting was Jacob's.

Fox locked herself in her room before she pulled the letter from the envelope. The written chatter confirmed that the real message was invisible. There were many ways to write invisible messages. Jacob always carried a nightingale feather. Fox whispered the words to make the message visible: "Through quivering branches only the nightingale's song resounds." The real message came

362

forth, weaving itself through the words like a second thread of ink.

The first sentences were Jacob's confession that he'd mixed a sleeping powder into her food. His lies were usually delivered very smoothly, but here he'd crossed out and rewritten much. Maybe that's why Fox believed him when he wrote that he'd only done it to protect her. Fox read on, her feelings wavering between fear, rage, and love. Fear for Jacob, fear for Orlando, rage that they'd both kept secrets from her. But her love was stirred by what Jacob had tried to hide, even in his invisible words: the jealousy and the shame he felt over it, his willingness to save Orlando even though he'd rather have shot him dead, all the courage—and love. Fox had to wipe her tears off the ink. So much love. It echoed through Jacob's excuses and explanations, like something that was too large to be hidden any longer. And, of course, he also needed her help. She had to help him deceive Orlando. As always, Jacob asked too much.

Fox memorized the meeting point, the time, and she ignored his instruction to burn the letter. She kept it, for those days when he would keep himself, and all that made him special, under guard again.

❃ ❃ ❃

It was touching how devastated Baryatinsky looked when she informed him that the Tzar's assignment meant she had to depart immediately. He ordered his servants to pack Sylvain's and Chanute's few belongings into his best travel chests (Fox was relieved they didn't find any of their master's possessions among theirs) and offered her the services of his personal coachman

363

(unlike the Tzar, Baryatinsky did not like automobiles). He was very disappointed when Fox assured him Jacob had already arranged for her transport. The provisions he'd had brought up from the kitchen would have fed an army on an expedition around the world: *khleb, zakuski, kulebiaka, blini...* The words tasted as good as the food. Their sound would forever remind her of a time when she'd been very happy.

Fox promised Baryatinsky they'd stay with him when they returned the carpet. She very much hoped he wasn't going to be charged as an accomplice—and that she might indeed return. If they could find Will. If by then she'd figured out whether to keep going with Jacob or to stay with Orlando. Was there even a question? She didn't even know that.

The Goyl by the gate was gone. Fox would've liked to know why. Hard to imagine Hentzau had lost interest in them.

55

DOUBLE CROSS

If you'd asked Ashamed Tchiourak why he'd been an informant for the Goyl for years, he'd have told you a sentimental story about a girl with amethyst skin whom he'd met in his youth and who'd taught him how to turn stone into the glowing colors that had made him the envy of his peers. Touching...so touching that Hentzau didn't believe a word of it. Tchiourak could say neither what had become of his muse nor why, despite those secrets, he was still such a bad painter. No, Hentzau guessed Tchiourak's real motivation was his origins. He was from Circassia, a province that had been plundered by Varangia for centuries. In Hentzau's eyes, that was good enough reason to make you a traitor.

Tchiourak's origins also explained why he was now selling information that didn't harm Varangia but Albion, the land that had just recently conquered his old home in a bloody campaign. And then there was the Wolfling. Brunel's liberators obviously weren't aware that long ago a Wolfling had made a cripple of Tchiourak's brother. Where would the world's spy agencies be without such stories? Private revenge, jealousy, ambition. Spies always claimed to have noble motives for their treason, but Hentzau had yet to meet one who really did.

Tchiourak described in great detail how the escaped prisoners in his workshop stank, and what a monster the Wolfling was, before he finally got around to what he'd heard. Brunel was to be taken out of the city very soon. Hentzau was sorely tempted to send some commandos into Tchiourak's workshop, but that would've exposed one of his most valuable assets, and even the Tzar's secret police were very reluctant to go into the neighborhood where the painter lived. No, it was better to set a trap and catch Brunel when they tried to sneak him out of the city. Tchiourak had told Hentzau the place, under the condition that the Goyl would let the liberators go—except for the Wolfling, of course—and that they'd keep the Varangian secret police out of it. Hentzau had no intention of keeping the first promise, but the second he had no problem with. He couldn't wait to embarrass those arrogant fools by presenting them with their escaped prisoners, proving once again how superior the Goyl were to any human, Varangian, Albian, or whoever. And as far as Orlando Tennant was concerned, Hentzau was toying with the idea of keeping him for himself. The Barsoi had valuable information about the Albian spy networks.

"You're saying they also have another man from Albion. What does he look like?"

Tchiourak shrugged. He was scrutinizing a speck of gold paint on his thumb. "Young. Mid-twenties. Dark hair."

Yes, that sounded about right. There weren't many men outside Nihon who knew how to use a melting-ax. So many flies with one stroke. Hentzau wondered what Jacob Reckless thought of his father. Or hadn't he recognized him?

366

56
PRIVIDINIY PARK

It was midnight, four days after they'd broken into the Magic Collection, when the Wolfling waved Jacob and Moskva's two most wanted men onto a sparely lit street. Jacob thought the two hearses waiting for them were much better than their previous conveyance. The smell of refuse was still in their clothes. Brunel wasn't so impressed, saying it was absurd to try to sneak past roadblocks in coffins. But then Ludmilla Akhmatova climbed out of a taxi parked behind the hearses. She was wearing mourning garments and assured Brunel that nighttime funerals were not unusual in Moskva and that there was no better way. It was the first time since the break-in that they'd seen the Dwarf woman. She directed the Wolfling to show them that one of the coffins did indeed contain a corpse, just to make the cover perfect. When Jacob asked her whether she also counted an undertaker among her lovers, she just smiled mischievously.

Thanks to the Dwarf doctor, Orlando had recovered reasonably well from the interrogation by the Varangian secret police. He looked quite amused as he climbed into his coffin. During their close confinement over the past few days, Jacob had wondered more than once whether his jealousy was worse because he actually liked Orlando Tennant. They had talked about everything — the political situation in Albion and Leon, about danger and how much they enjoyed it — but had studiously avoided talking about the one thing that was on their minds. The one person.

Ludmilla drove ahead in her taxi with the Wolfling on the coach box. The black veil made her beauty even more seductive, and Jacob would've liked to ride with her just to watch her convince the guards of her utter harmlessness.

It was an unusual journey through Moskva, lying on red coffin silk, feeling the cobbled pavement beneath, wondering what roads they were driving on. An unforgettable journey. Every time they stopped, Jacob got ready to play dead. The Wolfling had whitened their faces with powder, and he had put three dead cats into the real corpse's coffin, just to add the right scent. But Jacob's coffin wasn't opened once.

He'd made it quite clear they could use the Tzar's flying carpet for their escape only if Chanute and Sylvain came with them. Chanute had sent word to Ludmilla via one of her contacts that he and Sylvain had survived their firebranding, but they were hiding in a part of the city that was dangerously far from their meeting place. That had made it difficult for Ludmilla to accept Jacob's condition. The Dwarf was still a mystery. Jacob suppressed his urge to ask her why she was spying for Albion if she really loved her homeland so much. "The Walrus pays well" was all Orlando had said. But Jacob didn't believe that was the whole truth. One thing was certain: They all had their secrets, and they were all practiced in keeping them. Only Fox knew that Jacob didn't intend to fly Orlando and Brunel back to Albion, and whether they'd all spend the rest of the night in freedom or in prison depended on Fox and whether she'd gotten his message.

At the roadblocks, Ludmilla told the soldiers that they were headed to a cemetery on the eastern outskirts of town. But as soon as the roadblocks became fewer, the coachmen changed direction. The roads became rougher. Jacob could feel it only too well in his coffin, and soon he had no clue where they were anymore.

When the hearses finally stopped and the Wolfling opened Jacob's coffin, all he saw were old trees and wide lawns lined with weathered benches.

"Privideniy Park," Ludmilla whispered, lifting the veil off her face. "The Ghost Garden. Moskva's most popular place for duels. Has been for more than two centuries. Many of its most prominent citizens have died here. They say if you die in Privideniy Park, you stay here for eternity. So they're probably all still here."

And so they were. There were no lanterns to light the paths, and the ambling figures were barely visible. They all were the color of fresh blood, proof that they'd met a violent death.

Brunel stared at them wide-eyed.

"You should not let them walk through you," Jacob whispered to him, "unless you want to share a dead man's memories. But otherwise they're harmless."

Brunel's trembling hand brushed through his hair. Then he looked crossly at the white powder on his fingers. "Just too many allusions to death for one night," he said. "I find it hard to face my own mortality. The others don't seem to have that problem."

One ghost stopped by the hearses, as though they reminded

369

him of his own funeral. The red shape disappeared as soon as Ludmilla clapped her hands. Jacob caught himself scanning the park for glassy shapes, but the breeze billowing the hearses' black curtains was cool.

There was still no sign of Chanute and Sylvain. Jacob thought of all the times he'd waited in vain for his old teacher. Chanute was rarely aware what day of the week it was, let alone what time. And despite having been one of the most successful treasure hunters, he had a gift for getting lost. Jacob could only hope Sylvain was more reliable.

"May I ask what we're waiting for?" Jacob heard Brunel ask.

"For a carpet," answered Ludmilla Akhmatova.

57

FLY, CARPET, FLY!

There was the policeman who asked them gruffly why they were visiting Moskva. There were the suspicious faces of the guards as they eyed the valuable carpet on the simple cart. The officer who silently studied the warrants in his hand before finally giving the signal to let her pass. Fox's nighttime trip through Moskva offered plenty of reasons to be afraid. But the fear of arrest or of the rifles the soldiers trained on her was nothing compared to the prospect of seeing Jacob and Orlando and the worry that they would both be searching her face for whom she loved more. Her only consolation was that she didn't know the answer herself.

Still, she was glad when the wrought-iron gate to the park appeared in the darkness. Some of the ghosts who'd given this place its nickname were hovering right behind the gate, as if grateful for the diversion. The horses only dared to pass them when Fox took the reins from the young coachman. She'd met many ghosts,

371

not only on treasure hunts. The drowned whom she'd seen as a child had been as gray as the sea that had claimed their lives, but the soldiers she'd encountered with Jacob on an old battlefield had the same blood red color as the shadows in Privideniy Park. Fox feared the lingering dead only for one reason: their sadness.

The living were waiting by an obelisk commemorating a poet who'd been shot in a duel by his wife's lover. Fox wondered what the wife had thought of that. She climbed down from the cart. Jacob was standing next to Ludmilla Akhmatova and a man who smelled so much of Wolfling that her vixen's fur bristled. Orlando was leaning against the obelisk. Fox didn't know the man next to him. Probably Brunel. Strange—his face didn't match his scent.

Orlando spared her deciding whom she should embrace first. He came toward her and pulled her close, as though he'd been certain he'd never see her again. The first thing he said was Jacob's name and how he'd be in some anonymous grave now if it hadn't been for him.

Fox had never hugged Jacob so awkwardly. Could one love two men? She saw the concern in Jacob's eyes that she might not have forgiven him the sleeping powder, and she felt his relief when she hugged him closer—for the words he'd written but would never speak aloud.

Jacob was concerned that Chanute and Sylvain hadn't arrived yet. Fox suspected she knew why Chanute was in no hurry to face him, but she said nothing. It was going to be hard enough for Jacob to hear it from Chanute himself.

The carpet began to glow as soon as they unrolled it. It looked as though its colors had absorbed the light of the stars. The carpet was large enough to carry twenty people, but when Fox asked Ludmilla whether she would join them, the Dwarf shook her head.

"I don't like being in the air," she said. "Dwarfs are creatures of the earth. But I shall leave Moskva for a while. His brother" — she pointed at the Wolfling — "works for one of the Wolf-Lords in Kamchatka. I'm sure he can use a good spy, or who knows? Maybe I shall spy for the Tzar for a change? A woman is always on love's side, sister Fox," she added with a smile that would've done any vixen proud. "Men are always on the side of power. Even the Dark Fairy had to learn that. They will always betray us for power, so why shouldn't we do the same? If only it didn't make our hearts so cold."

She offered Fox her gloved hand. "I hope we see each other again. Soon. Watch your heart. The Golden Yarn weaves a painful bond."

The Dwarf cast a knowing look at Jacob.

Jacob approached the two figures who were now cautiously walking through the gate as though expecting to meet foe, not friend. Jacob was too relieved to notice it. Of course, none of that relief was in his voice when he shouted at Chanute to damn well hurry up.

Chanute pulled Jacob aside while Sylvain went to Fox. He was limping. Apparently, his night as an anarchist had taken its toll, but he certainly looked like he'd enjoyed himself.

"How do you think Jacob's going to take it?" Sylvain whispered anxiously.

Badly. How else? Fox couldn't hear what Chanute was saying, but she could read it on Jacob's face. If he was trying not to show his disappointment, his surprise, the hurt, his jealousy of Sylvain, then he was failing miserably.

Fox went to his side, just in case he needed comforting or

Chanute needed protecting.

"And what will become of The Ogre?" Oh, he was angry. Hurt like a boy who'd lost his best friend to another. Chanute, of course, pretended he didn't notice.

"I telegraphed Wenzel. He can have it. You'll see. We'll come back with our pockets full of gold."

Jacob didn't look at Sylvain. He liked him, but right now he wished him to the Devil, or back into his Elf-prison.

Ludmilla joined them.

"You have to leave."

Jacob nodded. *Did you know about this?* his eyes asked Fox. He could probably see the answer.

Sylvain almost crushed them both with his embraces. He couldn't even find a curse word to relieve his heart.

"Send a telegram to The Ogre when you get there," she said to Chanute. Wherever "there" was.

"Telegram? Nonsense. You shall read about our adventures in the papers!" Chanute always got loud when he got sentimental. He squeezed Fox almost as hard as Sylvain had.

"Look after Jacob," he whispered. "You know how bad he is at looking after himself."

Yes. Nobody knew that better. But if she kept looking after him, she'd break her heart one day.

Orlando was already on the carpet, studying its patterns. He probably recognized the words hidden there, but he didn't know about the memories Jacob had fed into the weave. How quickly would he notice they weren't flying to Albion? A gander could read the stars as well as a vixen could.

Ludmilla and the Wolfling led four of the horses onto the carpet. Brunel looked wary. He probably would've preferred to travel in one of his airplanes. Fox didn't know what to think of him, and that didn't happen often.

The carpet was soft and firm at the same time, like a mossy bed of pebbles. One had to step on it slowly to allow it to adjust to the weight. "You have to kneel on a flying carpet, like for a prayer," an old man in Maghreb, whose fingers had knotted the colorful patterns since his fourth birthday, had once told Fox. "They all have a soul, and they demand respect and a firm belief in their ability to defy gravity. Without that belief, they are nothing but rugs."

Jacob was still with Chanute. Finally, he embraced the old man as though he'd never let him go. Nobody had earned the title father more than Albert Chanute. Brunel watched them with a strange expression on his face.

Ludmilla was right. They had to leave.

Orlando knelt down next to Fox. It was good to feel him by her side again. It still seemed unreal how familiar he was, even though they'd spent only a few days together. His hands were blistered with burns, his neck showed signs of strangulation, and his eyes had a weariness Fox hadn't seen there before. He reached for her hand, and she returned the gentle pressure, yet the gesture felt like a betrayal, and her eyes sought Jacob.

When he saw Orlando kneeling by her, Jacob hesitated for the briefest moment. Then he knelt down as far away from her as the carpet's pattern allowed. And Fox's heart was sliced in two. Chanute actually wiped a couple of tears from his unshaved cheeks as he stepped back to stand next to Sylvain. Brunel only knelt down when the Wolfling prompted him with a curt nod. Ludmilla looked up at the sky, but if the Tzar's winged spies were looking for them, they were not looking at Privideniy Park.

A shudder ran through the carpet as Jacob read the hidden words aloud. Fox could read them as clearly as he, and she whispered along:

"Ride the wind
until my hand
touches the sky.
Fly, carpet, fly!"

The carpet rose as gently as Jacob's voice had coaxed it. Not even the horses shied as it left the ground, rising higher and higher. The night swallowed Ludmilla and the Wolfling below, Chanute and Sylvain...and the dead in the Ghost Garden.

Orlando stretched out on the carpet and closed his eyes. He was already asleep when they left Moskva's lights behind, and Brunel spared no glance for the stars, which would have told him Jacob wasn't steering the carpet toward Albion.

58

THE WRONG DEAD

For Hentzau, there was no clearer proof that humans were a
thoroughly absurd species than their graveyards. Burying their
rotting bodies in wooden boxes that would then rot along with
them, while erecting stones and statues on top to bemoan the
transience of all flesh, truly was absurd. The Goyl had so much
more dignity in death. The boulevards beneath the earth, lined
with the heads of their heroes, unchanged, stone in death as in
life. The rest of their bodies left behind wherever death had found
them, so they could again become one with the rocks and the
earth that had borne them... Now, that was how to end it.

Hentzau saw his own uneasiness reflected on the faces of his
soldiers as they entered the cemetery from where, according to
the icon painter, Brunel's liberators were planning to sneak him
out of Moskva. Why this cemetery of all places, Tchiourak hadn't
been able to explain, but he'd sworn that the Wolfling, who was

in charge of the whole operation, had mentioned this cemetery several times.

Hentzau suspected an underground escape route—a natural assumption for a Goyl—or a carriage sent by the Albian secret service. An automobile would have been too conspicuous. Yet all they'd found were graves.

They'd already been hiding for two hours behind the amateurishly hewn stones and sentimental statues that would've made every Goyl sculptor destroy them in shame. Finally, a white dove settled on one of the gravestones. Tied to her leg was one of the gold capsules the Moskovites used to invite each other to balls and dinners.

Nesser caught the dove and brought the capsule to Hentzau. The message inside was written in Goyl:

The painter didn't know better. He is a gullible man and as clumsy in his spycraft as he is with his brushes. Leave him alive. Better luck next time, Lieutenant Hentzau.

L. A.

The basement workshop was, of course, empty, except for the trembling, useless icon painter.

Hentzau left him alive, though Ashamed Tchiourak couldn't even tell him who L.A. was.

59

LYING MOUNTAINS

Onyx skin offered little help in staying undetected when there was nothing for miles but grass. Nerron wished he had Seventeen's mirror skin. He only dared follow the Pup within eyeshot during the night. The boy seemed to need as little sleep as a Goyl. *He is a Goyl, Nerron, even if he looks like a glass of milk.* All those days and nights of him playing nanny—forgotten. Betrayed by both brothers... But why was he more willing to forgive this one? Why was he still riding after the Pup even though the mere thought of his mirrored guardians sent silver shudders down his spine?

Ah, to hell with the why.

"Ah, the mirrors. Believe me, you'll never see them, or those who are waiting on the other side."

Really? He wanted what was his. He'd been cheated out of his loot too many times these past months.

Around him the grass finally began to give way to stone.

Mountains began to rise, higher and higher, until they gathered snow on their flanks and cast shadows to finally make him invisible again. Through onyx-dark ravines, following a baby face who was trying to kill an immortal Fairy... If he could find her.

What if he succeeded? Would Kami'en cry after his dead love? Would anyone miss her and her sisters? All the lovesick idiots who'd drowned themselves for them, princesses who'd slept themselves to death, their murderous swarms of moths... *Let him kill her, Nerron. You can still have your revenge once his Elf task is completed*. After that, the Mirrorlings would no longer protect him, and what would be lost with the Dark One?

Yes, what?

The jade.

Nerron hated that he had to just think the word to feel its power—and his longing. For what?

For what, damn it?

Around him the slopes grew steeper, and the Pup's progress slowed. His guardians wouldn't like that, nor the ever-damper shade cast by the mountains. Yet Nerron had the feeling the Pup was closing in on the Fairy. Black blossoms filled the rocky crevices with a heavy scent. Birds circled the ravines in excited flocks. And then there was that trail of a stag... Nerron couldn't make sense of it all, but that was usually a good indication of the presence of some powerful magic. What if he stole the crossbow before the Pup found the Fairy? Maybe he could cut him off in this rough terrain? Provoke him, call the jade. That the Pup didn't want it was a lie, a damn lie! His skin would protect him from the Mirrorlings—for a few seconds, anyway. They'd noticed that, and they hadn't liked it. Nerron pictured snapping their woody fingers, throwing their mirror eyes into the fire, grimacing at their faces as they turned to bark.

"Bastard... Bastard... Bastard..."

He reined in his horse.

Voices. Stone voices.

He heard them echo through underground streets, through malachite palaces, on plazas and stairs of deep green.

Nerron dismounted.

"Bastard Bastard Bastard...."

Where did they come from?

The malachite voices.

He climbed one of the rocks until he could see the mountains lining the horizon. Did they come from there? The voices grew louder, like a chorus carried by the wind. They came from far away. Ah, to the south was a mountain range, green like a hem of emeralds against the endless sky. The lost cities. Impossible. They were way north of here.

"Bastard Bastard Bastard..."

Nerron thought he saw the distant mountains take on the color of his skin. He saw them sprout pillars, towers, saw the Bastard on the throne, Hentzau kneeling in front of him, Crookback, the Walrus, and by his side four princesses, each as beautiful as the Fairy. He climbed higher, slipped, grazed his skin, climbed on.

"What took you so long, Bastard? What kept you? What kept you?"

It would be a five-day ride, maybe less.

Wait.

Wait, Nerron.

Stop, damn it!

He leaned against the craggy rock, panting.

What was he, a bat-brain? That wasn't the mountains whispering;

it was the wind. The wind!

A siren song for the stray dog who was so impertinent to follow them. And he'd fallen for it.

He pulled the looking glass from his belt.

Of course. No sign of the Pup.

Oh, he should hang himself from the nearest tree, feed himself to the vultures circling above!

Pull yourself together, Nerron.

He slapped himself. Once. Twice. Until his stone skin burned with pain.

He would find him again. Yes.

The Pup couldn't have gone far.

He would find him. The angrier they made him, the better.

60
THE RIGHT PLACE

A clear night gave way to a cloudy morning. Behind them lay
the wide steppes that stretched from Moskva toward the east.
A firebird attacked them over the old monasteries of Novgorod.
Maybe their carpet had cast a threatening shadow over its nest.
But it let them go when Fox shifted and bared her teeth. Brunel
couldn't take his eyes off her as he helped her gather the feathers
the firebird lost on the carpet. Maybe he'd never seen a shape-
shifter. The feathers were worth more than the advance the Tzar
had paid to Jacob.

When Orlando finally asked about their route, Jacob lied about
some storm that had made a more westerly course impossible.
Fox's presence distracted the Barsoi so much that he accepted the
flimsy explanation without question. His eyes hung on her with
such insistence it made Jacob wish he could make her invisible.
Fox stayed away from both of them. Unlike Orlando, Jacob knew

this mood—far away and by herself, in her own world. There was no reaching her when she went there, deep into the landscape of her own heart, formed from memories only she knew.

Beneath them the green of a cool summer turned into the brown of plowed fields and wide rivers. They flew over monasteries, churches, grand estates, and poor villages. The Tzar had banned the import of sugarcane because it was harvested by slaves, but most of Varangia's peasants were barely more free than the men, women, and children who were dragged from Oyo or Dahomey and onto Arabian slave ships.

By midday, the wind freshened and darkening clouds began to bulge above them. The carpet curled its edges up like a protective railing, but soon it began to rise and drop so abruptly that the horses shied and Jacob started looking for a spot to land. They couldn't risk asking for shelter in one of the large estates. Orlando was sure they were still over Varangian territory, and he was convinced the Tzar's couriers were faster than the wind. They must have already carried the news of Brunel's escape into the remotest corners of the empire. But the clouds looked like rain, and rain was something flying carpets could not tolerate. After all, they came from desert lands.

The first drops were landing on their faces when Fox pointed out some strangely-shaped hills. They turned out to be a Dragon's skeleton. The three skulls between which Jacob landed the carpet were each bigger than a train carriage. The neck vertebrae that had once supported those heads were so overgrown with dense grass that one could barely spot them, and they no longer indicated whether they'd been severed from the skulls. But there was an ominous hole in the rib cage. Varangia's Dragons had been famous for their strong urge for freedom—as much as those in Zhonghua.

Some had developed an appetite for royal daughters; others had hoarded treasure to build their nests and to give their young scales of gold and silver. Only a rare few had ever died peacefully.

The Dragon's ribs formed a spacious cave big enough even for the horses. They'd just dragged the carpet inside when the clouds broke. The bushes and trees that had covered the skeleton over centuries were so dense that the cave stayed perfectly dry.

Brunel was obviously fascinated by the skeleton. He soon began to explore it in more detail. When Jacob explained that the more valuable parts had probably found new owners already, Brunel just smiled enigmatically.

"I may have hunted treasure with my children," he said, "but my real interests are purely scientific."

Fox followed Brunel. A Dragon could, even after centuries, pose some serious dangers: Poisonous barbs, fire bones. Fox would know when to warn Albion's famous engineer. She was fascinated by Dragons, and she, like Jacob, dreamed of someday finding a Dragon's egg that still contained a spark of life.

Orlando's eyes followed her—Jacob wondered if his own face showed his desire for her as clearly.

"Why are we still not flying westward?"

So, the Barsoi's head was not only full of Fox.

"You saw the clouds."

Orlando smiled, but his eyes were alert. "Stop it. Where are we flying?"

"Not westward."

"Good. I assume this is about treasure? You think that can make the Tzar forget you freed his prisoners? Not likely, if you ask me."

"This has nothing to do with treasure."

Jacob didn't want to talk to him, just as he didn't want the Windhound staring at Fox or holding her hand. If only Alma were here. She knew some excellent recipes against jealousy.

"You do realize we'll all end up in the ice dungeons of Sakha when they catch us?"

"I never volunteered to be part of your rescue commando. You let yourself be caught like an amateur, and I got you out of there only for Fox. I warned you about the knife-wire, but you knew better, and then I had to risk my neck for you."

"Did she ask you to?"

"No."

The rain pummeled the old Dragon bones as though to provide the rhythm to the song of their mortality, but death was not what they had on their minds—or wasn't love sometimes called the small death?

"We have to take Brunel to safety!"

Of course. Politics. Always a much safer topic.

"The reward you'll get from Albion will be worth more than any treasure."

"I seriously doubt that. Don't explain my business to me. But as I said, this is not about treasure."

Ridiculous how argumentative Orlando's mere presence made him. Love made him foolish.

"Then what is it about? Is it so important you'd risk even Fox's safety?"

"She's used to it. Has been for years." *Heavens! Just listen to yourself, Jacob!*

"I assume appealing to your patriotic duty would also be in vain."

"I'm not even from Albion. That was a lie."

386

Orlando was about to reply, but he stopped himself when Brunel appeared from behind the bones. His hair and clothes were soaked with rain.

"She shifted," he said. "I'm to let you know she'll be back soon."

The vixen didn't mind the rain. She loved feeling it on her fur, and the scents it coaxed from the earth.

The Witch's comb Orlando pulled from his pocket was a particularly beautiful specimen. The teeth were shaped like feathers, which meant it could turn its user into any bird of their choice. Why was Jacob even surprised? Shape-shifting was perfect for spying.

"I wouldn't do that," he warned. "She wants to be alone."

Orlando went anyway.

Idiot.

But what did he know? Orlando had made her his lover, while Jacob couldn't even take her hand without fretting over the consequences. Jacob envied the other man for having met Fox at a ball, instead of when her bloody leg was stuck in the metal jaws of a trap. And how he wished it could have been Orlando who'd had to ask the Elf to save her from the Bluebeard.

But that was you, Jacob.

Brunel looked up to where the Dragon's heart would have been. Eating the heart supposedly made you fearless for life. Many Dragons had been killed for their hearts.

"We're not flying westward." Yes, in this world it was safe to assume most people knew their compass directions. "What's our destination?"

"Only the carpet knows that," Jacob said. "It looks like it's somewhere to the southeast."

"Ah. You fed it your memories. Such interesting magic. I once

387

tried to utilize it for airplane navigation, but it seems to work only on old-fashioned materials such as sheep's wool."

Jacob heard no irritation in Brunel's voice. He didn't seem to be in a hurry to return to Albion. The Walrus was dying, and his daughter was next in line to the throne. Maybe she was not as passionate about New Magic as her father?

"A friend of mine has a theory that this kind of magic is created not so much by the material but by the skill of the craftsman," Jacob said.

"Interesting. Which would mean that in this world, even a master mechanic could imbue his contraptions with magic."

Jacob wasn't sure what gave him more pause—that Brunel had spoken of "this world" or how he'd pushed his hair back from his eyes. So familiar...

Brunel was still looking up toward where the Dragon's heart had beaten. But then he turned. He did so slowly, like someone who'd decided to finally face down his fears.

"It won't last much longer," he said. "You can already see it, can't you? The Goyl took the last of my frost-fern juice. I had a few seeds sown into my shirt for emergencies, but even those are now gone. I hadn't planned for such a long trip."

Brunel's nose, the chin, his eyebrows, his whole face was shifting—not like it did on Spieler's creatures. No, Brunel's features were changing as if being kneaded by an impatient potter.

Tummetott magic. Therese of Austry had used it so she could mingle incognito among her ministers and listen to their intrigues. But the magic could leave permanent marks, and in the end Therese's vanity had proven stronger than her hunger for power.

The man into whom Isambard Brunel was changing was all too familiar to Jacob, even though he hadn't seen him in more than fourteen years. He felt hot and cold, was five, twelve, twenty-five years old. He'd imagined this reunion too many times to fully comprehend it was actually happening.

"So you recognized me in Goldsmouth." Jacob wished him away, far away, like his father had always been.

"Of course. But I had to keep my cover. Isambard Brunel guarantees my survival. Of course, I considered revealing myself to you, but after the sinking of the fleet, I had to assume you were dead."

His father. *You are talking to your father, Jacob*. How many times had he argued with him, screamed at him, ignored him in his mind? Years of searching for excuses for his betrayal, for answers to why he'd left them, him, Will, their mother. And now Jacob realized he no longer wanted to know.

He felt his mouth twist into a bitter smile, but his scorn was directed at himself. The yearning, the rage, the waiting, just to be standing there like an actor who for years had memorized the wrong lines. The heartless skeleton of a Dragon. What a stage for their meeting. Couldn't be more perfect.

"Drowned by the planes his own father built," he said. "That would've been ironic."

How he avoided his eyes. He seemed smaller. Of course.

"I assume it's too late for an explanation?"

"Yes, it is."

Jacob was going to leave him here. Orlando could stay with him if he wanted. For King, country, whatever. Maybe that's why Jacob had never understood the concept…because he'd never had a father. And he still didn't. Typical for John Reckless to steal the name of a famous nineteenth-century engineer to hide behind. *"John Reckless likes to stand tall — on the shoulders of others."*

389

His mother's father used to say that, but Jacob had never wanted to believe it.

He turned around a little too abruptly (oh, he was so angry!) and stumbled out from under the petrified bones into the pouring rain. Brunel called after him. Jacob wasn't going to think of him by any other name. A year ago he might still have had some questions, words he'd wanted to say, but too much had happened. And finding Will now was more important. Much more.

He walked faster, through the rain that blurred heaven and earth into a gray haze. He found it hard to breathe—as though the stranger with the two faces was stealing the world he'd called his own for so long.

"Jacob?"

The vixen appeared through the rain and shifted so quickly it looked like the woman's body was growing out of her fur. "What happened?"

He pulled her into his arms, just like when he'd nearly drowned without her. He sought her lips as if he needed to breathe through her, as if only she could keep him from choking on his rage. *Never, Jacob.* He let her go, stammered an excuse.

Fox pulled him to her, closed his mouth with her lips. She kissed the rain off his face, the tears, the rage, and Jacob returned the kisses, despite the Elf, despite his promise to himself, to her. Not lost. His. All his. For the first time and since forever. It had always been meant to be. Was that enough excuse?

Behind them a wild gander rose from the dripping branches of a tree.

61

THE DESTINATION

The landscape outside the carriage window had again grown sparse and wide. A sea of yellow grass washing up against rugged mountains in the bluish distance. Woolly horses and camels grazing among the nomad yurts. The people had black hair and dark eyes. They claimed to be descended from a princess who'd been born as a wild goose. Kazakh. She'd even given her name to the whole country. *Kaz* for goose, *akh* for white.

The Dark One now also traveled by day, asking every river, every brook, and the rain for the way. The answer was always just a direction. East. Always east. And Chithira drove the horses through a land filled with a magic so alien to the Fairy that she sent Donnersmarck into the villages and yurts to collect stories. He told her stories about a man who'd cheated Death for so long that in the end, Death turned into a snake and bit him. About men of gold, magic pillows made of black wood, eagle lords and rider hordes, but not a single word about the one she was seeking. They'd told stories about her in all other places, and the Fairy knew that meant she was getting closer. And still she felt her restlessness growing, fearing that the one who was following her might catch up before she reached her destination.

But then—she didn't know how—she suddenly knew she'd finally found the one she was looking for.

Chithira felt it even before she did. He stopped the carriage before she could order him to do so.

A giant spider's web, woven more artfully than the most precious lace, stretched between two wild apple trees. Thousands of drops of dew clung to the sticky threads, catching the world's reflection, and the spider sitting in the middle of the web was as green as the leaves of the trees between which she'd spun her silken trap.

"Make way," said the Fairy.

The spider obeyed only after the Dark One touched the web with her six-fingered hand. She scuttled up the threads until she was hidden in the trees' foliage. The giant web, now unguarded, stretched in front of the Fairy.

Are you sure? she heard a whisper inside her.

Who was asking? Not she. Not the one she wanted to be.

She stepped through the web, felt the silk threads tearing, and the cold dewdrops rolled down her skin like pearls.

62

COWARD

All those failed experiments to harness the magic of flying carpets for his airplanes—who would've thought they'd one day turn out to have their uses? One had to walk the pattern in a counterclockwise direction to erase its current destination. John struggled to drag the huge carpet out of the rib-cave. He had to hurry: the vixen could return any moment with Tennant or Jacob. It would be hard to forget the look in his son's eyes. It had contained something John had never seen in Rosamund, despite all her disappointment. Rage. And an unwillingness to forgive.

Forget it, John. He was good at forgetting, though he found it harder the older he got. In his mind, John was still lining up all the things he hadn't said to Jacob: explanations, reasons, excuses... Again and again, in endless variations.

The sky above the skeleton had turned a threatening yellow. *Get out of here, John!* But where to? Albion? He couldn't go back there. Even if the Walrus was still alive, they were going to accuse him of giving their best-guarded secrets to the Tzar. No, even though he felt homesick for Albion and his lover, he wasn't homesick enough to endure months of interrogations in the catacombs of the Albian secret police. There were too many countries that would welcome Isambard Brunel with open arms.

Counterclockwise... It felt like he was massaging a furry animal with his bare feet. The pattern had to be walked with bare feet, another thing John had learned during his experiments. He forced himself to walk slowly. Flying carpets were surprisingly stubborn. There was a theory that they took on their creator's personality. Hopefully, this weaver had not been too pig-headed.

As pig-headed as his elder son. John had always admired that about Jacob. Rosamund hadn't. The two had fought often. There had always been much love between the mother and her elder child, but they'd both struggled to show it. As though they'd been afraid of what the other would do with all that love. It was not true that his elder son resembled only him. Had Rosamund never noticed? Or had she been blinded by how much more Will was like her? Oh, how the memories kept sneaking out of that vault he'd built around them in his heart. No matter how tightly he thought he'd sealed it, the vault remained with his lost life inside. That's what John liked to call it; it made it sound more tragic, more fateful. As though it hadn't been he who'd discarded Rosamund and his sons like some old clothes he no longer thought suited him.

Where had Jacob been headed with the carpet? Probably toward some treasure. He was always looking for something. Had he ever looked for his father? One of the questions John could've asked him, though it was doubtful he would've gotten an answer.

Jacob's pride was another trait John had always admired. With him, ambition had always been stronger than pride.

John stared down at the carpet beneath his feet. *Same procedure as always, John. Your answer to all problems: run.*

What if he stayed this time?

What if he could win back the son he'd once loved so much? If he told him about the newspaper clippings he'd collected, of the treasure-hunting jobs given to Jacob only because of Isambard Brunel's recommendation? Maybe he could even explain that he'd only left Rosamund because he'd realized she could be much happier without him. It was not the whole truth, but it was a part of it.

So, he'd have to find a reason why the destination had been erased from the carpet. Maybe he could blame the rain.

The warm breeze suddenly brushing across his naked feet felt strange on this cool day. John looked back at the skeleton. Was it still giving off warmth, after all these years? Dragon bones as a source of energy? John slipped his feet back into his shoes. That would be an amazing discovery! These skeletons were everywhere.

The warm air seemed to be coming from the skulls. The first one had its jaws wide open. Something stirred between the teeth. John froze. A figure of glass. Through its limbs he saw bones and teeth, and the gray clouds. But then it suddenly grew a face, became more and more human. It was a girl. John reached for the pistol the Dwarf had given him. Not that he was sure bullets would harm it.

He walked backward until he felt the carpet beneath his feet. The creature jumped off the bony jaw into the grass. The eyes — they were mirrors. And the skin... It seemed human, but the hands were sharp-edged, like cut glass, with silver fingernails.

Yet the strangest thing was the face. It seemed to be a hundred faces in one. It looked as though a silver plate were being exposed repeatedly, every photograph slowly emerging from the previous one. Fascinating. John had never seen anything like it. This creature of glass and silver seemed to come from his world and time, rather than this one. No, it looked like a mixture of both, something he'd always dreamed of, but all his attempts to combine magic with technology had always failed. This one also seemed to have some problems. The face looked scuffed, and leaves were growing from the glassy shoulders.

The creature was approaching him. It? She? Yes, it was definitely a she, as beautiful as a painting. She had now settled on a face. Of course, he wanted to run, and this time it seemed more than reasonable. And he was standing on a flying carpet. *Say the words, John.* But even his mind was paralyzed, which didn't happen often.

"Hello, John!" The girl stopped in front of the carpet. "Or shall I call you Isambard? What a strange name."

John almost reached out to see if the skin was warm. The breeze that had announced her had been warm.

"You can call me Sixteen."

Her face changed again. Rosamund. A sick joke. But who was making it?

"A good idea. Take the carpet, John." Sixteen didn't have Rosamund's voice, but hers sounded almost as pleasant. "The horse lords in these lands don't think much of engineers. Your profession means the end of their way of life. If they find you here, they'll stick your head on a pike and let the eagles feast on your eyes."

Sixteen was very convincing. John scanned the horizon for

riders. Sixteen *what?* Were there fifteen others, or was she the sixteenth model?

She reached out. Being touched by her did not feel good. He felt like mercury was coursing through his veins. Sixteen no longer had Rosamund's face. The new one looked scarier, but at least it didn't make him feel so guilty.

"Kneel." She sounded impatient. Her fingers ran over her scraped cheek. Something was sprouting there, like a gray scab.

John dropped to his knees.

The carpet was already stirring. Sixteen whispered the words Jacob had used to wake it. The wet grass had made the carpet damp. It rose with a lurch.

"Where to, John?" Sixteen called. "West? East? North? South?" She was now barely visible. He could see the grass through her limbs.

John held on to the carpet's edge.

"Southeast! Alberica!" he shouted.

Yes. The New World. It was different on this side. Different alliances. Three nations, a war of independence that had been only partly successful, and apparently there was another war brewing. What more could Isambard Brunel ask for? They were going to fight over his services, and the longing for progress was so much stronger there than in Varangia, where the Tzar couldn't come up with a better use for him than to have him shot!

John had always struggled with languages more than with numbers, but Sixteen's pronunciation of the magic words was even more perfect than Jacob's. The carpet flew a wide arch and then faced the wind head-on.

John would've liked to ask Sixteen about her maker. Someone must have made her. There'd been an emptiness in her glass eyes — no soul, if there was such a thing. Fascinating.

The Dragon skeleton had already vanished behind the horizon.

One day he would explain everything to Jacob.

Everything. One day.

63

DIFFERENT PATHS

Orlando was leaning against one of what had been the Dragon's wings. The bones behind him spread out across the grass like an ivory fan. There were still a few goose feathers stuck to his clothes, but even without these, Fox could tell from the look on the Barsoi's face that he'd seen what had happened.

It had happened.

Yes, Fox.

A dream so often dreamed, a wish so often wished. Under Orlando's eyes, Jacob's touches turned to pitch and gold on her skin. Nothing made her happiness more real than his pain. Jacob left them. He disappeared between the Dragon's ribs, sparing the other man the sight of him.

Orlando forced himself to smile.

"The Golden Yarn," he said. "What can I say? Even Fairies are powerless against it."

399

Fox had never loved him like she loved him in this moment.

But Orlando looked past her. Jacob was striding toward them.

"Where is it?" There was something in his voice, and it had nothing to do with jealousy. "Where's the carpet?"

"Up in the air, I assume," Orlando replied. "I'm afraid Isambard Brunel thought his own safety was more important than ours. At first I thought he'd taken the horses as well, but I found two over there behind the skulls. They seemed very frightened. Maybe he chased them away, though I can't really make much sense of it."

She'd never seen Jacob paler, not even when Hentzau had shot him through the heart.

Orlando, of course, had no idea how monumental a betrayal he'd just witnessed. Orlando knew nothing of fathers who betrayed their sons. He talked about his own father the way one spoke about parents whose love one never had to doubt.

Fox felt Jacob's rage as clearly as if it were her own. Pain, rage, fury, against himself, because he hadn't foreseen what his father would do.

As a child, she'd always believed there could be nothing more painful than losing your father to death. Jacob had taught her otherwise. Fox wished John Reckless into the deepest caverns his fears could imagine.

"Did you see him?" Jacob asked.

"Would I still be here if I had?" Orlando plucked a feather from his sleeve. "I would've flown after him. Damn fool. It's going to be on my head if he doesn't make it to Albion in one piece. How's he going to find the way?"

"Albion? I don't think he's going back there," Jacob replied.

"Where, then?"

"Some place that won't hand him to either the Walrus or the

Goyl, somewhere that can afford to build his inventions." Jacob didn't sound like he was speaking of his own father.

Orlando looked south, to where the mountains of Kazakh were rising in the distance. "Fine. So I won't be returning Brunel to Albion. I'd better start looking for a new employer. The Shah of Bukhara is looking for spies."

Bukhara, Kazakh, Mongol... Fox knew little of the countries beyond Varangia. She wasn't even sure whether they'd already crossed any of those borders.

"I'd be grateful if you let me have one of the horses," Orlando said. "The people around here would rather sell their children than their horses, and the next town is at least a hundred miles away. I could fly, but I fear the gander is no match for the double-headed eagles."

"Sure," said Jacob, though he probably hadn't even heard Orlando's request.

Fox lowered her eyes as Orlando looked at her. Was she going to see him again?

Probably best not, his eyes seemed to say.

Orlando picked a splintered bone from the ground. Like birds, Dragons had hollow bones. The resinous material on the inside was a very effective explosive.

"Will you still look for the Fairy?" he asked. "Or are you done with that?"

"The carpet's gone," Jacob replied. "I guess that makes us done with that, right?"

"That depends. Maybe I know another way."

Orlando looked at Fox. *Don't hate me for not saying anything earlier*, his eyes pleaded. *You know why.*

Hate? She was grateful, even if Jacob would never understand

401

that. The days in Moskva had been hers, hers alone. Not Jacob's or Will's. Hers. And those days had let her find again what she thought she'd lost forever in the Bluebeard's castle.

Maybe Jacob did understand. He didn't ask Orlando why he was only mentioning this now.

He just said, "And? What do you know? Did you tell Fox?"

"How stupid do you think I am? What she knows, you know." Orlando tucked the bone into his bag. "I assume she told you who the Dark One is probably looking for?"

"*La Tisseuse*?" Jacob shook his head. "The Weaver? The Golden Yarn? You're talking about the Dark Fairy, not some village girl dreaming of true love. If the Dark One's looking for the Weaver, then it's to convince her to cut Kami'en's life thread."

Fox had never understood where Jacob's anger came from. All that harshness with which he shielded his heart. *He is gone, Jacob,* she wanted to say. *Your father is gone. Forget him.* But she knew too well how difficult it was to forget.

Of course, Orlando knew nothing of all this. He looked at Jacob as though he was doubting his sanity. *Are you really that ignorant?* his eyes jeered. *Oh yes, very often,* Fox wanted to reply. *And I love him anyway.* But Orlando knew that as well—and that "anyway" was at the core of love.

"So? Do you want to hear it?"

Jacob stared at where the carpet had lain in the grass.

"No," he said. "Fox and I are riding back to Schwanstein. The Weaver! If she really exists, then she won't be any easier to find than the Fairies, and probably just as dangerous."

He looked at Fox. *Let's go.* Anywhere. Never had that wish to just turn and give up been clearer on Jacob's face. His longing to just enjoy what they'd both been awaiting for so long, to forget the rest of the world, brothers, Alderelves, Fairies... just him and her.

It was hard not to say yes. But she loved him. She knew how unhappy he would be. And that he'd never forgive himself for abandoning his brother.

"Tell me," she said to Orlando. "Tell me what you know."

Jacob turned away and disappeared behind the Dragon's bones.

Orlando looked after him.

"I think I'd really like to duel with him," he said. "Pity we didn't get a chance in Privideniy Park."

He took Fox's hand. "I can still shoot him if he makes you unhappy. No, not quite right. I *will* shoot him." He bent to catch a spider crawling across one of the scattered bones. He opened his fingers, and it quickly ran up his arm. "The Weaver. Jacob is right. She's not easy to find, and that's putting it mildly. For mortals it's almost impossible. But one of my first jobs in Moskva was to make a list of all the magical creatures the Tzar could use in a war against the Walrus. Crookback had just lost a few colonies to strange magic, and the Walrus was preparing his war against Circassia. As far as I'm aware, the Tzar only ever recruited one Baba Yaga, and not with much success, as we all know. But of course I also learned about the Weaver. The stories about her are as plentiful as they are vague, when it comes to exactly where she lives. I was about to put her on the list of fictitious creatures when I met a man in a pub who claimed his village had recently rid itself of a particularly nasty landowner by petitioning the Weaver to cut his life thread. You can imagine how this kind of magic could be very useful to any ruler in this world. But here comes the part that might interest you." The spider crawled back down Orlando's

403

arm and onto his finger. "The Dark Fairy probably has her own ways, but for us mortals, even trying to find the Weaver can be deadly. Except if you ask a shaman. But not just any shaman..."

Orlando lifted his finger. The spider dangled off it by her thread.

Fox plucked the thread and spider from Orlando's hand. "A shaman who speaks to spiders. Of course. He and the Weaver are more or less in the same line of work."

"Smart vixen."

"And do you know where to find such a shaman?"

Orlando had tied the two remaining horses to one of the Dragon's vertebrae. One was already saddled. He went to it and tightened the surcingle. "I'm sorry. Shamans don't believe in a god who needs to be worshipped in golden churches. They worship the mountains and rivers," he said. "I've only ever met one, and he only talked to trees. But I'm sure the two of you can find one who speaks to spiders. You just have to promise me one thing: should you find the Weaver, I'd be most curious to know what the Dark Fairy wanted from her." He untied the reins from the brittle bone and threw them over the horse's head. "I'll take the better horse. Only fair, don't you think?"

Fox didn't know what to say. *I will miss you*? It would have been the truth.

Orlando swung himself into the saddle.

"You still have the feather? Just stroke it along the quill should he ever treat you badly. I will sense it and I will come. You can also call me if you're simply bored with him."

"What if I treat *him* badly?"

"I very much hope you will."

He leaned down and kissed her cheek. "We live dangerous lives. That's our choice, even though we may wish a different life for those we love. Use the feather! Whenever you need help."

He steered his horse toward the south. Pashtun, Bengal, the Suleiman Empire... Spies were always in demand. Fox stared after him for a long time. There went another piece of her—but she knew the Windhound would take good care of it.

Jacob was kneeling by the Dragon's petrified tail. The skeleton had been plundered thoroughly, but Alma had taught Jacob a few things not many treasure hunters knew. He'd scraped the moss off the bones and had broken some of the thorns off them. They were no bigger than rose thorns, but very effective on broken bones and torn tendons.

"We won't be very fast on one horse," Fox said, "but I could shift." The vixen could keep up with a horse, at least for a while.

Jacob put the thorns into his pouch in which he kept his medicines from two worlds.

"No."

"No what?"

"We're turning around." He got up. "We tried. Chanute is right. Will's not a child anymore. He decided to come here. Maybe he wants the jade back. Maybe he wants to take revenge on the Fairy. What do I know?"

He avoided looking her in the eyes; he always did when he was trying to fool her.

She took his face in both her hands, forcing him to look at her. "We don't run from anyone or anything. That's still true, isn't it?"

Jacob held her hand against his cheek. She loved him so much. Maybe even more now that she didn't have to hide it any longer. But what if they ended up betraying each other, just as Kami'en and the Dark One had?

Her heart pounded as he kissed her. Or was it his heart? She hadn't been able to tell the difference ever since he'd freed her from that trap.

64

EXPOSED

The spider was tugging on the web through which the Fairy had disappeared. The longer Donnersmarck watched it, the more he felt he was caught in its web himself. The stag now came almost every day. Leo Donnersmarck was keeping a journal of all the lost hours in an attempt to make them his again. The stag didn't count them. Donnersmarck tried to remember, but all he got were smells, images, the taste of grass, his quickened heartbeat as he scented a wolf, the memory of wind and rain. And her. But now she was gone.

A beetle had gotten caught in the spider's web. Was he dreaming or was it really a stag beetle? Its helpless buzzing grated at Donnersmarck's soul, but when he reached out to free the beetle, Chithira held him back.

"You still want to live, don't you? That door is not for mortals."

Chithira's voice always sounded like it was coming from far

away. Hardly surprising, since he barely belonged to this life anymore. How could one choose to become a fluttering insect, a bodiless shadow of one's former self—for love? Donnersmarck had never loved like that.

One got used to talking to a dead man, and it had been a long journey. Donnersmarck had learned Chithira had been married at the age of eight and his bride had died young. He'd told Donnersmarck how he met the Fairy. He'd described his birthplace and his place of death. But every time Donnersmarck had asked him about the other side, the land of the dead, Chithira had only smiled and talked instead of the green parrots in the temples and of his tame elephants that could wash pain and guilt off any human heart.

The beetle stopped humming. The spider was wrapping it in her silk threads until it looked like a cocoon. Life and death were so eerily similar. Donnersmarck had never noticed that before. Had the stag taught him that? He hated how the two overlapped, man and beast. She would've laughed at him for his useless resistance. Would she ever come back? What if not?

Would her dead coachman remind him of his name?

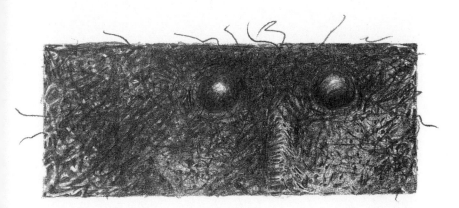

65

THE WEAVER

The Weaver's lake was much bigger than the lake from which the Dark One had been born. No trees lined its shores, just reed-like grasses and countless ponds reflecting the night sky. There were so many they reminded the Fairy of the eyes of the spider whose web she'd passed through to come here.

The webs of that spider's mistress were woven between the reeds and across the water. The silk threads caught all the colors of life, hope, fear, joy, despair… love and hate. Only the Weaver knew the patterns. She knew them all. Takushy was what they called her in this land, but she had as many names as she had woven webs.

The Weaver wove herself from the thread of night, hair of moonlight, skin of stars. So old. Without beginning or end.

"What are you doing here, sister who knows nothing of death?" The Weaver's voice sounded like a thousand fingers plucking the

409

strings of life.

"I need your help," the Dark Fairy replied.

The Weaver turned into a bevy of black swans. They settled on the lake, flapping their wings, and the largest one took the shape of a woman. Her body was made of threads as black as the night, as white as death, as translucent as spiders' silk. She walked easily through the water, and when she reached the shore, the Fairy had to crane her neck to look at her.

"You've come here in vain."

The Weaver's eyes were round and black, like those of her eight-legged guard. "You seek to sever what no one shall sever."

"I know," the Dark One replied. "But if you do it anyway, then I shall give you the only thread you can't spin. Free me from the Golden Yarn and I shall give you one of my three Yarns of Immortality."

The Weaver plucked something from the night. She had many fingers. "Your web weakens when you remove a thread," she said. "And you want to remove two?"

"Then give me others. Red, blue, green, even white, but not the gold."

The Weaver looked at the two threads she'd plucked from the night. One was silver, the other one glass. "Someone is spinning threads that don't belong here." She closed her fingers around the threads until they turned black as the night. "I don't make the patterns," she said to the Dark One. "I just weave them from the threads I find in the night. You don't want the golden one? Then you will have to spin your own threads."

With that she took one of the pairs of scissors she carried around her neck like jewelry, dozens of scissors, gold, silver, wood, and ivory. The pair she picked was made of gold.

The Weaver let the scissors snap open like a beak.

"It will weaken you more than you expect."

"I know," said the Dark One. "Cut it."

66

So Much to Lose

A shaman who speaks with spiders. A hunter they met knew of a man who spoke with lizards. A priest (looking around anxiously, worried about angering his god with such talk) whispered he'd heard of a boy who could speak to fire. And the days went by in this land where the past seemed more alive than the future. Jacob caught himself wishing they'd never find the spider shaman so he and Fox could just ride on and on to where nobody knew of Fairies or Alderelves.

He'd never been so happy.

Not even the thought of abandoning Will changed that. It felt so easy to finally indulge this love. Fox was the only one able to dampen the rage his father had stoked once more. If only it didn't scare him how much he suddenly had to lose.

They slept with each other for the first time while waiting out a storm in an abandoned shepherd hut. The hours the storm granted them, surrounded by raw wool and rusty shears, felt like a month, a year, all the years they'd been waiting for this, full of fear of their kisses, of their too-familiar skins. So far from all their memories, it felt as if they were meeting each other for the first time all over again. The horse scraping around in the discarded fleece, the storm, the sound of rain, Jacob gathered it all, like jewelry he would put around Fox's neck whenever they would remember this first time.

The next day they met a boy with an eagle that was almost as big as the shaggy horse he was riding. The boy told them about a holy man who lived in a tree and let spiders nest in his clothes.

No.

They still had only one horse, and Jacob could feel Fox's arms tighten around him. They probably both felt the same: They should have stayed a little longer in that hut, so they wouldn't have ever met that boy.

The boy described a remote valley and a forest of wild apple trees. They found the valley and the forest, but there was no sign of the shaman. Only when a murder of crows fluttered out of one of the trees did they spot the face among the branches, a face so weathered it barely stood out from the bark and leaves. The shaman ignored Jacob's calls, but when he saw Fox, he climbed down from his tree. His coat was crawling with spiders, so many it looked as though a Baba Yaga had put living embroidery on it. He picked a spider off his collar, one with pale green legs. Without a word, he placed it in Fox's hand, smiled at her, and climbed back up into his tree. The spider descended on her thread and began to weave a web into the grass.

It took a while until they realized she was weaving a map.

The white gossamer formed a mountain range, a river, the

413

shores of a lake. But then the web began to tremble. The fine threads tore, and Jacob felt a warm breeze on his skin. So warm it felt like rage. And pain.

He should have turned back. He shouldn't have listened to her.

Sixteen wasn't wearing Clara's face this time. She didn't even try to look like a human. Her body mirrored Fox, the torn web, the grass, the wild apple trees, but her glass skin was so jagged in places that the images were broken into a thousand facets, and the bark striped her like a tiger's fur.

The spider tried to flee, but Sixteen caught it and froze it into silver, throwing its body into the torn web. Jacob thought he heard a cry from the branches, but the shaman stayed out of sight. Smart.

"What are you doing here? My brother's warning wasn't enough?"

Jacob saw his fear reflected in Sixteen's eyes. She pointed at Fox with the silver blades of her fingers.

"Seventeen says silver suits her. And that you drove it out with Witch magic." She looked around. "But there are no Witches here."

She smiled.

Jacob tried to stand in front of Fox, but she wouldn't have it. She'd drawn her knife. It wouldn't help. Nothing would help. Sixteen eyed Jacob as though comparing his face to another's.

"You really look nothing like him."

Of course. His brother.

"He's so beautiful," Sixteen continued. "Even silver couldn't make him any more beautiful."

Jacob didn't ask her whether she'd already stolen Will's beautiful face. But maybe Sixteen could answer another question.

"Does he have human skin?"

The question didn't seem to surprise her.

"Yes. It only turns to stone when he gets angry."

Jacob tried to comprehend what that meant. *Let it go, Jacob.* What was it Dunbar's telegram said? Damp earth. Water. He looked around. Trees. Nothing but trees.

Sixteen leaned down and picked up the silver spider. "My brother has started collecting them. Insects, plants, a mouse, a snake. I wish this whole filthy world could be turned to silver."

She threw the spider away again.

"Let her go," said Jacob. "Please. Spieler is angry with me, not her."

Fox clawed her fingers into his arm so hard it hurt.

"He's lying," she said to Sixteen. "Before you can even touch him, I will shift and tear out your throat."

Sixteen flexed her fingers like a cat looking forward to the hunt.

"You won't be fast enough, fox-sister," she said.

Sixteen's features became human. And again Jacob recognized the face. It was his mother's, young, the one he knew only from photographs. The sight paralyzed him.

Fox yanked him away.

She screamed at him, pulled him along. They stumbled over roots and dead trees, ran side by side through the high grass that smelled of apples, their eyes desperately looking for the one thing that could protect them.

Damp earth. Water.

Sixteen was in no rush. She was obviously enjoying her quarry's fear.

Damp earth. Water. But all Jacob saw was rotting leaves. He wanted to stop, kiss Fox one last time.

Sixteen walked faster.

Jacob stumbled over a branch. Fox dragged him back to his feet. Shift! he wanted to shout. The vixen can escape. But what for? She would never flee without him. Together. Even in death. His fingers tightened their grip around her hand. A double statue of silver. Romantic. What would their faces show? Fear? Or love?

Jacob took a swarm of mosquitoes to be a figment of his desperate mind, but Fox pulled him toward them. A pond! Barely visible under the rotting leaves floating on its brackish surface. Jacob covered Fox as she slipped on the muddy bank. She waded into the water, and he dug his fingers into the damp earth, threw a handful into Sixteen's face, which was still that of his mother. The glass fingers quickly wiped the mud off, but the skin beneath had already turned to bark.

The pond wasn't very deep, the water barely reaching to their chests. But Sixteen stopped one step away from the bank, her eyes a kaleidoscope of a hundred stolen lives. Jacob wrapped his arms around Fox. The water was warm, and the rotting foliage surrounded them like a blanket. Would this be their end? In a muddy pond?

Sixteen's feet were growing roots. She stared at them. But then her head turned.

The muddy water rippled.

The wind, the wind, the heaven-born wind...

Sixteen smiled.

Maybe it was whispering to her.

"It's over," she said. "Your brother has found her!"

She briefly seemed torn whether or not to finish the hunt.

But then she turned to glass and was gone.

67

So Weak

The stag's head rose above the grass. He had no memory of ever not having carried the proud antlers. It was back, the melody that had been missing from the music of the world. But its song was weaker than usual.

The stag followed it, the one sound that contained everything he'd once been. And there she was, her dress covered in cobwebs. Only the thread in her hand was golden.

The stag went to her side, and the Fairy buried her face in his neck.

68

And Everything Will Be Just as It was Meant to Be

The leaves and blossoms growing on the carriage would have made good camouflage in any forest, but here, among the blue mountains and the yellow grass, they just announced from how far they'd come.

Will climbed off his horse and hid behind a dead tree.

He'd found her.

A stag stood next to the carriage. His antlers were wider than Will could stretch his arms. Two horses were searching the yellow grass for shoots as green as their coats. The man fitting the harness over their necks wore clothes that reminded Will of Scheherazade and the tales of a thousand and one nights. Those had been their mother's favorite stories. Will could no longer tell whether the memory of her was more of a fairy tale than what he was seeing now.

The Dark Fairy was kneeling in the grass a few feet from the carriage. The gathering dusk made her green dress as black as the approaching night. Will lost himself in the images brought back by being so close to her. Forgotten images: The day the Goyl had brought him to her. The time spent by her side. And the night she'd let him go. They'd all been so exhausted. Exhausted, betrayed, half of them dead. Who did he mean by "them"? Him and the surviving Goyl. Jacob had been there, and Fox, among the human prisoners. They'd come for him, but he'd had no memory of having a brother.

Maybe he didn't want to remember.

Enchanted.

The stag looked at him. What did he see? Even Will could barely make out Seventeen in the fading light of the dying day. And he hadn't seen Sixteen in hours.

He pulled the swindlesack from under his shirt.

The Fairy rose.

"Do not look at her, fool! Never." The Goyl who'd trained him had warned him over and over. Hentzau, yes, that had been his name.

Will tried to pull the swindlesack off the crossbow, but his hands seemed to resist. It's her magic, the silver under his fingers seemed to whisper. Fight back! But what if the Goyl was right? What if she took the jade with her? He so longed for the stone.

The Fairy looked toward him. She was as pale as the stars gathering in the strange skies above. So beautiful. The stag wanted to shield her, but with one swipe of her hand, his legs were caught in vines that wouldn't budge, no matter how he kicked and thrashed his antlers at them.

Shoot! the wind whispered. It brought a smell. A hospital corridor. A quiet room. Clara's motionless body on the bed. Like the princess in the tower. Dead because her prince had never come.

Shoot!

But he heard the Fairy inside his head.

"What did they promise you?"

He didn't know she could sound so weak. So vulnerable. The moths swarmed from her hair and clothes. Even the coachman in the fairy-tale clothes grew wings, and Seventeen disappeared under the fluttering mass, his scream frozen into bark. Sixteen's stiffening arms were raised in self-defense. The sight silvered his mind, but his heart was jade, the jade the Fairy had given him.

Don't look at her, Will.

He cocked the crossbow.

"No!" The Bastard sounded as if his tongue was silver, too. "Let her go!"

The moths let go of Seventeen and swarmed toward Will. Like black, winged smoke.

69

As in Her Dreams

He hesitated. Just like she'd seen in her dreams again and again. But even Fairy dreams didn't always come true. Was that why she hadn't hidden from him? No. Why lie to herself? She'd been too preoccupied with her own lovesickness.

The sickness was gone, as was the love.

The Mirrorlings who'd been shadowing the hunter had been born from her sisters' foolishness. So much rage. Payback for an ancient debt. More ancient than herself.

And she was so tired.

It was all she could feel. Tiredness.

Her hunter was still hesitating. No, that's not what she wanted to call him. His destiny was to protect her. That's why she'd sown the stone in him. But the crossbow had its own will. He'd just had to bring it here.

So much rage. So much ancient rage.

The stag wanted to jump in front of the bolt. He struggled desperately against the green shackles that protected him. They were all so keen to die for her. But why? The bolt would find her. Her sisters had been right. And still, she would've taken the same path again. Because it was her path.

The jade returned as soon as her moths attacked him. Her own magic shielded her assassin. All for Kami'en. Even that thought no longer hurt. The Golden Yarn was in her hand when the bolt struck.

So much darkness, so much light.

Was that what they called death?

The Golden Yarn slipped from her fingers as she surrendered to the element that had borne her. It was just a little trickle, but it willingly received her last spark of life.

Her sisters would perish, and it would be her fault. Again. That was the last of the Dark Fairy's thoughts before they dissolved and became as clear as nobody would ever allow them to be. And the rest of her died.

70
Gone

Yes. This was the convent Kami'en had described to the draftsman. It was the river he'd seen, and the nun who opened the gate wore a black habit. Her face showed the usual disgust as she took in his men. Her hatred baseless. When the Bavarian officer, who'd been sent along as their watchdog, asked her about the infant, her hatred turned to fear. Idiot. Was he trying to give them time to hide his son? Probably.

If they hadn't taken him away already.

Kami'en was no longer sure whether it had been wise to come himself. Two attacks on his train, farmers spitting at his sight, women crossing themselves, children staring at him as though they'd seen the Devil. Who was to say whether their fear of him and his armies brought more danger than protection to his son? Hentzau had been right: the Bavarians made no secret of their harking back to a time when all Goyl were simply killed on sight.

Now he could only hope Hentzau hadn't also been right about the trap. And that the child was still alive.

The nun spoke in a dialect Kami'en couldn't understand. He ordered the Bavarian officer to translate. The man's grasp of the Goyl language was quite good, but when he repeated to Kami'en what the nun had said, his soft human lips suddenly seemed to move without making a sound. All Kami'en could hear was his own heartbeat, loud, as though he was suddenly alone in a vast, empty hall.

She was gone.

The officer was still talking.

Kami'en turned his horse around.

His own men stared at him. The Bavarian officer wanted to stop him. One of his bodyguards reached for his reins. Kami'en shoved him aside, and he spurred his horse. He drove it beneath the trees behind the convent, ignoring the cries behind him. He'd always been a good horseman.

When he finally stopped, he no longer knew where he was.

Enemy territory. So what? For a Goyl, all territory was enemy territory.

She was gone.

And his heart was beating too loud and too fast.

Into nothingness.

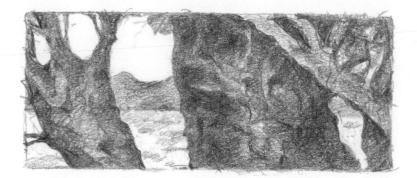

71

THE EXECUTIONER

The Dark One fell without a sound. Like a leaf. Nerron struggled to his feet. What had he expected? That she would die like a human? He looked speckled, like a bug, and his body ached as though those damn Mirrorlings had put him on a spit and roasted him. But the Bastard lived—though Sixteen had tried very hard to turn him into a hunk of precious metal.

Let that be a warning to your Elf masters! he thought as he scraped the silver off his face with his claws. They'd best remember not to mess with the Goyl when they return.

The stag was still trying to free himself from the Fairy's vines. It had really seemed like she didn't want to be saved. Hell, that stag was a monster. Nerron had never seen a bigger one, but the Pup walked past the snorting beast as though it weren't even there. He only had eyes for the still body lying next to the carriage. A lost boy was all he now was. *Oh, but no, Nerron. He now has a brand-new title: the Fairy Slayer.*

The moths were hovering aimlessly above her body, like drones who'd just lost their queen. They didn't attack the Pup, except for one who kept fluttering at his face. Will didn't even swat at it. Nerron went to his side. The Dark One's eyes were open. What happened when death claimed what was immortal?

The Pup was still holding the weapon that had ended her.

In his snail-skinned hand.

Nerron could've killed him. Why didn't he? The Pup no longer had bodyguards.

Seventeen was completely frozen. His startled bark-face was a welcome sight. Some of the leaves growing out of his arms were silver and glass.

Sixteen was still stirring. Will turned to her as she whispered his name. The Pup looked almost as startled as her wooden brother. He dropped the crossbow like a broken toy and stumbled toward what had been a girl.

Sixteen was on her knees, but in contrast to her brother, she still had her shape. She could even move one arm; all else had turned to wood. Will touched her face. She was trying hard to make it look at least a little human, but her skin was reflecting the gathering night. The Pup kissed her anyway. So touching. Smitten with a glass girl.

He didn't even notice when Nerron picked up the crossbow.

There. Won. Lost. Won. Lost. Won.

This wasn't quite the ending he'd hoped for, but that didn't make it a bad one. Except for the Fairy. The stag had almost freed himself. *Careful, Nerron.* Skewered by a stag with the crossbow in his hand? Well, why not try it on an animal for a change? Would all deer die with him? Whatever. The Bastard wouldn't miss them.

The bolt slid out of the Fairy's chest as though out of water.

Hurry, Bastard.

The stag reared up and tore through the last vines.

What antlers! The beast lowered its head, but it ignored the crossbow as well the Goyl who was aiming it at him. Surprise! He was going for the Pup!

Good. And why not? Let the stag take care of the Pup. Nerron liked it when others did the killing for him, and the stag would probably not object if Nerron claimed the head and sent it to Jacob Reckless.

Milk-face was still kneeling next to what had been a girl of silver and glass.

He didn't even look around!

Nerron cursed as he lifted the crossbow.

He cocked the glass string, though his fingers ached as if he'd bathed them in acid.

Damn, damn, damn.

The Bastard, who was so proud of thinking only of himself, was now playing the savior. And this time he didn't even have an excuse.

The stag still wasn't paying any attention to him. Maybe it was the crossbow. Magic weapons often made their victims blind to the danger they posed. Nerron caught him in midair. The bolt hit his unprotected side. The stag stumbled toward the Pup—he really didn't give up easily—and then he collapsed, with a groan that sounded almost human.

An onyx wouldn't have left the antlers behind, but the Bastard was no friend of hunting trophies. The crossbow was lighter in his hand than he remembered. The last time he'd shot it was at Jacob Reckless. Much more satisfying. He found the swindlesack on the ground and pulled it over the weapon. *Which leaves us with what's next, Nerron.*

The Pup was actually scraping the bark off Sixteen's body. He did it carefully, as though he were uncovering treasure. The jade boy and the glass girl. Well, if that didn't sound like a fairy tale. Time to give it a bad ending.

Yes. Who was to say he hadn't had a good reason to save him from the stag? Why leave his final revenge to some big buck, the revenge he'd traveled so far to get? Nerron didn't even want to know whether he was seeking payback for the humiliation he'd suffered at the hands of Jacob Reckless or for how the Jade Goyl had betrayed his maker.

But he did. He knew the answer.

Damn, he just had to look at the Pup to feel sick with disappointment. He wanted to make gloves from his pink baby skin, light a fire with his bodyguards and spit-roast the Pup over it. The Jade Goyl was now again nothing but a snail face. And that made the whole damn world seem as empty as the eyes of the Fairy, as dead as the stag. There should be a law against telling fairy tales to children, and anyone who broke it should have their tongue cut out.

He stepped behind the Pup and drew his pistol.

"Forget her!" he said, aiming at the pale dunce's head. "We're leaving. Why do you think she made eyes at you? She knew what would happen when she got too close to the Fairy. Why else do you think they needed you? I wonder what they have in common with their Elf fathers? Quite a lot, apparently."

There was something in the way the Pup turned.

Stop dreaming, Nerron.

"We can't just leave her here. She's still alive."

"Alive? I'm not sure that's what she ever was. Did you see her eyes? Maybe we should cut them open. Maybe then you'll believe me."

Yes. Oh, there it came. Pale green, like the old ponds in the royal fortress. Nothing more beautiful beneath the earth. Not beneath, and not above. The joy that flooded Nerron was as strong as when he'd last felt it as a child.

Once upon a time. *No, now upon a time.*

The Pup was one of them. Still. And forever. The rage in his eyes was Goyl in golden letters. Thank the Fairy!

"Shall I guess what you're thinking?" Nerron trained his pistol at the jade-green brow. "That you killed the Dark One for nothing, right? Fool! As though this was ever about you. Is that what they told you? I'm sure you handed your glassy girlfriend's master exactly what he needed. You could say the same about me. All's well that end's well. So will you get on that horse, or will I have to demonstrate how Goyl bullets can penetrate even jade skin?"

Sixteen groaned as she struggled to her feet. The pain made her draw blood as she bit her lips and straightened her back.

The Pup took her arm.

"I will find him," he panted. Oh yes, this was pure Goyl rage. "He deceived me. Me and her."

"He?" *Stop it, Nerron. You don't want to know.*

"Yes. He. Whatever he is. Wherever he is. I will find him."

"The only one we have to find is Kami'en." Nerron cocked the pistol. "I won't say it twice. Get on that horse."

The Pup didn't move.

The Pup was the Jade Goyl—the Fairy Slayer. "I'll show you the mirror if you let me go. You still want to see it, don't you? Come with me."

430

Oh no. No, Nerron! He had the crossbow. He had the Jade Goyl. It was never good to want too much. And Seventeen's warning had been quite clear.

Sixteen stood there looking at the Pup. Nerron couldn't figure out what he saw in her wounded face. She looked…guilty? Yes. "Do not look for him! Please." She sounded as though the bark was in her throat as well.

"Why? I'm not afraid of him."

"You should be."

She tried to flex her stiff arm, groaning with pain. The Pup attempted to help her, but she pushed him away. With her wooden hand. The one that couldn't harm him.

"Go with the stoneface. Why do you want to find him? You can't wake your love. Not as long as Spieler doesn't want you to." The Pup stared at her as though she'd just changed into a viper. "What do you know about Clara?"

"Don't be stupid." Sixteen flexed her wooden fingers. "The Fairies can't even see the mirrors. The thorn magic was never theirs."

The Pup grabbed her arm, but she flinched like a wounded animal. She was still dangerous. But the pistol was no help. Could he set her on fire? Sixteen looked at Nerron as though she'd heard him. She ripped the bark off her fingers with her teeth.

"It was all Spieler's plan. He's smart. So much smarter than the others."

The Pup looked at the dead Fairy.

That didn't feel nice, did it? Used like a tool, pushed like a pawn across the gameboard, not knowing for whom or what. Nerron knew the feeling. His own brother had been the last one to make him feel that way.

431

"Spieler." The Pup repeated it, giving a name to all the rage, the shame, the helpless pain Nerron could see on his face.

Put that pistol away, Nerron.

Who was he trying to fool? The Pup would never come with him, so what good would it do to shoot him? And it might not be so easy.

"Good," he said. "I'll come with you. Through the mirror. But I don't want anything to do with that... What's his name? Spieler? That's your war."

Sixteen smiled. It was a smile full of scorn — and pain.

"And how are you going to avoid meeting him, stoneskin? That mirror? It is his."

She looked at her hands. A couple of fingers were still glass. "But there are others," she said.

"Other what?" Oh no, Nerron did not trust her.

And the Pup didn't anymore, either. Even his jade face was easy to read.

"Other Alderelves."

Great! There were more than one left. He should have seen that coming.

"They all have mirrors," Sixteen added. "Spieler can't see those."

The Pup was still looking at the Fairy. "And? I only know the one in Schwanstein."

Sixteen tried to smile. Not easy when you had hardly any face left. "I can find them. We're made of the same glass."

She staggered toward the tree that had been Seventeen and stroked the face in the bark.

"I can find them," she repeated. "Oh yes."

Then she turned and hobbled toward the green horses still

standing next to the carriage.

Will wanted to go after her, but Nerron stepped in his path. The jade was still there. The Pup was on the warpath.

"You didn't stick to our bargain," Nerron said to him. "Don't try that again. You owe me. I want your promise that if you're still alive after you've settled your score with the Elf, then you'll come with me. The Jade Goyl swore an oath to Kami'en, and I will make sure he fulfills it."

The Pup wanted to say something, but then he just nodded.

The green horses let themselves be caught. They seemed as lost as the moths, but Nerron let Sixteen and the Pup have them. He caught himself the gelding he found behind the carriage.

Sixteen struggled to get on her horse. The Pup didn't look at her as he helped her.

Why are you riding with them, Nerron?

Why couldn't he stop asking questions?

Maybe he'd send Hentzau a telegram from along the way: *Bastard has crossbow. And Jade Goyl.*

Maybe. And maybe not. This world was now his. He had its most powerful weapon.

72

SILVER AND GOLD

It took Fox and Jacob four days to find the place the spider had shown them in its web. They were finally certain when they found a silver snake and the trail of two riders. Soon they came upon some bark, sticky with what looked like liquid glass. And then they saw the carriage.

They only dared to approach it after Fox had scouted a stream nearby to which they could flee. The memory of Sixteen's attack was still fresh.

Will was nowhere to be seen, nor were his guards, or the Bastard.

"Your brother has found her."

Yes.

Fox took Jacob's hand when she spotted the dead body next to the carriage. A few steps away, the grass was covered with blood, but it wasn't human. The trail Fox found was that of a wounded animal dragging itself away. The hoof prints were not from a horse but a stag.

Not once during their pursuit of Will had Fox realized that they were also trying to save the Fairy. She hated her and her red sister ever since she'd spent a year waiting for Jacob by the shores of their lake. They'd both caused her so much pain that Fox had often dreamed of being witness to their end. But now that she saw the Dark One lying there like a piece of bagged venison, she almost felt as if she were looking at her own corpse.

They could have made it in time. Jacob was probably thinking the same. If only his father hadn't stolen the carpet. If only Orlando had told them earlier about the spider shaman.

If only...

Jacob tried to read the ground for the answer he'd sought ever since he went to talk to the Bamboo Girl, but not even the vixen could see whether his brother had a jade skin. Will had ridden off with two companions; that much was clear. Fox would have bet her Man-Swan feather that the Bastard was one of them. But the second trail was a mystery. It was made by a lighter body, maybe a woman's. She seemed to have been injured, and there were bits of bark where the trail began, covered with the same sticky substance they'd found earlier.

Maybe they wouldn't have noticed the Alder, if not for the silver leaves. Fox approached the tree slowly. The face she spotted in the bark seemed familiar.

Jacob looked around.

They both knew who he was looking for.

"I think she's riding with your brother," said Fox. "She and the Bastard."

Jacob stared at the frozen tree-face as though it could tell him whether his brother had ridden with them willingly, and if so, why he'd chosen such dark companions.

Fox wrapped her arms around him and kissed him so she wouldn't have to feel the fear she felt stirring inside her, but the joy. Still so much joy.

You have everything you dreamed of, Fox. Everything.

Despite the Fairy.

Despite Will.

Despite the Alderelf, who was still waiting for his payment.

Despite. What a wonderful word, so full of defiance, freedom, courage, hope.

"The Elf got what he wanted," Jacob whispered. "Maybe he'll leave us in peace for now. But I'm not counting on it. I promise I'll find something. Some magic to protect you from him."

"No," Fox whispered back. "*We.* We will find something."

Jacob buried his face in her hair. He kissed her as though that could make him forget the dead Fairy and Will and his father, and the Elf who'd gotten what he wanted.

"Let's surprise Chanute and Sylvain," he said. "We can make it to Kamchatka before they get on the boat."

That sounded wonderful.

As wonderful as the stolen time in the child-eater's barn, and in the shepherd's hut. Or the precious moments on the beach, after they'd survived the sinking of the Albian fleet. They were good at stealing time. Together. But she couldn't let Jacob run away. "When, do you think, will you turn around again?" she asked. "Tomorrow? The day after? Who knows, you might even make it for three days. But then you'll ask me whether I can still find Will's trail despite his head start."

Jacob said nothing. His way of admitting she was right. To

never let the other forget who they are—love is also about that. One of the Fairy's moths was fluttering a little away from the others, hovering over a trickle left from the last rains. Something glistened on the water. Fox bent down and picked it off the damp grass.

A golden thread.

Maybe the Fairy had found the Weaver.

The moth settled on Fox's shoulder. The dark wings shimmered as if dusted with gold.

Jacob stood by the Fairy's body. He'd known her name and she'd tried to kill him for it. But she'd also given him his brother back and had saved them all at the Blood Wedding.

The moth fluttered after them as they picked up Will's trail. Fox didn't have the heart to chase it away.

73

No

Was there even one word from the others? Did anyone say, *Spieler, you were right*? Of course not. Krieger, Letterman, Apaullo — the whole helpers-on-the-other-side faction were too busy stage-managing their return. Who had found Will Reckless? Who had mingled the magic of this world with their own so they could at least send something of themselves through the mirror? Had Guismond been his idea? No! Krieger had wanted a knight. A knight! Who said immortality precluded stupidity? Apaullo had recruited conquistadores, Letterman a papal spy, not to mention all the Stilts, Thumblings, and child-eaters the helpers-on-the-other-side faction had bribed over the centuries. Backward. They were all so hopelessly backward in their thinking, in their dreams. But he wouldn't let them forget who finally ended their exile. Oh no.

It was simply ridiculous how excited he felt. Were the others nervous? He didn't even know whether any of them had gone back yet. They each kept the locations of their mirrors as secret as their true form. They'd all tried to find each other's mirrors, but usually without much success. Letterman's was most definitely in Fon, and Krieger's was probably in Nihon.

Spieler had chosen the oldest of his mirrors for his return, made from the first water they'd stolen from the Fairies. A theft they hadn't even noticed for the longest time...

Spieler ran his fingers over the artfully shaped frame. The lilies were so lifelike that insects often came to settle on their petals. They'd never found a silversmith quite as talented. Volund. He'd met with a very sad end. This world had not at all agreed with him.

The glass between these perfect silver flowers showed Spieler's true guise. The mirrors only allowed you to pass in that form. A huge disadvantage, and they'd tried in vain to change that. The others had also insisted that he give his face to Seventeen. A childish attempt to punish him for having pushed through with his idea. At least Sixteen had gotten Krieger's face. A shame that they'd lost both of them, but Spieler had always thought the probability of the Mirrorlings surviving the mission was vanishingly small.

Eight centuries. Eight centuries in the wrong world.

He lifted his hand.

This world had been good to him.

More than you could say about the other one. In this moment, which he'd yearned for so painfully long, everything seemed to wash up behind the mirror's glass: defeats, old foes, the backwardness, the terror of those last days...

No, Spieler.

He pressed his hand on the glass.

439

Home...

He kept his eyes closed for a moment, listened to his own breathing, sensed the changed room surrounding him, its width and depth. He didn't like the smell. The air smelled of lost time, of defeat, and of a past so long forgotten it had lost all its flavor. And it smelled of the Fairies' elements, of water and earth.

Spieler opened his eyes, and what he saw was familiar, made strange by too many years of absence. The most painful aspect of exile was how home became a dream, cleansed of all that was bad. One never returned to the dream one had nurtured over centuries, but to a reality that would always look shabby compared to the romanticized memories. The silver pillars, the balconies, the chandeliers, the glass floor—how dusty, how old-fashioned. Yesterday. Was there a more merciless word?

His steps echoed through the empty hall.

He'd once been so proud of this palace. Touching. Now it struggled to compare with the glass towers that could touch the sky.

Spieler stopped. He touched his forehead.

What was that?

The skin above his left eyebrow was rough. His fingers felt a bark-like scab. No, this wasn't a scab.

He pulled his mirror eye from his pocket. But there she was. Her beautiful body was already crumbling into petals. *Come on, show me her sisters.* There. The lake. Wilting trees, the water clouded by dying lilies. No sign of life. Was their curse dying more slowly than their bodies? Yes. That had to be it.

Spieler put the medallion back in his waistcoat pocket—the clothes of the other world were another thing he'd gotten too used to—and stared at his right hand. Small spots of bark were

440

forming on it.

"No!"

Spieler said it aloud, in his empty palace that smelled of their elements, of water, of the earth, so stuffy, so heavy, so alone with his rage and all the immortal disappointment.

Some remnant... Was it possible? That something remained? He touched his face, his neck... Nothing. Not yet. *Stay calm. The curse is broken, Spieler, or you'd already be a tree.*

But something must have survived. What if that final spark had found a keeper? One of their dead lovers, those human weaklings who'd found them so irresistible.

He again reached for the medallion, but it just kept showing him the decaying body and the images he'd seen before.

No.

No!

He would not go back.

He would find it. Whatever it was, whatever remained.

He would make new creatures, better ones. Immortal, untiring, more terrible than anything that had hunted in this world before.

Oh, he didn't like himself when he lost his patience.

CORNELIA FUNKE
RECKLESS

THE PETRIFIED FLESH

CORNELIA FUNKE
RECKLESS

LIVING SHADOWS